"Read *Chateau of Echoes*. Take this wonderful chance to escape life's pressures for a few hours and revel in a delightful story beautifully told."

— GINGER GARRETT
author of *Chosen: The Lost Diaries of Queen Esther*

"Siri Mitchell weaves a witty, double-edged tale of intrigue, romance, and French culture that is expertly researched, carefully spun, and deliciously satisfying. You will want to pack your bags for a never-ending vacation in France when you turn the last page — this multi-dimensional story is that alluring."

— SUSAN MEISSNER
author of *Why the Sky Is Blue*

Chateau of Echoes

Siri L. Mitchell

NAVPRESS®

BRINGING TRUTH TO LIFE

OUR GUARANTEE TO YOU

We believe so strongly in the message of our books that we are making this quality guarantee to you. If for any reason you are disappointed with the content of this book, return the title page to us with your name and address and we will refund to you the list price of the book. To help us serve you better, please briefly describe why you were disappointed. Mail your refund request to: NavPress, P.O. Box 35002, Colorado Springs, CO 80935.

NavPress
P.O. Box 35001
Colorado Springs, Colorado 80935

© 2005 by Siri L. Mitchell

ISBN 1-57683-914-1

Cover design by The DesignWorks Group, www.thedesignworksgroup.com
Creative team: Rachelle Gardner, Darla Hightower, Arvid Wallen, Glynese Northam
Author photo by Dave Jazdyk

"The Rules of Love" on page 200 are from Andreas Capellanus, John Jay Parry, trans., *The Art of Courtly Love* (New York: Columbia University Press, 1990).

This novel is a work of fiction. Names, characters, places, and incidents are either the product of the author's imagination or are used fictitiously. Any resemblance to actual events, locales, organizations, or persons, living or dead, is entirely coincidental and beyond the intent of either the author or publisher.

Published in association with the literary agency of Alive Communications, Inc., 7680 Goddard Street, Suite 200, Colorado Springs, CO 80920 (www.alivecommunications.com).

Mitchell, Siri L., 1969-
  Chateau of echoes / Siri L. Mitchell.
    p. cm.
  ISBN 1-57683-914-1
  1. Widows--Fiction. 2. Castles--Fiction. 3. Treasure troves--Fiction. 4. Bed and breakfast accommodations--Fiction. 5. Americans--Europe--Fiction. I. Title.
  PS3613.I866C47 2005
  813'.6--dc22
                                    2005018510
Printed in Canada

1 2 3 4 5 6 7 8 9 10 / 10 09 08 07 06 05

FOR A FREE CATALOG OF
NAVPRESS BOOKS & BIBLE STUDIES,
CALL 1-800-366-7788 (USA)
OR 1-800-839-4769 (CANADA)

To Tony

My favorite dreams are those I've dreamed with you.

août

S'il pleut pour Sainte-Radegonde,
misère abonde sur le monde.

August

If it rains on the day of Sainte-Radegonde,
misery abounds in the world.

On the third day of August, I received a letter from America. The envelope indicated no name, simply an address in California.

It was a glorious summer day for Brittany, France. The temperature was hovering around 75, and the clouds thinned to let the sun through now and then. That made it warm enough to slip a cornflower blue halter over my black capris. A breeze fingered my hair and tipped my straw gardening hat over my right eye. I am blonde but not in a striking sort of way. I belong to the shade rather than the sunlight, being pale and having eyes the iciest shade of blue.

I paused at the mailbox, clamping the letter between my upper arm and my body, put a hand to the brim of my hat, and played tug-of-war with the breeze to tie the strings of my hat more tightly underneath my chin. As I walked from the mailbox up the mile-long pea-gravel drive toward the chateau I call my home, I relished the crunch of the stones beneath my feet, welding me to the present.

The chateau, which dates from the fourteenth century, has four turrets. It definitely isn't the biggest in France, and it isn't the most beautiful, but it is mine. And looking at it as the sun filtered through the clouds, drenching it in a golden haze, I felt an unreasonable sort of pride. The chateau had existed over half a millennium without me, and it would probably exist another half after me. I was only borrowing it during the brief period of my existence. But for that short moment, it belonged to me.

Friends expected that I would be lonely, learning to live alone again in a huge chateau, but it was here that I began to reorder my life. To carve out a space for myself in the world. It had never felt too big or too empty.

It used to be just perfect.

But that morning, I had been working in my potager garden and had the familiar feeling of not being alone. Of a gentle tapping in my heart. And as I sometimes do, when I feel offended by the monolith of a God who refuses to stay away from me, I said out loud, "Would you leave?" And, as usual, I felt an emptying in the air around me.

More and more, I had found myself talking to a God that I didn't want to acknowledge. A God I didn't know I believed in anymore. I wished I could be as sure as Peter, my late husband, that God didn't exist. But I wasn't, even though I'd effectively bet Peter's life on those atheist beliefs. But if God did exist, then where did that leave Peter? And what kind of person did that make me?

It was just easier to ignore God. So I did.

❧

After walking past the two square stone pillars that separate the chateau from the grounds, I stopped, surveying the gravel drive and the barren courtyard that lay in front of me. I meant to convert the gravel into a formal garden. Someday — after I'd renovated the stables and taken care of other more immediate improvements. I wanted to channel the driveway into a defined loop and turn the enclosed expanse into a Daedalus labyrinth of cotton, lavender, and yew. Or maybe a knotwork design in a combination of privet, yew, and box. I tried to imagine what the enclosure would look like, shrouded with green geometric patterns of clipped hedges.

I had compiled a collection of books on historical landscaping and had spent many pleasant hours flipping through them, accumulating ideas. I just didn't know yet what I wanted. But for the moment, it was fine. It looked like 90 percent of the other chateaux in France.

I walked on, kicking up dust from the gravel. Then I scaled the steps of the chateau and swung the massive oak door shut with a kick from my foot. I slipped out of my shoes, took off my hat, and set it beside a vase of flowers on a round table in the vaulted entry hall. The flowers were bunched too tightly, so I stopped to pluck and poke at them. Their purples, pinks, and yellows lightened the mood of the heavy stone walls.

There are three narrow arches leading from this hall. The one on the left provides access to a tightly wound staircase that both descends to the kitchen and allows access to the three floors above. The one in the middle leads to a hallway with another, more generously proportioned, spiral staircase and, past it, the reception hall. From the reception hall, the dining hall can be seen to the left and the council room to the right.

The archway to the right descends to the cellar.

Opening the letter, I walked through the central archway and then sat on a settee in the reception hall. The wavy leaded panes of clear glass set into the thick stone walls diffused the light, and the rectangles of colored glass along the tops of the windows made puddles of color on the black and white tiled floor. I like this room. It's not meant for use, but rather as a stopping place on the way to a meal or a gathering area for people to meet up before embarking on their day's business. There are several settees, a *dressoir* sideboard, three pairs of chairs and a table, all lined against the walls in true medieval fashion. The ceilings are of painted wood and beamed. A geometric pattern decorates them in colors of mid-green, gold, and scarlet. The fireplaces at each end are wide and are nearly six feet tall. The mantels are carved from stone and have twisted columns supporting them on either side. Several framed antique maps are hung on the walls.

Sliding the letter from the envelope, I admired the heavy, expensive cream paper on which it was written and the assertive slant of the handwriting. It contained a request from an author to rent a room from me for a period of six months. I recognized the name, Robert Cranwell, even after having lived in France for nine years.

Apparently, he'd had the ingenious idea to write a novel that would be loosely based on the life of Alix de Montôt, *comtesse de Kertanuan.* He'd decided that staying at my chateau, reputed to have been her home, would surely inspire greater authenticity in his work.

I couldn't help but roll my eyes when I read that line.

Alix de Montôt.

Had I known the trouble she would cause, I would have burned her journals the day I'd found them. For a fifteenth-century waif, she'd caused a disproportionate amount of chaos in my life.

❧

I'd found her journals in an old trunk in the *cave,* or cellar, of one of the estate's outbuildings in a meadow a mile and a half from the chateau. It was the meadow that served as the halfway point of my three-mile jog. I'd had the structure torn down for safety reasons and the foundation stones scattered. The day I discovered the cellar, I had come to make sure the work had been done properly. I noticed a trap door near what had been a corner of the building. Of course, being American, I immediately envisioned a blonde, blue-eyed angelic child falling through the ancient door, breaking a leg, being trapped inside, and slowly starving to death. My next thought was of the inevitable million-euro lawsuit that would follow. The French aren't a litigious society, but I'm sure eventually they will become one.

In any case, I tried to pull the door up to see exactly what it guarded. I was surprised the wood hadn't rotted, as the building's roof had fallen through decades before. The planks forming the door had to have been a good four inches thick, and the hinges and ringed door pull, though rusted, were equally as sturdy. It was the rust that kept me out that first day.

But the next day I was back, armed with a spray can of heavy-duty oven cleaner. I had learned all sorts of tricks as I renovated the chateau's kitchen. For that room, at least, I'd trusted no one but myself. The oven cleaner smelled worse than a ripe *Mont d'Or* cheese, but it worked. I had to walk back to the chateau to get a crowbar from the stable-*cum*-garage, but once levered, the door swung up and I was soon walking down a steep, narrow flight of stairs.

Like stairs on ships, they were narrow and deep. Layers of chill enveloped me on the way down. By the time I'd reached the last step, I was blowing into cupped hands to warm my fingers. Without a flashlight, I couldn't see much, but I had the impression of a low ceiling and a dead space. Not of any *thing* dead, but of a space that was not in use.

In climbing back up, I was careful not to touch anything for fear of cobwebs or mice. Thinking still of lawsuits, I let the door drop back with a bang and decided to head home and fix myself lunch. I had a creepy feeling, as if I'd collected an assortment of spiders on my short adventure, so I turned every way I could, trying to get a look at my back. When I couldn't, I reached around, swatted my back, and did a hokey-pokey sort of dance right there in the old ruins.

Starting out on the trail I'd worn through the meadow, my imagination began to populate the landscape with the people who must have lived there during the region's long history.

People assume King Arthur and the Knights of the Round Table lived, fought, and died in Britain. The Bretons believe that some of the legends actually took place in *Brocéliande*, this haunting area of *Bretagne*, or Brittany. To my understanding, which was gained over the course of a four-hour dinner in the company of the Embassy's cultural attaché, Celtic tribes had bounced from Brittany to Britain and back again so often that historians get whiplash.

Celtic society on the Armorican peninsula of Brittany was all but obliterated by raiding bands of Saxon pirates. And then those same pirates turned their boats toward Britain. The threat of raids and pressure of population groups fleeing in advance of the Saxon menace led to a full-scale evacuation of the southern part of the island. The evacuees came to the depopulated peninsula of France. And when those British came, they attached their name to the land and the population. Brittany, or *Bretagne*, would forever after be populated by Bretons. But the new residents ran into some of the old residents who had retreated inland, and two families of the ancient Celtic Diaspora reconnected.

Until a new threat came to the peninsula: the Vikings. Once more, the Bretons fell victim to barbarians, and this time, some of them chose to flee back to Britain. And some of those who did not, chose to cross the Channel instead with William the Conqueror. Many of the fine old families in Britain are descendants of a Breton — who may at one time in fact have lived in Britain after having emigrated from Brittany.

So when Brittany declares herself the land of King Arthur, the country of the fairies Viviane and Morgane, she might not be lying. For to whom do the Arthurian legends belong? To the first Amoricans who battled the Saxons? Or to the British who battled the Saxons? Or perhaps the legends are more ancient. Perhaps they were told in whispers that crossed a continent during the dispersion of those original Celts. How many times does a story boomerang before it forgets who first sent it wheeling into the sky? Before it forgets whether it is part of the warp that underpins the fabric of a culture or a fabulous golden thread that has embellished it? Regardless, on one point everyone agrees: Arthur still lives.

I often imagine the lives of those legendary characters, wondering what they must have seen as they walked this land. But this time, my musings felt personal. Not as if I was walking through history, but as though I had walked into it. Turning around, I gave the area one final look before retreating to my chateau.

Three days passed before I felt nervy enough to go back. It's difficult for me to explain exactly how that cellar made me feel. This is the closest I can get: It had been like walking into a pool of still water. As if by prying open the door, I'd disturbed and set into motion something that had settled for centuries.

Knowing what I do now, I wonder if I imagined all those feelings. If maybe I was using knowledge gained afterward to interpret those past events, but I don't think so. I think it was God. A God who rules over time and history. A God who can use the diaries of a centuries-dead girl to bring healing to the heart of a modern woman.

When I finally went back, I took the crowbar and a flashlight. It was a beautiful morning. A fog was rising from the grasses and winding through the trees. The sun hadn't yet beaten its way through the gloom, but it had enough power to light the mist and make it shimmer. It was the sort of fog that puts shadows in motion and makes you think you see things that aren't there. Or things that haven't been there for centuries. I always imagine knights on horseback on mornings like this, searching for Marzin, or Merlin, the Magician. Some say he still haunts *Brocéliande*, imprisoned forever by a fairy's spell.

The trapdoor was easily pried open, and the flashlight made a friendly circle of cheer in front of me as I descended the stairs. I had a winter hat and gloves on this day to guard against the room's chill.

The flashlight probed the recesses of the space. After descending the eight-foot shaft of the stairway, I saw a rectangular area no more than twelve feet by thirty feet that had been carved out of the ground and completely lined with fitted stone. The ceiling was about fifteen feet high. The cellar would probably have been used to store food for the chateau, although there was no evidence left of any shelving system.

The space was clean swept. No mice or mouse droppings. No spiders or webs. In fact, there was absolutely nothing in the room. I was disappointed because I'd been so certain I would find something.

My shoulders must have sagged, because the flashlight moved about a foot down the wall opposite me, until it lit the junction with the floor and came to rest on a small chest two feet high and two feet long.

I walked forward and poked at it with the flashlight. It seemed rather heavy for its size. Its top was curved into a half-barrel shape. It was completely covered in leather, which was attached to the wood by rivets. They had been placed to form curving, decorative shapes. I had seen chests of this sort in museums like the Cluny in Paris.

Trying the lid gently, I thought that, like the door above, it might have rusted shut, but it lifted easily, silently, the flashlight revealing the contents. I was enough of an antique lover to know that the twin stacks of books inside were extremely valuable, but I was too much a bibliophile to resist opening the cover of one and turning the vellum pages. I had expected to see an illuminated manuscript with vivid filigree embellishments, but the book was more journal-like, the letters more individual than those made by the first printing presses or even those formed by scribes. They had more personality.

☙❦❧

The chest and the books stayed with me for a week before I decided to turn them over to the University of Rennes II, asking only that they keep me informed of what the books revealed. They were quickly devoured by both the Department of Archaeology and the Department of Celtic Studies, which confirmed that half of them were journals, and that they had been kept by a woman named Alix de Montôt from 1459 to 1462. The other half were popular books of the era.

The discovery was reported across France. The importance lay in both the gender of the diarist and the period during which the journals were kept. Women weren't well educated during the late years of the Middle

Ages, and it has been rare for any journal to last five hundred years, let alone the journal of a woman. So, since the first report of the discovery, the university has been inundated with requests from researchers to access the volumes.

That was two years ago.

Now that the first two volumes of the diaries have been translated into modern French and English and published in academic journals, I have been hounded by researchers. They seem to think that since I live in what is assumed to be Alix's chateau, they should have the right to stay at my inn free of charge. At least twice a month I catch someone skulking around my property trying to "walk in Alix's shoes."

Not that I scorn all academics. I have one graduate student from Rennes staying with me, but Séverine is different. She's charming, even though my American brain still wants to spell her name "Severing." She asked if she could explore the chateau and its grounds. Nicely. And at the moment, she even helps me with the inn.

And now, Robert Cranwell. An American. An author.

Alix's popularity had spread across the Atlantic. It was bound to happen. But if he wrote Alix's story, then it would probably get turned into a movie, and then I might as well be living in Disneyland for all the visitors I'd have.

2

*D*eciding that I deserved an espresso, I shoved the letter into my pocket and walked back into the entry hall and downstairs into the kitchen. As I went, I knotted back my hair. It's wavy, so when I twist it into a cord and tie it in a knot, it actually stays. I always knot my hair when I walk into the kitchen; it's a habit left over from cooking school.

I counted coffee beans, ground them into powder, and pressed them into the filter basket of my espresso maker. I love the smell of freshly ground coffee. And I don't care what the French insist: Starbucks beats *Carte Noire* any day of the year. I perched on the stool in front of my desk and fiddled with a pencil, waiting for the espresso.

The kitchen has no direct light, but half-moon windows high on the walls allow enough indirect light for the stone vaults to multiply; I've never had a problem reading recipes. And for the short winter days, I have several halogen lamps that streak light up the ribs of the vaults and down into my workspace, lighting the marble-topped island in the center with its stools and providing enough light to see into the doorless wood cabinets that line the walls. My pots and pans hang from a hand-wrought iron rack suspended above the island.

Six months.

It was difficult to keep from making a face as I poured the espresso into a demitasse. Six months would be a huge commitment. And I was in the habit of turning down prospective guests. I can afford not to run my inn full time, and so I don't. If Cranwell came in September as he planned, he'd be with me through . . . February. That was grim. January was not pleasant in northern Brittany, so I usually spent a few weeks after Christmas in Rome and Sorrento, enjoying the mild Italian sun.

Although I would never describe myself as a hedonist, I did live a life that pleased me. Following the death of my husband in 1998, I used the money from his insurance policy and an inheritance from the estate of my parents to purchase the chateau. While my husband had been working at the Embassy in Paris, I had put my time to use studying for a diploma at *Cordon Bleu* cooking school, and I had graduated at the top of my class.

Following renovations to the chateau, I had opened my inn during the spring of 2000 and was given a rave review by a Paris magazine that keeps the jet set informed of what's trendy. Apparently in the world of quaint inns, it's me. I charge a ridiculous amount of money for each of my seven rooms and an equally absurd amount for breakfast, lunch, and dinner. It keeps away the crowds, but I still only agree to one reservation in eight.

A remote location in northern Brittany, chronic bad weather, and outrageous prices: my secret to success.

Since I could afford to be choosy, Robert Cranwell would just have to find somewhere else to stow his pen. I dropped the letter into the garbage can on my way out of the kitchen.

For the rest of the afternoon, I worked in my garden. It supplies my chef's need for fresh herbs and vegetables, and I had planned it so that something is always in season.

Guests usually expect me to have a medieval garden, but I don't. My garden is purely practical. The only flowers I grow are my favorites, and they're used to decorate the entry hall and guest rooms. The edible flower fad in France is long gone, except perhaps in Provence where lavender has always been used in cooking.

If I catered to the tourist trade, I would be more interested in medieval gardens and medieval cooking, but my guests aren't here to gnaw on haunches of venison. They want the type of cuisine they eat at France's three-star restaurants. I'll never make that list: I don't have the staff or necessary level of service, and the wine list begins and ends with me. If a meal needs a $300 bottle of wine, then I provide it. I make the choices. But that's what my guests pay for.

My garden is parterre style: laid out in geometric patterns. It's situated behind the chateau close to the kitchen so that I can climb out the back door and quickly gather what I need. Most French formal gardens use low-clipped hedges to outline beds. I use rocks. My garden is a forty foot by seventy foot rectangle. Along the edges are beds of flowers. Tall flowers like cheerful yellow *rudbeckia*, sweeping blue perovskia, lavender asters, and the pink spear-like *Lythrum virgatum*. They're meant to fill the large spaces between the floors and ceilings of the chateau. Around the foundation of the chateau I placed flowering shrubs of *hortensia*, spirea, forsythia, and heather to mix with the ivy that has climbed the stone walls for centuries.

Down the middle of the garden are three rows made of square beds divided into four sections each. These squares are mostly herbs. Between the flowers and the squares, I have several long rows stretching the length of the garden for things that need space: tomatoes, raspberries, peas, and beans.

My garden is not meant to be pretty. It's meant to be serviceable. I spend at least a quarter of my day tending to it, and I make my menus from what is ripe and ready to be picked. In the fall, I pay local hunters a premium for whatever they bring me. I prefer wild duck and rabbits, but I've also been known to use squirrels, deer, and geese.

I live in a personal paradise where I get to do what I love: create recipes, cook them, and eat them. For me, life is filled with pleasure. At that moment, I was savoring sweet melons, crisp cucumbers, and the sunny taste of eggplant.

I was having dinner that evening, listening to R.E.M. and reviewing the newsletter of the foundation I'd set up in my parents' and husband's names. My father had been a loud voice in the U.S. Senate and spokesperson for the trade-as-diplomacy brand of politics. After they had all died, I'd formed an intercultural foundation in their memory. Although it expressed my own ideas about politics, it did emphasize the importance of intercultural education. The foundation sponsored lecture series at influential universities. It also sponsored visiting professorships on high-profile campuses. That summer I had also decided to investigate possibilities for business exchanges among people in similar industries.

The foundation required more work than I'd imagined, but I kept reminding myself that the rewards to humanity were worth the effort.

The phone disturbed me. The phone always disturbs me. I glanced at the calendar, counted ahead five weekends, and decided I'd only accept the reservation if it were for that weekend. Some people might think me eccentric, but I can't help it, I need my solitude.

After turning down the CD, I picked the phone up from the desk and then walked back to the stool where I'd been enjoying my dinner.

"Chateau de Kertanuan, je peux vous aider?"

"English?" If the question was rude, the voice that asked it was rich, mellow, and deep.

"Yes."

"Is Frédérique Farmer in?"

Frédérique. I'd never identified that name with me. Any other 'ique'-ending name would have been better: Monique or even Angelique. My father had his own nickname for me, but he was dead, so I hadn't heard it in years. Hadn't been that person in years.

"Speaking."

"Hey. This is Robert Cranwell. Did you receive my letter?"

"Yes. Just this morning." As often as I refuse to make reservations, I have never learned to lie. Some faded memory of childhood Sunday school classes made the guilt unbearable.

"Great. So how about it?"

"Six months is a very long time. I can't make that sort of commitment." I stabbed at my pasta with a fork.

"Sure. I understand. What about four months? All I really need to do is get the feel of the place and do some research. You know: walk where Alix walked. That sort of thing. If after two months you hate me, I can always move to a different place in town."

The smile that curled my lips couldn't be stopped from coloring my reply. "Mr. Cranwell, there is no town. Alix's chateau might have been the center of life in her time, but there's nothing left now for at least twenty miles."

"Oh."

"Sorry to disappoint you. Good luck." I was ready to hang up the phone.

"Wait. Please. I need to write this book. I can explain it when I get there, but this is important. How long can you put me up? Whatever you say, that's how long I'll stay. Even if it's just a week."

My eyebrows were making exclamation points. Cranwell had to be worth millions. He was a moneymaking machine. His novels had been made into movies by the dozens. I even had a few on my bookshelf. But the life of a fifteenth-century French girl wasn't his genre.

"Please."

It felt as if the entire weight of the book were resting on my shoulders. Guilt could always motivate me. "Let me look at my calendar." I put my hand over the phone and sat for a minute, staring at my plate, debating with myself. I hated being chained to someone else's schedule. If Cranwell wanted to come, then he'd have to adapt to mine. I could probably put up with him for a month. I looked at that second weekend in September and counted back four weeks. "If you can be here next Saturday, you can stay for a month."

"Great! See you then."

My disgust with my inability to say, "No," was so great that I couldn't finish the rest of my penne pasta with *fines herbes*. I got up and made an espresso instead.

After climbing into bed at 9:30, I picked up my *International Herald-Tribune*. I always read the paper at night. I like knowing the news I read has already been analyzed and reacted to by the time I see it, and that, in spite of everything, the world hasn't come to an end. But I couldn't concentrate that night, so I finally dropped the paper to the floor, punched my pillows into a more comfortable position, and tried to sleep.

And found I couldn't.

So I gave myself permission to enjoy a *nuit blanche*. A white night. I decided that if I couldn't sleep, I might as well enjoy it.

First, I plugged in my laptop computer. Then, I climbed into bed with it and searched the Internet on "Robert Cranwell." I found listings for all the books he'd ever published: reviews, sales, collectors trading first editions. I was looking for an interview or some insight into his character, but it was like wading through *gelée*. There were 5.7 million sites that had the words Robert Cranwell hidden somewhere in their listing.

So I searched on the names of several Hollywood-gossip magazines and then searched those sites for Cranwell listings.

It took several hours to read through the snippets of "Cranwell sightings." He'd casually dated many A-list actresses, had seriously dated several models, and was engaged briefly to a rock star. One article, dated three months earlier, trumpeted his supposed conversion to Christianity. After all the other articles I'd read about his life, that particular claim provoked an unladylike snort. The longer I read, the greater my unease became. It looked as if I'd have a giant ego on my hands for the next month.

My own dating life had consisted of just one person: Peter.

My father had made a career out of being a senator and my mother a career out of being his wife, but the high-profile, high-society friends they kept and the lifestyle they led just made a shy little girl grow more into herself. I had a small group of friends in high school — okay, one friend, and I managed never to have to talk to a boy, let alone go to a dance with one. This is not to say that I was a mouse. I had definite opinions. I was on the debate team and I never had trouble expressing myself in the classroom. It was the one-on-one I had a problem with.

The college I picked was as far away from home as possible. That's where I met Peter. I was forced to speak with him because a professor paired us together for a group project. From the first time he made me laugh, it seemed as if he'd known me forever. When I was with him, he made me feel beautiful. I went from wearing baggy sweaters and jogging pants to clothes that actually followed the shape of my body. And I discovered along the way that I had a waist!

It never crossed my mind to question Peter's confident assumption that he and I would spend our lives together. I never had to make that decision — he made it for me. We married the week after we graduated, moved to DC, and then, several years later, to Paris. With him to teach me, I finally became comfortable with myself. Even developed a sort of flair for fashion.

But my years in junior high and high school had marked me. Though I had not taken part in the social scene, I had watched. What I learned was this: The more popular and better-looking the male, the less trustworthy he was. This equation increased exponentially the moment a male realized he was good-looking.

So how had I ended up with Peter the Blond, the Fair, the Blue-eyed? He had disarmed me.

And then he'd died.

In that same calamitous year, my parents had also died. I did the smart thing and enlisted the aid of a counselor in Paris, spending a year working through my grief. I'm cured now. At least I think I am. The counseling was in French, so it's hard to know for sure. I do know that at the end of the year, she waved good-bye and shoved me back into the world. I surfaced in Brittany, stripped of any rose-colored delusions about life or the role God plays in all of it.

Twisting Peter's ring around my finger, I glanced back at the computer screen.

Robert Cranwell smiled confidently back at me, his dark eyes wrinkling at the corners, the precise sweep of his dark hair back from his forehead betraying a hundred-dollar haircut.

Giant ego might be an understatement.

After trying so hard to keep my life simple, it seemed as if I'd sabotaged myself by answering a single phone call. Gazing out past the glow of my computer screen, I appreciated the homegrown elements of the room: stone and wood. Life couldn't get much simpler than that. Letting my mind drift back to the days when the chateau was first built, I imagined the servants who would have been relegated to this top floor. At some point during my reverie, after 3:00 a.m., I fell asleep.

I woke at 5:00 a.m. It's rare that I ever sleep later.

⚜

By Thursday evening, I was in a testy mood. I hate it when I say yes to people when I should have said no.

Friday's rain made my mood even worse. I had heard fistfuls spatter against my window as I slept. I woke to pouring streams of it. And Séverine did nothing to help. She was in the clutches of one of her own dark moods.

"Frédérique. This rain is not good." She shot me a worried look as I placed a demitasse of espresso in front of her.

"No kidding." I sat on the stool across from her, propping my chin up on a hand.

She muttered something in French and crossed herself.

"*Pardon?*"

"*S'il pleut pour Sainte-Radegonde, misère abonde sur le monde.*"

In spite of her years of education, Sévérine was extremely superstitious, but that knowledge did nothing to stop the chill that crept up my spine. "If it rains on Sainte-Radegonde, misery abounds in the world?"

She crossed herself again.

Needing to do something to shake off the chill, I got up from my stool and turned the halogen lamps up. The increased light did nothing to decrease my unease.

Sainte-Radegonde. Today, 13 August. Was the misery worse if it fell, like it did this year, on a Friday?

And just how long would the misery last?

3

On Friday evening my guests arrived from Paris. They splattered around the loop of my drive in a Bentley and parked it right in front of the door. Why not? They were my only guests for the weekend.

Except, I reminded myself, for Cranwell.

The driver, a gentleman, got out, popped up an umbrella, and opened the passenger door for a woman. He helped her climb out, kissing her before releasing her. Then he adjusted the sweater that was flung around his neck, she adjusted the scarf that was around hers, and hand in hand, they climbed the stairs.

As they approached, I pulled the door open wide in welcome.

The gentleman was well known in France; the woman, not known but very beautiful. I'd lived long enough in this country to realize that she was probably not his wife. I sternly lectured my puritan conscience to mind its own business as I led them toward the reception hall and then up the winding central stairs. Their second-floor room was already glowing from the fire I'd lit to counter the chill of the evening. She kicked off her brown Gucci loafers, unwound her blue and brown-colored Hermès scarf, and dropped it over the back of a chair before I closed the door behind me. They requested breakfast in the dining hall at 10:00 the next morning.

By 10:15 that next morning, my sole staff member had failed to appear. "Monsieur is probably becoming very hungry," I muttered while I arranged the serving tray yet again. I would have delivered it myself, except for the way that I was dressed. I mix all the breads the evening before, then shape and bake them in the morning before I serve breakfast. It's a job that makes for sweaty work, so I've eliminated most of the traditional chef's wardrobe. I've kept the classic baggy white and black micro-checked pants and comfortable shoes. I tossed the oversized white jacket and replaced it with a simple white tank top.

And though I look good in my modified outfit, I don't look good enough to appear in front of a French cabinet member who expects a lot more for his money. I don't know what I'd do without Séverine.

We have an arrangement, she and I. Séverine has been with me for two months and has another ten to go. I provide room and board, and she provides wait service and cleaning for my guests. It's a perfect arrangement. Except for the fact that she's chronically late. But she has such classic French beauty that everyone — including me — forgives her. I turned the dial on the espresso machine as soon as I heard her shuffle down the stairs.

"Frédérique. I am so sorry." She appeared, breathless, at the bottom of the staircase. Her short black skirt and high-heeled pumps accentuated her long legs, and her deep red V-neck sweater managed to make her lips look even more red and her long black hair even more shiny.

"*C'est partie!*" I shoved a basket full of freshly baked *pains au chocolat* into her hands, and turned her around back toward the stairs. No one stays mad at Séverine. She started off with a slow ascent that would have been maddening had she not been so elegant. I knew the moment she entered the dining room, the French cabinet minister and his friend would be completely charmed.

"*Je suis bête.*" I am stupid. That's the first thing Sévérine says to any of my guests, and it's offered by way of apology: for being late in answering the door, for being late in serving breakfast, for being late in picking them up at the nearest train station. My guests would see what everyone saw in Sévérine: long, graceful French legs, a handful of wavy dark hair pulled back into a twist, random strands of that hair pulling out of the twist to frame an animated face, and impish green eyes.

Just as long as they were never subject to the schizophrenic moods that swept over her like tidal waves. I blamed it on her work. She was more passionate about her research than any academic I'd ever met. She'd never yet snarled at one of my guests, but if she ever did, I would have to reconsider our arrangement.

It was after I had turned back to the counter to begin cutting fruit that I realized I had left the sugar bowl off the coffee tray. *Quelle horreur!* No self-respecting Frenchman drinks an espresso without sugar. I grabbed the bowl and took the stairs two at a time, hoping to catch up with Sévérine before she made it to the dining hall.

After taking two tight twists of the spiral staircase at a fast pace, I was dizzy when I emerged on the ground floor. I meant, of course, to sprint through the narrow door into the front hall and then past the big staircase into the reception hall. As it was, I dashed right through the archway and into Robert Cranwell.

If I hadn't dropped the sugar bowl to grab a fistful of his sweater, I would have tumbled backward and down the stairs into the kitchen. If he hadn't dropped his briefcase to grab me around the waist, he would have been propelled back into the table holding the flower arrangement. We wobbled back and forth for a moment until we obtained a collective balance; then I released his sweater and had the chance to look up into his face. I'd have to say that at first glance, I found him even more attractive than the picture that appears on all the jacket covers of his novels.

But he's exactly the kind of man I don't trust. If I hadn't known his age, I would have guessed him five years short of forty-five. He had dark wavy hair, cut short on the sides and slicked back on top. It was graying at the temples, which gave him a look of distinction I was almost certain he didn't deserve. At least he had a sense of humor; his dark eyes were sparkling. They were probably brown. I didn't spend time looking. To top it off, he seemed the type that has a perpetual tan, and I could see a handful of chest hairs peeking through the open collar of his long-sleeved carbon-colored polo sweater. In certain circumstances, that has the ability to drive me crazy.

His tan wouldn't last the week in Brittany.

An apology had almost formed on the tip of my tongue, but then I realized he still had an arm around my waist. I slid out of his grasp, trying to pull myself together and be professional.

"Welcome to Chateau de Kertanuan." At that exact moment, my hair inexplicably spun out of its knot, and cascaded down around my shoulders. "May I help you?"

"I'm Robert Cranwell. I'd like to see Frédérique Farmer, please."

There were two choices: I could admit to being me, or I could pretend that Séverine was me. But I couldn't go through with the lie. He'd find out the truth sooner or later. It was better to choose humiliation and get it over with. I'd dealt with worse situations.

I held out my hand. "I am Frédérique. Pleased to meet you."

Something flashed in his eyes that I couldn't interpret. He clasped my hand in his. "The pleasure is mine." Then he bent down to the ground and started collecting pieces of the broken Quimper bowl. "I'm really sorry about this."

Kneeling on the stone floor beside him, I placed a hand on his arm. "Please. Let me. It's not a problem." *Only two hundred dollars worth of antique ceramics.* I cupped my hands and he emptied his shards into them. "If you'd like to have a seat in the reception hall," I indicated the general direction with my chin, "I'll be with you in a moment."

Séverine walked into the entrance hall just then. She and Cranwell exchanged glances as she sailed past me and spiraled down the stairs. She always makes me feel as if I'm a klutzy teenager.

Taking a deep breath, I turned on my heel, leaving Cranwell to find the reception hall on his own. I trudged down the stairs shaking my head. At some point, I had to take on the persona of a professional hotel manager, preferably at some point before Séverine left the following June. She was my face to the outside world, and I depended on her completely. I tossed the pieces of the bowl into the trash.

Séverine hooked her foot around the leg of a stool and pulled it out for me as she filled another bowl with sugar cubes. "I will take this up, yes?"

"Please." I buried my face in my hands as she ascended toward the dining hall. It wasn't that I wanted to impress Robert Cranwell. I didn't care a thing about him. In fact, he was already becoming a nuisance. It's just that I didn't want to have one more person assume that I was twenty-one years old. When I lived in Paris, I made a conscious effort to look my age. With my even features and round face, I'll probably still look twenty-one when I'm fifty. As the proprietor of an inn, a well-renowned inn at that, I should have commanded more respect. I put a hand up to my hair and thought once more about cutting it, but then my hand glided down its length and I thought how much I'd miss it. It was probably my best feature. I sighed and threw my upper body across the marble-topped island, my arms flung out, my palms accepting the coolness of the stone. I turned my head so that my cheek rested on the tabletop. It felt like ice to my burning cheeks.

A small movement at the bottom of the staircase drew my attention, but I realized it had to be Séverine. She knew her way around my kitchen well enough to be able to take the fruit from the cutting board and arrange it on a small platter. I closed my eyes and let my body melt into the marble.

A suspiciously male-sounding cough made my eyes fly open. "Cranwell?" His name leaped from my lips before I could stop it.

"Ms. Farmer?"

How dare he invade my space. Reluctantly, I scraped myself off the marble and turned on my stool to face him. "What can I do for you?"

He held a large Louis Vuitton suitcase out in front of him. "I was just wondering . . ."

"Your room. Follow me."

I have to confess that I bypassed the formal stairs and led him up to the second floor straight from the kitchen. I might also have taken the coiled steps two at a time, leaving him gasping for breath and struggling to keep the rough stone walls from marring the leather of his suitcase. But then again, chateaux were not made for modern convenience.

The chateau has a tower at each corner. This gives both the dining hall and the Council Room a round area at both ends. On the three floors above the ground floor, there are four or five rooms on each floor, with central, tapestry-hung halls that provide access to the central staircase. On each floor, the towers have been converted into bathrooms, turning each of the guest rooms into suites. Seven of the rooms have been renovated for guests. One of the larger rooms, I turned into a library; another smaller room, next to my own bedroom on the fourth floor, I turned into a lounge. The remaining space on the fourth floor, I had renovated into an apartment for staff.

I had opened the door to Cranwell's room and drawn the dark rust velvet curtains from the windows by the time he had joined me.

The olive brocade curtains enclosing the bed had been whisked back and secured to the posters, exposing the rich rust and olive tones of the duvet. I walked across the stone floor toward the tower end of the room. "Bathroom," I announced, indicating a small door in the stone wall. "If you'd like a fire in the evenings, and if you're responsible enough to tend it, I'll have some wood delivered."

"I'd like that." He was making a tour of the room, touching a corner of the sixteenth-century tapestry that hung on one wall, fingering the key to the armoire that stood beside it. "This is very nice."

"Thank you." The room's deep autumn tones fit him. I'd decorated specifically with those colors, thinking it would make a man feel at ease.

He half-bowed in an oddly endearing manner as if by way of compliment.

I found myself smiling before I could think not to.

When he straightened and saw me, he smiled too. He pulled a pair of glasses from his pocket. Raising them to the light, he frowned, polished them against his sweater, and then perched them on his nose. Then he bent to look more closely at a small painting that sat on an easel on a rectangular table.

"You're welcome to move that if you'd like to do your writing there."

He turned to look at me, his left eyebrow raised.

"I assumed you'd want to work on the table. There's an outlet right beside it and a plug-in for a laptop."

"Oh. Thank you. Yes."

"Once you've settled, come downstairs, and I'll make you coffee."

"Espresso. Thanks." He cleared his throat and looked at me over the top of his glasses. "I didn't mention it in my letter, but I'll be having someone stay with me."

Someone else? Two people were a lot different than one person in the language of innkeeping. So now not only would I have to cater to a famous author, I'd also have to deal with his groupie.

"Lucy is . . . "

Holding up a hand, I put a stop to his explanation. "As long as you pay, you may do whatever you'd like with whomever you want. No explanation required." I didn't want to hear about it. One of the most pleasant things about living overseas was being disconnected from the Hollywood scene. Cranwell's personal life was nothing I cared to investigate.

But I don't like it when plans change.

When I left Cranwell's room, I headed up the stairs instead of down. It was probably too late to change an impression, but I wanted Cranwell to see me in something besides my tank top and baggy pants. It was always possible I'd make him leave before the month was up, so establishing myself as a figure of authority was necessary. I spent two minutes in the shower to freshen up and then about fifteen minutes in front of the armoire trying to figure out what to wear. I finally settled on trim black Capri pants and a light blue sleeveless ballet-neck sweater. My arms get a workout from kneading bread dough and stirring pots of soups and sauces for myself or for my guests. They've become muscular, so I like to show them off when I can.

As I made my way back to the kitchen, I lectured myself. Cranwell was here because of the chateau. No matter his thoughts of me, he could hardly fail to be impressed by it.

I had decorated with furniture that spanned five hundred years of French history. Most family-owned chateaux are furnished in that fashion. Each new generation would make their mark on the structure by redecorating. I had tried to stay with a single period or theme in each room. The dining hall is Louis XIV: The chairs have crossed, curved supports connecting their legs. The backs are tall and broken by a horizontal rectangle of upholstered material, hung with a fringe. The colors are deep red and wheat gold. The table is more narrow than its modern counterpart, but is considerably longer. It is simply made with no ornamentation save along the legs.

The reception hall is a showcase of high medieval period furniture. The settee, on which I choose most often to sit, is softened with a moss green velvet cushion. The chairs that line the walls are of basic shapes and basic construction. The walnut *dressoir*, however, is a masterpiece of medieval skill: Its dark wood is carved and shaped into a procession of panels decorated with repeating vegetal designs.

The guest rooms of the chateau run the gamut from Louis XV to art deco styles and are decorated in colors as varied as canary yellow and deep plum. When I have time and the weather isn't cold, I scour flea markets to pick up accessories to fill them: books, candelabras, linens, timepieces. French furniture styles fascinate me. Each epoch has its own look, its own colors, its own politics, and its own expression. The only period for which I do not care is postmodern.

Medieval and Renaissance period pieces are difficult to find, outside of chests and trunks, so I purchase reproduction furniture at a fraction of the cost. At least with the sturdy fakes, I could be certain that no one would fall through a chair or lift a door off an armoire.

All the guest beds are also reproduction. Antique beds are generally so short and narrow that my guests would have been sleeping with their knees pulled up to their ears. But at least I draped and hung and canopied them in an authentic style. Though sleeping enclosed by curtains or swathed in material makes me claustrophobic, I find the look romantic and knew my guests would too.

When I started decorating, I made a conscious decision to try to divide the decoration of the guest rooms evenly between feminine frills and masculine scrolls. If I took a reservation from a woman, I would give her the Louis XV room with its pink and baby blue upholstered furniture or the Napoléon III room filled with gold-plated, crystal-dripping glitz. If a man booked a reservation, I would reserve the Roman-looking Napoleon I with its colors of avocado and aubergine or the Louis XVI room with its simple straight-lined, columned shapes.

Do I name my rooms? Do I have a Marie Antoinette? A Blaise Pascal?

No.

The French have particular sensitivities and often choose their furniture styles based on their political and philosophical preferences. I might have a guest request the Revolution Room, but the Marie-Antoinette? Never.

Do I collect English or German antiques?

No.

In my opinion, the former are often clunky, of awkward shapes and oddly colored wood. The latter are usually rubbed with finishes so dark and heavy the artistry can't be seen.

I'm both a Francophile and a snob, and I feel absolutely no remorse.

Besides, it's my chateau.

4

*C*ranwell had already made himself at home in the kitchen by the time I arrived. He was deep in conversation with Sévérine, who was seated on a stool next to his at the island. She had her arm resting on the countertop with her chin propped in her hand. She was looking at Cranwell as if he were the only man left in Brittany.

Spare me.

While they talked, I made espressos and placed a basket of breads in front of them.

He laughed at something she said and then glanced at me.

Turning my back on him, I poured the espresso shots into their demitasse cups.

He laughed again and she joined him, her melodic giggle joining his baritone chuckle.

Chancing to look at him when I set the cups in front of them, I found his brown eyes gazing at mine.

"Sugar?"

"Please."

As I took the new sugar bowl from the cupboard and set it in front of them, my toe hit something under the island. I bent down to investigate and found myself nose to nose with a dog. A slobbering, pug-nosed Boxer. It was fawn-colored with a jaunty white blotch that covered its nose and curved into its muzzle. The sturdy chest was marked with a blaze of white.

"Ms. Farmer, Lucy." Cranwell made the introduction with great aplomb.

Lucy was a dog! She licked my face with her large wet tongue, and I couldn't help myself from grinning, but I managed to wipe it, and the slobber, off my face by the time I straightened to face Cranwell.

He was looking at me innocently, as if finding stray dogs in kitchens was a normal occurrence.

"If she barks — "

"She doesn't bark."

"If she tries to chew my furniture — "

"She won't."

"If she even starts to go — "

"She doesn't. Not in the house."

We stared at each other for a long moment before being distracted by Séverine, who had climbed off her stool and was down on all fours making cooing sounds at Lucy. Dogs or babies — the French will go crazy for either. But apparently, Lucy wasn't crazy about Séverine. She growled and pushed herself farther beneath the island.

"Fine. She can stay."

"She prefers beef."

"Really." I scowled at the beast. "I only make one meal. The rule for her is the same for you." I fixed Cranwell with my most withering glare. "You eat what I cook, or you go hungry." I gathered my dignity and stalked up the stairs to my room.

Séverine's voice floated up the stairs behind me. "You are not to worry. She is really very good cook."

Séverine knew enough about my routine to be able to find lunch for Cranwell in the refrigerator and warm it for him. My other two guests would be out of the chateau until the evening. For myself, I decided to skip the noon meal. I just didn't feel hungry.

I did, however, feel like a run. I've never been accused of being wiry, but I'm slender. And running every other day ensured I stayed that way. I changed into a jogging top and shorts, cinched my shoes on, and galloped down the stairs and out the front door. I jogged slowly down the drive, my feet sliding slightly backward as I pushed off the gravel with every step. But as I turned right, toward the forest, onto my well-trod path, I found my stride. I ran, savoring the scent of the forest and the soil. I wound through the trees and then burst out into a meadow. Alix's meadow. My halfway point. I'm an out-and-back runner. The meadow was at exactly 1.5 miles.

As I pushed through the grasses toward its middle, a sparrow-hawk streaked out of the forest from the opposite side. I saw its gray wings flap once. Twice. Its white and brown mottled body torpedoed toward the ground. It snapped up a mouse without even slowing its flight and rose, triumphant, into the cornflower blue sky.

Having jogged a wide loop in the middle of the meadow, I sped back toward the chateau. With a mind refreshed, I looked forward to an afternoon of working in my garden and cooking. As soon as I saw a glimpse of the drive, I increased my speed, breaking into a full sprint once I touched the gravel. At the front gate, I slowed down and did three circles around the chateau, gradually easing into a walk. On my last circle, I heard a call from above. I looked up to see Cranwell leaning out his window.

I waved and made sure I didn't slow a step.

That was the third time the man had intruded upon my life that day.

It was a bad sign.

Without changing clothes, I went straight from my run to the garden. I was merciless with the weeds that afternoon. Just before 2:00, when I usually started working on dinner, I turned to my border of flowers to decide what to cut for the front entry. I had already taken several stalks of aster and was debating what to take next. Again, I sensed that irritating, gentle presence. I was hoping that at some point God would just give up and leave me alone. "Would you leave?"

He didn't.

"Please?"

"Okay. Sorry to disturb you."

I screamed, and the lavender blooms fell to the ground.

Lucy barked. Once.

"I'm sorry!" Cranwell bent to pick up the asters. "I was just trying to let you know I was here."

Must the man surprise me every time he happened to be in my vicinity? "It's just that sometimes . . . "

"I think the *rudbeckias* would look nice with these." The suggestion was gently offered, so I rudely rebuffed it.

"Perovskia." I hurriedly clipped three stems and grabbed the asters from his hands and began to speed-walk up the flagstone path.

"Don't forget your spade," Cranwell called from behind me.

Detouring back into the garden, I found it sunk into the earth beside a row of peas. I must really have been daydreaming to have left it like that. It didn't occur to me until later to ask how Cranwell had seen it there, covered as it was by the leaves and tendrils of the plant.

Cranwell and Lucy sauntered to the chateau behind me and watched as I arranged the flowers in the vase. He was right. The *rudbeckias* really would have been the best choice.

Later that afternoon, as I climbed the stairs to my room to rest before dinner, I noticed that someone had added several stalks of *Lythrum* and a branch or two of spirea. It looked much better than it had before.

Cranwell and Lucy appeared as I was setting the table in the dining hall. He silently armed himself with the forks and knives I'd brought out and followed me as I laid out three plates. "If it's all the same to you, I'd rather not eat up here."

That comment surprised me. "Why?"

"It seems as if the other couple staying here is rather . . . " He grinned.

"Rather." I nodded in agreement. "I'll have Séverine bring your dinner up to your room." I couldn't blame the man for feeling like a third wheel.

"We — Lucy and I — could always just eat with you." He looked at me from under his dark eyebrows, imploring.

How come brown eyes can't be just brown? Why do they have to include such fascinating shades of honey and amber, fawn and walnut?

"In the kitchen?"

"Isn't that where you eat?"

"Yes." But it's also where I unwind. I put on a CD, read a book, enjoy my food. I have a routine. A routine that I like. Even Séverine eats in her own room.

"You could explain to me what the chateau was like when she lived here."

She. Alix. It defied explanation how a centuries-dead person could have continued to cause so many complications in my life.

"I need to know so that I can start to write."

Anything to get him out of my life as quickly as possible. "Of course. Come down at seven."

My reward for surrender was a wink.

I hate men who wink.

Cranwell and Lucy appeared promptly at seven. He'd just taken a shower: His hair was slicked back and he emanated a masculine scent of soap and woodsy aftershave. In spite of myself, I breathed it in as hungrily as the scent of fresh-baked bread.

He smiled what I might have labeled a shy smile had I not been better informed of his character.

On a stool, at the island, he watched as I took plates of eggplant bruschetta out of the oven, and napped them with Mediterranean vinaigrette.

Bending down, I set a bowl of raw cubes of steak in front of Lucy. She eyed me, then leaned toward the bowl and swallowed them whole. She must have, because she could not have chewed them in the thirty seconds it took the meat to disappear.

"Do you have a cup? I'll give her some water."

After handing him a heavily leaded crystal tumbler, I watched in amazement as he tipped it for Lucy and as she daintily lapped it up.

"If I give her water in a bowl, she slops it all over the place." He put the glass in the sink and resumed his place.

Lucy walked slowly to the stairs, sighed, and then walked her paws out in front of her until her belly touched the floor; she lifted her head regally. Then she rolled out her hip, stuck out her back legs, and crossed them, as delicately as any lady, at her ankles.

We both smiled as we watched her.

"I call her Queen Lucy. You know: *The Lion, the Witch and the Wardrobe*."

No, I didn't know, but it irritated me that he had read my thoughts. The plates had absorbed the heat of the oven, so I used oven mitts to place them on the marble.

Cranwell pulled at the tips after I'd finished and drew them from my hands. Then he stacked them together and laid them on the counter.

Half an hour before, I had opened the wine, a Chinon, to allow it to breathe, so I poured two glasses and handed one to him. We clinked our glasses together. "To Alix," he ventured.

"To Alix."

Wondering just how much he knew about wine, I watched him take the first sip. I was impressed.

He took a small sip, and opened a crack in his lips, to draw in air. I saw his lips purse as he exhaled through his nose, knowing that the berry notes would be filling his sinuses, as they were filling mine.

"'90?"

"'95."

"Cassis, cherries, violet."

Okay, so I wouldn't be serving him macaroni and cheese while he was at the chateau.

"Bread?" I held a baguette in one hand and a bread knife in the other.

"Please."

I sawed off a generous slice for him and another for myself. And then it was time to eat.

"Is Frédérique a family name?"

"In a sense. I have my father, Frederick, my mother, and my grandmother to thank. Mother was so sure I was a boy that she'd decided that I was going to be Frederick Jr. She never even picked another name. When I came out as a girl, my grandmother, who is French, suggested Frédérique."

"So did your friends call you Ricki when you were growing up?"

"No."

He ate several minutes in silence, and then lifted a piece of bruschetta. "This is excellent."

It *was* excellent. The olive oil-based vinaigrette had sweetened the eggplant, and I'd broiled it to perfection. I thanked him for the compliment. It had been so long since I'd been in a social situation that I had no idea what to say to him. I talked to Sévérine every day, but it was a vocabulary limited to the inn. I felt like a person coming into a warm house from the frigid cold: My cheeks were stiff; my mouth wouldn't work right. I tried to make words; I tried to say phrases, but they came out haltingly, as if I hadn't spoken in years.

Cranwell, bless him, ignored my false starts and stutters, orchestrating the conversation.

"And how did you come to be here?"

"I bought the chateau in 1999, spent a year renovating it, and opened up the inn. I had some good publicity — "

"I saw. In *à La Mode* magazine."

"Yes. That was good for business."

"I can imagine. But how did you come to France?"

And there it was. Would he pity me? "With my husband, Peter. He worked at the Embassy."

"In Paris? State Department?"

I nodded; it was just easier than explaining. Although diplomatic work is the purview of the State Department, there are many other federal agencies with staff at embassies — some of them with a higher profile than others. "It was a three-year assignment. He was asked to go to Tanzania the month before we were to leave."

"Tanzania. I've been there on safari. The Serengeti is like nothing I'd ever seen."

"It was August of '98."

He was quick. It took only a moment for him to realize the significance. He absorbed the information faster than I had. At the time of Peter's death, the bombings at U.S. embassies in East Africa had seemed like a disturbing dream. Disturbing and disconnected from anything real. It took weeks for me to connect the rubble of those ruins to my own grieving heart.

Cranwell glanced down at my hand. His gaze lingered on my wedding band; then he lifted his head and looked at me. "And you decided not to return to the U.S.?"

A wave of relief buoyed me. There would be no pity. No awkwardness. Just a simple acceptance that, as I had fought to claim, life moved on. "No. I mean, yes. I couldn't go back. Too many things had changed. I wasn't the same person, and I didn't want the same things I'd wanted before."

"Did you cook before you came to France?"

I shook my head. "Peter was so busy at the Embassy that I needed to find something for myself. I decided on *Cordon Bleu*."

"Sounds glamorous."

"It wasn't. I spent two weeks just learning how to use a knife. When it came to actual cooking, I made recipes over and over, memorizing them. Sometimes we ate the same thing for a week and a half."

"If it tasted anything like this, I can't imagine he would have complained."

"He didn't. Ever."

At that point, I got up and removed the plates from the table. Then I quickly sautéed three chicken breasts, adding melon jam at the last moment. I took a breast from the pan, arranged it on a plate and reached for the next. Cranwell had anticipated this and was already at my side, offering the plate. He did it easily, smoothly, fitting himself into my rhythm of work but not invading my space.

I heard a familiar shuffle on the stairs and arranged a tray of food for Sévérine.

Lucy growled and moved from her position by the stairs to take refuge underneath the island.

"Excuse me. I do not mean to interrupt." Sévérine stopped at the foot of the stairs when she saw Cranwell; then she came forward to collect her tray.

Cranwell did what every man does when they see Sévérine: He got to his feet, saying, "Please. No. That's quite alright." And then he managed somehow to touch her. Sometimes men touch her arm, sometimes her shoulder. Sometimes they even clasp her hand and pull her closer. The magic of Sévérine is as old as Eve. And it never fails.

"I see you later, Frédérique."

Nodding, I confirmed, "At eight." She would serve dinner to my guests.

Cranwell followed her with his eyes as she left the room, and with his ears long after she had disappeared from sight.

Waiting until he was done goggling, I tried to restart the conversation. "And how did you hear about Alix?"

"A lecture in L.A. 'Feminism in Medieval France.'"

I bent to pick up a scrap that had fallen on the floor. I eyed Lucy and then decided against tossing it to her; she was definitely too high-class for scraps. "How enlightened of you."

As I set a plate in front of him, he looked into my eyes. "A prospective girlfriend."

"It didn't work out?"

"She wasn't any fun. But the lifestyle of medieval women was fascinating."

How typically male. "Maybe for you, but I'm sure it wasn't for them."

He had been cutting his chicken but waved a hand as if to brush away my remarks. "I asked for a list of references and did some research. I came across an article by — "

"Let me guess: a Ms. Dupont?"

"You know her?!"

"You do too." The thing that is most irritating about Sévérine is how smart she is. It really is not fair. "Sévérine."

"Sévérine — ?"

It was impossible not to catalogue the emotions as they crossed his face. "That's perfect."

Just perfect.

5

After I'd cooked for my guests and Sévérine had finished serving them, Cranwell came back down with Lucy for an evening walk. They returned as we were putting away the last of the dishes.

He rapped on the kitchen door, startling me. It wasn't the normal entrance for guests.

Sévérine let him in. Lucy barked at her.

"I hear you're the expert on Alix de Montôt."

"The expert!" Sévérine laughed. "This is me."

Cranwell pulled out a stool for her and then one for himself. "What was she like?"

"What was she like?" Sévérine gave the slightest shrug. "Who can say?"

"I mean, was she . . . a daredevil? A prude? A tomboy?"

"I do not know these words, but you are asking me of her character?"

"Yes."

"Her character . . . " Sévérine thought a moment, a slight 'v' appearing on her forehead between her eyes, just pronounced enough to make a person want to lean over and smooth it away. "This is difficult, you know, because she is not of our age. This is the problem of history. You see, we cannot expect that a woman in the fifteenth century would be the same person in the twenty-first century. The society are different and they affect the behavior of each person. You understand this, yes?"

Cranwell nodded.

Sitting at my desk behind them, I decided to get a head start on the next week's menu.

"For her century, she was . . . I do not know how you say this, ahead of her time?"

"Yes."

"She was educated. She wrote very much. She had her own thoughts . . . "

"You mean she thought for herself?"

"Yes. This is what I mean."

"Thoughts that were not common?"

"Maybe thoughts that were common for a man to think, but not for a woman."

"That sounds modern. Advanced."

"Yes, but we find this is because she is not taught."

"You just said she was educated."

"Yes. Educated. But not . . . she was *mal élevée.*"

The silence stretched and I couldn't help but interject. "She was poorly raised."

"Yes. That is the one!" Sévérine turned and smiled her thanks at me. "She was poorly raised, so she does not know what is expected of her."

"In what way?"

"As a woman. As a wife. She knows how to read and write and do the maths, but she cannot manage a chateau. She knows nothing of food or of servants. She does not do *broderie* or sing or play music. And of life, she does not understand that she does not have choices, and so she thinks and makes as if she does."

"So, she's ahead of her time, but she's also behind it."

"No. Behind it would be no education. It is that she is not . . . "

Again, I intervened. "She's not socialized."

"Yes. Not socialized."

"So did she not want to get married?"

"No. She did. She knew she must because she was a woman, but she did not know what this meant."

"You mean leaving her home?"

"This she knows. She does not know, by example, about sex. She does not understand what a correct wife does."

"So what does she do?"

"Nothing."

"Nothing?"

"Nothing." Séverine sighed. "This is complicated. You could perhaps read my notes and the journals and understand the marriage better."

"But what about the history? In her era, Brittany was not a part of France."

"This is correct. Many parts of the republic of today were not ruled then by the King of France. They owed fealty to the king, but the lands had their own kings or rulers. Brittany was one of the most powerful, but there were many others."

"Exactly what was 'France' then?"

Séverine shrugged. "It is hard to know, but normally we say Normandy, Champagne, Poitou, Langedoc, Dauphiny, Touraine, and the area around Bordeaux to Cahors."

"And Alix's family came from this France?"

"Yes. Her father's family from Touraine, near Chinon. Her mother's family comes from Provence, from the land of a different king, King René."

"Was Brittany friendly with France?"

Sévérine sucked air between her teeth. "Yes. But she is also friendly with England."

"And England and France hate each other."

"Yes. The Hundred Year War is not long over. Not even ten years."

"So Alix's marriage is strategic."

"Yes. And this is correct for her family."

"Was her family close to the king?"

"They are related. Cousins, but not close."

"And Brittany, did it have a king?"

"No. In *Bretagne* we have the duke. The *duc de Bretagne*. He is the king."

"The family Alix married into, were they close to the duke?"

"Yes. They are cousins also, but more close than the family of Alix to the king."

"Is it possible then that Alix could have been a spy?"

"A spy?! I do not think so. There is nothing we have to say this."

"But is it possible?"

"I do not think a spy."

Again I turned from my cookbooks to interject. "Cranwell writes fiction Sévérine. *Les romans d'espionnage*. He's not writing a story about Alix. He's writing a story about a girl of Alix's time. Is it possible such a girl could have been used by her father to get information on Brittany's relationship with England?"

Cranwell sent me a grateful look over his shoulder.

"Yes. Yes, this is possible."

The way things sounded, Séverine and Cranwell might talk late into the night. So I went upstairs and left them alone. The sooner he got the information he needed, the sooner he would leave. I craved my solitude, and it had been lacking that day. I decided to take him out in the forest the next day and trot him around the boundaries of the old estate.

I sank into bed, enjoying the peaceful familiarity of the room around me. My room is on the top floor of the chateau at the end of the hall. The ceiling low and beamed. The fireplace, small and utilitarian. I have several windows, but they are tiny. At the time the chateau was built, archers would have used them to shoot at enemies. Some people might think it gloomy, but I'd never been one to linger in a bedroom. If I retreated, it was to the kitchen. I have a double bed set into a dark wood carved frame; it looks ancient, but it is a reproduction. I'd chosen furniture for my room that I'd fallen in love with. *Les coups de coeur.*

There is a carved wooden blanket chest that I use as nightstand, the top made of smoothly joined planks, the sides carved with a menagerie of animals. There is a simple oak Louis XIII-style chair that has more dignity in its simplicity than any curvaceous Louis XV I'd ever seen. I also have an armoire of walnut. It is a cross-period piece that mixes Louis XV and Louis XVI. The sides are columned, the top and bottom curved. The ironwork around the lock and the hinges is flowery. At the top of the piece in the center, an eighteenth-century craftsman had cut out a circle and filled it with ivory, bone, and ebony fitted together in the shape of a star. My one luxury item is a huge oriental Tabriz rug with a cherry red background. I had found it at the *Puces* in Paris when Peter was still living, and I could not tear my eyes from its vivid colors. It also has the benefit of keeping my feet from freezing as I walk across the stone floor to the bathroom. Apart from the carpet, my room is composed of the gray of the stone walls, the dark sheen from the wood furniture and beams, and the soft white of my duvet cover.

That next morning, after a breakfast of *tartines* of bread, chocolate-hazelnut spread, and espresso, I took Lucy and Cranwell on a tour. The overcast sky and hint of chill in the air were harbingers of the weather to come. I wore a pair of old jeans and a thick mariner-style long-sleeved shirt striped in cream and red, with work boots laced over thick socks. Cranwell too wore jeans and a light yellow button-down shirt, but his loafers were more suited to a day at the Louvre than a walk through the countryside.

Glancing at the forest, I decided to steer him first through the woods to the remains of the old outbuilding in the meadow.

"What was the size of the old estate?"

"It depends on what you mean by estate. The Forest of Paimpont used to extend for miles. Alix's husband held this chateau and the hectares surrounding it, but the *duc de Bretagne* had also given him lands in other parts of Brittany."

"Where?"

"Off to the west, as far as Chateaulin and up north toward Morlaix."

"So he had several chateaux?"

"No. Just extensive properties. He was given rights to various mills and other commercial operations, which allowed him to collect a percentage of their profits."

"He was wealthy."

"Extremely."

"And where did the king . . . the duke sit?"

"In Nantes, to the south."

"But Alix and her husband lived here . . . ?" We walked along together in silence for a while, Lucy bounding ahead and then stopping to wait up for us. "Was he involved in sea trade?"

"No. Not that they've found. The Hundred Years War was hard on trade in this part of Europe, and it never fully rebounded."

Cranwell frowned. "But for such a wealthy man, this location seems isolated."

"It is. But you have to imagine what can no longer be seen. A chateau of this size would have required many people to support it. And there would have been fields which would also have needed people. And if people were needed to support the chateau, then others would have come to support the needs of those people. There would have been a baker, a cobbler, a smith, a miller. There would have been a dairy and a church—"

"Here?"

"Yes. An entire village."

Cranwell stopped and looked around at the trees that seemed to stretch to the horizon. "It's just hard to believe."

Lucy barked, urging us forward. Ahead of her, I could detect the meadow through the trees, but we needed another minute to reach it.

We walked toward the middle of the meadow where the old building had been standing. "This is where I found the journals."

"Here?" Cranwell stopped in mid-step. "Why would they have been placed here? It's so far from the chateau."

Good question. As far as I knew, no one had asked it before. As far as the university was concerned, the important thing was that they had been found at all.

We stepped over the foundation, and Cranwell crouched down and reached toward the ring to open the trap door. "Do you mind?"

"Not at all."

What had taken me a crowbar to accomplish, he seemed to find effortless. He went nimbly down the ladder and spent several minutes in the cellar before climbing back up. Lucy was uneasy, spending the whole time whining into the darkness of the hole.

I gave him a hand as he climbed out, and he let the door drop with a thud. He wiped his hands on his jeans and then stood for several minutes, looking once again at the forest surrounding us. Lucy sat at his feet, practically on his toes, a sentinel.

Finally, he nudged Lucy, and we ventured further out into the meadow. "I've visited strange places before, but here it seems . . . "

"Like you're being watched?"

"Yes." He sent a keen glance my way. "You feel it too."

"Ever since I've been here. That's why in the garden . . . when you . . . "

His lips split into a grin over his white teeth.

I shrugged.

"Does it help?"

"He goes away. For a while."

"Who?"

"God."

"Ah. But he always comes back, doesn't he?" The way Cranwell said it, it almost sounded as if he were grateful.

Feeling uncomfortable discussing private business with someone I hardly knew, I changed the topic. "The history of this area is very old. And legendary. King Arthur. The Knights of the Round Table. Merlin. His fairy lover. Assorted druids."

"Here?"

"The Forest of Paimpont is part of the *pays de Brocéliande*, the Country of Brocéliande. This is where the search for the grail took place."

That comment stopped Cranwell in his tracks and brought his eyes to bear on mine. "I recall it being in Britain. Near Glastonbury."

"Most people think that, but it's not true. Some of the legends took place here."

"Why would you think that?"

He was beginning to bother me with his insistence. "Why else is the birthplace of Viviane the fairy just up the road? And why is Merlin's tomb just a few kilometers farther? And why can I visit the spot where Merlin first met Viviane?"

"You sure you're not making this up?"

"Yes!" I stalked ahead of him several steps. The man was insufferable. How can a person have an opinion of something he knows nothing about?

"Why would they search for the grail in France?"

By that time, I was ready to tear my hair out. "Because of Joseph of Arimathea."

"Who?"

"Joseph. The owner of the tomb in which Jesus was buried. Come on, Cranwell. King Arthur is a classic of Western literature."

"Joseph rings a bell, but I know next to nothing about him. So shoot me."

Lucy looked anxiously up at Cranwell and then over at me. She placed herself between us and sat on her haunches.

"The grail, from which Jesus ate during the last supper, was given to Joseph, and it was used to collect Christ's blood when his body was taken from the cross. After Jesus' body disappeared, Joseph was convicted of its theft and thrown into prison. While in prison, Christ appeared to him and blessed the grail, allowing it to sustain Joseph during his forty-two years in chains. When he was released, he and his family fled Israel for a place in the Roman Empire where they could live in peace. He brought his family, and the grail, to Gaul."

"To France?"

"Yes. It was a familiar part of the Roman Empire."

"And so then what happened to it?"

"No one knows."

"And you claim the good king Arthur came over to recover it? But how would he have known about it?"

"All the Celts, all the Breton peoples knew about it."

He shrugged. "If you say so."

For such a well-traveled person, he had a surprising lack of information about this particular part of the world. I wiped my nose against my sleeve and shot a look at him over my arm. I wasn't used to feeling like an idiot.

Lucy shifted her weight between her feet and let out a strange whimpery bark that made Cranwell look down at her with a piercing glance.

"Lucy wants to go."

"Fine." I turned my back on him and started toward the opposite stand of trees, tramping the dewy green meadow grasses under my feet. When I reached the edge of the forest, I turned, expecting to find Cranwell behind me.

He was still standing in the meadow where I'd left him, looking around. He shook his shoulders as if to ward off a sudden chill and then ran to catch up with me, Lucy at his heels.

"This place is strange." He said it with an unsettled look in his eyes.

"This place is old. Ancient. Its past infused with all sorts of pagan religions."

"I've never felt this way in any other part of France."

"This is not France, it's Brittany. *Bretagne*. Different country, different history."

my thirteenth year
year thirty-seven of the reign of Charles VII, King of France

one day before Saint Dominique

I am Alix de Montôt. I have thirteen years. I am the only child of the first wife of my father. I was left motherless at two years. My father has been married these seven years to Hélène, his second wife. She has had three children. Sons.

But I am the one who was taught the magic of letters by the hand of my father. I am the one to whom he chose to reveal the mystery of numbers. I was betrothed at birth to honor an ancient promise my before-before-grandfather made during the Crusade.

It was said between he and the comte de Barenton, his companion in battle, that their offspring should marry. For two hundred years, the families have had only boys. I am the first chance that the promise can be kept.

And fortunate for my father. After these years of strife between France and the duchy of Bretagne, and France and England, it is a wise match; I am promised to a Breton. If Bretagne turns to England as some say she will, or if Bretagne turns to France, as the king wishes, there will be ties of marriage to Bretagne through me. And father will profit from it. This he has explained to me.

I understand my value.

I am to be fiancéed next month.

one day before Saint Matthieu

My fiançailles will take place tomorrow. I am to marry Awen de Kertanuan, comte de Barenton. He is Breton and so he must be rich from trading by sea.

Agnès, my woman, says me that I shall always have beautiful gowns and will wear only blue and gold.

He has thirty years, which is very old, but I shall be glad if he has still his teeth.

day of Saint Matthieu

My fiançailles took place today. I wore an houppelande of leaf green and lined within and without by fur of gray squirrel. It ceintured about my waist with a length of willow green velvet fastened with a green jasper. Hélène says me that this is to symbolize my faithfulness in fulfilling the ancient promise of my family.

I have been told that my lord does not live near the sea. He is inland, south of Dinan. My lord is dark, as Agnès says me that Bretons are. He is more tall than father and he has his teeth, of which I am glad. And they are still white. I did not speak to him, but as a gift of our fiançailles, he gave me a chest which is studded with nails. And inside a crucifix cloisonné and threaded with gold. I should rather have liked a necklace of gold, but Agnès says me that the gift is very pretty.

The trunk at least is practical. I can place in it this journal, with room for many more.

one day after Saint Matthieu

I spoke with the comte today. I curtsied and said, "My Lord," in the pretty way I had been taught to do. He said nothing for so long that I rose.

He looked at me so strangely. Then he gave me his hand and drew me near. He touched my face and says me that he had once a sister my age. He spoke it so quietly I could hardly hear him. He seemed to me sad.

I demanded of him if she had been gay.

He smiled and replied to me that she had been quite gay. He looks kind when he smiles.

two days after Saint Matthieu

My lord left today. Hélène says me that I shall join him when I become grown.

five days before Saint Dionysius

Something happened today. My insides started falling out. I screamed and would not be quiet until Agnès had come.

Agnès told Hélène what was happening.

Hélène had fear. I heard her tell Agnès that this means I must leave soon.

two days before Saint Martin

I am being sent to my lord, the comte.

My father says me that I must go. He will give me Agnès.

I do not know how to speak the language of Bretagne. I do not know the people. I feel myself alone. I begged father to let me stay, but he replied to me that he is bound by the contract of fiançailles.

four days after Saint Martin

I spend this week in preparation.

day of Sainte Cécile

Father has given me a present of the most valued possession of my mother. It is a small circular baton made of leather. Twelve jewels the color of violets ring the top. There is a curious 'N' inscribed on front with a curved line set on top of it. I shall treasure it always. He has given me also the Book of Days of my mother. I had not before seen it, though my father says me that she read it each day.

From himself he gives me the books of King René d'Anjou, the brother of the King of France. These are the Livre du Cuer d'Amour, Espris, and Mortiffiement de Vaine Plaisance and these please me.

Agnès recounts me still stories of the Emprise de la Joyous Garde at Saumur, the famous tournament of King René. This happened before I am born, but my mother went to see it and Agnès says me that she was more beautiful even than Isabel d'Anjou, the wife of King René.

I have seen, from not so far away, Jeanne de Laval, the present wife of King René. They tell me she is Breton. She is pleasant, but I have heard it said that she is not so gay as Isabel. Perhaps it is because she misses Bretagne the way I shall miss France.

two days after Sainte Cécile

I am sent away. At least I have been given Agnès. She was the woman of my mother, and now she is mine.

We passed by Chinon and I could not stop my tears. Will I never again see the chateau, which projects so mightily from river Vienne? Will I never again walk its infinite length, never visit the home of Richard

65

the Lion-Heart or imagine the persuasion of Jeanne d'Arc on Charles VII against the English?

Chinon is my heart. Touraine is my country. I wish for no other.

two days before Saint Andrew

There has been little time to write these five days. We passed by Saumur. I wished to stop and demand of Jeanne de Laval would she go to Bretagne in my place. We stayed the night before at Chateau de Montsoreau after having passed the Abbaye de Fontevraud where Richard the Lion-Heart and his mother and his father lie entombed. The chateau is all new. The square towers are more like Saumur than Chinon. It is much less big than the both.

We crossed the river Loire the next morning. We lodged at the Chateau de Treves.

This next night we stayed at St. Remy la Varenne.

And now we have gained Angers.

I have never seen a chateau so formidable. It is immense. And outside it is striped by stones of lighter colors. The towers cannot be called well-portioned or graceful and the ramparts are low and ugly. Inside I changed my mind. This is the place of birth of King René. How could it not be pleasing? There are many gardens, pavilions, and galleries. Had it not been so cold, I might have made a promenade about the grounds.

Would that I could stay forever in this city of books and songs and learning.

Time presses. My lord awaits.

four days before Saint Nicolas

Angers is but a memory.

These days between Angers and Chateaugiron are difficult. The more long my journey, the more strange the countryside appears. I miss being able to see the land. And the river. There is nothing here but trees. And more trees. They press themselves up to the road and I cannot breathe.

The songs of the birds are strange. Even the sky, when I can see it, appears different.

three days before Saint Nicolas

My jennet enervates me. She has no mind, only following the palfrey of the man of my father, who rides first. She is too quick and too eager to finish this journey. This means that for every step of the palfrey, she takes two. My brain is so shaken by her gait that it is numb. I can no longer think. The trees, the hills, the road, the villages pass. And ten minutes later, I cannot remember what it is that I have seen. I am become dull.

two days before Saint Nicolas

I have gained Bretagne.

Agnès says me that I am blessed by fortune to be married into the line of Barenton.

I have only thoughts of returning to Chinon. My soft, gentle country. I do not like it here.

one day before Saint Nicolas

We gain Chateaugiron. The man of my father says me that it is one of the nine great baronies of Bretagne. The chateau is being restored, and so we pass by. It pleases me, with round, tall towers made of stone from the countryside.

Perhaps one day I will come back here and visit with my lord.

I hope my chateau will look the same.

day of Saint Nicolas

This night we lodge at Rennes. We entered through the stout Portes de Mordelaises. Passing between the two squat, round towers, I felt as if I were being swallowed up by the country of Bretagne. My jennet fought for rein to move forward and into the city.

I have been met by the man of my lord, the comte. From here he rides with us.

one day after Saint Nicolas

This day we passed the river Ille and many millers, launderers, and tanners who do work upon the banks. This night I am told we are two days ride from Chateau de Kertanuan.

three days after Saint Nicolas

Today we will reach Chateau de Kertanuan. When I rose, Agnès aided me to wear one of my new robes. It is an houppelande the color of vert-de-gris, a green of gray, and the sleeves and neck lined in fur. The all is covered by silvered broderie and it is rather elegant. A ceinture pulls tight beneath my chest, but it has a clasp of gold which is decorated with stones of chrysoprase which glow a gray-green.

Agnès says me that they symbolize virtue.

I would rather a stone symbolizing intelligence or wisdom.

My shoes of soft leather have a long curled point, as is the fashion.

I write this night of the chateau of the comtes of Barenton, Chateau Kertanuan. It is not so large as Chateaugiron. It is constructed of stones of the countryside, and it has four tall round towers, one for each corner. The enceinte encloses a chapel and a large courtyard in front of the chateau. This is filled with mud and stone and hay. In time, perhaps, I shall make it a garden.

The village is not small, there are both a tavern and a carpenter. But it is not large: I saw no butcher, no fishmonger, no smith.

At least the trees do not assault the chateau. This I could not support. And one can see clearly down the road and into the village. It is not far.

I have my own room.

Agnès sleeps on the level above me, and her room too has much space.

For my own, I have a bed. And a large one. It is four columned with a drape the color of blueberries broderied with silk the color of wheat to make flowers and vines. And the duvet of the bed, the same material. I have been given a bench for by the window and several chairs. There is a large fireplace in which I can stand and lay two of me end-to-end. And it is made certain the fire never goes out during the day. There is a fur all near on which I might sit. On the walls are hung several carpets of the orient. Their patterns are exotic and of blue, gold, crimson, and cinnamon.

There is also an armoire large enough to hold all my clothes.

But the best is a table on which are several sharpened quills and a pot of ink. And it is here on which I write.

This is my new home.

one day before Saint Damase, pape

The noces took place this day inside the chapel for cause of rain. And I am glad of it. If not, my martin blue velvet houppelande might have been ruined. As it was, my cloak protected the outside, but the crimson satin lining of the skirt has been spotted from the underneath. And I shall have need of a new pair of silk slippers.

But still, in spite of the rain, there were musicians who promenaded before us. They played the saqueboute, and the drums, and an instrument of which I have never heard: a biniou. It gives a strange, wild, screaming sound that raises the hairs of my head.

I pledged to give my body to my lord, and he pledged to receive it. And then he pledged the inverse and I did the same thing.

My lord gave me a band of gold with a ruby. I have never seen a ruby so large. And that he placed upon the thumb of my right hand and on the next two fingers in turn, invoking the blessing of the trinity. It remains even now on the middle finger of my right hand. I must become accustomed to the weight of it.

The man of my father placed my hand in the hand of the priest and the priest joined my hand with that of my lord.

And then, we celebrated the Mass with a veil covering myself and my lord as we kneeled in front of the altar.

I spoke to my lord, the comte, after.

He is dark as I remembered. His hair waves beneath his hat. His brow and jaw are strong, his eyes are dark. He speaks French. This day he had dressed in a costume of blood red velvet. His houppelande was short and Agnès says me that he has a very fine leg. As his leggings do not sag, I must believe she is correct. Around his neck hung a chain of gold so thick that my smallest finger would not equal it. And on it, a disc studded with pearls. From his ceinture I saw hung a small dagger with a handle encrusted with jewels of many colors. I know this dagger for my father carries its twin. They are the weapons our before-before grandfathers came by during the Crusade.

I smiled to see it and found that when I looked at him, my lord smiled back.

He has also a cousin, Anne, who lives with him. She speaks also French.

There was a great feast after the noces. We had oysters, and partridge, and suckling pig. There were jongleurs who threw balls and blades. And always the musicians.

And after the food, the dance.

We started with the danse basse large which began when my lord bowed to me. This dance I prefer, for with the short gliding steps my lord does not dance far from me and with the music slow and dancing up on the toes I find it graceful, like the swimming of a swan. And for this the music of the vielle and the recorder.

And after the danse basse, the conjé which my lord calls the trihoris. This I like also. There are eight figures, the all more quickly made than the danse basse but of equal grace.

And after, a surprise. A branle danced with torches to fête our marriage. It is danced by the guests and all holding tapers of many colors. It was as beautiful as if the stars themselves were dancing.

And after, my lord extended his hand and I placed in it the palm of my own, for all the persons with joined hands danced. And after, the next couple led the branle double; and after, the next led the branle single; and the couple behind, the branle gai. And then we left the children to dance the branle de bourgogne and the music more fast until they fell, laughing.

And after, Agnès and the man of my lord danced the branle du haut barrois.

And there followed the cinq pas in which we leapt and skipped and danced in all directions and that very quickly.

And this after: I took rest.

It was late when Agnès and Anne came to take me to bed.

Agnès and Anne made much over my dressing for bed this night. They unmade my hair and combed it until it shined. Agnès rubbed perfumed rose oils into my skin and pinched my cheeks to make them red. They dressed me in a fine silk chemise with long hanging sleeves and a low neck which had broderie throughout in the shapes of curling vines. Then they made me drink cinnamon water to sweeten my breath. They told me my lord would come to me after they had left and they bid me do what he will demand of me. They left me smelling of rose and cinnamon, standing in front of the fire.

My lord came in, as they had said, after they had left.

I curtsied and greeted him.

He took my hand to aid me rise and then demanded what Agnès and Anne told me would happen tonight. I told him that they had not told me. They said only that I must do as he bid.

He looked very angry then.

It frightened me and I trembled.

He saw it and drew me to the fire and made me sit and covered me with a fur. He stood beside the fire and watched me for a long time before speaking.

He demanded of me if I should like to hear a story.

It was a rather stupid question. I always like to hear stories, but I was getting sleepy and tried not to yawn.

He began to tell me about a fée, a fairy, but then he saw me yawn and he stopped.

I apologized, but demanded of him if I could go to bed.

He was very nice to pull the duvet back for me. Then he kissed me on the cheek and demanded of me if he might stay until the fire burned down and I consented if he would not wake me. He blew the candle out and I heard him sit beside the fire, although my eyes were so tired I did not see him. But just before I slept, he told me I must tell them the next morning that I did as I was bid. And that he was very gentle. And that it did not hurt so very much.

At least I think that is what it was.

He was not there when I woke in the darkness of the night, so I could not demand it of him.

day of Saint Damase, pape

When Anne and Agnès came in this morning and looked so anxious, that I told them what I could remember of the words of my lord.

Agnès hugged me.

Anne was arranging the bed and must not have heard.

Agnès made me cover my hair this day. As I have wed, it is not right that my hair be loose any longer. She pulled it tightly from my head and fixed a henin on top. She says me that this tall pointed hat is of my mother. She draped it with a gauze. To balance it on my head all the long of the day has given me a pain in my neck that she has tried this evening to rub out.

My lord spoke to me this day in the hall where I was reading. He demanded of me if I had told Agnès and Anne what it was he had told me to speak to them.

I replied to him that I did not know if I had remembered correctly, but I repeated what I had told them.

He smiled and told me that I had remembered exactly.

So I began to tell him about the druids and how they had games for remembering everything, but I could tell he was not listening, just like I can tell when father does not listen. I demanded of him if he would mind if I returned to read.

Before excusing me, he told me he would come by times to tell me stories at night.

I suggested that he might come earlier so that I could better enjoy them. He made me a present of a brooch of pearls and told me that I must wear it and explain to Agnès that he gave it me this day.

one day after Sainte Damase, pape

Anne, the cousin of my lord, is from Beaune. Her family disappeared by the pox. He is her relative the most close, so she has come to stay with him. The mother and father of my lord have been long dead since his youth, and so she has served as the lady of my lord, as the chatelaine. Anne has twenty-two years. She is dark and gay, and laughs often. I know she will be my close friend.

Agnès does not like her, and I do not know why.

But I am a woman. I am thirteen. I can do as I please.

day of Saint Thomas, apostle

Agnès says me that I must take charge of the household: the servants, the tradesmen, the meals, and the accounts.

I demanded of her who these had done before.

She replied to me, Anne.

As I am now chatelaine, I must tell Anne she can do still these things. It is for me to make progress in my studies.

Agnès told me it is my duty as an honorable wife to manage the chateau. And she remembered to me that I ignore the duties of a wife. I know neither how to make broderie, nor how to make music, nor how to sing.

How to sing? Better to write the songs. Recite poetry? Better to write the poems.

Agnès recalled to me the example of Anne.

And I recalled to her that as much as I have seen, Anne does nothing. She plays at broderie. She plays at music, and at singing. But I have both seen and heard better. The thing Anne does most well is talk to her woman. Perhaps Anne has also been playing at chatelaine. But if it is so, then it cannot be such a difficult role to play. And as a complaint of my lord has not reached my ears, I must assume he is satisfied with her efforts. So Anne may play all that she wants. I shall study.

As a wise wife, I will let those duties to the one who has been properly managing them. And more since the feast of Noël is nearly upon us. I know that Anne has been always arranging this.

It is me the chatelaine. If I must be in this strange land, I will do as I please. And it pleases me to let Anne guard these duties.

day of Noël

After the work of yesterday, in cleaning, in giving the animals double their food for the day, when it seemed everyone of the house was distracted, we passed this day playing cards, in prayers, and by singing. They have found a log as big around as six persons and as tall as two persons and have lit it in the hall of dining, in the hearth; this is to last for the three days that come. And on it we throw salt and wine and bread in honor of the holy trinity.

And then the midnight mass. This mass is my preferred of the year. This night we had chants and offerings, and even a nativity theater. I made certain not to rise a moment early to leave the church, for I had no wish to see the dead march in procession through the village.

And outside, after, on the path to the chateau, I listened to hear the animals speak, or to see the stones rise, or the fruit trees flower during the twelve rings of the church bell at midnight; we must have been too late, for I neither saw nor heard anything. I kept close watch also for witches or demons that come out this evening. I gave myself fright for I did not remember having left the door open for bad spirits to leave the chateau, but on our return, I saw that someone had it done.

For the meal we had a roasted boar and oysters and cakes and chestnuts and a potage of truffes. And everything served on the table this night. Anne says me that this is so the dead can serve themselves and take part with us in the fête. And there must have been some dead among us, for at the end of the meal, I saw no food uneaten.

day of the new year

Anne had some men find a ball of mistletoe and had it hung between the hall of reception and the hall of dining.

Anne and my lord walked in to dinner together.

The rest of us had already assembled.

As they passed beneath the door, my lord realized there is mistletoe and he must kiss Anne. He did it, and Anne blushed. She is very pretty.

I demand of myself why she is not yet wed.

day of Epiphanie

This day, we celebrated Epiphanie, the coming of the kings. The galette des rois, was served. And in his part, my lord found a fève.

He was crowned king, and he must choose his queen.

I was saddened at first that I was not chosen to be his queen, but then he had chosen Anne, and I was glad. It is kind of him to look after her interests, as she is left unmarried at such an old age.

We instructed the cook to give the part left of the galette, the part of the Virgin, to the first mendiant leading a horse decorated with laurier who will pass by the chateau.

two days after Sainte Agathe

My lord came to my room this night to tell me a story.

I have taken the decision that if my lord is to tell me stories, then I will write them down. As they are Breton, I have heard nothing of them before. It will also serve as good practice for my penmanship. The follow is the story he told me this night:

Trédamial has many people in good health. This is because the Chapelle de Notre-dame-du-Haut is possessed of seven healing saints. They are: Eugénie who heals head-aches; Houarniaule who heals fear, anguish, and nervous illness; Hubert who heals rage; Lubin, who heals joints and eyes; Mamert, who heals intestinal difficulties; Néen, who heals troubled minds; and Yvertin who also tends to head-aches.

I demanded of my lord what good this story is. It does not amuse.

He told me again of the saints and the maladies they heal and bid me remember in case I will have need of them.

I reminded myself at this moment here that his young sister caught an illness and died. And also, my mother.

My lord sat by the fire, morose.

I rose from bed, pushed back the curtains, and sat at his feet. He seemed in need of company.

We stared into the fire together for a long while.

septembre

Ce que le mois d'août n'a pas mûri,
ce n'est pas septembre qui le fera.

September

That which the month of August
does not ripen will not be made
ripe by September.

8

*C*ranwell and Lucy spent their time in September just roaming the estate. I would see him sometimes while I was jogging, sitting in the forest on a fallen log scribbling in the notebook he always carried in his pocket, or throwing a stick for Lucy in the meadow. He would wave at me and then turn back inside himself.

At dinner, as a rule, he was attentive and made for good company. I asked him about his walks one evening over *gougère bourguignonne* and *braisé de boeuf*. The spongy texture of the cheese bread was a perfect foil for the meat.

"So what is it that you do out there in the forest with Lucy all day?" I asked this as I unwound my hair from its bun and combed through it with my fingers. The uncommonly nice weather was drying out my skin, making my scalp itch. Of course, I wouldn't be caught dead scratching in Cranwell's presence, but the feel of my fingers gliding through my hair was soothing.

"Hmm?" He looked up at me over the rim of his wineglass.

"You've been wandering around out there for the past three weeks."

"I'm getting ideas. Talking to God. I think best when I walk." He reached toward his back and pulled his fisherman's sweater over his head, leaving his hair in an uncharacteristic sprawl across his forehead.

I resisted an urge to reach out and push it back into place.

He unbuttoned the sleeves of his faded denim shirt and rolled them up. I'd like to know why denim shirts always look so good on men.

"How's it coming?"

"Well." His eyes were glazing again and their focus moved from my eyes to my hands, to my hair. He stared, as if mesmerized, and reached out a hand, fingering the ends of my hair.

I could feel my chest constrict.

"What color hair did Alix have?" It was clearly a question he was asking himself. I couldn't have answered if I'd tried. My voice had disappeared.

He put his other hand to his chest as if to search inside a pocket on his jacket. When he realized he wasn't wearing his jacket, his lips curved into a self-deprecating smile. "I think I'll take Lucy for a walk."

He let go of my hair. I watched him rise like a sleepwalker and snap for Lucy.

She rose and sighed, sending me a beseeching look.

I gave her a pat and then shook my head as they walked up the stairs to the back door.

"Don't forget your coat."

He paused and then turned, staring at me for a long moment. "Right." Reversing directions, Cranwell came back down the stairs and then went up the spiral staircase toward his room.

Watching them leave, I put shaking hands to my hair, gathered and rewound it, and knotted it back into place.

That week I dedicated to making *confiture*, or jam. I'd put foundation correspondence on hold, canceled my regular trip into town, and decided to skip the week's regional flea markets. September is the traditional month for jam making in France. In fact, in the 1700s, when the revolutionaries renamed the months of the calendar, September became Fructidor, identifying it with the fruit processing done during the month. In case of questions regarding my cooking diploma, I do adhere to the laws of jam making. (In France, birthplace of bureaucracy, you cannot doubt that there are laws governing this skill.) For to make jam is not to make marmalade; neither is it to make compote. Jam is composed of great quantities of both sugar and fresh fruit, whole or juiced. Marmalade, of course, includes gelatin and purée, while compote violates the jam rules by including very little sugar.

My boxes of *fruits verger*, or orchard fruits, covered every available space of the kitchen. There were apples, pears, peaches, plums, figs, gooseberries, and black currants, as well as a mound of lemons, a pile of vanilla beans, and bag after bag of sugar. I also had a selection of hazelnuts and chestnuts to add to several of the jam mixtures, and I had an assortment of jars and lids.

Standing back to survey the work before me, I suddenly felt very tired. Over an espresso I organized my work according to the ripeness of the fruits in front of me. The prep work wouldn't take too much time: squeezing the lemons, crushing and chopping the nuts. The more perishable fruits I would process first: peaches, pears, gooseberries. The others could safely be left for the end of the week.

After my espresso, I rearranged the boxes in accordance with my plan of work: Those I would process first were nearest my work area; the rest were placed farther away toward the back door.

I'd made sure I'd taken no reservations that week, and I'd stocked the freezer with food from Picard . . . but that was my little secret. The Picard frozen food grocery chain sold anything one could imagine from *sauce béarnais* to *coquilles St. Jacques*. And the preparations were extremely well done. Serving Picard wouldn't damage my reputation in the least. I only hoped it wouldn't help it!

It was in the middle of my jam week that things began to rearrange themselves. At first I assumed it was Cranwell, so I mentioned it at dinner on Wednesday evening. We were enjoying *filets de pintade aux cèpes et aux girolles* — so much that I'd almost decided to let Picard do my cooking more often. The fowl was perfectly moist, and the sauce that accompanied it, studded with mixed mushrooms, was divine.

Between courses, I got up to check on a batch of jars and happened to realize how stained my white tank top and pants were; at that point in the evening, it wasn't worth changing clothes. And besides, Cranwell didn't care. And that was what reminded me.

"Cranwell? If you need to move my boxes when you take Lucy out, could you remember to replace them afterward?"

"What boxes?"

"The ones by the back door. The fruit. I lined them up in the order I'll be needing them."

He turned on his stool to take a look at them. "We haven't been going out that way. I didn't want to interfere in your production line." He turned back around to face me. "What's been going on?" The color of his burgundy crew-neck sweater was echoed by the color of the wine we were drinking. As he took up his glass and put it to his lips, the color was reflected by a glint in his eyes.

I swallowed. "Nothing. It's probably just me." I picked up the baguette and sliced a piece for myself. But the problem was, it wasn't me. I knew myself, I knew my work habits, and I knew exactly how I had laid out the boxes. They were no longer in the same order I had placed them.

"Maybe Séverine cleaned down here and moved them around."

My brow couldn't be stopped from wrinkling into a frown. "She never cleans down here. The kitchen is my responsibility. She helps me serve meals and clean up after them, but that's it." But even as I was speaking I remembered that I *had* come upon Séverine in the kitchen at an odd time earlier that day. It had been in the mid-afternoon, long after lunch had been put away and hours before she was due for dinner. I had gone out into the garden to do some weeding but then decided to snip some basil for dinner while I was thinking about it. I gathered some leaves and returned to the kitchen to put them in the refrigerator.

As I came through the back door, I saw Séverine crouched along the bottom of the kitchen wall by the stairs.

Pausing in my step, I almost lost my balance and cried out. Séverine whirled around and came up to her feet, a dinner knife in her hand.

She'd said something about wanting a baguette and dropping the knife when she had been buttering it. At the time, I remember being surprised: The French only butter their baguettes at breakfast. Now that I'd remembered, I decided to ask her about it.

But when she came down for dinner, Cranwell plied her with questions. She was still responding as she made her way back up the stairs.

"How broad was education during Alix's time? I know that she was a scholar. Would she have read books in Latin, French . . . Arabic, Hebrew, Greek?"

She paused on the staircase. "We know she read Latin and French. Arabic is not popular. With the Crusades, the church is not so pleased with the Arabs. All their knowledge is thought stained by their religion, and so they keep their sciences and their maths to themselves. Hebrew is difficult. The Jews of course know Hebrew, but they have been chased from France in the fourteenth century. Before this, there have been many in this region. But they must leave and settle in the Kingdom of Provence and in Spain and Italy. There are no official Jewish populations in France during the fifteenth century. There are people in France who are Jewish who pretend that they are not. Understand? But we have no documents written in Hebrew and no schools of Hebrew because they are not allowed. And Hebrew is difficult whatever is the case because at that time it is used as both alpha and numeric. Each letter represents also a number. I will show you this."

She came back down the stairs, set her plate on the table, and took a pad of paper and pencil from my desk. "By example, the letter Y and the letter A. The tenth letter of the Hebrew alphabet, *Yod*, may be used like our letter J or like Y. And *Aleph*, like our A, is the first letter of the Hebrew alphabet." She drew what looked like an N with a wavy line on top of it. "In Hebrew these are also the numbers ten and one. So you might add them together and make eleven. And the fun is that an eleven such as this might be just the number eleven or it may be a symbol."

"A symbol?" Cranwell looked thoroughly confused.

"Yes. The ancient language is read on many different levels. Some numbers were special and some were not. Twelve by example is a complete number and very significant. Eleven misses one, and because it is not quite twelve, it symbols for not complete. You see?"

"I think so."

"*Bon.* As for Greek, according to her journals, Alix did not know this. I have answered your question?"

Cranwell nodded.

As Sévérine continued her ascent, my eyes dropped to the place I'd seen her crouching earlier. The mortar between the stones looked as if it were crumbling. Either that or I had mice. I grabbed a broom and swept up the debris. As I was sweeping, I thought of Sévérine picking up that dropped knife and then using it to cut and spread a pat of butter. My nose wrinkled. After dumping the crumbled mortar in the wastebasket, I decided to throw away the butter Sévérine had used. No point in contaminating food with what might be mortar mixed with mice droppings. I opened the refrigerator, found the butter dish, grabbed it, and took it to the sink. When I took off the lid, I was surprised to see that it was still wrapped in paper. It had never been used.

Why would Sévérine have lied to me? And what had she been doing with the knife?

༄

The next week brought a conference to my chateau. It was sponsored by the French *Ministère de la culture et communication* and it was meant to address the significance of Alix's journals to the current record of late-medieval French history. Mostly it was a chance for six professors from the University of Rennes II and the University of Paris IV (the Sorbonne) to come together and debate their interpretations of the journals.

The significance to me? It was the first conference I'd ever hosted.

During the restoration of the estate, I had made the decision to put off restoring several of the outbuildings as well as the stable that I currently used as a garage. I could have easily added another six guest rooms to my total, but I wanted instead to narrow the scope of my efforts. I had also been tempted to close off the council room on the bottom floor.

There was no real need for it; I'd already placed a library on the third floor and had a pseudo-office in my kitchen. Besides, the room was huge, stretching the entire width of the chateau, with the towers flanking it on either end. It might have been used as a ballroom in an earlier period of history. The windows had retained their integrity, and the fireplace was functional; no immediate work was necessary. It had been my first guests who had inquired whether I had any meeting facilities. At that point, starting my business, I'd had no idea of the ridiculous fees I could charge, and so I was interested in anything that would bring in more money.

The conversion of the space to a conference room had been easy. It necessitated the purchase of modern amenities such as a large screen that could descend from or roll up into the ceiling; an overhead projector; a VCR and a computer hooked up to a ceiling-mounted one-gun projector; a printer; a copier; a fax machine; a telephone; blackout shades for the windows. And also pieces to lend the room atmosphere, like a huge, respectably faded and worn carpet, purchased from Drouot auction house in Paris; a large, long reproduction table in the best Renaissance style; a dozen comfortable folding leather arm chairs of a sort of medieval "director's chair" model; a map desk filled with paper, tape, scissors, and paper clips; a long, waist-high, hand-carved cabinet on which I had placed a coffee maker, a thermos for hot water, and a selection of teas, demitasses, and cups and saucers. I even had the ceiling's beams painted in rust, green, and gold with coats of arms and *trophées de guerres*, military trophies.

To enhance the "Council of War" theme, the walls were decorated with all the shields, pikes, helmets, and spears that I had been able to pick up at flea markets. I'd even acquired two full suits of armor to guard the fireplace.

On the whole, it was a room to be proud of, and I had to admit that if I wasn't looking forward to the horde of guests that week, I was looking forward to seeing the room used.

In planning for the conference, I'd been certain that I'd thought of everything. I designed the breakfasts around breads and fruit, making sure that they would not require time-intensive preparation. I'd planned lunches and dinners around easy stews or roasted meats with simple desserts such as sorbets, cakes, and cheese platters. And everything would be served from a buffet table. It had been perfect.

Until Séverine announced that she wouldn't be able to help.

"But —"

"It is impossible for me to be here."

"But this is a conference on Alix. Think of your dissertation. All the experts in your field will be here."

"I have not been invited."

"So invite yourself. Offer to take notes. I can't believe you would want to miss this opportunity."

Séverine just shrugged and that was the end of it. At least as far as she was concerned. It wasn't the first time she'd dumped the duties she'd signed on for. A month earlier, she'd left me short-staffed as I was preparing lunch for some guests. She hadn't returned until late the following day.

Maybe that single-minded pursuit of knowledge was an asset as an academic. It certainly wasn't appreciated by this employer. Our arrangement wasn't formal — it had been verbal. That left me with more power, but Séverine seemed to act, at times, as if she were doing me a favor by showing up to help at all.

If I hadn't been so busy with my work at the inn and with the foundation, I might have asked her what was going on. I was familiar with the symptoms of a workaholic, and I knew Séverine was consumed with her academic pursuits. Peter had been the same way with his career. But my role as his wife had precluded me from saying anything because when I voiced my concerns, it sounded like I was nagging.

Séverine had become my friend. And this time, maybe I could say something.

But not right now. My job had just doubled. Not only would I be making meals, I would be serving them, tidying the guest rooms, doing unending loads of laundry, and trying to wedge in a few hours of sleep when I could.

Deciding to prep as much of the food as possible in advance, I spent an entire day chopping vegetables like celery and carrots and creating pear, apple, and cassis sorbet, as well as delicate chocolates that would accompany espresso during the conference coffee breaks, and *oeufs en gelée*, eggs in gelatin. I made *terrines*, both of vegetables and meat, and simmered stock for several of the dishes I would prepare later.

Cranwell appeared promptly that evening for dinner, Lucy ambling along beside him. Frankly, I hadn't put much thought into dinner, but I made quick work of slicing into one of the vegetable *terrines* and tossing a baguette on top of the island. Then I seared two steaks and made a quick reduction of wine and mushrooms to accompany them. For dessert I decided some of the aged Roquefort I'd had delivered would sit well with an old Porto I had in the cellar. And I was right.

Cranwell thought so too. "I've never tasted a better Roquefort."

It was the perfect combination of salty tang and cream. "It's from my secret source."

"Have you had any other strange happenings lately?"

"No." I was embarrassed at ever having brought the subject up with Cranwell. "Have you had any other encounters with God in your wanderings?"

He looked surprised and took time to spread cheese on a piece of baguette before answering. "Yes. Quite a few —"

I heard Séverine coming down the stairs and excused myself so I could prepare her steak. Cranwell never finished his thought.

"Robert, you are well?" Séverine appropriated my stool and sat down next to Cranwell.

He put down his bread and smiled at her. "Yes. And I have some questions about Alix I'd like to ask you."

"Of course. I can answer after I have eaten. I will meet you at your room."

I smiled to myself. Her response was so typical: Never mix business with food . . . at least not until dessert.

Cranwell glanced at his watch. "Nine?"

Séverine nodded. Then she rose and took her tray from me and climbed back up the stairs.

"It's a good thing you caught her tonight. She won't be here next week."

"Where's she going?"

That question stumped me. She hadn't really said.

9

*F*ortunately, the conference guests staggered their arrivals the following afternoon. I was able to give each one an individual tour of the chateau, ending with their assigned rooms. And in between the arrivals, I set the dining hall table and prepared dinner.

At 7:30, they assembled for paté and *cornichons* pickles, sauced-veal *blanquette de veau*, rice, and *haricots verts* green beans, followed by a luscious *gâteau au chocolat* that was much richer than any "death by chocolate" dessert I've ever tasted. I had portioned out enough of everything for Cranwell and me to have the same for our dinner and left it all on the counter, telling Cranwell to help himself. I meant to eat between serving, but after delivering espressos, taking orders for *digestifs* and clearing off the table, it was well after 10:00. Thankfully, Cranwell had placed all my food in the refrigerator, but it no longer looked so appetizing. I ended up scrambling a few eggs, scavenging some baguette, and calling it a meal. Preparing the bread doughs and setting the table for breakfast took until midnight. When I finally managed to crawl up the stairs to my room, it was all I could do to take off my clothes before falling into bed.

The alarm rang much too early the next morning.

As the conference was to start at 8:30, the guests had wanted breakfast available at 7:30. By the time the breads were shaped and put in the oven, I had to hurry to slice fruit and get a tray set up with espressos.

It was around 10:00, after the table was cleared and breakfast dishes put away, that I finally had a breakfast consisting of leftovers: a slice of melon and half a peach. A glance at my watch warned me that lunch was right around the corner, so I reset the table and then started cooking.

I'd decided on small individual *salades composées*, broiled chicken breasts with ratatouille, and an apple-rhubarb crumble. Crumbles were all the rage at the moment, even at the most exclusive three-star restaurants in Paris. I composed the salads first, leaving them to chill in the fridge, then I sautéed the vegetables for the ratatouille. At the last moment, I broiled the chicken breasts. The crumble, I began to cook after the guests had started to eat. That way, I could guarantee it was served warm.

Cranwell came in about the same time the guests began to eat. I pointed at the fridge, the stove, and the oven in turn, and told him to help himself as I flew up the stairs to check on the guests.

After they had disappeared into the council room, I cleared the table and was beginning to fix myself an espresso when I remembered that I needed to collect their sheets and towels to do the laundry. I raced up the stairs to the first guest room before I even thought about needing my master key to gain entrance to the rooms. Half an hour later, I was out of breath, out of energy, and in general need of a break before I started on dinner. Running usually lifted my spirits, so I decided to slip out for half an hour and take a jog.

I made it into the forest before I began to feel lightheaded. I can recall seeing Cranwell and Lucy up in front of me in the meadow, and I think I raised my hand to wave at them, but that's all I can remember.

When I came to, I was seated on a fallen log with my head between my legs and Cranwell telling me to take deep, slow breaths. He had his hand around the back of my neck as if to make sure I wasn't going to jump up and run away. I stayed bent over that way for a while, long enough to realize a trail of ants was working hard at storing food in the log. And long enough for Lucy to thoroughly lick my face.

"Are you okay? Did you hurt anything?"

From my doubled-over position, I inspected my ankles and my knees. "I don't think so."

"What happened?"

Too tired to answer him, I contemplated the ants, wondering when they were going to stop. Would they ever take a break?

"Do you feel sick?"

"No."

"Do you have a history of heart trouble?"

"No." I tried to shrug his hand away from my neck. "Is it all right with you if I sit up now?"

"Sorry."

He rose to his feet as I closed my eyes, stretched my back, and then sat up straight on the log. When I opened my eyes, it was to find Cranwell staring at me. The furrow in his brow told me he was worried.

"It's nothing. It's probably because I haven't eaten much in the last twenty-four hours."

"Why not? You definitely don't need to be on a diet." He put a hand to my waist as I attempted to stand.

"It's this conference. I don't have time to do anything but cook and clean."

He had shrugged out of his jacket and slipped it around my shoulders, leaving himself clad in jeans and a white button-down shirt. I had to admit that I had been starting to get cold. A jogging top and shorts work well when I'm actually running, but once I stop, I tend to cool off fast.

"Then why didn't you ask for my help?"

Why? Because I hadn't thought of it. "You're a guest. I can't ask you to help. It's my inn, not yours."

He muttered something to himself and then, with a firm grip around my forearm, marched us off in the direction of the chateau. "When we get home, you're going to sit down, and I'm going to make you something to eat. Then you're going to tell me exactly how I can help you."

True to his word, he did find something for me to eat. He made me eat an apple for an immediate injection of sugar, and then he gave me a plate of pasta with *gruyère*.

He watched me closely while I ate. It almost made me feel uncomfortable.

Finally, I finished and pushed the plate away.

"Feel better?"

Actually, I did. Surprising what a big difference a little food can make.

"What do you need me to do?"

Looking around at the kitchen, I couldn't think of any cooking that he could help with. I began to shake my head.

"What do you need me to do?" The way in which he said it demanded some sort of task.

"Laundry?"

"Where is it and what do I do with it?"

"All the towels and sheets are in the washers. Could you put them in the dryers and then make the beds and put the towels back?"

"Just tell me where the laundry room is."

After I had explained the location to him and pressed the master key into his hand, he headed up the stairs like a man on a mission.

Dinner for that evening would be easy to prepare. The *oeufs en gelée,* halved eggs, were just waiting to be pried from their molds. The *civet de sanglier,* wild boar stew, only needed to be assembled and put on to simmer; I would add boar's blood to thicken it. The sorbets were done. The only thing I would need to do at the last minute was boil potatoes to go with the stew.

An hour later Cranwell still had not returned. I wondered for a moment whether he actually knew how to make a bed, but I put the thought out of my mind as quickly as I could.

He appeared in the kitchen several minutes later and insisted on helping me set the table in the dining hall.

When I started up the stairs afterward, he demanded where I was going.

"I was thinking of changing clothes. If that's all right with you ... ?"

He scowled and then climbed the stairs behind me. "I'll change too."

After I'd taken a quick shower and changed into black pants and a black boat-neck knit top, I returned to the kitchen. And found Cranwell waiting for me. He was still wearing his white button-down shirt, but had exchanged his jeans for a pair of black slacks.

As I finished the dinner preparations, he watched me like a hawk.

"I'm not going to faint again. I promise."

He grunted as if he didn't believe me.

Irritated by his constant surveillance, I finally began to give him platters of things to take up to the dining hall, just to give him something else to do.

One good thing about his help: I was actually able to eat after the guests were served and before I had to run dessert up to them. Cranwell

helped me clear the table after they were done and stayed up wit
while I mixed dough for the next morning's croissants and baguet
even had time to read the paper and learned of the horrendous floo
that had been plaguing Provence that week. France can be a country
meteorological extremes; everywhere else in the country the sun h
been shining, the skies unmarred by clouds.

When I got to the kitchen the following morning, Cranwell wa
waiting for me. "What can I do?"

My eyelids were refusing to remain open. I fumbled for the espresso-
maker, but Cranwell took me by the hand, seated me on a stool, and slid
a demitasse toward me.

"How long have you been up?"

Cranwell shrugged. "Half an hour."

Well, he sure beat Séverine on punctuality. I took my time and savored
the espresso as he drummed on the marble island top with his fingers.

"So, what can I do?"

The espresso was starting to kick in. I left the stool and went to punch
down the bread dough.

He trailed me. "Unless you give me something to do, I'm going to
take over here, and your guests will have milk and cereal for breakfast."
He was serious.

"Can you divide this into twelve equal parts?" I would need twelve
baguettes for the combined meals that day.

"Not a problem."

Leaving Cranwell to dig his hands into the dough and figure out how
to separate it, I turned my attention to shaping croissants. When I was
finished and able to turn my attention back to him, I found him leaning
his back against the counter, arms crossed in front of him. Twelve equal

balls of dough were sitting beside him.

I moved to shape them, and as I took a ball of dough and began to mold it, Cranwell mirrored my actions. In ten minutes both the baguettes and croissants were in the ovens.

Since Cranwell had exhibited such sincerity in wanting to help, I set him up with a cutting board and knife and left him to slice fruit while I went upstairs and set the table.

When I came back, he had the fruit neatly separated into different piles. It was sliced, I'll give him that, although it was a little roughly done. For the sake of expediency, I just dumped it all into a large bowl and asked him to take it upstairs and set it on the buffet.

I'd never before allowed anyone to help me cook. Of course, I'd never before hosted so many guests at one time. But having Cranwell around had been a lifesaver.

Séverine came back into town just after the last guest had left. I had been in the council room, opening the shades and putting it back to order, so I saw her drive up. And I couldn't help but stare, because it looked like her car had wallowed all week in a gigantic mud puddle.

I caught her before she went up to her room. "Is everything all right, Sévérine?"

"Yes. Everything is as it should be."

"Was it a family emergency?"

She frowned. "No. This was for research. I have no family."

"None?"

"My mother is dead. My father is . . . " She finished her sentence with an eloquent French shrug.

"You don't get along with him?" I could relate.

"*Non.*" She laughed. But it wasn't filled with mirth. "You are an

American, so perhaps you do not understand this, but my mother was a mistress. Of a very powerful man. A nobleman."

"But that's . . . " *wrong . . . immoral . . .* ". . . fine."

She looked at me. "For my mother perhaps. But not so fine for me. We French do not progress like you Americans. We still have class structures. We are still the same as King Arthur and his knights. Much is forgiven here, but never a child without a name. Because you cannot make one for yourself in France. It is given you."

"He ignored you?"

"*Non.*" She set her bag down. Put her purse on the table. "He would tell me the most wonderful stories when I was a child. Of Arthur and of the search for the grail. But it was only to make my mother happy. When she died, there was no more connection. No more reason."

"But you're his daughter."

"By blood, not by name. And I must never be named. I do not exist. Anywhere. Not anymore."

"But — "

"You do not know what it is like to be the child of an affair. Not a one-night stand. An affair is two people, for life. Two people, never three. It was my mother and me during the weekend, the very best of friends. But during the week? At night when my father came? I might as well not have been born. I ceased to exist. So is everything okay? Everything is fine. Better than fine. Because one day my father will want, more than anything, to call me his daughter. Will be proud to claim me as his. One day very soon." She picked up her bag and her purse and tramped up the stairs. I was left staring after her, uncertain how to respond, because I couldn't decide what emotion her eyes had been glinting. Triumph? Anger? Defiance? Was I supposed to congratulate her, protect myself from her, or commiserate with her? That evening, even as I was eating dinner with Cranwell, I still hadn't decided.

⚜

If Cranwell had to be around, at least he hadn't shown himself to be demanding. And since he had been so eager to help with the conference, I didn't have very many qualms about enlisting his aid for the *Journées de Patrimoine*. The Days of National History. Every September, historical sites in France opened their doors to the public. They included museums, monuments, parliament, the president's and prime minister's mansions . . . as well as provincial sites of interest like my chateau. The chateau is a *site classé*, the equivalent of being listed on the National Register of Historic Places. To encourage the maintenance of historic buildings, the French heavily subsidize restoration of those buildings. The price of the subsidy? Letting the public climb all over the properties for one weekend every year. It wasn't demanded, but it was highly encouraged. And in the next few years I was planning on doing some renovations to the outbuildings and the grounds. I would need all the friends in high places I could make to help speed my applications through the bureaucracy.

If it sounds like I was making a big deal out of nothing, you should see how long it takes me to clean and straighten up after all the visitors. The previous year, I had to have all the carpets professionally steam-cleaned. And I'd need all the help I could get, making sure that fans of Alix didn't walk away with everything they could stuff inside their pockets. I wouldn't have thought academics could be such kleptomaniacs.

It was fortunate that I could count on support from both Sévérine and Cranwell. I'd decided that Séverine would be in charge of the third floor. She had an affinity for the library and I knew she would guard my collection with her life.

Cranwell I would place on the second floor. He didn't speak French, but that wouldn't stop him from being able to keep an eye on people.

As owner of the chateau, I would guard the ground floor and the garden area.

The fourth floor of the chateau, housing my room and Séverine's apartment, would be off limits. And without extra bodies, I'd have to entrust the outlying grounds to the visitors' conscience.

The week before the *Journées* began, I explained my plan to Séverine and Cranwell.

"Do you mind helping?"

"Pardon me?" Cranwell had clearly not been listening.

"*Journées de Patrimoine.* Can you help?"

"When is it again?"

"Next Saturday and Sunday."

"Sure. No problem."

"Séverine?"

"Yes, Frédérique. Of course I will help you."

10

*T*hat following Saturday dawned gray and misty. It looked as if the carpets could look forward to another steam cleaning.

The first visitors arrived at 9:30. I had sworn off cooking that day, figuring that mouthwatering smells wafting up from the kitchen would only encourage people to stay longer. I had dressed in the standard French uniform of black pants and a black V-neck sweater, wrapping a silk scarf around my neck to provide the requisite splash of color. I even went so far as to pin my hair up in a twist.

Those first visitors were students from the University in Brest and they came in a caravan of three minivans. Séverine went out to greet them. The dark jeans and high-heeled boots she was wearing only served to accentuate her long legs, and the citron green silk shirt she wore made her eyes sparkle and her teeth gleam as she smiled and laughed. She spent some time talking to the professor who had accompanied the students. The students themselves milled around on the gravel drive, smoking cigarettes.

Watching them, I ground my teeth. I'd forgotten how many days it had taken the previous year to locate and dispose of all the cigarette butts my visitors had left behind.

Séverine was gracious enough to give the students a private tour of the chateau. I stayed by the front door to welcome any guests that followed.

And did guests follow!

It was only when I stopped to take a breath an hour later that I realized

I hadn't seen Cranwell that morning. Racing up the central staircase to the second floor, I prayed that I'd find him in the hallway exactly where I'd asked him to stand.

No such luck.

I poked my head into the rooms, stopping now and then to answer questions from the guests.

He was not to be found, so I sprinted up the stairs to the third floor, hoping he'd attached himself to a group of visitors.

The only person I saw was Séverine, and she was at her station in the library.

"Have you seen Cranwell?"

"*Non.*"

Had he materialized just then, I would gladly have poked his eyes out. "I can't find him. Could you rotate between this floor and the second?"

"Of course."

I flew down the stairs, berating myself for having trusted him.

Cranwell drove up at six o'clock that evening in his Jaguar, waving at me as I stood in front of the door watching the last of the visitors leave.

As I watched him walk up to the door, his good-natured grin and dashing tweed overcoat did nothing to soften my heart. In spite of all the things I had to say to him, "Where were you?" was the phrase that popped out of my mouth.

"In Nantes. It was terrific. I was doing some outlining last night and realized I didn't know anything at all about the city. And it was the capital of Brittany. You were the one who told me that, right? So I decided to spend the day looking around." He was practically glowing. "Almost every museum in Nantes was free. And they were crowded. The French take their history seriously."

"I know. Because it's the *Journées de Patrimoine*."

"Which are . . . ?"

I just stood there glaring at him. Because I knew if I moved, even a muscle, I would do something I might regret. Like permanently disfigure him.

Expressions swept across the contours of his face like clouds across a landscape. "Oh no. I stood you up, didn't I? I am so sorry. I just — this is going to sound like an excuse, and I suppose it is, but at this stage in writing, I'm really not reliable. I can't be trusted. Half the time I don't even know what I'm saying."

"I was counting on you."

"I know. And I'm sorry."

"And what are your plans for tomorrow?"

"When I was driving back from Nantes, I got some great plot ideas. But I really need to walk around with them. Try to place them in location. I thought I'd take Lucy and just — "

"Wander around the grounds? Walk where Alix walked, that sort of thing?"

"Exactly."

"So what you're saying is you're not going to be around to help me tomorrow?"

"With . . . ?"

"Forget it." I had to give him credit. At least he'd warned me about himself. And he was right: He wasn't reliable; he couldn't be trusted. If he couldn't concentrate for two minutes on a conversation he was contributing to, there's no way I was going to count on him showing up tomorrow.

And it's a good thing I didn't.

Sunday was no less busy than Saturday had been. By the time I'd closed the door behind the last guest, I was ready to fall into bed and sleep for a month. I'm sure Séverine felt the same. I stripped off the black uniform I had worn that weekend, shook down my hair, jumped into a pair of comfortable jeans, and pulled on Peter's old cherry chamois shirt.

And Cranwell?

He'd spent the day wandering the forest. When he finally appeared, shedding his disheveled barn jacket and coming to dinner in a plain black turtleneck and grubby black cords, his greatest concern was his own stomach. I wanted to slap a baguette into his hand, give him a jug of water, and banish him to his room!

But then he looked into my eyes and gave me a smile. It was a happy smile — the kind of smile that usually comes from three-year-olds. And what can I say? I'm a sucker. My heart melted, and I put a heaping plate of *moules marinaire*, mussels steamed in aromatic broth, in front of him.

His dark head bent over the plate, that distinguished nose funneled in the rising vapors, and he let out such a blissful sigh of pleasure that I couldn't help but forgive him.

Besides, writers are a type of artist. Aren't artists supposed to be flaky?

His wanderings must have taken him far out into the woods, for he ate at least two pounds of mussels, using nearly an entire two-and-a-half foot baguette to sop up the broth. Finally, he pushed the plate away, took a deep breath, and then slowly exhaled.

"I didn't really eat all that myself, did I?"

I said nothing.

"Good grief! Is there any left for Séverine?"

"I saved some for her. No worries."

As I got up to clear the plates, he made a move to help me, but I waved him back to his seat. "I take it you don't want any *profiteroles*?"

"How big are they?"

I put four small pastry puffs filled with vanilla ice cream on a plate, smothered them with steaming chocolate sauce, and set them down in the middle of the island. "Not very."

His hand was reaching toward the plate even before I'd set it down. "Maybe just one."

Smiling as I started the espresso-maker, I watched as the caramel-colored liquid filled the glass carafe. "Cranwell, how do you go about writing a book?"

"It depends on what sort of book it is. I start with the idea — "

"But how do you get ideas?"

"I don't know, really, they just come. I guess God gives them to me." His lips curled into a wry twist. "I wouldn't have admitted a year ago that it has anything to do with Him, but it does. Sometimes the characters come first. Sometimes it's the plot. If I need to research, I research. For some books, I just leave holes and go back and fill them in later."

Deciding to leave all thoughts of God alone, I focused on the process. "How do you know you've done enough research?"

"When the characters start talking. When they start telling their story, I start typing."

I poured the espresso into demitasse cups and placed one in front of him. "But how do you know *how* to write?"

"I don't. It's a gift I've been blessed with. I just listen to the characters. If they're strong enough, they write the story for me. The trick is to be able to type fast enough or to take notes if I'm not near a computer."

"You don't have an outline?"

"I do. But characters don't usually talk to me with chronological precision."

"How long does it take you to write a book?"

"If I work on it for half a day, I can count on about 2,000 good words. A book has about 100,000 words. If I were able to write flawlessly, in fifty days I'd have a book. It usually takes several drafts for me to get it right."

"Which stage are you at with this one?"

"Still deciding who's going to tell the story. It's different this time. I'm not exactly sure how to approach the writing process anymore. I feel like I'm starting on my first book again. I just became a believer several months ago . . . " He looked up then, and his eyes were piercing. "Maybe you don't quite understand, but for me, knowing God changes everything. There's a new presence in my life, a new awareness. And the things I did before automatically, without thinking, aren't necessarily the right ways to go about life anymore. I find myself questioning everything I do."

He wanted to say more, I think, but he seemed at a loss for words. That must be disconcerting for an author.

"I think I'll work on reading Alix's journal first to get her point of view in her own words; I'll see what that looks like. Maybe I'll let Alix tell the story. Maybe I'll have her husband tell it. We'll see."

It was difficult for me to even imagine what it took to write a book. Cranwell might be a playboy, he might even be a flake, but writing a book was something I could never dream of doing.

"You do understand — about God?" he asked.

"Can we not talk about Him?" The mention of God evoked thoughts of eternity, and thoughts of eternity were irrevocably entwined with my thoughts about Peter. If I had ever bothered to have an honest discussion with him about God; if I had ever bothered to challenge his atheistic beliefs, then thinking about eternity wouldn't cause such guilt. But I hadn't; so it did. There were many ways to deal with grief, and I had tried most of them, but so far, I had found nothing to help me deal with guilt. And instead of diminishing over time, its burden had only increased.

Cranwell's eyes registered disappointment.

"Don't get me wrong, I know all about Him. I grew up going to church. I just don't approve of Him." I hoped I didn't sound too defensive; Cranwell would never understand the dialogue I wasn't having with God.

"Because of your husband?"

"Because of lots of things. Anyway, I'm going to put a bottle of champagne in the fridge. When you finish that last draft, let me know and we'll pop it open."

"Thanks." Cranwell got up from his stool and stretched toward the ceiling; mid-stretch, he asked if I had any armagnac.

Did I have armagnac? Any chef worth his toque would be humiliated to be discovered without armagnac.

"If I don't have something to help all this food digest, I'm not going to be able to sleep tonight."

"We can't have that." I poured out two large snifters.

"Can we have these in the library?"

Shrugging, I lifted an eyebrow in surprise. I had my own lounge on the fourth floor, so I'd never thought of using the library as one, although it made sense. It was cozy enough.

He ambled to the stairs, and I followed him to the entrance hall and then up the central stairs to the third floor.

In the library there are several floor lamps and a lamp on the large table that serves as a desk. I had decided during renovation that they would be more intimate than a huge chandelier.

Cranwell stopped me as I walked around the room turning on the lights. "Let's have a fire instead."

Backtracking, I turned off the lamps and then settled into a leather armchair, kicking off my shoes, and tucking my feet beneath me.

Cranwell arranged the firewood. I saw the flare of the match light his face. The fire caught, and the room began to glow with light.

Looking around at the rich red oriental carpet, the walls lined from floor to ceiling with books and the Louis XVI leather upholstered *fauteuils* armchairs, I felt peace. The niggling anxiety of the mystery of the fruit boxes fell away, and I decided I should end my evenings here more often.

Cranwell sat across from me, stretched out his legs, crossing them at the ankles. He took a sip of armagnac and savored it.

Mirroring him, I felt the slow awakening of taste in my mouth. I let the sip kindle my tastebuds and then I swallowed it, felt the pleasant burn that trailed into my stomach. I held the snifter in the palm of my hand, letting the liquid absorb my warmth.

Cranwell caught my eye. "What would this room have been used for?"

"In Alix's time? A bedroom or drawing room. Might have been used to store books, but there probably would not have been nearly as many. Books were worth a fortune. Even an avid reader might only own twenty or thirty in a lifetime. It was kings and princes who had the money to collect them."

"What would they have been reading?" It must have been rhetorical. Cranwell's eyes were fixed, unblinking, on the fire.

I'd lost him.

Frankly, I had begun to feel ignored. It was surprising how Cranwell had started to grow on me. I missed his undivided attention even as I understood the reason for his introspection.

Not wanting to disturb him, I relaxed into my chair, sipped my armagnac, letting my own thoughts wander. My eyes swept the bookcases that surrounded me, many of them lined with books I considered to be old friends. Some books I read on an annual basis and found as much pleasure in them as the first time I discovered them. Some were reference books. A set of encyclopedias that I used when I was in grade school. At least three dictionaries. Books on history. Atlases. Two entire cases filled with books on political science and government, beloved by Peter. He had always read ravenously, two or three books at a time. There were classics, of both ancient and modern times. Biographies. Autobiographies. The only section absent was my cookbook collection. I kept it down in the kitchen so it would be close at hand.

Taking another sip, I got up and walked toward my favorite bookcase: the one filled with rare and ancient books. The temperature in the chateau stayed relatively constant, so I could afford to keep these books on shelves rather than in glass cases. I hadn't dared read many. Just cracking open their covers and flipping through the pages was luxury enough. Some were so old they were written in Latin. Others in old English and French. Some even dated back to Alix's time. They were my birthday and Christmas gifts to myself.

"Cranwell, you might be interested in these."

He started in his chair. I'd disturbed his reverie, but he walked to my side, snifter in hand.

"These are from Alix's period." I waved a hand at a shelf's selection of books. "They're in French, so I don't think that you could understand them, but if they'll help you, you're welcome to them." This part of my library, I had arranged in chronological order; the other bookcases were arranged by subject and by height, but this section was my treasure. I ran a finger along the shelf in front of the books. I never touched them gratuitously. They were too valuable. I recited their dates for Cranwell.

"1352. 1365. 1380. 1412. 1430. 1433. 1451. 14 —." I stopped, confused. The book I was referencing *was* the book from 1451. I'd confused myself. I started over at the beginning of the shelf, but when I came to the book in question, I had again given it the wrong date. I looked past it toward the end of the shelf.

"Is something wrong?"

It was when I began again, purposely matching titles with the dates, that I found it. There was a gap between 1412 and 1430. I felt like I had been kicked in the stomach. "One of my books is gone."

"Maybe you reshelved it in the wrong place."

"I don't take these books from the shelf. The last time I touched that book was when I first put it there, about three years ago."

"Are you sure?"

"Positive."

"What kind of book was it?"

"It was a book found during the renovation of my room." The only book on that shelf I had not bought. "It was a Book of Hours."

He looked at me blankly.

"A medieval book of devotions. It was illuminated. Illustrated."

"Why would anyone want to steal it?"

"I have no idea."

"Maybe Sévérine borrowed it."

"It predates Alix by a generation. Her research is specifically tied to Alix. It wouldn't be of interest to her. Besides, I invited her to use anything that I have. She looked at the shelf, but shrugged me off. She said there was nothing here that pertained to her work."

Someone must have taken it during the *Journées de Patrimoine*. It was the only explanation. I felt like crying. If only Cranwell had been there, then Sévérine wouldn't have had to cover both floors; the book would not have been stolen.

Cranwell was looking at the shelf, but his eyes were focused on a point beyond it. "What would your room have been used for again?"

"A servant's room. Probably a servant with some status. The lord or lady's personal servant."

I drank the rest of my armagnac and glanced once more around the room.

The peace had vanished.

The last days of the month provided a warmth I would have expected from July. An *été de la Saint-Martin* had found us. An Indian Summer.

My cupboards were full of jam. The carpets had been steam-cleaned; the pictures straightened; the fingerprints waxed out of the furniture; the folds shaken out of the duvets where visitors had sat on the beds.

I even had time to spend drafting letters to my father's old friends in the Senate on behalf of the foundation. The wording can get tricky when you're trying to evoke an old friendship, prick the conscience, and lobby for new legislation at the same time.

My life had returned to normal.

Ash Wednesday

Agnès says me that if I leave Anne the management of the chateau, I must at least manage her.

I told Anne that I must see menus and read accounts once each week.

Now it might be that Agnès will leave me to my books.

six days after Ash Wednesday

The follow is a story my lord told me: At Chateau de Trécesson, a poacher saw two young men burying a young bride alive. The chatelain arrived and tried to save her, but it was too late. The men would not reply to him why they had committed the offense, and the bride had perished before being able to tell her story.

In demanding around the countryside, it was revealed that the two young men were, in actuality, the brothers of the woman. They were punishing her for having married a man of which they did not approve.

In honor of the bride, the chatelain hung her veil in the chapel. Now young women from all over the countryside come to touch it in the belief that she will help them find a husband.

I told my lord that I was glad I had no need of a husband, for touching the veil of a dead woman does not please me.

He laughed at me and replied to me that some women will do

114

anything to catch a husband. And other women will do anything to keep one.

I demanded of my lord what must become of women who do not marry.

My lord says me that someone can usually be found to keep them. Even the church.

And I demanded of him why women may not keep themselves, as do men. Men may marry, they may join the church, or they may join a war. Why is it that women may not do the same?

My lord replied to me that women are not suited to life alone. They must be kept. And it is for men to keep them.

Or God, I recalled to him: men or God.

But I demand of myself, if women might join in wars, would the battles grow greater or lesser in number? Agnès guards bad thoughts of Anne and has since we have first arrived. I have not been witness to any battles in this war, but it seems to me there is one still the same. A war without reason. Perhaps it is better that women make not war with weapons.

two days after Saint Grégoire le Grand

This is not the country of Touraine. I am habituated to a land that is gentle, divided by rivers and streams. A land of green that gives fruit and wheat, a land on which the sun shines.

This land is savage. It is gray. And filled with trees. And they are mean, these trees. They have none of the generosity of spirit or of shade of the trees in my country. They are thin and spindly and they stand so close that no light can penetrate. And it is rare that I have seen the sun. I have seen fog grow lighter and begin to shimmer and warm with the hint of it, but I have not seen the sun these thirty-nine days.

All is dark.

The forests, the countryside, the people.

I demand of myself how a God who has created the sun and flowers and birds can make also a land so savage as this. Can He take pride in such a thing? Must it give Him so well a pleasure as my country? If it is true, I must not have known Him also as well as I thought.

day of Annonciation

This holy day, we heard mass in the chapel.

At least this one thing changes not. As I listened to the words I know by heart, I felt a tear start from my eye, and roll down my cheek. I closed them and wished myself back in the house of my father and I could imagine his chapel: the smell of the incense and the sound of the priest, and I felt the touch of his hand. But then I opened my eyes and saw it was only my lord, and he had patted my hand as he had seen my tear.

I have heard my lord praying this day, and in a language I could not comprehend. And so I demanded of him if he speaks in holy tongues.

And he did laugh and replied to me that if Breton be considered a holy tongue, then this is what he must be speaking.

I demanded of him why he must pray in Breton when he speaks so well in French and when the masses are spoken in Latin.

And he replied to me that prayer is a language of the spirit. His head may be French and his soul may be Latin, but his spirit must always be Breton.

I demanded of him to teach me Breton. And he replied to me that it is very difficult.

And I recalled to him that I know Latin as well as French.

And he says me that he will find a tutor.

five days after Annonciation

My lord began to tell me the story of the Song of Roland.

I stopped him as I have heard this story and demanded of him please to tell me another.

He replied to me that contrary to the Song of Roland that I have heard, this comte de Bretagne and nephew of Charlemagne did not die in Roncevaux in Spain, but rather at Dompierre near the valley of the Cantache in Bretagne.

This I had not known, so I told him to proceed.

It happened while he was returning from Spain, after having fought the Sarrasins. Roland came to the valley of the Cantache and wanted to leap across on horseback, for she whom he loved was waiting for him on the other side.

With the help of God, he succeeded.

He decided to try it again, in the name of the Holy Virgin. And succeeded.

When he tried the third time, in the name of she whom he loved, his horse slipped and they both fell from the precipice to the valley floor.

My lord says me that one can go there today, and if one looks closely enough, it can still be seen: the marks the horse made as it tumbled.

Nearby sits the Pierre Doutante, a rock from which drops of pure water fall; they are the tears of she whom Roland loved.

I had my own tears when he had finished telling this story.

He dried my eyes and demanded of me why I cried.

I demanded of him if he could not imagine the sadness of she whom Roland loved. The comte was so close, but then had slipped away and was lost forever. I think that the grief of the woman will stay with me forever. I demanded of my lord if he did not think so.

He told me that the only thing he thought was that Roland was stupid for trying to jump the valley three times when the first had done well enough. Then he rolled himself up in a fur in front of the fire and told me to go to sleep.

nine days after Annonciation

I demanded this day to see the accounts and the menus. This I should have done two months past. Anne has kept these since three years. I know not what is normal for quantities of food or for prices, but the handwriting of Anne is poor.

In the future, she will bring me receipts and I will keep the books. I promised to make time each week for these accounts.

This has satisfied Agnès.

thirteen days after Annonciation

The priest has come to teach me Breton. I took many notes of explanations, but after he left, I found I could not remember the sounds the letters must speak. They look the same as my own, but they speak with different accents, and sometimes so different an accent that they might as well be another letter entirely.

sixteen days after Annonciation

I worked all the long of the day on Breton, but I cannot guard it in my head. The structure is strange. The sounds are foreign. The words have no cousins in either of the languages I know.

seventeen days after Annonciation

Again the priest has come. I have fear that I do not please him. I had translated the phrases he had left into sounds using my own letters in the manner I am habituated.

And he says me that I cannot learn this way. And that it is not worth the effort to educate a woman. And if it were, why would I not wish to learn to write in Latin or in French.

And so I have shown him my journal, in which I write in French, and I have shown him my books, which I read in Latin. And I have told him also that he must keep his language for himself. There is no value in knowing a language which is no longer spoken at court.

day of Saints Jacques et Philippe

This day was a feast of which I was ignorant. On waking, Anne says me that this is the day of Saint Brieuc, but she had not the time to tell me of this saint, nor what he had done. And so I found my lord and demanded of him to tell me of this saint.

He replied to me that this is a founding saint of Bretagne. One of the seven who had given Bretagne the Christian faith. Saint Brieuc was taught by Germanus and performed many miracles and converted Cynan.

And I demanded of him who is Cynan, for of him I have heard nothing.

And he says me the follow:

Cynan was the son of the brother of Octavius the Old of Wales. And when Octavius will die, Cynan had thought to take the place of his uncle.

But the daughter of his uncle was wed to a Roman, Magnus Maximus, and so Cynan must defeat the Roman before he can gain power. And this he tries, but in this he also fails. And so in place of becoming enemies, the Roman and Cynan become friends.

When the Roman takes the decision to travel to the Continent to become Emperor of the West, Cynan takes the decision to come with him. And so Cynan kills the ruler of Armorica, here in Bretagne, and takes this position, and he and his men stay. But one problem is that they have no wives. And so Cynan demands of Donaut, the friend of his uncle, for many Cornish women. And it is decided that Cornwall and Armorica will be united when Cynan marries Ursula, the daughter of Donaut. But Ursula had wished to be a nun, and so she demands of Cynan some time to make a pilgrimage with eleven thousand girls. And this done, she and Cynan are wed in Rome by the pope.

But Ursula dies and Cynan does not marry again for many years, but becomes very powerful. And as his second wife, he takes the sister of Saint Patrick of Ireland. And when Cynan is dead, Armorica is divided in two to give to his sons who are Gradlon and Gadeon.

day of Ascension

This day I reminded myself that I have not learned of the other founding saints of Bretagne. And so again, I have searched my lord and in finding him, demanded the identity of the saints who remain. They are:

Saint Samson of Dol, who has the same day as Saint Nazaire. It was King Childebert who had named him bishop of Dol. Like the Samson of the Holy Bible, he had refused alcohol.

And there is Saint Pol Aurelian, also a bishop, who has the same day in spring as Saint Grégoire le Grand. He is said to have performed many miracles.

And Saint Tugdual, whom King Childebert named bishop of Tréguier. He had come from Britain with his mother, sisters, and other relatives.

Saint Patern, who shares the day of the Vénérable César. He is come from Wales and was much known for his charity and mortifications.

Then Saint Malo who came to Bretagne with Saint Brendon himself.

And the last, Saint Corentin, the first bishop of Cornouaille.

My lord told me that the large part of the saints have come from Britain. Perhaps they will have sympathies with me, who has come to Bretagne from France.

octobre

Vilaine veille de Toussaint
ne présage rien de bien.

October

A nasty day before All Saint's
foretells nothing good

12

"Freddie?"

"Hmm?" I glanced up from my saucepan over my shoulder to see Cranwell's brown eyes spark at me. He was wearing a ribbed oregano funnel-neck sweater over black moleskin pants. Somehow that particular shade of green added depth to his eyes.

"I knew it!"

"Knew what?"

"That somewhere, sometime, someone must have called you Freddie."

"You're very clever." How he gloats! "My father. He started when I was thirteen and only continued because it annoyed me so much." I knew the rising color in my cheeks probably matched the crimson color of my long-sleeved envelope-necked sweater. If I hadn't been so intent on finishing the sauce, I would have glared at him. As it was I decided to ignore him. "Aren't you supposed to be writing or something?"

"Freddie, I'd really like to stay longer."

"When you came you knew it would only be for a month."

"I know. And I appreciate you having let me stay for a couple more weeks, but I need more time. I feel like I've only just begun to get the rhythm of the story."

"This isn't really your kind of book. There aren't any guns. No terrorists."

"I know. But this is the novel I've always wanted to write. Historical espionage."

"That's ridiculous. You only found out about Alix a few months ago."

"Then I used the wrong words. This is the novel I've always *meant* to write. When I first started, I wrote a novel like this one, but it wasn't very good. I knew I had to make money if I wanted to keep writing, so I wrote what I thought people would want to read."

"And you've done very well at it."

"But now I want to write something *I* want to read. I love history. And the fifteenth century of France was a tumultuous period: The independent duchy of Brittany at odds with the King of France. Given her husband's position at court, Alix could have had access to confidential information. Even if she weren't a spy, I can fictionalize her story. At least her journals provide a glimpse of what life must have been like then."

What could I say?

"I'll wash dishes for you. I'll scrub my own toilet." He didn't even crack a smile. This man was serious.

"I don't mind toilets, but I hate vacuuming."

"I'll do it. I'll even do it tonight. Where's the vacuum cleaner?"

He was out of the kitchen and halfway up the stairs before I called him back.

"You can stay. But I need my space. And I'm not going to change my plans just because you're around. I have some trips planned."

He wrapped his arms around my waist, spun me, and kissed me on the cheek. Then he set me back down on the floor. "If you need to go somewhere, I'll stay with friends in Paris."

When I caught my breath and the scent of his cologne had stopped making my head spin, I agreed. "Deal. The vacuum cleaner is on the first floor in the small closet to the right of the stairs. But dinner's almost ready. You can worry about it tomorrow."

I was stuck with him now for the duration, and it was my own fault. One of my virtues is that I always take responsibility for my actions. I'd done it to myself. I desperately needed to learn how to say no.

☙❧

Two days later, box after box of books began arriving from an Internet bookseller. They kept coming for the remainder of the month and in small packages of one or two for several weeks thereafter.

"What did you do, order one of each?" I shivered, having come from the warmth of the kitchen in my tank and chef's pants up to the cold vault of the entry. After signing for what seemed like the twentieth delivery, I had called Cranwell down from his room. I didn't mind signing for him, but I didn't have the strength to cart a box full of books up those spiral stairs.

Cranwell glanced up from the box. "Basically." He paused to push up the sleeves of his black boat-neck sweater and then returned his attention to the books.

I looked over his shoulder. *A History of Medieval France. Women of the Fifteenth Century. Atlas of the Medieval World. The Church and the State in the Middle Ages. The Hundred Years War. The Economy of Medieval Europe. A History of Costume.*

At the least he would be widely read.

Cranwell hefted the box and started up the stairs with it.

Following him halfway up the first spiral, I made sure he didn't stumble. I may also have been admiring the way his jeans fit and the sheen of his black venetian loafers. "What do you plan on doing with these when you've finished with them?"

"Donating them to you." He flashed a smile over his shoulder at me as he disappeared around the bend.

During October, Cranwell was much more present inside the chateau than he had been in September, although he was never without a book in his hand. Séverine and I would run into him in all manner of odd places.

One afternoon I found him sprawled on my bed, his back to the door.

I'd just come up from the garden and wanted to take a shower. Good thing I hadn't started stripping off my mineral blue wool shirt or black flannel work pants; I was used to having my room to myself.

Walking up to him in my stocking feet, I tapped him on the shoulder. "Excuse me, I hate to displace you or seem rude in any way, but would you please leave?"

"Hmm?" Cranwell rolled toward me, glancing up from his book over his reading glasses. "I'm sorry?"

"What are you doing in my room?"

He closed his finger in the book, played with the collar of his shirt, and looked around as if mystified. He turned the book over and read the title aloud. *"Fortified Castles of the Middle Ages."*

He looked at me. Looked at the book, flipped back through some of the pages. Looked at me again. "Studying fireplace and ceiling construction."

He rose from my bed, shoved something into the pocket of his cognac-colored plants, and sauntered out, reading all the while.

I bolted my door behind him. The man was a menace to polite society.

Except at dinner.

It was as if he worked from 8:00 a.m. until 7:00 p.m. and then flipped a switch and became the Cranwell I had known in August. An enjoyable, if flirtatious, companion.

"Where did you grow up, Freddie?"

"California."

"Really? Me too."

This I already knew from my Internet research.

"Where?"

"Near Hollywood."

"Me too."

I smiled. "On the other side from you. Toward the west."

"You lived there all your life?"

"Until I was old enough to escape."

"You didn't like it."

"Not particularly. Did you?"

"Loved it."

That figured.

"Only child?"

I nodded.

"I have one sister."

I knew that too. Her name is Laura. She is a dental hygienist.

"What did your family do?"

"My father was a senator."

"Which one?"

"Howard."

"Duke Howard? No kidding! I knew him well. I was sorry to hear of his death. Of your mother's too. It was just, when? — '98?"

I nodded.

"That must have been a hard year for you."

A renegade tear sprung to my eye. I couldn't believe it. I'd never been that close to my parents, but being around someone who knew them opened the floodgate of my memories. It had been comforting to know that somewhere in the world, I had belonged to someone. And someone had belonged to me.

"They threw the best parties."

Smiling was difficult with my chin beginning to tremble.

"I never knew they had children. How come I never met you?"

I shrugged. "I was never really a party girl."

"But when they had a party, everyone would come."

Pulling my hands inside my arctic blue sweater, I wrapped my arms around my waist. "I wasn't presentable, Cranwell. I was pudgy, I was covered with zits. My hair was stringy, and I was introverted in the extreme. I wasn't the kind of daughter Duke needed." I didn't compare favorably with my parents' glamorous clique.

"It's hard for me to imagine he ever would have thought that."

My shoulders tipped up in a shrug.

He leaned between our stools and lifted my chin with a finger. "Freddie, you're lovely."

To avoid having to look at him, I closed my eyes, but I felt a tear trickle down my cheek. I had no power to stop it. I was reliving my childhood in front of one of those very same beautiful people. It was my fate to live my life in a purgatory of humiliation.

Cranwell let go of my chin and then reached an arm around my shoulders, hugging me to his side.

I turned my head into his chest. My fists clutched handfuls of his wool polo as my anguish found voice in my sobs. They were deep and ugly sounding. I was embarrassed; I was mortified, but the hurt of those years was so deep I could not control them.

Cranwell smoothed my hair while his arm offered firm support for my back.

Eventually, my sobs quieted, my hands slackened their grip, and my arms found their way around his waist. I attempted a deep, quivering breath.

Cranwell never stopped smoothing my hair.

I stayed there, with my cheek against his chest, listening to his heartbeat.

"Freddie, I wasn't lying. You really are lovely."

"Thanks, Cranwell."

Gathering what strength was left in me, I made a move to turn away, trying to hide my face from his eyes. I knew how hideous I looked when I cried. My face swells up, and the ice blue color of my eyes only accentuates how bloodshot they are.

Cranwell stopped me.

He cupped my face with gentle hands and turned it toward himself. I thought for a moment that he was going to kiss me, but then he used his thumbs to press away the last traces of my tears.

He let me move away and then offered to help me do the dishes.

A man after my own heart.

I spent several hours that night tossing in my bed, remembering my childhood. My self-imposed exile from my parents' life. Maybe Cranwell was right; maybe my feelings of inferiority originated in me rather than my parents.

Summoning a vision of myself as a teen, I subjected that person to an honest examination. That appraisal revealed exactly what I had told Cranwell — but did that mean no one would have wanted to talk to me? That I wouldn't have been interesting? That my parents weren't proud to call me their daughter? Maybe what I had perceived as rejection was only their attempt to shelter me, to keep me from situations they knew I wasn't comfortable with. To protect my privacy. My anonymity.

In the final analysis, the problem had been my self-esteem. I couldn't imagine anyone being interested in knowing me. And the thought of meeting new people terrified me. I was so self-absorbed I was incapable of directing my focus from myself to others. That's what college, and Peter, had helped me to do.

Although I still wasn't comfortable at parties, and given a choice, I would rather read a book, at least I no longer thought of myself as a social pariah.

I was an interesting person.

I was well traveled. I was an expert in my field. I was intelligent; I could hold my own in any conversation. I was an excellent hostess; I threw fabulous dinner parties . . . at least while Peter had been alive.

I had achievable goals for my future and considered myself successful.

I was not beautiful, but I was pleasant looking. I would never be a model. I didn't care to be one. I knew my best features, my eyes and hair, and I accentuated them. I kept my weight under control.

In fact my life seemed perfect. But why didn't it feel that way? I could almost sense the spectre of God hovering at the edge of my thoughts. I wrestled with Him. Tried to push Him away. Why did He always keep popping up? Like a spiritual jack-in-the-box? Would I ever be able to push him back down? Put a definitive latch on the box?

Staring up at the ceiling, I let go of the rein I had on my thoughts and let them gallop away. I closed my eyes, hoping for sleep, but Cranwell's brown eyes haunted me.

What if I *had* met him at my parents' house?

My thoughts had veered off in a completely unforeseen direction. I kept thinking of his thumbs wiping away my tears. Of those brown eyes, looking into the depths of my soul. He was the type of person I'd always worked hard at staying away from. He was the type of person I had never allowed myself to trust. The type of person I'd listened to from the safety of my room while my parents had entertained. And yet . . .

And yet, he was forty-five with a whole life full of people and places and experiences that I'd never known and frankly never wanted to. I decided, in a searing flash of insight, that I had developed a crush on Cranwell.

But crushes were something I had experience with. As long as I didn't feed the fascination, didn't fixate on the object of my affection, I knew it would go away. Especially when it lacked encouragement from him. Which it did.

Which it would.

The only reason he paid me any attention was because of my position. If he were kind to me, it was only because he wanted me to let him stay longer. If he flirted with me, it was only because he flirted with everyone; I knew his type. And if he had an interest in anyone in the house, it would be Sévérine.

And that proved to be the happy thought to which I fell asleep.

*C*ranwell and Lucy found me one afternoon on my third run-recovery lap around the chateau. It was one of the rare times I'd seen him without a book.

He caught me near the garden and began to walk beside me, fitting his stride to mine. "There was a call for you while you were out."

I glanced at him. He looked scholarly in a pair of chocolate wide-wale corduroys and a cardigan. "You don't have to answer the phone."

He shrugged. "I was in the kitchen."

Doing who knows what. "Who was it?"

"Some people looking for a room."

"I'll call them back this afternoon. I'm probably booked."

"I found your booking calendar and there was no one scheduled, so I booked them for you."

That brought me to a halt so fast I almost fell over. "You what?!"

"I booked them. Two couples, two rooms. I even remembered to ask for their credit card numbers." He looked supremely satisfied with himself.

"First of all, Cranwell, it's not your job to answer the phone for me. Séverine does that. Second, it's not your place to book rooms for me." I hadn't been that angry in years.

"I looked in your schedule and you don't have anyone coming until after Christmas."

"That's because I don't want anyone. I refuse most of the people who call."

"That's not any way to run a business, Freddie." The louder I responded, the quieter Cranwell became.

"It's my business. I like it this way. I need solitude."

Lucy had clamped her ears to her head and was crouching close to the ground.

"Don't you think it's a little strange to be refusing guests when you run an inn?"

His mild tone infuriated me, but I could think of nothing to say.

He snapped a finger at Lucy, and she stood up, rolling her eyes toward the forest, looking eager to get away. They had started for the trees when he stopped and turned around. "By the way, I forgot to take down their phone number. You can't call them back to cancel. Sorry."

I was steaming when I resumed my walk. The worst of it was that my calves had cramped while I'd stopped to argue with Cranwell. I spent a good five minutes stretching them out against the chateau's wall. By then, even zipping my black jogging fleece up to my neck failed to keep me warm.

Taking a deep breath, I held it for ten seconds and looked up at the steel gray clouds. I saw a flock of *hirondelles*, sparrows, heading south. Their cries skirled across the sky and echoed in my ears, reminding me that fall was upon us. Which meant that winter would soon arrive. The chill that tinged the air would only get worse.

Clapping my glove-clad hands together for warmth, I jogged around to the front door.

"I'm sorry, Freddie. I thought I was doing you a favor, and I can tell now that I wasn't. I didn't mean to infringe on your territory."

At least Cranwell had apologized before I served dinner. Now I would be able to enjoy the food. I washed my hands and wiped them on my twill pants and tugged on the long sleeves of my lagoon blue U-neck sweater to pull them back down. Then I served him a thick slice of *paté de lapin aux noisettes* before I answered.

"I'm sorry for yelling at you." I set a plate down for myself and broke a crisp baguette in two, handing half to him. Then I took my place on my stool. "After Peter died, this was my sanctuary. It still is. I'm redefining my place in the world, and I like to do it at my own pace."

"I can understand that. It's what I'm doing too. Redefining myself as a Christian. This is a sort of sanctuary for me too."

We ate in silence for several minutes, savoring the rabbit and hazelnut spread. "I don't take many guests." I didn't reveal to him my decision mechanism. It sounded juvenile even to me.

"Nothing wrong with that. If you had too many, you wouldn't be able to pay individual attention to me." He winked at me.

I wrinkled my nose at him.

"So what was Peter like?"

"Blond. Blue-eyed."

"I mean, what kind of a person was he?"

"At least give me some place to start, Cranwell."

"What did he want out of life?"

"He wanted to be the head of his agency."

"That's it?"

"It? Cranwell, that's like saying, 'I want to be the president.' Very few people get to that point in their careers."

"What did you want out of life?"

Why did Cranwell have to be so nosy? "For Peter to be the head of his agency. I was a good wife."

"I'm not saying you weren't."

"He would have made a good executive. He was smart. He worked hard. People listened to him. He was a natural leader."

"What attracted you to him?"

"He knew what he wanted from life. And because he knew where he was going, I didn't have to. He had everything planned. When you met him, you knew it would all work out. And he made you want to be around when it did."

"Where would you be if he were still alive?"

"Belgium? Switzerland? Morocco? Côte d'Ivoire? Somewhere in French-speaking Europe or Africa. And after, we would have gone back to DC."

"What about you?"

"What about me?"

"I just can't see you living that sort of life."

"I was good at it. We entertained a lot; I enjoyed it. And I'm a patriot; I felt honored to serve my country as a diplomat's wife. If life hadn't turned itself upside down, I would still be doing it."

After clearing away our plates, I portioned out the *pintade aux figues sèches*, a guinea fowl prepared with dried figs. I loved cooking with dried fruit. They always lent an earthy flavor to food. The fowl was cooked to perfection. As I carved, it fell away from the bone. I served it with buttered French-style macaroni sprinkled with chives.

I brought the plates to the table and then took my seat.

"So, are you happy here?"

Surprised at his question, I looked up at him from my food. "I'm very content. I like it here."

He took a bite of *pintade* and chewed a moment before speaking. "This chateau suits you. Classic, but comfortable. Traditional, yet surprising. Welcoming, but guarded at the same time."

"Thank you." I ripped a piece of bread from my half of the baguette. "I think."

"It was a compliment. You're welcome. This is excellent. What's in it?"

The next several minutes I spent explaining the recipe to him, realizing, over the course of our conversation, how good it felt to have someone to talk to. And someone to listen. Any lingering irritation from earlier in the day had vanished.

We savored our ginger-spiked pumpkin mousse and sipped espresso afterward.

❦

The next weekend, I bought a fortune in game from local hunters. They brought venison, partridge, duck, rabbit, squirrel. The only thing I refused was pigeon. Pigeons don't have gall bladders, and if not cooked to perfection, their meat can be tough and chewy. And worse, when it's raw, the flesh is dark, almost purple. In contrast, I love squab, but I don't cook it. Because squab are baby pigeons, just four weeks old. And that seems cruel. But for the most part, I try to keep ethics out of my kitchen.

Sunday evening I spent dressing the game and portioning it for freezing. I laid aside a nice rabbit to make *lapin au moutarde* and several squirrels and a hare to make a *terrine*.

I love fall. It's my favorite season.

Cranwell's guests came the next weekend. They weren't very old, but I could tell they were well-connected. The French would have called them *branché*. Fashionable. Trendy. And I'm sure the only reason they wanted to stay at the inn was so they could brag to all their friends.

The two men I pegged right away as X-graduates. They had the same arrogant savoir faire as other graduates of Ecole Polytechnique that I had known from Embassy connections. As France's premier engineering school, it was the most elite of the country's elite schools. Graduates hired only other graduates, and even a diploma from Ecole Polytechnique with poor grades was more valuable than perfect scores from any other university.

The women I labeled as ENArques; they seemed less Silicon Valley and more Wall Street. ENA, Ecole Nationale d'Administration, was the only other school in France that rivaled X.

They were all pleasant, but in a detached, judgmental sort of way.

The moment I saw them walk up the front steps, I completely changed the menus I had planned to offer them.

Even though I love cooking, I hate it when people criticize my food. And had I served anything classically French, I know they most certainly would have. If I had served duck, then I would have had to serve a Saumur-Champigny wine. Had I served *foie gras*, then I would have had to offer Sauternes.

So I decided to serve them food they might never have tried before. Not knowing how it "should" be, they'd have no reason to snub it. Their first evening with me, they sampled the delights of prawn-stuffed avocadoes with cumin sauce, green enchiladas, fajita-style flank steak, and salsa verde. I served flan with cinnamon sauce for dessert. And a Chilean wine that I'm sure they would have protested against had they known it cost fewer than 10 euros.

As it was, Séverine relayed to me nothing but their compliments.

The next morning, I made the most delicate of New Orleans-style beignets, sifting a generous portion of powdered sugar over the heaping platter. I actually waited until I laid eyes on Séverine before I began to fry them; I wanted to ensure that they would still be piping hot when they were served. I saved enough batter to make a half dozen for Cranwell and myself. It had been ages since I'd last made them.

The couples sat in the dining hall through lunch, debating and laughing until they finally jumped into their car and roared down the drive for their afternoon adventures.

For dinner that evening, they started with an American-style shrimp cocktail, which was followed by broiled salmon paired with a cranberry and cilantro relish. In celebration of the next day, Halloween, dessert was a pumpkin cheesecake served over a pool of rich ginger crème.

For their last morning, they ate tottering stacks of hotcakes served with authentic Vermont maple syrup.

By the time they drove away, I was exhausted. I had meant to spend that day putting the chateau back in order, but dawn had brought a raging storm, and the accompanying gloominess inspired lethargy rather than industry. Thankfully by nightfall the storm had blown past and left in its wake a clear, if cold, darkness.

As I walked across my rug from the bathroom to my bed that evening,

I glanced out the window and noticed the haziest of rings surrounding the moon: frost. And the moisture left from the storm would make the damage worse. My garden needed protection. I still had tomatoes and herbs that I wanted to cook with. I hurried to my armoire, threw on my robe, and got out my slippers, then I pounded down the stairs, running out the front door to the garage. I stopped only long enough to gather an armful of rags. When I got to the garden, I tucked them around my plants. I had just finished wrapping a rag around the last tomato plant and had risen to step across the row to the herbs when I heard a footfall on the flagstones of the pathway.

I froze. I'd never before felt frightened on my own property.

"Freddie."

My knees almost buckled in relief. It was just Cranwell. "What?"

"Lucy and I were out for a walk. Can I help you?"

"I'm trying to save these from the frost." I tossed a handful of rags at him, and Lucy jumped to grab at them. "Drape these across the chives."

He immediately stooped to the task.

We worked together in silence until the plants at last were covered. He gave me his hand as I stepped back over the rows. Releasing it as I set foot on the path, I was suddenly very aware of my thin cotton batiste chemise. Had the moon not been full, I would not have been so worried, but as it was, the moonlight sharpened every image it touched. I comforted myself with the thought of my robe. The medieval-inspired blue-gray velvet garment fit tightly over my torso but fell loosely from my waist and from its bell-shaped sleeves. I was safe.

"Freddie."

"What?"

"Come here."

Why did I find myself suddenly backing away? All week I'd been aware of his lips. All month, I'd been fascinated by his eyes.

He took a step closer as I took a step back. Unfortunately, his steps were bigger than mine. And I tripped over the hem of my robe. He slipped an arm around my waist and steadied me. "Freddie. You shimmer in the moonlight. You look like a fairy." His gentle fingers immersed themselves in my hair. Began to swim through it. It had been so long since anyone had done that. I wanted to melt.

I moved my head so his hand slid to my cheek. The sleeve of his pea coat felt rough against my neck.

He pulled me closer. "You beguile me." His face hovered above mine. His nose nuzzled my cheek; his breath frosted my eyelashes.

His words were so soft and gentle it was as if he'd whispered them inside my head.

My arms rose of their own volition and wrapped themselves around his waist.

He cradled my face between his hands and stood back and looked at me. Then his hands slid to my neck and he brought my face close and kissed my forehead.

My eyes fluttered shut.

He kissed my eyelids.

I sighed.

He kissed my nose.

A frenzied burst of barking came from Lucy.

We broke apart, staring at the dog.

Her stance was rigid, and she was glaring fixedly at the end of the forest.

I knew what it had to be: one of Alix's admirers. Alix ruined everything.

His eyes were full of regret. And — were it possible — shame. "Stay here."

I couldn't find the voice to tell Cranwell not to worry. I was floating. I was sinking. I couldn't remember the last time my head had spun so fast.

He took Lucy with him and walked straight toward the forest. They rustled through the woods for about five minutes, but of course, they didn't find anything. Or anyone. The moonlight from behind drenched his form in its glow as he emerged from the woods. I couldn't see his face; it was shadowed, but I could feel the heat of his gaze.

I stood, rooted to the brick pathway for a moment. Then I turned and fled.

As I neared the back door, I came upon Sévérine. Emerging from the shadow cast by the forest, she had just become visible as she slipped around the corner of the chateau. Her figure appeared ghostly in the moonlight, but still, it seemed as if her hands concealed something long and quite real behind her back. I gasped as I looked into her glittering eyes and then continued in a stumbling run, pulling open the door and continuing my flight upstairs. And there's no other word to describe it, for when I reached my room, I bolted the door behind me.

In that last conscious second before sleep claimed me, a searing thought flared in my mind: What had Sévérine been doing in the forest?

my fourteenth year
year thirty-eight of the reign of Charles VII, King of France

day of Sainte Anne

My lord had not come to me for several months, but this past night he came. He placed me on the bed as normal, and let the curtains drop around it, then I heard him pull a chair close to the fire and he began to speak. He told me of Salaün. He was a simple soul who lived alone in the woods of the Lesneven region. He was avoided by all and lived the life of a hermit, only begging bread and repeating Ave Marias without cease. He lived in harmony with nature and slept outside. He never bothered a soul. At forty years, he fell ill and was found dead near a fountain. He was buried and quickly forgotten, until one day, a Lys flower was noticed growing from his tomb; Lys are the symbol of purity and innocence. They opened it up and found that the root of the flower was growing from the mouth of Salaün. In fact, the leaves had "Ave Maria" written on them in gold. And that is why the tomb of a simple hermit has become Notre Dame du Folgoët.

I demanded of my lord if the hermit had not one friend.

My lord replied to me no.

But if he were such a simple kind soul, surely someone would have wanted him as a friend.

My lord says me that everyone avoided him.

I told him that did not make sense. If he were a kind man then people would have been near.

My lord says me that perhaps he was mean.

At this, I climbed from under the covers and pulled back the curtain at the foot of the bed. I told him that then in that case he would not have been called kind.

My lord turned in his chair to face me, but then rose and sat on the rail of the bed in front of me. He says me that perhaps the hermit warned people away.

I told him that if he were repeating Ave Marias without ceasing, then he would not have had time to speak to anyone.

And then my lord replied to me that the men he knew had better things to do than to repeat Ave Marias.

I do not think this story makes sense and this I told him.

He told me that if I did not want to hear his stories, that there were others who would gladly. He commanded me back to bed, and began to replace the curtain, but then stopped and demanded of me how many years I have.

I told him. Fourteen. I feel I do not please him. I told him he does not have to tell me stories. I had never demanded of him to.

He replied to me something I could not hear. It seems to me it was, "You demand of me nothing at all."

two days after Assomption

Agnès says me that the trades people come to see Anne.

This seems to me normal.

Agnès says me that they should come to see me. I am the chatelaine. It should be me to make decisions on who to buy from.

I am ignorant of trades and the people who do them. It does not interest me. Anne has done well since four years, and I am certain does still.

Agnès recalled to me that the tasks of a wife are dictated by God and that in all my studies perhaps I should study this also.

Perhaps I will do.

five days after Saint Augustin

I occupied myself this day in copying expenses into the accounts. I should have done since three months. And God who all sees, the things I will not do and the things I do not do, will see this also. And tomorrow I shall see the priest and these confess.

day of Saint Etienne

My lord had promised to tell me of Arthur King of Bretons this night. But he began by telling me of a king called Marc'h, which is 'horse' in Breton. This king had a palace in Plomarc'h near Douarnenez. King Marc'h had the most handsome horse the world has ever seen. He walked on the sea also as well as he did on the land. And mountains made the same to him as valleys. The horse was called Morvarc'h and there was nothing the king liked more than to hunt with this horse.

It arrived that one day, as the king was hunting with his nobles, that he saw the most beautiful white hind the world has ever seen, and he turned with his men to pursue her. Morvarc'h was the only horse that had speed enough to chase her and even he could not catch her. The chase finished as the hind ran up a rock that rose above the sea.

The king drew an arrow from his quiver and fit it to his bow. The hind let forth a pitiable cry and then the king let fly his arrow. At the moment when it would have hit the hind, the arrow turned in its path and flew back toward the king. It hit Morvarc'h in the chest and the horse threw the king and hurtled off the cliff into the sea.

In a rage complete, the king drew his dagger and advanced upon the hind. At this moment there, the voice of a woman cried out. And in the place of the hind there is a beautiful girl.

To punish the king for having pursued her, this girl gave the king the mane and the ears of his horse. King Marc'h drew his cloak over his head and returned to Poulmarc'h. He had a wall of gold bricks as high as the head of a man built around his throne and commanded that no one would look upon him or they must die.

He has a coiffeur come to cut his mane, but so that no one may know the secret of the king, the tongue of the coiffeur is cut out the moment he has cut the last hair. But the hair grows, and in two weeks when he calls the coiffeur to come back, he cannot be found, for he has taken his wife and his children and has fled the kingdom in fear. So the king calls another coiffeur and when he is finished, his tongue also is cut out and when the coiffeur is called back in two weeks time he also cannot be found, for he has fled the kingdom the same as the first. And soon all the coiffeurs in the kingdom have fled in fear of the king, save one: Yeunig. This is the favorite of the king and the one who has cut his hairs always before this happening. And so the king does not wish to cut out the tongue of this coiffeur. And so he will wait and wait. But the hair must keep growing and soon it is too heavy to bear. And so the king will call Yeunig.

And seeing the mane and the ears of the king, Yeunig demands of
him, why did you not send for me more quick? I have the enchanted
scissors and whatever hairs the scissors cut will never grow again. But if I
will cut your hairs, then you must promise not to cut out my tongue.

And the king will do this, only Yeunig must never tell anyone that the
king has the mane and the ears of a horse. And Yeunig swears this. And
the hairs are cut and Yeunig leaves.

But all the world has envy to know the secret of the king, and so
they offer Yeunig money and women and power if only he will repeat it
to them. He refuses all. But he fears he must speak the words aloud or he
will explode.

For that no one may hear, he goes to the beach and digs a large hole
and puts his head into this and screams, The King Has the Mane and the
Ears of a Horse! And then he covers up this hole. And he feels himself
much relieved: he has spoken these words and no one has heard them.

But three reeds begin to grow from the hole.

King Marc'h takes the decision to marry his sister to the King of
Léon, who is Rivalen. But there must be a big fête with all of the royalty
of Bretagne. And how will King Marc'h be the host and yet not be seen?
Yeunig counsels him to wear a hood about his head and tell all the world
that he has a maladie. The musicians arrive to make the music and as they
play their instruments, they have great hunger and thirst. And they go
about the palace eating and drinking whatever they find. And that, the
food left for the korrigans.

And at this moment here, I demanded of my lord who are the
korrigans.

My lord replied to me that they are small creatures, like dwarves, who
are very secret and only appear at night. Some are friend to humans and

some are foe. The korrigans are of different types: some belonging to the woods or the lakes, some to the houses.

And I commanded my lord to continue.

When the korrigans have come at midnight, to clean the palace, they find there is neither food nor drink for them. And so, they have taken the reeds from the binious and all the bombardes of the musicians. And the next day, when the musicians must give the branle and the other dances, they have realized they have no reeds. And so they search something that can be made into reeds. At this moment here, a small boy says them that he has seen three reeds which grow on the beach. And so he is sent to take them and give them to the musicians. And new reeds are made and given to each musician. And so they make ready to play. But the first note is not music, but this: The King Has the Mane and the Ears of a Horse!

And all the world demands of King Marc'h if this is true and he removes the hood and declares it so. And as all the people know now his secret, the king can no longer reign. And he must disappear from Bretagne.

At this point here, I found that my eyes would not stay open. When I woke myself in the morning, my lord had already gone.

day of Saint Matthieu

When my lord rendered me a visit this night, I demanded of him to tell me the part that rests of the story of King Marc'h.

He replied to me that he has told me the story, the two weeks which have passed.

And this confused me for he had told me he would tell me more of the story of Arthur King of Bretons when he had begun the story of King Marc'h.

And then my lord remembered to himself that he had not finished the story. What he added is the follow:

After leaving his kingdom, King Marc'h has crossed the Channel and is living with his cousin who is Arthur King of Bretons. And Arthur demands of Marzin if the spell placed on the king cannot be broken. And Marzin replies to him that he cannot break the spell, but he can make it less. And he gives King Marc'h a potion that disappears the mane and the ears of the horse so long as he is in Britain. But if the king ever returns to Bretagne, then the mane and the ears must again appear. And so King Marc'h takes the potion and then Arthur gives him the kingdom of Cornwall for to rule.

One day King Marc'h has word that his brother-in-law, Rivalen, has been killed by a duc named Morgan. And also, his sister is dead of grief. But before she had died, she has borne a son. And all the world is ignorant of what has become of this child.

Many years after, a handsome boy appears in Cornwall. He is a strong warrior with all the skills of a chevalier, and he becomes the favorite of King Marc'h. The boy is called only Tristan and knows not his family.

At this time here, a Breton noble is searching an adopted son who was taken of him by pirates. And he is told of Tristan who is arrived in Cornwall. And this noble comes to King Marc'h and explains to him that Tristan is the son of Rivalen, and that the noble had hidden him from duc Morgan while making of him a chevalier.

And because it has been revealed that Tristan is the nephew of the king, the king takes the decision to leave his kingdom to Tristan when he will die.

The jealous nobles demand that the king must marry and have an heir of himself. King Marc'h wants no other heir than Tristan, but he is fatigued by the complaints of the nobles. And in seeing a long golden hair that has been dropped by a bird, he tells the nobles he will do as they demand of him as soon as they will find the owner of the long fair hair. He will marry no other.

And the nobles agree if the king will tell them to whom the hair is belonged and in which country she must live.

And the King replies to them to demand of the bird who has dropped it.

But Tristan knows the owner of the hair. Before he is come to Cornwall, he has killed a monster in Ireland and this monster is the uncle of a girl named Yseult. And the Irlandais will kill him if they will see him, but because of his loyalty to his uncle, he searches for Yseult. For he knows he must not advance in power only because his uncle cannot advance.

But when Tristan has convinced Yseult to return with him to Cornwall, they have drunk a love potion in mistake and ever after they are bound by a passion they can neither comprehend nor rid themselves of. And the encounter of Tristan and Yseult brings much unhappiness to everyone who once has loved them. It brings exile for them both and sends Tristan to the kingdom of Arthur. And, at end, it must bring death to the lovers.

But at this moment here, I demanded of my lord what has happened to King Marc'h?

My lord replied to me that for cause of the betrayal of the two persons he has most loved, he will return to Bretagne and take again the mane and the ears of a horse. He retakes his throne, but he is never the same king as before. He is destined to excess in debauchery as well as excess in charity.

But that, my lord says me, is another story. And it will not be told this night.

four days after Saint Dynys

My lord began the proper story of Arthur King of the Bretons. This I already heard many times, but it is not polite for me to say this, and so I listened. Here is how he told me it:

It is told that the great king lived here, in Brocéliande. He was born of King Uther. As his mother was not the queen, King Uther gave his son to a chevalier who trained Arthur in all the arts of war so that when he is grown, he can also be a chevalier. When Arthur had sixteen years, his true father, King Uther, died without an heir.

At the death of King Uther, the leaders of the clans demanded of Marzin the Magician, to name them a new king. Marzin answered them to wait until heaven touches earth, the dead come back to life, and those who cannot speak are given voice.

One day, in the parvis in front of the cathédrale in a place which had been empty, a stone appeared with a handsome sword sunk into its mass. This stone was not like those of the country. It was so large that no man could move it and it had writing on it so strange that no man could read it. And all the people came to see it.

It was Marzin, the last one to come, and the first one to be able to read what the stone would say. It was written on the stone: The one who is able to take from the stone this sword is the one who must be king. Marzin remembered to them that neither family of birth nor richness make nothing to do with the decision of who must be king. It is for the store to decide to whom it will yield the sword.

Each of the leaders stepped up to the stone and placed his hands around the sword, but each of the leaders failed to pull it from the stone. After all of the leaders had not succeeded, it was given to any person to try to take the sword. Many of the men of the town tried this, but none of them, even not the smith, had success. At this, the leaders made their sons try. And after the sons had failed, then the sons of the men of the town were given it to try. And after, even the servants and their sons. And then even the most young, those who could not yet walk, were let to try. And finally, although all had tried, none had succeeded, and still the sword remained in the stone.

At this moment here, Arthur was searching a sword for the chevalier who had kept him since birth. When he walked into the parvis and saw the sword sunk into the stone, he demanded if it did not belong to any person. When he was replied that it did not, Arthur placed his hand on the sword and pulled it from the stone. At this, Marzin named him King of Bretons.

At this, the people of the town are very happy, for they have known Arthur and he has lived among them, but the leaders are unhappy and they demand of Marzin that Arthur return the sword to the stone so that they might try once more to succeed in pulling it out. Once more, all of the leaders try at this and fail. And the men of the town try and fail. And then the sons of the leaders try once more without finding success, as well, the sons of the men of the town. And still, once more, the servants and their sons are given to try and when they also fail, then the young and babies are given a chance. Again, as before, it is Arthur the only one who has success.

But even at this, the leaders refuse him as their king until Marzin says them that Arthur is, in actuality, the son of Uther. At this, Arthur gathers a great army made not of the sons of the leaders, but of the sons of the people of the town and Arthur leads his army with Kaledvoulc'h, his sword; Gweneb-Gourzhuc'her, his shield; and Rongomyant, his lance.

My lord began to tell me more, but I found myself falling into sleep. He saved the rest of the story for the next time.

I dreamt this night that someone came beside me and combed through my hair with their fingers all the long of the night.

This seems to me bizarre because it is normal that I do not remember my dreams.

one day before Saint André

Anne demands me of the feast of Noël, what I would like served. I am ignorant of the customs of the Bretons and I cannot remember what was served this past year. I do not know why she demands this of me so I have given her permission to do as she likes.

Agnès says me that I must take interest in the affairs of the house. A good wife is certain that things are managed according to the desires of her husband.

I replied to Agnès that as Anne has managed these past years, she must know what my lord requires. Far better for her to plan the feast than for me to plan and have it disappoint my lord, the comte.

one day after Saint Hilaire

My lord finished his story from three months past: soon after Arthur became King of Bretons, Marzin the Magician tells him that the Saxons have come to take the land of the giant Gogvran Gaor. As Arthur comes to help Gogvran Gaor, Marzin suggests to Arthur to attack first.

The lady of Gogvran Gaor and her daughters watch the battle which follows from the safety of the chateau. The fight is long and very bloody, and at one point, Gogvran Gaor is taken by the Saxons. Arthur, seeing this, plunges into the middle of the battle, overtaking the Saxon lord and rescuing the chevalier. When the Saxons have seen this, they lose their morale, gather their men, and draw back, leaving the lands of Gogvran Gaor.

Arthur is carried back to the chateau of the giant by his army, much wounded and in danger of death. The oldest daughter of Gogvran Gaor, Guenievre, commands that all leave the presence of Arthur and allows no person but herself to aid him.

My lord says me that Guenievre means White Ghost. She is so fair she is said to glow in the moonlight, her step is so soft it is said that none can hear it, and her voice so low it is said that it sounds like the call of a bird in the night. She is the girl the most kind of all the world. Her touch is so cool it gives life to Arthur as a spring in the middle of the forest.

Gogvran says to Arthur that he is happy to have as a son-in-law the man who has saved him from death, even though he has not yet been told the identity of this man.

At this moment here, Marzin says to Gogvran Gaor that the name of this man is Arthur, King of Bretons, and son of the great king Uther.

The marriage takes place the next month, and all the world has never been so happy.

I told my lord that Gogvran Gaor was a generous man to give his oldest daughter to Arthur, thinking him just a brave peasant; the chevalier might have given Arthur gold or silver in her stead.

My lord replied to me that sometimes daughters, and sisters, are more dear to men than riches.

novembre

A Sainte-Flora, plus rien ne fleurira.

November

At the day of Saint-Flora,
nothing else will flower.

15

The first day of November came cold and clear. It served to magnify the barren trees against the sky, and the dusting of frost over the dead grasses highlighted the hardness of the ground. It was entirely appropriate for *Toussaint*. All Saint's Day. A day for remembering the dead.

I didn't like *Toussaint*. I didn't know what to do on it.

My memories of Peter were private. I had mourned. I had worked through all the cycles of my grief. He would always be a part of me, for the person I am is due, in large part, to him.

I didn't know what to do on *Toussaint* because he was buried in a family plot in Massachusetts. I had no grave to visit, no place to leave flowers. But I felt guilty if I didn't do something in his memory. So in the past, I had honored his memory by making his favorite meal: clam chowder and sourdough bread.

The only problem with that ritual was that I happened to hate clam chowder, and I much preferred a normal baguette to sourdough. My heart just wasn't in it.

I pulled on my checkered pants and tank top and lumbered down the stairs to the kitchen. I made the breads in autopilot and sipped my morning espresso without enjoying it.

What would Peter have done if the situation were reversed?

I tried to picture him, tried to imagine where he would be were he still alive. He certainly wouldn't have given his whole day over to morose thoughts of me. He probably would have done something I'd liked to do. Read my favorite poem, drunk a glass of my favorite wine in toast to me. Something of that sort.

So why did I feel the need to make a crock of clam chowder that I'd never eat?

Rousing myself from the stool where I was sitting, I grabbed a bottle of Bushmill's, Peter's favorite whiskey, and a shot glass and marched up the stairs.

I flung open the door to my room and stood in front of the picture of Peter that graced my night table.

After pouring a shot of whiskey, I raised the glass in his memory. As I downed the shot, a ray of sunlight fell directly on the photo. I'd done the right thing.

Satisfied, I started toward the kitchen, but I ran into Cranwell and Lucy on the stairs.

"That bad a day already?" Cranwell was eying the bottle of Bushmill's I held in my hand.

"It's *Toussaint*."

"Oh." Cranwell left it at that. At least with me. I heard him later that evening asking Séverine about it.

"Have you heard of Tucson?"

"*Toussaint*? Yes. It is the first day of November. The English call it the day of All Saints. In France this is the day to remind us of the dead. We visit cemeteries if we live not so far away, and we clean tombs and leave flowers. Chrysanthemums."

I went to bed early.

I heard a soft knock on my door after I had turned out my light. I was wearing a silk chemise and didn't even think of throwing on a robe until after I had reached the door.

I turned the handle and opened it, using the door to shield my body.

It was Cranwell. He was in his silk pajamas and was shifting his weight between his bare feet. He looked about ten years old.

"I'm sorry. About the whiskey crack."

"That's okay. You didn't know."

"No, but I do know you."

"I had a drink in his memory. One. Bushmill's was his favorite."

"I just wanted you to know that I was sorry." He turned to leave, but I came out from behind the door and placed a hand on his forearm.

"Thanks."

He put a hand over mine and squeezed it, clearing his throat as if to say something.

I waited.

His eyes searching mine made me aware of how little I was wearing.

"Good night."

"Good night, Freddie."

❦

Cranwell's public reading tapered off, but he'd started asking questions. Lots of questions. He was no longer looking for facts, but rather for opinions. The topics ran the gamut from politics to gender. And they were not always the easiest to answer.

He caught me at work in the garden one overcast, gusty afternoon, as I was tidying it up for winter. The gusts kept catching the tail of my gray plaid wool shirt, trying to pull it over my head. Thankfully my black wool turtleneck and trousers kept the bite of the wind from my body. And the thick gray stocking cap jammed over my braided hair trapped my body heat. But clouds were beginning to scour the steel-colored sky, and I was in a hurry; it felt like the onslaught of the first winter storm.

"Freddie, pretend you were married in the Middle Ages at the age of thirteen. What would you have taken with you when you left home?"

"At thirteen? That's asking for a lot of imagination." Not to mention a lot of thought. And that's something I didn't really have time for. The wool of my hat was making me itch. I tried to scratch through the wool yarn, but I only succeeded in smearing mud across my forehead.

He squatted beside me, in blatant disregard of his mulberry cashmere sweater, pleated pants, and five-hundred-dollar driving moccasins. He casually took a handkerchief from his pocket, hooked a finger around my chin to turn it toward him, and wiped the mud away. Then he began to help me pull up the few weeds that had lingered after the frost. Wouldn't you know he'd be the type to carry a handkerchief?

"Really Freddie, what would you take?"

"My favorite things."

"But what *are* a thirteen-year-old girl's favorite things?"

I thought back through the years to my preadolescent days and the box of treasures that I had kept underneath my bed.

"Yo-yos, art projects, dried flowers, insect collections." I stopped for a moment to tug at a particularly stubborn root. "Paper dolls, gum machine jewelry. Favorite books. Notes from friends." Rain began splotting around us. The wind had begun to blow more forcefully. Three rows left. I wouldn't be able to finish. "Time to go inside."

Cranwell helped me to my feet and picked up my pail of gardening tools. "Would you like me to run this to the garage?"

The raindrops were starting to fall faster.

"No. I'll just leave it in the kitchen and take it back tomorrow."

We sprinted the fifty yards to the kitchen's back door. Cranwell helped me shove the door shut and bolt it.

"It's going to storm all night," I commented as I pulled the hat from my head and stuffed it into my pocket.

"You think?"

"I know." I'd gotten used to the weather's rhythm during the three years I'd spent in Brittany. As if the wind's chill fingers had followed me inside, my teeth began to chatter. "Espresso?" I asked as I made a beeline for the machine.

"Great. It'll help take the chill off."

Primed by the jolt of caffeine, I opened my mouth and started talking; I soon found I couldn't stop. Before I had the presence of mind to censor my words, I heard myself talking to Cranwell about the day Peter died.

"I was always nervous when I knew he was flying somewhere. And I was always nervous when I knew he was on assignment. But that's the funny part: He wasn't flying that day, and he wasn't on assignment. I always thought that if something happened to him, I would know. I would feel it.

"I felt nothing. I thought they were joking when they told me. I just could not believe that he would leave this world and that I would have no knowledge of it. That's what was most devastating.

"That and the fact that I have no idea whether or not I believe in heaven anymore, and even if I did, I don't know whether or not he'd be there."

"He wasn't a believer?"

"Not that I know of. And I knew him very well." If Cranwell really wanted me to talk about my ongoing feud with God, I'd decided that the time was now. "I just don't know if I can be part of a religion with a God like that."

"What did you do after he died?"

"I went to a therapist in Paris, and that helped." The French are great humanists and humanism is noble. It's very big on human potential and relatively silent on guilt and sin. "But mostly I cooked. I cooked these fabulous five-course meals. For myself. It was the second year, when I moved here, that I really worked through it. This chateau was my therapy. I worked on one room at a time, contracting out what I couldn't do myself. By the time it was finished, I had worked out the grief."

"Do you miss him?"

"Of course." I'd had enough of talking about Peter. I shrugged out of the heavy wool shirt I was wearing and set it on top of the island. "What made you want to be a writer?"

"Don't know, really. I just always knew I had the ability to write a book. I finally got to the point where I had something to write about."

"I've always heard you should write about things you know. Is that true?"

"In certain ways. I write about international espionage, politics, and conspiracy. I don't know anything personally about that sort of lifestyle. But I do know about betrayal. I know about loyalty and what it costs. I know about love and the sacrifice it requires."

I caught myself gazing deeply into his eyes, leaning toward his voice. I blinked and reoriented myself on my stool.

"If I strictly wrote what I knew, I would continually be writing an autobiography."

"Your life must be so different."

"Than whose? Than yours? We have quite a bit in common, I think. I go underground when I write, and you live your life hiding out."

"I do not."

"Yes, Freddie, you do. Why else do you refuse guests? Why else do you live twenty miles from the nearest town?"

"I need solitude."

"So do I. When I write. But I always surface afterward. You need to reconnect with the world."

"I go to Italy every January."

"And visit whom?"

"I go to the Forum. I go to the Coliseum. I go to Capri."

"To visit whom? You visit ancient sites when you travel; you live in a forest populated by ancient, mythical characters. You even try to push away God, the giver of life, the healer of broken hearts. Your whole life is one long communion with the dead. It's time to move on, Freddie. Let Peter go."

"That's ridiculous. Peter died four years ago."

"And now it's time to move on."

Just what I needed: an amateur psychologist. Refusing to listen, I turned my back on Cranwell and my attention to cleaning our coffee cups. After a while, he left.

I felt like swearing, but even that overwhelming urge couldn't override a childhood of sermons and Sunday school.

The only times I'd thought of Peter all autumn were the times Cranwell had brought him to mind.

When I started on a tart crust for dessert, I'm afraid I was a little more vicious with the pastry than I needed to be. I ended up throwing it away and starting all over. It would have been too tough.

I thought about what Cranwell said the next morning as I worked in the kitchen. Although most of it was garbage, he did have a point about moving on. And I had moved on.

In my head.

But I still wore my wedding ring. I looked at it in the clear morning light which filtered through the windows. It was a simple solitaire set into a platinum band. Peter had picked it himself, and I had always loved it. But maybe it was time.

As an experiment, I took it off.

Kneading and shaping baguettes and brioches, my finger felt naked. When I went up to deliver Cranwell's breakfast that morning, I felt exposed. The ring had protected me for so long that I had taken it for granted.

Cranwell was seated at the table, with his butterscotch-colored robe flung over his caramel and burgundy paisley silk pajamas. He looked up from his computer, glancing at me over the top of his glasses.

I handed him the tray, and then I spooned a cube of sugar from the bowl with my left hand. It rolled into the coffee with a plop.

It was just a test, to see if he'd notice.

He took the cup from my hand, looking at it, but not really seeing it.

But when I turned to leave, he caught my hand, stopping me.

"I can help you later." He was trying to tell me something with his eyes, and I could not look away from them.

"Help me what?" I swallowed.

"Look for your ring."

My hand trembled; my cheeks flamed. I couldn't help it. "It's not lost." I tugged my hand loose and left the room.

On my return to the kitchen, I pulled the ring from my pocket and screwed it back onto my finger. It seemed safer.

That afternoon, as I made crêpes for dinner, I tried to decide what it was about Cranwell that was so attractive. I'd always thought that self-delusion was reserved for cowards, and so I could not deny that he was attractive and that I was attracted to him. That is not to say that I trusted him. I absolutely did not.

Would not.

As I slid pats of butter across the crêpe pan, poured pools of batter on the metal surface, and spun a rake across the mix to spread it out, I had to be honest with myself. Cranwell was attractive.

His eyes were hypnotic.

But my feelings for him were not all based on the way he looked. They had something to do with his laugh. It started in his chest as a 'humph' and then ricocheted inside him until it burst out into a chuckle.

I enjoyed making him laugh.

It was also enjoyable to see him smile. Smiles started in his lips, and sometimes, if I were lucky, they would crimp lines beneath his eyes and cause them to glint. They were quiet smiles.

In myriad ways Cranwell seduced the senses. His eyes, his laugh, his smile. The way he carried himself. The clothes he wore. The textures and layers that made the man.

Sliding a spatula under the last crêpe, I flipped it onto the top of the pile.

At least I had identified him. At least I knew who my nemesis was.

The problem was that, in spite of everything, I liked Cranwell. And maybe he really had changed. Maybe he wasn't the playboy he had been. I decided that the challenge would be to avoid falling in love with him. And that was going to cause some difficulties. I could tell already, because on top of everything else, Cranwell liked to listen. And heaven help the woman who finds a man who will listen to her.

I comforted myself with the thought that the first step in waging war is taking measure of the enemy.

16

The next evening, when Sévérine came for her dinner tray, I remembered to ask her a question that had been on my mind. "Is this the year of your *Catherinette*?"

"*Oui*." It was the first time I'd seen her blush. In fact, she blushed so badly, her cheeks matched the color of the scarf she'd wound around her neck.

"What's a *Catherinette*?" Cranwell was looking at Sévérine with interest.

"Oh, Robert, it is nothing." Sévérine waved a graceful hand at Cranwell as if to swat his question away.

"What is it, Freddie?" He fingered the collar of his moss green v-neck sweater the way he always did when he was curious about something.

"It's the year of Sévérine's twenty-fifth birthday. And because she's single, we celebrate. And she pleads with Sainte-Catherine to send her a husband."

Sévérine shushed Cranwell's laughter. "It is not done so much any more."

"Of course it is!" I'd had friends in Paris who'd celebrated. "Especially the twenty-five kisses."

"The what?" Cranwell was getting into the idea. I could tell.

"It is an old custom. Very *vieux jeu*." Sévérine had jammed her hands into the back pockets of her tight-fitting indigo jeans.

"Let us celebrate with you. It'll be fun." Cranwell's eyes held a dangerous twinkle.

Séverine looked from Cranwell to me; I could tell she didn't quite trust us.

"Seriously. It will be fun." I handed her a dinner tray. "Tell me what your favorite meal is and I'll fix it."

"*Foie gras, homards, et croque-em-bouche.*"

I lifted an eyebrow. Liver paté, lobster, and a pyramid of tiny puff pastries filled with cream and wrapped in spun caramel. Since I'd insisted on celebrating, she was going to make me work.

But she deserved a celebration. Especially since she had no one else to celebrate with.

Cranwell waylaid her on her route to the stairs. "I wanted to ask you about the grail."

She stopped so suddenly that she lost her grip on the tray. It clattered to the floor. "Frédérique! I am so sorry."

"It's fine. Don't worry about it." Nothing had broken and most of the food had stayed on the tray. I got out a new plate and began to reconstruct her dinner.

"You had asked me about the grail, Robert? What does this have to do with Alix?"

He shrugged. "I don't know. Probably nothing. Just following a thought."

"I am only an expert on Alix."

"But surely you've studied the legends if you've studied medieval history."

"*Oui, oui, oui.* Of course. In the context of the time period of Alix."

"So it left Israel with Joseph of Arimathea and then came here? To Brittany?"

"This is one story. But there are many others."

"What are the other versions?"

She blew air from her cheeks. "There is the one where it is not a cup or a chalice at all. This is a Celtic one. The grail is a graal or a cauldron."

"A kettle?"

"For cooking? Yes."

"And the quest for it was a search by Arthur?"

"By his knights. But it is more than a search. It is an obsession of all of his knights. But only Galahad succeeds. Because he is the most pure. And in the end, it kills him."

"So it's dangerous."

"Obsessions are always dangerous. And this obsession takes away the best knights from the *Table Rond*."

"And leaves it undefended?"

"*Non*. Not this so much as it lowers the moral."

"Morale?"

"No. The moral. The character of the kingdom. But remember, it is just a fairy story, Robert."

"Maybe. But then people still search for it, don't they?"

"I have a problem." Cranwell probed me with insistent eyes.

So did I. I'd given myself ten minutes to put dinner on the table, and the meat was taking longer to cook than I'd expected. "What?"

"It's too cold in my room."

Don't start with me. "Generally, fourteenth-century castles were built for defensive purposes, not for warmth. Have you tried wearing a hat?"

"Really. I can't type."

Turning my head, I glanced at him over my shoulder. To his credit, he was wearing moleskin trousers and a heavy cream fisherman's turtleneck sweater. "Did you try—"

"A fire doesn't help. Opening the flue only creates a draft."

I didn't have time for his complaints. I checked the meat again. Almost done. "Do you have any solutions?"

"Can I work down here?"

I dropped the pan. It banged onto the stove. Thankfully, it didn't fall to the floor. "Here?"

"It's warm. You have an outlet. I could just set myself up right there." He was pointing at my desk. *My* desk. He had invaded my house, captured my thoughts, and kidnapped my heart. Now he wanted my desk.

There are limits.

"Cranwell, you can't have my desk. You can bring down a table from elsewhere in the house, but you cannot have my desk."

"Great. I'll do it right now." I was finally in a position to turn around to talk to him, but all I saw was his back disappearing up the stairwell.

The next morning, when I made my way down to the kitchen before dawn, I discovered that Cranwell was already hard at work, sitting at the table he'd placed at the back of the kitchen, in his robe and silk pajamas.

Lucy lifted her head when she saw me, then sighed, and dropped it back on her paws.

"Has she been out?"

"Yes."

"When?"

"About —" he paused to look at his watch. "An hour ago."

"You've been here since four?"

"Yes."

He hadn't turned from the computer since I'd walked into the kitchen.

"Espresso?"

"No. Already got it."

Really? Good for him.

After making my espresso, I carried on with my routine, rolling out croissants and then folding them. By 6:15, I was taking them out of the oven.

I put together Cranwell's normal tray, with an espresso and two croissants, accompanied by a small pot of *confiture*.

"Thanks." He looked up from the computer long enough to flash me a smile. "They're talking to me, Freddie. I have to keep typing."

Two weeks later, I was in the kitchen and working on my breads by 5:30, but Cranwell and Lucy were nowhere to be seen. It looked, in fact, as if they hadn't been down at all that morning.

After I had shaped all six baguettes, placed them in the oven, and baked them, I took a break and had an espresso. Happening to glance at the calendar above my desk, I was struck by how quickly November had passed. It was already the 24th, Sainte-Flora day, which seemed odd. If you were going to dedicate a day to a person named Flora, why not give her a day in the spring?

A chill suddenly passed through my shoulders and down my spine.

I decided to run up to my room and get a sweater. I took the central staircase because it came out closer to my room.

As I came back down, Cranwell's door opened. Something made me hold my breath and shrink into the shadows. I saw Sévérine slip out of his room, clad in a black lacy scrap of nothing, and climb the back stairs to her own.

I felt like I'd been hit in the heart with a sledgehammer. Oh, but I'd been stupid. I stumbled back up the stairs to my room and jumped into the shower. I stayed until I'd stopped shaking.

It didn't take much debate with myself to decide to tell Sévérine that I was sick. She knew enough about cooking to scrape together the day's meals. I knocked on her door and shouted the message at her and then sprinted back to my own room before she had a chance to respond. I climbed into bed, wet hair and all, and pulled the duvet over my head. I pretended not to hear when she came and knocked on my door.

I'd known it from the beginning.

Cranwell was exactly the type of man I didn't trust. Men are weak; that's what my mother always warned me. She was right.

Je suis bête. I was so stupid.

By the end of the day, I was beginning to imagine that I could be sick for the entire week. I found myself becoming very philosophical. It wasn't that I minded Sévérine being his lover; I was humiliated at having let myself trust him.

In fact, I was glad they had found each other. It was obvious Sévérine needed a father figure in her life. And Cranwell was perfect for that role. He was old enough. He was forty-five.

That was the end of my crush on Cranwell.

I almost stayed in bed the next morning, but then I remembered what day it was: 25 November. Sainte-Catherine's day. The day of Séverine's *Catherinette*.

What perfect timing.

A shower did little to rouse my spirits. I threw on my usual chef's attire and then rooted around in the closet to find the bonnet I'd bought for Séverine. It was tradition that a Catherinette receive one . . . and usually they were decorated in the worst Minnie Pearl style. This one was no exception.

After pulling back my hair into a ponytail, I slipped on my shoes and trudged down to the kitchen. Thankfully, Cranwell wasn't there. I put some brioches in the oven and then made a plan of the dinner's preparations.

The only thing I'd have to do for the *foie gras* was toast some of the brioche and make beef-flavored *gelée*. That was easy.

The lobsters I planned to cook at the last moment, although the tagliatelle I'd serve with them would need a little more preparation.

The *croque-em-bouche*, the *pièce de résistance*, would take the most time, so I decided to start it right after lunch.

With no sign of Cranwell, and although I had no desire to see him, I put together his breakfast tray and carried it up to his room.

He looked up with a smile, from buttoning his shirt, as I entered the room. He looked as if he'd just come from the shower. "Freddie, the book is really coming along! Did you know there was a love triangle?"

Not until just yesterday.

Cranwell jabbered on about the count and his cousin and Alix, but

I had no interest in poor Alix and her love triangle. Triangles no longer seem so symmetrical.

"You're feeling better."

"Much. In fact, I'm making plans to go to Italy." I set the tray on a chair and turned to leave.

"Can I come?"

I turned back to face him. "No. You'll have to take yourself off to Paris and visit your friends."

"What does Sévérine do when you leave?"

"Whatever she pleases." And I could almost watch the thoughts work through that crafty mind of his. Some Christian he was. I was trapped. I couldn't stay in my own home because I couldn't stand to see them together, but if I went, I didn't know if I could stand to think about them at the chateau . . . alone, while I was sipping limoncello on some shaded terrace in Sorrento.

I closed my eyes. Some bread dough to knead would have been perfect at that moment.

Cranwell came to stand behind me, and I felt his hands on my shoulders as he began massaging them. His voice, close to my ear, said, "You look tense."

Is it possible to want to throw yourself at a man and kill him at the same time?

The dinner turned out perfectly. I would have served champagne, but Sévérine had been so moody lately that I didn't want the evening to end in maudlin tears. And although I had envisioned a casual dinner, both

Cranwell and Séverine showed up dressed to the nines. They must have coordinated at some point. Why else would Cranwell have been wearing a tuxedo and Séverine a floor-length designer knockoff? I wouldn't have chosen pale green for Séverine, but the shimmer of the material set off sparkles in her eyes and made her teeth even more white.

My own outfit was more traditional: I was wearing a very nice pair of faded jeans and a plain-Jane blue oxford button-down shirt. I had the sleeves rolled up for extra panache. I would have taken my hair down for dinner, but considering Séverine looked like she'd spent hours getting hers just right, I decided to leave mine in its knot.

For several moments, I considered not giving Séverine the bonnet. But then again, what would I have done with the hideous thing?

"Séverine, I have a gift for you."

As soon as she saw the hatbox, she knew what it was. "No, Frédérique. This is not necessary."

Oh, but it was.

"Cranwell, maybe you can do the honors while I get the *foie gras*?"

"Of course." He took the box from my hands, opened the lid, took the hat from the box, and burst into laughter.

Séverine could not have made a more ugly face if she'd tried.

"Is this part of the tradition?" Cranwell asked through his laughter.

"It's part of the tradition."

Cranwell placed it on Séverine's head and ceremoniously tied the hot pink ribbons underneath her chin.

She pouted.

At that point I turned around to cut the *foie gras*. When I turned back, Séverine was all giggles and Cranwell was whispering in her ear.

Okay then.

Somehow dinner passed. I don't remember saying much. I can't even remember how the food tasted, although I do know that the *croque-em-bouche* looked magnificent.

When Cranwell decided Séverine needed twenty-five kisses, I excused myself to go to the bathroom.

When I returned, Cranwell was clearing the table, and Séverine was untying her bonnet. "Thank you, Frédérique. This was very kind."

"You're welcome." I tried to smile. I'm not sure if I succeeded. What I really needed was to be alone in my kitchen. "Cranwell, Lucy looks as if she needs a walk."

She really did. I wasn't lying.

"If you don't need any help —"

"No. I'm fine. You and Séverine should . . . let this be. I'll clean up."

Séverine didn't wait to hear another word; she made a beeline for the stairs. And Cranwell strolled out the back door with Lucy.

It's the last I saw of either of them that night.

my fifteenth year
year thirty-nine of the reign of Charles VII, King of France

day of Easter

It has been three months since my lord has rendered me a visit.
But this night, after he commanded me to bed, instead of drawing the
curtains, he demanded of me if he might sit on the bed beside me instead
of the hard floor. My cheeks became red because, had I noticed before, I
would have made offer.

I must learn to be a better wife. And in fact, I do know how, for I had
done the study of the Holy Bible as Agnès had demanded of me. I must
begin to practice it.

He sat beside me for a while, but then laid himself the length of the
bed, with his head at the foot, crooked his arm at the elbow, and placed
his head in his hand as he told me this story:

There lived in Bretagne a prince named Kulhwch who had fallen
in love with a lady named Olwen, daughter of the giant Yspaddaden
Penkawr. Olwen had hair the color of broom, exactly, my lord says me,
like mine. She had eyes the color of doves, just like mine, and cheeks
stained the color of thrift. The prince demanded of the giant the hand of
Olwen.

The giant gave his accord, but only if Prince Kulhwch would go to Eire, a kingdom across the sea, and take from them the Graal, a cauldron which must be used in the marriage fest.

The Graal was so strong in magic that in spite of the number of persons taking food from the Graal, it never went empty; but food from the dishonorable could not be cooked in it. And when dead chevaliers were thrown into the Graal, they are alive the next day, more fit than before, but without a tongue to speak.

The prince demanded the aid of Arthur King of Bretons. To refuse would have been dishonorable, so Arthur sent a message to Odgar mac Aedh, King of Eire, and demanded of him the Graal.

Odgar the King told Diwrnach the Gael, keeper of the cauldron, to give it to Arthur.

Diwrnach promised God Arthur would never have it.

Arthur took a group of chevaliers and sailed on his boat to Eire. They rendered a visit to Diwrnach the Gael, who offered them to eat and sleep. Arthur and the chevaliers ate and slept and then demanded of Diwrnach the cauldron.

Diwrnach refused.

Lancelot du Lac took Kaledvoulc'h, the sword of Arthur, and killed Diwrnach the Gael. Then the Graal was given to Hywydd, the servant of Arthur, for to guard it.

And ever after this, it is for Hywydd to be keeper of the Graal and be ready to light the fire underneath it.

I demanded of my lord if I wasn't as fair as Olwen.

Then he raised himself and came to sit by my side. He took a lock of my hair and stroked it and told me that I was still more fair.

This pleased me.

four days before Saint Barnabé

One month since my lord told me a story, he came again this past night. I reminded myself of Marzin the Magician, and demanded of my lord if he had not a son or a family.

My lord says me that he is the son of the devil and a nun. That he has not family, but that he is the lover of the fairy Viviane.

It is Viviane who made him prisoner in nine magic circles of light, invisible as air, but more strong than stone. He wanders still the Brocéliande, although he is very rarely seen.

Viviane met Marzin at the Fontaine de Barenton and then enchanted him at the Fontaine de Jeunesse Eternale. She used the chants of Marzin himself to turn his age into youth.

Marzin built for her a crystal stronghold beneath the lake at Concoret. It falsely reflects the Chateau de Comper. My lord says me that if one plunges into the lake and looks far enough down, the stronghold of Viviane can be seen.

I demanded of my lord to take me to the lake and to teach me to swim.

He laughed at me and replied to me that girls swim not.

I replied to him that I am not a young girl, but a woman. And that his wife. And if he can swim, than I am sure to be able to. I have two arms and two legs as has he.

He laughed the harder, his head falling from his hand and onto the bed.

At this I came from the bed, walked to beside him at the foot, and lifted my robe that he could see how sturdy were my legs.

He stopped laughing.

one day before Saint Jean-Baptiste

My lord has gone to Dinan these two weeks. He left Anne and I. I have tried to interest Anne in books.

She says me that reading gives her pain in the head and tires her eyes.

I told her of an invention in Italy of glasses one puts in front of the eyes to be aided to see.

She says me that they must be ugly or they would be the fashion, and that no man loves a women with red eyes, crossed from reading.

one day before Sainte Marie-Madeleine

My lord rendered me a visit.

I demanded of him information on the chevaliers of Arthur and how many there were.

My lord says me that there were 350. And when they feasted, they sat at a great round table so that there was no first or last among them. They were the most strong and most courageous chevaliers in all the world. And they went out from Arthur in search of adventure, and returned to him only when they had overcome many things and obtained much glory.

As Arthur became aged, he began to think they must lose respect for him, for he had not fought a battle in many years. He made the decision to show the chevaliers that he was still the most strong and the most courageous. He called them to battle against the Romans.

Before his leaving, he gave his kingdom to the keeping of his nephew, Mordred. Mordred was Lord of Verre, where there was neither summer nor winter.

When Arthur came near to the Romans, the army came out to meet him. The fight lasted three days. At the finish, only seven of the chevaliers of Arthur had life. The rest of the 350 had been killed. But still, Arthur made the Romans retreat. At this moment here, messengers brought news that Mordred had taken Guenievre to the Land of Verre and had there married her and made of himself the King of the Two Bretagnes.

Arthur left the Romans and returned to Bretagne. There, Arthur and the chevaliers discovered that Mordred had made an alliance with the Saxons, and led an army of 50,000. There was much fighting and the sea became red with blood.

The final battle took place in Kamlann and was the battle the most bloody the world has ever seen. There were 100,000 deaths. Of the seven chevaliers that had returned from fighting the Romans, only three remained: Morvran ab Tegit who was so ugly people thought him the devil; Sanddey Bryd Angel who was so fair people thought him an angel and feared to touch him; and Glewlwyd Gavaelvawr who was the last chevalier to see Arthur alive.

Arthur and Mordred found themselves face to face in the middle of the field of battle. Arthur pierced Mordred through the chest with Rongomyant, his lance. But, before his death, Mordred stuck his sword in the sides of Arthur.

Faithful servants of Arthur carried him to a chapel by the sea.

Arthur demanded of his servants to help him gain the sea. Then he took his sword and took his leave of it. He demanded it be thrown into the sea.

The faithful servants then took the sword and launched it at the sea. At the point where it touched the waters, an arm appeared from the sea and lifted high the sword three times, and then drew the sword beneath the waves.

Arthur took his leave of the faithful servants, saying, "Where I am going, you cannot follow, but one day I must return."

Then the faithful servants took leave of their king, but in their leaving they saw a boat that reached the shore not far from Arthur. And in the boat sat the Fairy Morgane, the sister of Arthur, who, when she saw the king, left the boat and touched him. Arthur got to his feet as if healed and leapt into the boat.

The boat sailed to Avalon where Arthur lives still.

I demanded of my lord why I have not heard before of Morgane, the sister of Arthur. He says me that the name of Morgane is spoken with reverence. She is a healer and a prophetess and a magician.

I have made note that all good women are fair, as are Olwen and Guenievre.

Must that mean that Anne is wicked?

day of Saint Dominique

I see many children of all the tradesmen. It is my duty as a wife to have children for my lord.

I demanded of Agnès how I might have children and she replied to me that sometimes God is slow: she told me that I must say extra Ave Marias, and then God will hear my prayer, and that if my lord renders me visits more often this will help.

day of Saint Laurent

I have taken the decision that I will write a mystery, a play in verse, for the services this year for Easter. The first task must be to choose a story. For a mystery, perhaps something Breton, the life of St. Ivo or Saint Guénolé. Or something more pious: the life of Jésu Christ. If I will work hard, and write well, then I may have 1,000 verses.

day of Assomption

I have explained to my lord that which I will try to accomplish: a mystery with 1,000 verses. He says me that the priest is not decided what importance these mysteries have to the church.

But I tell my lord that he has much power, and why should the priest not listen to the advice of a comte?

My lord looked at me, an appraisal I must imagine, and says me that I begin to think like a comtesse. But also that he must read the mystery in whole before he will recommend it to the priest even in part.

I will begin my work tomorrow.

one day after Assomption

This day I have chosen St. Ivo as my mystery. I had wanted the life of Jésu Christ, but then have reminded myself that the scene of the crucifixion must take as long as it did for our lord, the Christ. If the priest is not decided on the value of a mystery, then perhaps a mystery which will take fifty of the peasants the day entire to perform, would not be a wise choice.

And now, I must educate myself on the life of St. Ivo. Who better to tell me the story of this saint than my lord? Surely it must number among the dozens of which he has knowledge.

two days after Assomption

I have demanded of my lord to come to my chamber this night.

He replied to me to be certain that this is what I desire.

I replied to him, but of course I am.

And in leaving, he raised my hand to his lips and kissed it.

When he is come, he has seen me at my desk. And he says me, I had thought to come to your chamber of your heart and I come instead to the chamber of your head?

At this phrase I turned, and found him clothed in a costume of blood red velvet which seemed to me too warm for the weather, but is his most fine, and I had fear that I had taken him from some important affair. I presented all my excuses and told him of why I wished him present: That I must know the life of St. Ivo before I can write the mystery of it.

At this he had the look of a soule of which the air has left. And he took from his shoulders the outer houppelande, with clenched jaw, and placed it around my chair and laid himself the length of the bed and began to speak.

Ivo, patron saint of Bretagne, is also advocate of the poor. Ivo was born in Kermartin near Tréguier, the son of a noble man. When he is grown, he is gone to Paris to study the laws of the church and when he is done he is gone to Orléans to study the laws of the state. And all this time, he drinks no wine, eats no meat, and many times takes only bread and water. And often he wears a shirt of hair and he sleeps less than he would like.

When he is returned to Bretagne, he is become a judge of the church, first in Rennes and then in his own town of Tréguier. There it was that he began to seek justice for those who could find none. It is said of Ivo that he was a lawyer, but was not dishonest. He refused bribes. He tried to arrange cases outside the courts so the peasants must not pay. And if they must pay, then St. Ivo would give the money himself. He defended the poor, and went to them in prison. He fought against unfair taxes and gave to the poor much that he had earned. And even those he must judge against later returned and thanked him for his judgments.

And then he became a priest to preach at Lovannec. And there he built a hospital with his own monies and himself cared for the sick who were poor. He gave his own clothes to those who had none and his own bed to those who had only ground on which to sleep. And when there was harvest, he gave to others all of the fruits of his field.

The miracles of Saint Ivo are many according to my lord. And these not occurring while Saint Ivo has life, but after his death. Among them, a sick man falling into a well who calls on Saint Ivo for aid and neither drowns, nor is lost beneath the waters.

A man who is condemned to death by hanging who swears to Saint Ivo that if he is delivered from death then he will visit the tomb of the saint; the man is hung and will not die. And although the hangman tries three times to kill him, he is not able.

A man crossing a bridge falls with his black horse into the river in a spot so deep they cannot touch the bottom; and as they flounder, the leather bag in which are important documents detaches itself from the horse and sinks. They are certain to drown, but the man calls on Saint Ivo for help. At this, the horse bounds from the water onto land, and as the man watches, the bag also comes to the surface. And the man retrieves this from the water and he finds after he has this opened that not one of the papers has become even wet.

One day, as a knight and fifteen persons take a boat to gain the ile of Teven, they are overtaken by a storm which breaks twelve of the oars and engulfs the boat. They have fear of being drowned when they pray to Saint Ivo for aid. And their boat, filled still with water, is pushed to the land in the place exact where they had left.

And then my lord gave pause and I demanded of him if these were all.

He replied to me that if I had three days then I might hear the end of them.

And so I have begun to record these four. And most commendable to me are not the miracles and not the fact that Saint Ivo quit the law to take care of the poor, but that he was honest in law from the start.

And while I am writing still, my lord has fallen asleep. It has taken my prodding and poking to wake him, but now that he has gone, I may finish the transcription.

four days before Saint Etienne

I surprise myself with the effort the writing of a mystery must take. Habituated to translating texts and to keeping record of my days, I had not anticipated that writing verse must be so difficult. I have but ten. I miss 990. I suppose that I could leave writing for reading and no one would know what I have done not. But I remind myself that I have told my lord what I have thought to accomplish. I must still finish this task. And with enough time for the peasants to learn their verses.

two days after Saint Michel

I but write this day. And have only twenty more verses to add to my meager total.

four days after Saint Dynys

My lord has rendered me a visit this night. And has found me at my desk. My verses number 100 at this moment, but this is not enough. My lord demanded of me on what I work.

I replied to him on my mystery.

And he demanded of me if I will read these verses to him.

I trembled for what he will think; for myself, I think them poorly formed. But he must hear them on Easter the same.

He stopped me on the fifth verse and demanded of me who has told me Saint Ivo has worn a shirt of hair.

I replied to him that it was himself. Not two months before.

He commanded me to read on, but then stopped me on the fourteenth verse and demanded of me who has told me that those Saint Ivo has judged against return to thank him?

I replied to him again that it was himself.

He commanded me to read on, but again then stopped me on the seventeenth verse to tell me that perhaps the hangman does not try only three times to kill the man who is supposed to die.

I demanded of him if he had told me the story incorrectly at the first instance.

And he replied to me that stories change. It makes no difference if the hangman tries to kill the accused three times or twelve. He says me that I try to make history from legend and that to write a mystery, one must attend to the mystery, not the verity.

And so I demanded of him whether there ever was in existence a Saint Ivo.

And he replied to me for certain that there was. But perhaps the horse crossing the bridge was white and not black. And perhaps ten oars were broken in place of twelve. But that it matters not what exact parts of the miracles have been performed, but that they have been performed and witnessed at all.

As I surveyed my verses I reminded myself I spent one hour searching the rhyme for black. And one day to phrase 'the waves had taken the oars of twelve; then snapped the sticks; left the boat to wend; through the waves, their souls to heaven were giv'n.' And I looked up from my papers to the bed and found that my lord had risen to stand behind me.

And he says me that I have become too earnest. That the pleasure of a story is in the recounting, in the sound of the words, not in the small details. He says me that I must fit the story to the verse, and not the verse to the story.

That seems to me dishonest, but he demanded of me to try this for one week and then compare the results with what has gone before.

This I agreed to do.

two days after Saint Malo

My lord has rendered me a visit this night. He demanded of me how many verses I have written.

I replied him since, as truth matters not, 479. He looked well pleased, but I tell him this includes the 100 I have written before, and have returned to re-write.

I demanded of him if, in re-telling the stories he has recounted me, this day Arthur King of Bretons might have 100 knights at his great round table in place of the 350 my lord told me before.

He replied to me that this day here, he might even have just 12.

I demanded of him if in re-telling the story of Arthur fighting the Saxons, whether this day there might be 60,000 Saxons instead of 50,000.

He replied to me that this day here, there might even have been 100,000.

I demanded of him if in recounting the story of Arthur being cured by Guenievre whether she might have dark hair and high color of her skin.

At this, he replied to me that some elements in stories must never change. And Guenievre must always be fair. That beauty like hers and like mine is an idée fixe that must remain no matter who will tell the story.

day of Noël

We went to mass this night. Anne had fear on the way and says me that she did not leave the door open.

I explained to her that this does nothing. It is superstition. As well, the ghosts, the beasts that talk, and the trees which flower at midnight.

I could see she believed me not, but kept her fear.

day of the new year

Save Noël, this month has passed in mist. I must have taken food, for I am not faint; and I must have taken sleep, for I do not have sleepiness, but I remember having done nothing but write. I have finished this day the mystery. I think there are some verses which are very beautiful. I think there are other verses which are quite dull. And I think that were St. Ivo to hear it, he would not even guess the subject of this mystery. I will give this to my lord and he will decide whether it must be given to the priest.

one day after Epiphanie

My lord has rendered me a visit this night. And with him, the mystery. He recounted to me the story of I-do-not-recall-whom who did I-do-not-recall-what. I had no concentration for the words or the story. I only wished to know what my lord has thought of the mystery.

And then he demanded of me what I must reply to his story.

And I tell him that, as I know now his secret, which must be to lie at every instance, that I cannot reply to him since I know not that it even is the real story. This story might, when told in truth, be a different one altogether.

At this, he made to leave the bed, with my mystery in his hand, but I ran to his side and begged him to stay and to tell me what he has thought of the mystery.

He says me that he found it very nicely done and that I might make of myself a Breton after all.

And I demanded of him will he show it to the priest.

And he replied to me that he will. If I will come with him.

And we agreed to do this tomorrow.

two days after Epiphanie

This day I went with my lord to give the mystery to the priest.

My lord explained to him that I had it written with hopes that it might be performed at services of Easter.

The priest has agreed to read the mystery.

four days before Sainte Agnès

This day I went with my lord to demand of the priest what he has thought of the mystery.

It lay in disarray upon his desk, the pages spotted with candle wax and marked with grease.

He first disparaged the verses as being too full of fancy, the life of St. Ivo portrayed as though a romance.

My lord remembered to him that a mystery is performed as a drama and to convey the emotions, they must by times be overwrought.

The priest then replied to him that the length is too long, that the peasants would find sleep before they found the end of the mystery.

My lord replied to him that many villages enact the entire life of Christ, which must take more than one day, and no one ever has complaints.

Finally, the priest replied to him that he cannot accept a work written by a woman. That mysteries of the spirit are better worked out by men.

I could see the jaw of my lord clench and I had fear for what words he might speak, but then he spoke no words at all, only held out his hands for the pages.

The priest these gathered and placed in the hands of my lord.

And on leaving, my lord told him that sorry he was the mystery was not received, for it was he, my lord, who had it written. And that he had feared the verses were not well made, and so I had agreed to claim them as my own.

On hearing this, the priest took the pages from my lord and clutched them to his chest and made much over their loveliness. Their perfectness. Their form.

My lord placed a hand on my arm to keep me from leaving until the priest had agreed to choose fifty persons to enact the mystery on Easter Day.

On the return, my lord demanded my pardon for claiming the mystery for his own.

I replied to him that I understood the why of what he had done and I thanked him. For had he not claimed it, the mystery would never have been heard. By any.

And he recalled to me that in all cases, it is for God the glory of such a work and not man.

And this I know, and this I had intended, but it does not make the offense seem any less.

décembre

Après Noël, brise nouvelle.

December

After Christmas comes a new breeze.

19

*C*ranwell was talking to me about Alix's journals. I hadn't read them myself, but apparently, if Séverine's translations were correct, for the first three years, Alix had been a neglected wife.

"Not abused." Cranwell put down his fork of *joue de lotte* fish and leaned toward me to emphasize the point. "Neglected. Her husband didn't even consummate the marriage."

I fixed the appropriate shocked look on my face that Cranwell seemed to expect. Personally, I was all for Alix's husband. They married when she was thirteen and he was thirty.

Trying to focus on what Cranwell was saying, I tore my thoughts from the barbarity of the Middle Ages. I found myself looking at the slight wave in his hair, wondering if Séverine liked to push her fingers through it. My eyes strayed to the top button of his navy cashmere polo. I could just imagine Séverine undoing that button, and the next, and pushing the sweater up over his shoulders . . .

"And then she grew up."

Men! It all had to do with looks. Of course Alix's husband hadn't been interested in her. At least not until she grew breasts and hips and obtained the allure of an adult. Men are pigs. I glanced down at the low square neckline of my hyacinth blue jersey shirt, making certain it hadn't slid too far down my chest.

When I looked back up at Cranwell, I discovered that he'd been doing the same.

He had the grace to look guilty, and he took another swallow of wine.

Refusing to be embarrassed by his transgression, I considered his words. "So she grew up. Most girls do. What was it that caused him to notice?"

"She was mistaken for his cousin. An older man, a count, made a pass at her. And later in the evening, her husband realized that none of the guests was treating her as if she were his wife; they were treating his cousin, Anne, that way. He got angry, and he reminded the guests that Alix was his wife. His lady."

"Why would that have made him angry? If he wasn't paying attention to her, why should he care that anyone else wasn't? That seems completely out of character. You could hardly portray him as a jealous husband."

"He wasn't jealous. He was making Alix a player. There were very different ideas of love in the Middle Ages. And strange rules governing how people should act when they were in love." He reeled off a score of them. Cranwell had a phenomenal memory. "Rules like, he who is not jealous is not in love. One cannot give one's heart to two women at the same time. No one may be deprived of a loved one without reason. Love is not miserly. A new love chases away the old one. Once love has diminished, then disappeared, it cannot come back. Jealousy makes love grow. Tormented by love, the lover sleeps and eats little. The lover must act while thinking of his beloved. The perfect lover likes only that which pleases his love. The smallest suspicion incites the lover to suspect the worst in his beloved. Nothing stops a woman from being loved by two men or a man from being loved by two women. Love is necessarily adultery. And most of all, the lady of the castle is to be adored by the knights as the perfect woman."

"So by naming her his lady, he was, by definition, turning his knights' attention from Anne to Alix."

"That's right."

"But did he do it because he wanted Anne's attention for himself or because he'd begun to like Alix?"

"At least begun to respect her. Maybe it was because he simply felt the knights' attention was Alix's right."

One of the rules he'd recited earlier had caught my attention. "Why was love assumed to be adulterous?"

"It wasn't always. Not among the lower classes. There was much more freedom for women of the peasantry to marry whom they wished. But the women of the upper classes were considered property. As property they were bargained for and consigned into marriage. The heart was a separate consideration. Marriage concerned property, love concerned the heart . . . and fidelity of the heart was never considered part of a marriage contract."

"How convenient. And by Alix's own words, she had become a woman?"

Cranwell nodded. "And by her husbands actions, he'd finally noticed. My problem is that I just can't bring myself to believe she didn't know anything about what was going on between Anne and Awen."

"Why should she?"

"Come on, Freddie, they spent so much time together! She reports that herself. How could she not know?"

I shrugged. "Who was going to tell her?"

"Agnès."

"Her maid is going to tell her that her husband is cheating on her? I don't think so."

"It's not natural to be so naïve. Besides, part of the legality of a marriage involved its consummation. Alix could have had her marriage annulled on that basis alone."

I thought about that. "Well, from what you've told me, I'd bet her father didn't tell her the facts of life. He probably assumed his wife would do it. But you told me that Alix wasn't close to her stepmother. The stepmother probably assumed Agnès would do it, but in that period, you'd be as likely to shoot the messenger as not. Besides, by telling her, Agnès would be humiliating her. The only possible person who could have told Alix the facts of life was her husband. And he wasn't telling."

"It's not like it's any big secret."

"It would have been to a high-society medieval girl of thirteen."

"She was sixteen at this point."

"Men are more experimental. I was a virgin when I married Peter and—"

"You were a virgin?"

"Yes."

"You mean you didn't have sex? Not even while you were engaged?"

"That would be the definition of virgin, wouldn't it?"

"Not even—"

"No."

His fingers were fingering the collar of his polo sweater. "Why not?"

"You know, Cranwell, virginity used to be the default condition of a woman. Unless she were married. And I am not one of your actresses or models."

He must have seen how irritated I was becoming because he dropped it, although I saw him shoot a look at me from under his eyebrows.

Ignoring him, I continued with my argument. "So, yes, it is entirely possible that Alix had no idea what sex was about."

After clearing our dinner dishes, I retrieved the *crème caramels* from the refrigerator. The dessert was a custard, typical of what a French grandmother might have served in the 1950s. It was nothing fancy, but sometimes I had a craving for plain, homegrown food.

I put a ramekin in front of Cranwell and set one at my own place, then I turned on the espresso-maker.

"So Peter's the only man you've ever been with?"

I turned to face him with a hand on my hip. "And when did this become your business?" Yes. Peter was the only man I'd ever been with.

"Sorry. I didn't mean to pry. It's just so interesting." There he went again, his fingers toying with his collar.

"Don't you mean quaint?"

"No, I mean interesting. I've never met anyone like you before."

"Exhibit three — virgin girl in natural habitat."

"Don't make fun of yourself."

"Cranwell, enough has been said."

"Okay. Fine." He held up his hands in surrender and then picked up a spoon and dug into dessert.

The next morning, I delivered Cranwell his breakfast, the way I usually do. I plunked a cube of sugar into his espresso and handed him the cup. He took it from me, set it down, and then put a hand on my arm.

"Freddie, have I done something to make you upset with me?"

He had no idea. If he hadn't safely stowed his espresso on the opposite side of the table, I would have doused him with it.

Smiling was difficult. "Why do you ask that?"

"You haven't been . . . *you* lately. I miss the time we spend together. I miss you."

Cranwell, you have a funny way of showing it, sleeping with Séverine. "I've had other things on my mind."

"Are you sure? If there's anything . . . ?"

Well, now that you mention it, could you keep your pants zipped? The problem with me is that I never say what's on my mind. "No, there's nothing."

❧

That weekend, we had guests. Friends of Cranwell's under the auspices of his Freddie Improvement Project. When they pulled up the drive in a limousine, and I saw the chauffeur hand them out of the car, my eyes must have popped out of my head.

Cranwell was halfway out the door and had raised a hand in greeting when I grabbed ahold of his shirt and yanked him back beside me.

"You might have warned me."

"About what?"

If looks could kill, Cranwell would have been drawn and quartered that very instant.

"About the bowing and scraping I'd have to do. I would have said no."

"Then you would have missed out on becoming acquainted with some very charming people." Cranwell's eyes swept from mine to the couple now ascending the steps. He lifted a hand in welcome.

"You're an American. You can be forgiven for your uncouth behavior," I whispered. "I have to live here. Do you even know the protocol involved in hosting someone of royal blood?"

Cranwell rolled his eyes and blew me off, reaching to grasp the hands of the guests who had by now reached the front door.

While they exchanged European-style kisses, I fled to the kitchen and began flipping through my Miss Manners book.

Several minutes later, Cranwell snuck up behind me. He wrenched the book from me, closed it, and returned it to the bookshelf. "Listen. It's not a big deal. They don't expect any 'Your highnesses' or 'Your graces'. This is a weekend getaway."

My lunge for the book was quick, but he managed to step in front of me fast enough to block it. He held onto my upper arms and gave me a shake. "For this weekend, just pretend they're Carl and Fran."

"When you booked them, you said they were Carlos and Maria."

He released me and threw his hands into the air. "Forgive me. Maria was last month. This month it's Francesca. Next month, it will be someone else. It's not a big deal. The reason he came here is because I said he wouldn't need a bodyguard, that they would never mix with the general public. So don't make me regret my advice."

"I'm not going to do anything differently."

"Fine."

"I'm not changing the menu."

"Okay."

"And I won't bow or kiss anyone's hand. It's not democratic."

Cranwell didn't even bother to respond. He just brushed past me as he walked toward the stairs.

❧

Carl and Fran turned out to be perfectly pleasant. Mostly because I had Séverine deal with them. Like most French women I'd met, she seemed to have an intuitive grasp of how to treat people from all stations in life.

"Did you know that she is the *Princesse de Kohn-Bavarie*?" she asked as she waited for me to prepare a breakfast tray.

"I had no idea."

"And he a crown prince."

"That, I knew."

Glancing over at the island, I saw her sitting on a stool staring off into space with a smile on her lips. Séverine must have been reliving those childhood fairy tales her father had told her.

Uh-oh. Carlos was a magnificent specimen of a human being, but definitely not of the over-the-counter variety. Bending down, I drew a cutting board from a cupboard. Putting it in front of Séverine with a knife and a mound of mushrooms, I commanded her to chop.

"Now?"

"Now."

"But they will brown."

"It doesn't matter. I'm using them in a sauce later."

She sighed in protest and then took up the knife and began to chop. She brightened a moment later when she heard Lucy skitter down the stairs. Where Lucy went, Cranwell could not be far behind.

"Espresso?" he asked me when he appeared.

"Help yourself." I didn't have time that morning to wait on him personally. And should he even think of complaining, I planned to remind him that Carl and Fran were his great idea.

"Want one?"

"No, thanks."

"Sévérine?"

"*Non, merci.*"

Sévérine sounded suspiciously listless. I'd never seen her that way before, and it had the potential to put a damper on my reputation as an innkeeper. She could flirt all day with my guests as long as she was professional. Sulky, however, was another matter. Not everyone of noble blood was a louse like her father. But then again . . .

"Cranwell, please tell Sévérine what a rat your friend Carl is."

"Rat?"

"Playboy. Philanderer."

"He dates around, but in his circle, it's not unusual." Cranwell was looking at me as if confused.

"A new girlfriend every month? You'd think he'd run out of eligible women."

"He is a crown prince, Frédérique." Sévérine was staring at me with the same look of confusion as Cranwell. "This is normal."

"Normal? He's a lecher."

"Maybe to some people, but in his mind, he's just having fun. At some point, Daddy will put his foot down and make him marry some suitable sort of woman. Morals aside, he's a good guy. Very smart, actually."

"And someday he will be king." Sévérine put down her knife and shoved the cutting board away so violently that several mushrooms tumbled to the floor.

Lucy growled at Sévérine and then gave them a good sniff before deciding that they were better left alone.

Oh no. Sévérine had that look in her eye again.

I tried to distract her. "But what kind of king?"

"It does not matter. There have been many kinds of king. All of them have left a page in history. It matters only that he is king. And that he choose a queen."

Rolling my eyes, I looked to Cranwell for help. Surely he could see Sévérine needed a reality check.

"Well, he's certainly trying." Cranwell drained his demitasse and then loped off outside with Lucy. A big help he was.

"Not everyone can be Arthur and Guinevere."

The eyes that looked across at mine glittered. "And why do you think I search so hard for—" She untied her apron and folded it. Then she placed it on the island and left. And then I was left alone wondering why loutish behavior was forgiven in royalty and wondering what Sévérine was searching so hard for. Love? Acceptance? What else could it be? Alix's journals had already been found.

Sévérine served dinner that evening. I started Carl and Fran with a pinot gris and a salmon mousse served with tarragon sauce, followed by pork with kiwi and onion sauce, and a dessert of key lime pie.

Cranwell, Sévérine, and I dined on pot roast. There are times when I need the food I grew up with. That night was one of them.

For Cranwell's epicurean taste, I had also offered a generous selection of cheese with our baguette.

"Delicious, Freddie. Dessert?"

"What would you do for a plain old brownie?"

"Almost anything you wanted me to." He clapped a hand to his mouth. "Did I just say that? I'm sorry." He really did look very contrite. "Sometimes I speak without thinking. I'm working on it."

"Relax, Cranwell. We're all working on it."

It wasn't stretching the truth at all to say that he looked irresistible in his hand-knit Norwegian sweater. I offered him a steaming brownie with a large scoop of vanilla ice cream melting across the top.

We savored the marriage of chocolate and cream and talked for a while about how the book was coming. Then Lucy scrambled to her feet, and we both knew that meant she needed to go for her walk.

20

*L*ate that night, I awoke to shouting.

It had wafted up the stairs and was just pointed enough to make sleep impossible.

Propelling myself from bed, I threw on a robe and pushed my feet into my slippers. By the time I reached the third floor, Cranwell had poked his head out of his door.

Reaching out an arm, he caught me as I walked past him. He was wearing his signature silk paisley pajamas. His bangs were sticking up as if he'd leaned his head against his palm for some indefinite period of time.

"What should I do?"

"Nothing."

"Nothing? How can you say that? He could be beating her."

Cranwell shook his head and drew me into his room. "He's not beating her. Do you hear any fear in her voice?"

Cocking my head, I listened for a moment. "No."

"Lover's quarrel."

As I looked around the room, I realized that he'd probably been working. If the argument had disturbed my sleep, it had probably disturbed his concentration.

I sagged into the extra chair by the desk. "Is he always like this?"

Cranwell shrugged. "He's temperamental." He looked at his watch.

"It'll probably be over in fifteen minutes." He sprawled into the chair in front of the desk, making it look like an extension of his body.

We were facing each other.

All I really wanted was sleep. I drew my feet out of my slippers and tucked them up underneath me. I also slid my hands up into the sleeves of my robe. "Why do people stay in relationships like that?"

"Some people need it. At least if someone's yelling at you, they're paying attention to you . . . and then there's always the making up afterward. Some people think it's romantic."

It didn't seem as if he thought so. At least we were in agreement about that.

A door slammed.

"Did you ever have a relationship like that?" The lateness of the hour must have loosened my tongue.

"Never really stayed in one long enough for it to deteriorate into something like that. I've always relied on more polite forms of communication."

"Letters? Faxes?"

"E-mail." He smiled and pushed back his chair. His hands joined behind his head and he closed his eyes. He looked tired, and his five-o'clock shadow made his face pale.

"Seriously?"

"Seriously. Surely you know that I don't have a fabulous track record on relationships."

I clamped my lips together so that I wouldn't say anything I'd later regret.

"I'm not sure why. They've just never worked out."

At that moment, I was biting my tongue so hard I thought I'd punched a hole in it. Clearly, it was not the time to talk; it was the time to listen.

"I've never felt like anyone has wanted to be with me for the simple reason that I am me. I've had people want to be with me because it makes them look good. I've wanted to be with people because they make me look good. I've been in relationships where both of us were using the other for some ulterior motive."

At that point, he opened his eyes. They were empty. Denuded. And they made him look a hundred years old.

My heart reached out for him.

"It tends to make a person cynical."

There was pounding on a door downstairs.

A corner of Cranwell's mouth lifted. "See? She wants back in."

"She can't be older than twenty-one."

"Nineteen."

"She's so young."

"And tonight, they'll be together. And they'll drive back to Paris tomorrow, and they'll fly out next week. And once they're home, he'll forget to call her. She'll call him. He'll promise her a weekend somewhere exotic. And then he'll cancel: unforeseen circumstances. And she'll still be waiting for a call when she reads in the paper about his latest girlfriend."

"But she's so innocent."

"The problem with innocence is that once you pluck it, it's all gone."

We listened for a moment to the silence, felt the chateau go back to sleep around us.

I stretched and got up to leave.

"You've managed to keep yours, Freddie."

Facing Cranwell, I found him looking at me as if I were a rare antique.

"My what?"

"Innocence."

"I've been married." If we were talking about sex, I'd had plenty.

"I'm not talking about that." He stood beside me and cupped my chin in his hand. "I'm talking about your soul. And don't tell me you don't have a soul and that you don't believe in God, because you do. You wouldn't fight Him so hard if you didn't. But you're not jaded. I still haven't figured out if you were well loved, but I can tell that you loved well."

He kissed me on the forehead and led me out into the hall.

When I had been with Peter, I had felt well loved. In retrospect, I had given much more than I had received in return. Not that love is selfish, but the person I was now would have demanded better treatment.

Mid-stride, I paused as I walked up the stairs.

How had Cranwell known that?

And what did he mean that I believed in God?

⁂

Carl and Fran left the next morning, practically attached at the lips. The chauffeur bundled them into the limousine and sped away down the drive. I couldn't help pitying her as I watched the car turn onto the road.

I didn't think it was worth it.

⁂

The next week, my thoughts turned toward Christmas. And not voluntarily, for I hadn't celebrated the holiday since Peter had died.

There was no one I bought presents for and no one who bought them for me. There had been no one to cook for, no one to decorate for. I wasn't even sure where I'd stored my Christmas tree ornaments. In fact, it was Cranwell who brought it up.

"What's the plan for Christmas? Is Séverine going to be around?" He'd been writing in the kitchen as I worked, but had slid back his chair and stood up for a stretch. His turmeric-colored chamois shirt was tucked and belted into a pair of olive twills. The month before, I might have thought he looked good, but by December, I was immune to his charms.

"I'm pretty sure it's on the twenty-fifth, just like last year, Cranwell." I gritted my teeth to answer his second question. "Séverine's going away for Christmas, but she'll be back by New Year's." Why hadn't he just asked her if he were so interested?

He bent down so he could scratch Lucy's stomach. "You don't do anything for Christmas?"

"What's there to do?" I turned from the vegetables I was chopping and unsnapped the sleeves of my red denim shirt so that I could roll them up. The close-fitting cut of the shirt allowed it to stay close to my body and wear it untucked over my jeans without it becoming a hazard to cooking.

"I don't know. Cut down a tree. Sing carols. Go to church. Drink eggnog."

"What do you usually do for Christmas?"

He smiled. "Not a whole lot. Go out for dinner. Take a walk with Lucy. I'd hoped this year to go to church somewhere."

"I'm planning on being here for Christmas, so I'll definitely be cooking." I shook some pistachios into a bowl and set them on the island.

Cranwell joined me at the island as I sat down on a stool.

"Seriously."

"I am being serious. If you'd like a tree for your room and if I can find my ornaments, you can have them."

"We should do something."

"Like I said, I'll cook dinner, but beyond that, it's up to you." I took a pistachio and used a thumbnail to pry it from the shell. As far as I was concerned, the full-blown Christmas experience was best saved for small children. I remembered my parents' extravagant holiday parties and I wanted nothing whatsoever to do with them. When I was young, planning for Christmas began in October.

"How about I take care of the whole thing?"

"The whole thing?"

"Decorations, Christmas dinner. Everything."

I felt my eyebrow lift in surprise. I took another pistachio and cracked it open, buying time to think about his proposal. I was no grinch. I had nothing against Christmas in general. It was the energy, the time, the pressure of tradition that made me pretend the holiday didn't exist.

"Freddie?"

"Dinner too?"

"Dinner too."

"Deal."

The next morning I began to pay for my error in judgment. Every ten minutes, Cranwell came down to the kitchen to ask me for something: an axe, a hammer, nails, screws, wire, wire-cutters.

"Do you have a —"

Tu danse sur mon dernier nerf! I tugged at the hem of my white tank top then gave my pot of soup a vigorous stir. "Cranwell, anything I have that's tool-related is in the garage. Did you look there?" He was tap-dancing on my last nerve.

"No."

"Then I probably don't have one."

"I'm sure you've got to at least have a couple."

At that point I was very close to ripping my hair out. I put the ladle on the counter and turned to look at him.

He put a tentative hand up to his hair and came away with what looked like a few pine needles. There were a few more sprinkled on the shoulders of his plum zip-neck sweater too. He frowned, glared at them over the top of his reading glasses, and then let them drop to the floor. His eyes zoomed from the floor straight up toward mine. "What I wanted to know is if you have a minute to spare."

Okay, so at that point, I felt foolish. I pushed my arms into a black shawl-collar cardigan, tied it around my waist, and accompanied him up the stairs.

He led me past the central stairs, through the reception hall, and into the dining hall.

What I saw amazed me.

He had fixed pine boughs to the primitive iron chandelier, woven red ribbon around the anchoring chains, and replaced the lightbulbs with candles. I had to admit that it looked good. So did the trail of intertwined holly and ivy that wound down the center of the table and the myriad ivory candles of various sizes that covered the mantle of the fireplace.

He was staring at me, his brown eyes begging for approval, as I took in the extent of his handiwork.

"Very nice, Cranwell." Even though I wanted to wring his neck most of the time, I couldn't help but acknowledge that he'd done well in his Christmas decorating endeavor.

"Where do you think your ornaments are?"

"They could be anywhere. The garage. The cellar . . . "

He held out a hand, "Let's look!"

"Cranwell, I have things to do."

"Lunch can wait."

Easy for him to say. He wasn't the one worried about scorching a soup.

He'd already grabbed my hand and was tugging me toward the reception hall.

I pulled it from his grasp and planted my feet against his persistent tugging. "What do you need them for?"

"I'm going to cut down a tree — "

The laugh escaped from my lips before I could stop it. I couldn't imagine him swinging an axe, let alone carrying a tree through the woods.

" — and decorate it."

"I have to check on the soup. Why don't you go to the cellar and I'll join you in a minute?" I pointed to the arched doorway to the right of the entrance hall and saw Cranwell start down the stairs before I ran down to the kitchen.

Thankfully, the soup hadn't boiled over. I pulled it from the stove and then cut a lemon and squeezed it on the fruit I'd cut earlier to keep it from turning brown.

Quickly, I scraped the undesirable odds and ends into the trash and scrubbed the cutting board and knife clean. Then I retied the cardigan, shook out my hair, and climbed the stairs to join Cranwell.

The light wasn't the best in the cellar, so it took me a moment to realize what he had in his hands.

Livid sums up how I felt when I realized he was looking at my wedding photos.

Apparently, he read the anger in my face, because he immediately shut the album. "I was just looking for the ornaments."

Snatching the album from him, I tucked it back into the box labeled "Wedding" and then hefted it back onto one of the storage shelves that lined the cellar walls.

"I'm sorry, Freddie." He'd come to stand behind me and had placed his hands on my shoulders, coincidentally squeezing a knot right beneath my left shoulder blade.

Wincing, I ducked away from his grasp and whirled to face him. "You have no right to poke your nose into my private things."

"You're the one who sent me down here."

"To find Christmas ornaments, which are probably located in the box labeled 'Christmas.'" I stabbed at the box as he moved to take it from the shelf. "What gives you the right to pry?"

"Nothing really. I was just interested." He knelt beside the box, remorseless, and began to dig through it.

"Well, did you see everything you wanted?"

"No." He looked up from the box and there was no humor in his eyes.

"What is it that you want from me?"

"Evidently, something you're not prepared to give."

Not like Séverine was.

His eyes darted back to the box. "I was curious. You've never talked much about Peter. I just wanted to see what he was like."

"And did you?"

"Yes. But then I saw the pictures and I wanted to know what you were like. You looked happy . . . "

"I was happy. It was my wedding day!"

"But you didn't look like you. You've changed."

"Of course I have, Cranwell. Everyone changes." My words might not have conveyed it, but I did know what he meant. I had looked different then. I'd been the prototype diplomatic wife. My hair had been conservative, my smile had been level, my clothes had been appropriate, my makeup discreet. I'd devolved into the wild-haired, cynical, take-it-or-leave Freddie that he'd encountered. But I liked the new Freddie.

"I like you, Freddie. The you that I know. I didn't know who that other person was."

He'd done it again; he'd nailed it on the head. That *was* the problem with that other person. The former me. She *hadn't* known who she was.

He shrugged. "So that's why I was curious, but I am sorry that I violated your privacy."

How could I be angry with him? I wrapped my arms around myself and tried hard to glare at him anyway. "You're forgiven."

He rose to his feet, hefting the box. "These are all ornaments."

"Fine." I went before him up the stairs, waiting until he'd reached the entry before I turned out the lights and shut the door behind him.

Cranwell placed the box on the entry table.

"Where are you going to put the tree?" I couldn't imagine any place in the chateau that wouldn't dwarf the average Christmas tree.

"I'm not sure yet."

Walking past him, I began the descent to the kitchen.

"What about mistletoe?"

I paused on the third step. "If you want to climb a tree and find some, be my guest."

"It grows in trees?"

"Yes. It's a parasite." Just like love.

*C*ranwell must have followed my advice, because by dinner, he'd suspended balls of mistletoe around the chateau. There was one dangling from every arched doorway on the ground floor. I saw them as I came down from my room to serve dinner.

They were festive, but they made me wince. Holidays hurt. Holidays were markers, days that occurred each year in which thoughts turned to how you celebrated in years past, and with whom. For a person like me, holidays were a point in time at which you were forced to reconcile the life you used to have with the life you now lived.

Christmas with Peter had been cozy. Christmas *à deux*. Our Christmases for two had consisted of traditions we both found meaningful. That meant chocolate truffles instead of cookies; jazz instead of carols; *Life is Beautiful* or *Amelie of Montmartre* instead of *It's a Wonderful Life*. Sometimes even exotic vacations to Morocco or the Canary Islands. Our holiday had ambience, but no religion. And looking back on those years, I realized I had missed the wonder of Christmas and the contemplation of the divine. I missed meditating on the sacred moment when God reached down and touched the earth.

Peter viewed Christmas as an opportunity to ease the collective guilt our culture had accumulated throughout the year. If people were really as kindhearted as they pretended to be at Christmas, then he thought food pantries and soup kitchens should be stocked and staffed year-round at consistent levels. If people hadn't kept in touch with their friends for eleven of the year's months, then they used the twelfth one to make up for it, clogging the postal system with holiday-themed junk mail. If companies hadn't paid their employees a fair wage, then they distributed a Christmas bonus to make themselves look like heroes instead of misers. Poor man. He wasn't as churlish as his rhetoric made him sound.

Peter and I had talked about the religious heritage of Christmas. I had asked him, just for the sake of argument, what was so wrong about humanity's desire to communicate with heaven. And, for the sake of argument, we'd had an argument about Christianity's exclusiveness and other religions' tolerance. But the argument had ended when he reminded me that not only didn't he place faith in any God, but he also didn't even believe a God existed. I'd never before stopped to consider how very great a distance there was between believing in something and believing nothing. There may have been less of a culture clash had I been married to a Hindu or Muslim. At least we both would have been approaching life with the idea that there was some sort of higher purpose for it all.

There was a profound difference in our attitudes toward others. Peter wanted to review the financial statements of any nonprofit he was contemplating donating funds to. I was much more spontaneous. If I glimpsed TV coverage of a disaster, if I were stopped on the street by some collegian canvassing for rights in Third World countries, I always gave what I could. I figured if situations were reversed, I would be the one benefiting from the kindness of strangers. Peter could never understand that. The "there but for the grace of God . . . " argument was never able to sway him. And it was that age-old wisdom that said it all: the grace of God. I believed in it, and he did not. The people he gave to needed to be deserving of his help. The people I gave to sometimes didn't deserve my help at all.

The idea of a Creator reaching down toward his people didn't make any conceptual sense to Peter, didn't evoke any sentiment, didn't inform any of his decisions. Say nothing else of my parents, at least they introduced me to that idea. For even on the chance that it didn't have any eternal importance, it made a great difference in terms of human spirit. Love made my world go around. To this day, I can't say for sure what made Peter's.

Maybe faith complicated ambition. Maybe his linear analyst's mind couldn't handle the divergent thoughts that faith must have thrown in his direction. But if that was so, I had discovered that I was disappointed in him. I'd thought him courageous. I'd thought him intelligent. And now I had decided that an atheist's proclamation is neither. It's a cowardly rejection of all that adds color and life and meaning to the world.

Which was not to say that I had made my own peace with God or decided that I should climb back into his boat.

If anything about Cranwell held any attraction for me, besides his physical appearance and in spite of his relationship with Séverine, it would have to be his claim of conversion. For a man in his position with power, influence, and money to have turned his attention toward faith proclaimed to me his intellectual honesty.

But only, of course, if it were true.

So, I'd gone from holidays as part of a crowd, to holidays as part of a couple, to no holidays at all. And now I'd have to negotiate what sort of role they would play in my life. Because it was clear I would no longer be able to ignore them. At least not with Cranwell in the house.

I had exchanged my chef's outfit for a pair of brown suede pants, cognac leather heels, and a navy long-sleeve shirt with an extended placket and horn buttons that I thought were particularly flattering. For some unknown reason, I took an extra moment to smooth on lip gloss and smudge eyeliner around my eyes. When I stepped back to look at myself, I realized the eyeliner made my pale lashes fade, so I had to swipe on mascara. And after the addition of mascara, my eyes had become such a focal point that my skin looked dull. I rooted around the bathroom for blush, as I reminded myself why I rarely wore makeup. I rolled my eyes at my reflection before I left the room.

In the kitchen, I discovered Cranwell typing like a maniac. The distraction of Christmas decorating must have set him behind schedule. Mistletoe was the farthest thing from my mind as I set the table and puttered around the kitchen.

"Ready for dinner?"

"Hmm?"

"Dinner?"

Cranwell turned around to look at me.

"Are you hungry?" I prompted.

"Oh. Sure."

He uncorked the wine and poured glasses while I divided marinated leeks between three plates. I left Sévérine's on the counter and took ours to the island.

"Bread?"

"Please."

I began to saw off a chunk for Cranwell, but I made the mistake of looking into his eyes. They roved across my face, and I knew he was taking in the lip gloss, the eyeliner, and the mascara.

By that time, my natural ability to flush tomato-red had overcome the demure rose-colored blusher I'd stained my cheeks with. I felt Cranwell's hand wrap around my wrist as an electric tingle vibrated through my body. It must have been the magnetic force of those russet eyes which drew my body across the island toward him.

I've never been known to have trouble swallowing, but at that moment, I did. I licked my lips in an effort to provide them with some moisture.

It only succeeded in drawing Cranwell's attention like a beacon.

My eyes fluttered down toward the countertop, and when I looked back up, Cranwell had nearly met up with me halfway across the counter. He was so close that I could feel his breath fan my hair.

"Mistletoe."

"What?" I was intercepting such loud messages from his eyes that I couldn't hear what he was saying. That didn't stop me from being fascinated by the way his lips had formed that one word. I wrested my eyes from them and tried to pay attention to what he had said.

"Mistletoe." It looked as if his eyes were having trouble straying from my lips, but he directed them to a spot in the air above our heads.

It was at that point, when I looked up, that my weight shifted to the outside heel of my right shoe. It was enough to cause it to slip, slide forward, and pitch me backward onto the floor. I ended up at a perfect angle to view the ball of mistletoe he'd cleverly suspended from the middle of the iron pot rack.

"Freddie?"

I saw Cranwell's head appear over the edge of the counter.

"I'm fine." Of course, I would have been better had the floor swallowed me whole.

"Let me . . . " I heard him push back his stool and start around the island.

"I'm fine." The edge in my voice must have stopped him.

"Are you sure?"

"Yes." Now I remembered the reason I hadn't worn those shoes for a while: they were prone to slipping at the worst possible moments. As I lay there, I began to get angry. Not only because my tailbone was throbbing, but also because Cranwell, Mr. Christianity himself, thought he could string me along while he was doing who-knows-what with Séverine. That was not going to happen.

There was an awkward moment when I scrambled to my knees and pushed myself off the floor, but I managed to rise to my feet gracefully, with my back toward Cranwell.

"Do—"

I held up a hand to stave off any comments. After looking at the stove, the sink, the countertop and realizing that there was nothing that needed to be done—that the leeks, the wine, the bread were waiting for us at the table—I took a deep breath and turned around.

Cranwell was sipping his wine.

It was clear to me that I was beginning to manifest a personality disorder. Half the time I wanted to kill the man. The other half, I wanted to jump into his arms. A tremendous longing for Peter welled up inside me. Our relationship had been so stable, so adult. I didn't need the complication of Cranwell. I reminded myself that any attraction I felt for him was purely physical. That there was nothing about him that I admired; his entire character was one big flaw. Buoyed by my own propaganda, I was able to look him in the eye again. *"Bon appétit."*

one day after Saint Matthias

My lord takes Anne and me to Dinan this week. He must do business and it is said the duc de Bretagne may be in the city at this time.

Agnès says me that Anne must be found a husband before she becomes too old. I will give it thought.

This first night we lodged near the Val Sans Retour. It is said that the Fairy Morgane laid a spell on the vallée that he who has done wrong or has been faithless may enter, but never return. It is said also that if one finds the hidden lake while the moon still is shining, the reflection seen is of one he is destined to love.

This vallée I wished to see. And Anne also wished it.

My lord promised he would take us.

I replied to him that it was only worth the effort if seen at night.

He laughed and then declared it would be so.

We took with us the men, as brigandes are known to patrol the ways at night.

We rode to the vallée singing and talking and making much noise to warn of our strength and presence.

It was beautiful, this vallée, in the light of the moon and with the lake set into the cleft. We dismounted and bid the men watch our mounts, then we stood beside the lake, all the three, and found in it a reflection. A curious thing then happened.

What began as a reflection of three became a reflection of two. As we watched a wind stirred the waters and the reflection of Anne was slowly erased as the reflection of myself and my lord remained.

Anne ran weeping.

My lord stared at the reflections as if bewitched. He turned to me and made as if to speak, but then heard Anne cry and left me to follow her.

I stayed and watched my reflection and made note of another curiosity. My reflection aged me. I lifted a hand to touch my face, and the reflection also did, but it was not the same face.

Would that I look the same two or three years hence.

I waited for the return of my lord and Anne, but when they did not appear, I made a place for myself by a rock on the edge of the lake. I pulled my cloak around me and slept.

When I woke, my lord and Anne did not yet come again. I found the men and we mounted finally our horses and made the return to the inn.

two days after Saint Matthias

At day, the men of my lord made a search for him and found him, still at the vallée, and brought him back.

We stay here one more night which makes one night the less in Dinan.

I have heard from Agnès that my lord tried to find his way from the vallée but could not.

I demand of myself to whom he has done wrong.

four days after Saint Matthias

On the way to Dinan, we stopped at the Temple de Mars. Some people call this the Tour de Courseul and say it is the most ancient building in Bretagne.

A storm blew in and we were obliged to take shelter in the parish church nearby. I read tombstones to Anne. The most ancient I found looked Roman. It read: Consecrated to the god Manes. Silicia Namigidde who from Africa, her country, moved by an admirable tenderness for her son, followed him, rests in this place. She lived 65 years. Cneius Flavius Jannaris, her son, to her erected this tomb.

I demand of myself what it would be like to live 65 years. I suppose if one lived near those one loved, it might be satisfying. To leave a homeland for a son. Would I dare to do the same? If I did it for a husband, might I do it for a son?

My lord installed me first in my chamber, and then he installed Anne. I did not see the two of them until my lord passed to take me to dinner.

one day before Shrove Tuesday

We have come to Dinan this day. We mounted to the city through the vallée of the River Rance after having passed over a new bridge composed of four arches.

It is a powerful city with strong walls, a city rich from trade. We entered through the Porte du Guichet, with two towers flanking it and thick doors of wood. It looks as if it could withstand any assault. And near to it the donjon where we will rest these coming days.

There are many strange buildings made of stone and plaster, separated by lengths of timber. It seems an odd way to build and not nearly as strong as stone. Perhaps it is a fashion that shall pass in these next years.

My nose is assaulted by the smell of this place and the air is foul. As the wind blows always through these streets, the scent of the fishmongers and tanners comes by times to overtake us. Glad I am that

Agnès has commanded me to travel with a sachet of spices. The mace invades my nostrils, leaving no room for the stench of the tanner.

I have pain in the ears from the noise of the city. At home, none speak but speak softly and none sings but songs of gladness. Here men cry in the streets and people shout from the windows and the horses and the carts make much noise.

I surprise myself by longing for the chateau.

Shrove Tuesday

My lord presented me to the duc de Bretagne, François II, which is not a grand thing, as I have already met the King of France. But this duc has much power and I reminded myself of the position of my father and so I curtsied most deep and talked to him of pretty things.

Ash Wednesday

My lord came to tell me a story this night, but before he did it, I demanded of my lord where a husband for Anne might be found.

He demanded of me why one must be found.

I explained to him that Anne is old and it may be that next year few men will want her. And as he knows those at court it is possible he may inquire.

He demanded of me if Anne does not please me.

I told him that she does. That if Anne were not here that I would have no friend. That if it were to me, I would have her stay forever, but that this is too much to demand of her, for she would make someone a good wife.

He bid me to speak of this to Anne to discover what she will reply to me.

And the follow is the story that my lord told me: There was one time
a King called Gradlon. He had great riches and a fleet of boats of war.
There came a time when his sailors became fatigued from fighting in
cold, strange lands. They left King Gradlon, took the boats, and returned
to Bretagne.

The King was very sad, but felt a comforting presence. He looked up
and saw a woman with hair red like a fox. It was Malgven, Queen of the
North, who ruled the lands where it is always winter. She told the King
that her husband was old and that if Gradlon helped her to kill him, then
she would return with him to Bretagne.

They killed the husband of Malgven, took a chest filled with gold,
and leapt onto Morvarc'h, the horse of Malgven. The horse made a path
over the waves of the sea, galloping through the night, and delivered
them to one of the boats of the king and they lived there a full year, on
the sea.

And at this point here, I demanded of my lord how the horse
Morvarc'h can be in two stories at the same time. I recalled to him that
Morvarc'h also was the horse of King Marc'h who was killed by the hind
he had chased.

And my lord replied to me that Morvarc'h is the magic horse of the
sea who can gallop on water as well as on land. And then he made as if
he would continue.

And I told him that even if Morvarc'h gallops on water it does not
mean that he can be the horse of every king.

And my lord replied to me that perhaps it may not be so in Touraine,
but in Bretagne these things are possible. And he continued with the
story.

Malgven came to give birth to a girl child she named Dahut, and then became ill and died.

King Gradlon took his child and returned to Bretagne. The child grew to be more beautiful than her mother. The only pleasure of the king was his daughter, but the only pleasure of Dahut was the sea.

One day Dahut convinced her father to build her a city beside the sea. Thousands of workers labored to build the city. The city became the most beautiful of all the world. To keep the sea from engulfing it, a high dike was formed. It was closed and locked by a brass door; King Gradlon was the guardian of the key. The city was named Ys.

Ys soon became known for great feasting and mariners came from all over the world to take part in the revelry. But Dahut bored herself with these fêtes.

It came to be that each day she would choose from the men a favorite and place a black mask around his face. She would take the favorite into her bed and he would stay with her until the rising of the sun. At this point here, the mask would tighten, suffocate the favorite, and he would die. A rider on horseback would take the body from Dahut and throw it into the sea.

One day, a chevalier arrived in Ys. He was clothed in red. Although Dahut smiled and spoke to him, he did not respond. As evening approached, he at last consented to speak with her. She took him as her favorite and took him to her bed, but he would not wear the mask.

A storm rose from the sea and began to batter the walls of the city. The chevalier demanded of Dahut if there was not some way to open the door of the dike. Dahut explained to him her father kept always the key around his neck. The chevalier suggested to her that as her father, King Gradlon, was asleep, she could take the key from him without trouble.

Dahut this did.

Immediately, a wave washed over the chateau and woke King Gradlon. Dahut realized that the sea had pushed over the dike and that the only escape was on the horse Morvarc'h.

The King and Dahut mounted the horse, but the sea was too violent and the horse began to sink. Dahut cried for the king to save her. At this moment there, a lightning flashed and a voice called for King Gradlon to throw Dahut to the sea.

The voice was Saint Guénolé. He told the king that Dahut was being punished for the sins she had made Ys to commit. Saint Guénolé repeated for King Gradlon to throw his daughter to the sea. The waves had almost over risen the horse Morvarc'h, so the King pushed his daughter into the sea.

Immediately the horse mounted the waves, and reached the land, and delivered the king to Quimper, the city of seven hills.

All from Ys were drowned. It is said that when the sea is calm, if you stand on the shore, you can still hear the bells of the disappeared city ringing. My lord says me that Lutèce was formed on an island in the middle of the River Seine. It is called Paris because "Par Ys" in breton means "Like Ys." One says that when Paris is engulfed by waters, then the city of Ys will re-emerge from the sea.

I told my lord that it is better to live a life of purity than to live in a wicked but beautiful city.

I told him also my secret, that I repeat Ave Marias each day that I might bear a strong son for him. I told him if he will come at night more often, then God will see and send a child.

He looked at me then and kissed me on the cheek.

I demand of myself what did Dahut do all night with her favorites?

Is it possible that they told each other stories? My lord has told me his stories are ancient. Perhaps they are the same that Dahut was told.

one day after Ash Wednesday

I demanded of Anne this morning if she does not want a husband.

She began to cry and prayed me not to turn her out of the door.

I began to cry also and promised that I inquired only after her happiness and that I would never send her away. Only if she would want a husband for herself.

I promise myself to write to my father demanding of him if there is anyone in our family who will suit Anne. And I will keep his reply against the time when Anne will want to marry.

two days after Ash Wednesday

We visited la Cohue, the shops where we found materials and friperie for new robes for Anne.

Agnès says me that I should have at least as many as Anne and one more.

I told Agnès that the robes I have do well. It is only three years since I have come to Bretagne and my robes were all new at that moment there.

She says me that if Anne has new, that I must too.

I told her that if she desires it so strongly, then she must pick the materials and have done with it. And also that a more comfortable hat would please me.

I passed from the dressmaker to the bookseller.

This evening, Agnès showed me the materials she has bought for me. They please me. There are several good silks, one of which is the color of turquoise through which gold threads are woven. Another is the color of thrift.

She has bought also a velvet of green which reminds me of spring and a second velvet the color of lavender. And the last length is of fine wool the color of a ripe peach. For these, she found some furs of sable, for which I am pleased, as these have become rare. She has also squirrel and fox, and then some lengths of gold braid and of the most delicate lace from Bruges.

Tomorrow, we quit Dinan.

three days after Saint Grégoire

My lord made a gift to me of a trunk filled with books! They have cost a fortune. I know this as I have made note in the accounts, but they will keep me for the next year. I am blessed with good chance.

To Anne he made a gift of a collar of pearls. They show well against her high color.

Agnès shook her head as she saw this and says me later that better pearls to a wife than a cousin.

I told her it should please her that my lord knows I value books more highly than jewels.

day of Easter

The mystery was performed this day. And all did well, save for one man who had inversed several of the verses. I had thought I would wish that all would know that I had written it, but in the end, it did not matter. Much more important to watch the faces of the peasants as they listened to the play. To realize that they cared not who had created it, only that it had been created. It made no difference the color of a horse, or how many oars had been broken during a storm, only that God allowed a miracle to have taken place.

But my lord says me that he has much pride in his little comtesse, that she should create such a wonderful work.

And if he is the only one who knows this, then perhaps it is the only thing that must matter.

six days before Ascension

Agnès is angry. I have received my new robes this day from the materials she bought for me in Dinan. The colors please me, but the fashions please not Agnès. She says me that they are not of the styles the most current as Anne has had made.

The styles most current have a small difference of neck and a small difference of skirt. The underskirts of Anne have broderie of flowers and vines. Anne says me that this is because I am still young.

It makes the least of things to me. I care not.

But Agnès will not be calmed. She claims Anne conspires against me. This I cannot believe.

two days before Saint Jean-Baptiste

My form has taken shape.

Agnès says me that I am as lovely a girl as she has seen.

My hair falls still to my waist. It still is golden and curls. My eyes are still gray, but my cheeks have become more sharp. My chin has become more pointed. My chest has more at the same time my waist has less.

I wish still the high color of Anne.

My skin is pale.

At least it is clear.

And I suppose that I can pinch my cheeks for color when I have need of it.

nine days before Sainte Marie-Madeleine

Apropos of my lord: his men respect him. I know it by the way they stand near to him, always ready to hear what he commands, to respond to what he demands of them. And why should they not? He is clever, I have seen this when he plays at chess.

He is strong, I have seen this when he plays at soules.

He is wise in money, for all in his house are cared for and his table is neither that of a miser nor that of a spendthrift.

He has also a temper, though it is rare when he shows it. It is kept in control by a clenching of his square jaw, but is betrayed by a glint in his dark brown eyes. And glad I am that I have never received his harsh words, for words such as those, he chooses very carefully so they cut into the heart and leave wounds as lethal as that of a knife.

The woman of Anne watches him. But for this, he cannot be blamed, for he is tall, he stands a head above his men, and he has the grace of a lynx. And the carriage of a mastiff.

He is well-wrought and well-thought.

three days after Sainte Anne

We have come to hear that King Charles VII is dead. May God guard his soul. He is disappeared the day of Sainte Marie-Madeleine from a long maladie. One first heard news of his troubles since three years.

Louis, his son, will be King.

My father will not be pleased.

Louis had been the cause of many problems for his father. He was not permitted to live in France since many years. Even now, he must come from the north, from the Low Country, to take the throne.

I find myself content to be living in Bretagne, for who can tell what this new King will make of France.

May the King live long.

janvier

Un mois de janvier sans gelée,
n'amène pas une bonne année.

January

A January without frost
doesn't bring a good year.

23

*M*uch of New Year's Day I spent wondering whether or not to be thankful for the turn my life had taken the previous year. The week before, I'd wondered if I'd even make it to January.

Cranwell had been a man with a mission. He'd tramped through the forest and identified a fifteen-foot tree that he just had to have. Unfortunately, he didn't foresee the effort it would require to transport it to the chateau. He'd ended up dragging it through the trees, grass, mud, and gravel, straight through the chateau and up the central stairs.

I nearly cried when I saw the trail of dirt and needles he'd left strung behind him like a sort of demented Hansel. But when I saw what he had done with the tree, I nearly laughed.

Cranwell decided to set it up in my room. He and Séverine decorated it while I was busy cooking. It would have been a nice surprise except that, being so suddenly brought from the cold into the warmth of the chateau, it dropped all its needles. And because Cranwell forgot it needed water, sap from the trunk seeped all day from the tree directly onto the stone floor.

I hate Christmas.

Of course, Cranwell apologized and Séverine cleaned up the mess, but the thought of that naked tree laden with luxurious ornaments still made me smile . . . when I didn't think about the cost of cleaning all the carpets he'd soiled on the way up to my room.

Cranwell had redeemed himself on Christmas Eve. He'd had a seven-course meal delivered from Fauchon, the gourmet grocery store in Paris. It was fabulous. From the *foie gras* to the three-chocolate *bûche de Noël* served with Maury wine. And he had truly excelled when he'd selected the cheese course: eight cheeses which ranged from a mild chevre to a strong Roquefort and came complete with all the right wines.

That evening, we drove into the nearest town and attended midnight mass. I wouldn't have gone with him except that his heart was set on going to church. Somewhere. Neither one of us understood a word, but the liturgy was so familiar that it seemed as if no one was there to actually hear it, but to experience it. To enter a stone country church lit by candlelight on the holiest evening of the year. To hear a priest intone those precious phrases in so solemn a voice they evolved from mere words into a priceless blessing. To see the incense from the censor spread its fingers out over the congregation. To belong to a ritual so ancient that, more than anywhere else I'd been, it provided a glimpse of a little manger in Bethlehem and a connection with saints both past and present. I could feel my soul relax. And when I felt like God was sitting on the pew beside me, I didn't have the heart to tell Him to leave.

The wonder on Cranwell's face at the end of the mass was worth any misgivings I'd had about coming. He looked very humble. At that moment, I was almost able to believe that his conversion had been real. But then I remembered Séverine.

The moment she returned to the chateau, he bombarded her with questions about Alix. She didn't even have time to take her coat off. He ran up the stairs when he heard the door slam, and he came back down dragging her behind him.

I poured them both a Lillet and happened to be handing one to

Sévérine when Cranwell asked her his question. "Could Alix have been a Jew?"

Sévérine's face froze, but her eyes registered a dozen emotions before she answered. "Why would you think this?"

"You said her mother was from Provence."

"Yes, this is true, but not everyone in Provence is a Jew. In fact, there would not have been many left in France at that time. And recall that her father was of noble birth."

"But her mother was very beautiful."

"And this makes of her a Jew? I do not understand."

"I'm just trying out different angles. Maybe that one won't work. But what if she was?"

"If she was, then she may not have known."

"Why not?"

"For her own protection. For the advancement of the family. If she was a Jew, the comte de Barenton might never have agreed to marry her."

At the time, Cranwell's thought about Alix seemed like a non sequitur. But Sévérine's answer seemed to satisfy his curiosity. And I was too busy preparing the New Year's meal to draw any of my own conclusions.

The champagne was my favorite, from a small but prestigious maker. For the meal I had decided on *magret de canard* with puffed potatoes and French green beans. The appetizer would be *foie gras* — to serve anything else would have been a huge gaffe. Dessert was still undecided. I pored through my cookbooks trying to find something special. When I saw the recipe for chocolate cheesecake soufflé with Chambord sauce, I knew I'd found my dessert.

The meal was fabulous, and by the time the clock struck midnight and we toasted in the New Year, I was exhausted. Cranwell and Séverine convinced me that they could handle the cleanup, so I stumbled up the stairs and fell into bed.

During my New Year's Day reverie, I decided to keep my Italian vacation plans. It wasn't that the weather was particularly terrible — that January had been one of the warmest on record. It was just that watching Séverine work her charms on Cranwell was becoming tiring, and I didn't want to watch anymore. I counted down the days until the fifteenth, when I took the train into Paris and from Paris to Charles de Gaulle Airport.

It wasn't until the plane lifted off and Paris disappeared beneath gray clouds that I finally felt able to relax.

It didn't last long.

Once in Rome, I stayed two nights. That first morning I spent pacing up and down the Forum. I bought a slice of pizza from a sidewalk vendor and ate it in the shade of the Basilica of Maxentius. Then I stalked down the ancient streets and stayed what seemed like ages at the House of the Vestal Virgins. Was their life as wonderful as it sounded? It was difficult to tell with everything in ruins, but how easy it would make life to know that you were forbidden to be intimate with a man. I wanted to shove back the rose bush and leap over the crumbled walls. To throw myself into what used to be their courtyard and beg their spirits to take me in.

After, I went to a hill south of Rome and spent an hour eating gelato, draped over the railing, looking down on Rome, envying the anonymous problems of the anonymous people scurrying through the streets.

That evening, I tried to climb the Spanish Steps, but gave up halfway for lack of interest. I even entertained thoughts of eating dinner at the fast-food restaurant just around the corner from the plaza. That's how depressed I was.

The tragedy was that I loved Rome. I was used to tramping all over the city, losing myself on purpose just to pretend I was a part of its history.

Even eating at La Pergola and La Terrazza held no special thrill. In previous years I had looked forward to the occasions, had looked to them for culinary inspiration. I had divided my time between the masterpieces of world-renowned chefs and hole-in-the-wall mamas and papas, equally satisfied and equally inspired to things both great and small. It is just as difficult to turn out a perfect veal marsala as a perfect gnocchi. But this trip, food didn't interest me at all.

So depressed, so listless was I, that even the street urchins and gypsy gangs left me alone.

Having ruined my own good time and not knowing quite what to do with myself, I took the train to Sorrento on the third day. I stayed at the Imperial Hotel Tramantano, overlooking the Gulf of Naples, and insisted on a bayside room. Then spent hours on the balcony watching the hydroplanes ferry tourists to and from Capri.

In Sorrento, I prefer to eat not downtown among the winding streets filled with pottery and souvenir shops, but at the harbor of Marina Grande where I can watch the fishing boats come in, see wedding parties taking pictures in front of the old church, and watch grandmothers go to mass. I usually love the walk that plunges steeply down the hillside, twisting through narrow streets and passing underneath the city's ancient gate. And there's nothing like eating outside at a table on the crude dock that hovers just above the lapping waves. But that year, I couldn't get excited about the long walk back up the hill to the hotel, and I decided not to make the trek.

The second afternoon, I did, however, visit a marquetry shop run by a family who sells antique boxes pieced together from miniscule bits of colored wood. Among all the containers and plaques and trivets, I saw a box that would have been perfect for Cranwell; he would have appreciated the artistry required to make it. I punished him by not buying it, and on my walk back over to the hotel, I purchased a bottle of limoncello for myself instead.

I spent that night parked in a chair on my balcony, sipping lemon liqueur, watching the activity, hearing the humanity in the town around me.

The next day I spent on Capri.

And that year, I found no pleasure in the hydroplane ride across the bay. In the past, I had loved the strength in the wind as the boat rounded the corner of the peninsula and pointed its nose toward the island. That year, it required too much energy to keep my hat on my head, so I went inside the boat and sat on a bench. If I wasn't happy, at least I could nurse my self-pity in the relative warmth of a southern Italian winter.

My thoughts kept stalling on Cranwell. I kept wondering what he was up to. And even as I climbed the hill that the town of Capri clings to, I tried to decide whether or not he would be doing whatever it was with Sévérine.

Even the view from the top of the hill at Tragara, of the wedge-shaped Faraglioni formations jutting from the sea, seemed mundane. In past years, I had followed the path beneath the hillside terrace to the water. That year, I found a bench beneath a tree and, hidden by my sunglasses, closed my eyes and dozed in the breeze.

From hundreds of miles away, Cranwell had managed to ruin everything.

From Sorrento, I took the train back to Rome and flew out of the Eternal City seven long days after I'd landed there. It was only after I reached Paris that I realized my thin black pants, black tight-fitting long-sleeve sweater, and hair spun into a French roll were reminiscent of Audrey Hepburn. And wasn't her Roman holiday nearly as pointless as mine?

I returned to find Cranwell waiting on my doorstep with Lucy beside him. He was wearing a black leather jacket fastened with toggles over a pair of jeans. Forlorn little kids sitting on the stoops of their tract homes in mid-America have nothing on forlorn grown men sitting on the huge steps of a gigantic chateau.

He shot up like a rocket and a grin creased his face as soon as my car looped around the drive. He practically skipped to the car, opened the door for me, and then insisted on carrying my suitcase up the stairs.

"And where is Séverine?"

"I have no idea. I haven't seen her in a week."

For the first time since I'd left on vacation, I felt my spirits lift.

We had dinner together, as was our habit. I had to admit that it was nice to see him again, although I still clenched my teeth whenever I thought of Séverine.

His soap and woodsy scent overpowered the smell of everything else. And it was not the first time I'd noticed that it had a dizzying effect on me.

As I placed an espresso in front of him after our meal, he cleared his throat as if he had something important to say. I suddenly felt very nervous.

"I have something for you Freddie."

"Oh?"

"I saw it in Paris. It made me think of you. Merry belated Christmas."

He passed a small rectangular package to me. I opened it. Found it to be an antique cookbook that was at least three hundred and fifty years old.

"I know it's not quite fifteenth century, but I thought it might be interesting all the same."

When I clenched my teeth that time, it was to keep from crying. All I could see was that perfect box sitting in the marquetry shop in Sorrento. I kept my head bowed until I regained control.

How did the book come to be clasped to my chest?

I smiled and looked at him. "Thank you. It's really very . . . " I couldn't help myself: I burst into tears.

"Freddie." He drew me close and put his arms around me. "What's wrong? Why are you so unhappy?"

He pressed his cheek to my hair and stroked my back as I allowed myself the pleasure of being held by him. His shoulder was the perfect height for me to rest my head on. Closing my eyes and feeling the roughness of his taupe wool sweater against my face, I imagined for just a moment that he loved me.

If only he weren't with Séverine.

As if on cue, the door slammed in the entry hall.

"*Cou-cou.*" Séverine's voice drifted down to us. I pulled out of Cranwell's arms, turned my back to him, rubbed a hand across my face, and took a tremulous trial sniff.

"Frédérique?"

I walked toward the stairs and shouted up at her. "Down here."

Quickly walking back to the table, I palmed Cranwell's present and slid past Séverine as she came down the stairs. She was wearing a well-cut black blazer and a jaunty red chenille scarf over tight-fitting jeans.

Leaving the lovers to themselves, I took my misery upstairs.

❦

I passed the week kicking myself for breaking down in front of Cranwell again. My emotions didn't usually live so close to the surface. Finally, I was able to look Cranwell in the eye, and by that time, my next guests had arrived. They came, surprisingly enough, on a Tuesday.

They drove up in a Mercedes and parked exactly in the center of the drive.

As I watched, a man opened the driver's door by degrees and appeared in increments, first a foot, then a calf, then a leg. An arm. The top of his head. Finally, he straightened. Although he was old and hunched, he had a magnificent head of hair and a regal cut to his suit. Pausing for a moment, he put a hand to his tie and then made his way around the car to the passenger's side.

He opened the door and offered a hand to the passenger. In contrast to the gentleman, she floated out of the car to her feet, and after settling a sweater over her shoulders, she slipped a hand around the gentleman's arm.

Together they turned toward the chateau.

My jaw dropped.

Never had I seen a more beautiful woman.

She, like the man, was probably at least eighty years old, but where he was stooped, she stood straight as a ruler and carried her head high. At a younger age, she would have had the blackest of hair, for that was the only way to account for her brilliant white locks. They had been drawn back from her face and then curled up at the ends. And her body was one that even I would envy. The drapey crepe dress she wore recalled the sirens of the 1940s.

And then, she turned her face to the man and smiled. The glow in her eyes and the round apples that appeared in her cheeks cast the illusion of a woman in her thirties.

They came up the steps toward me, and I opened the door wide for them.

"Monsieur et Madame Duroc." I inclined my head as I greeted them.

The light went out in the woman's eyes and she extended a slender jeweled hand toward me. "Please. Call me Sophie."

Surprised at her informality, I took her hand and shook it.

We walked, at a slow pace, up the central staircase, and I gave myself credit for having placed them in a room on the first floor near the stairs. I made sure they knew where the bathroom was and asked if they required anything.

Sophie walked me to the door saying, "We require nothing."

I'd never been brushed off so politely.

They came down to dinner late that evening. Both had changed into more formal clothing. M. Duroc was wearing an honest-to-goodness tuxedo, and she was wearing a backless floor-length gown.

They spent four hours on dinner: *foie gras* on toasted brioche with Sauternes, *Coquilles St. Jacques*, scallops, *filet mignon de porc* with mushrooms and steamed green beans, and a *gâteau aux trois chocolats*.

Séverine sat with Cranwell and me in between serving courses. At one point she came back down in the middle of a conversation Cranwell and I were having.

"I haven't seen it that often," I told him.

"It's not so rare." Cranwell shoved up the sleeves of his butter cream cotton sweater.

"Maybe between an eighty-year-old man and a thirty-year old woman, but not with a pair of eighty-year-olds."

Cranwell scoffed at me. "You just haven't been to Florida lately. Happens all the time."

I whipped his plate away from him, meaning to carry it to the sink.

"Do you mind?"

"Sorry. You weren't done?" I placed it squarely back on the island in front of him.

"No." He reached for the remaining baguette that rested between us, tore off a piece, and began sopping up the mustard sauce from the rabbit we had been eating.

"Honestly, Freddie, love can come at any age."

"I know . . . " I just hadn't seen a love so passionate. At any age. Not in a long time.

Séverine perched herself on a stool beside Cranwell and tore off a piece of baguette for herself. She began to run her bread around the rim of Cranwell's plate. Her hand bumped into his. She let a tiny giggle escape and smiled into his eyes when he looked over at her.

He dug an elbow into her side. And winked at her. Then addressed his next comment to me. "Freddie, you're the one who insists King Arthur's nationality was French."

"Breton."

The glance Cranwell sent me let me know he'd been teasing. "The love story between King Arthur and Guinevere is a classic. Passion that's withstood the passing of centuries."

"But they weren't really in love, were they?" I was unclear about the finer details of Arthurian legend, but I knew someone who had believed in fairy tales. I looked at Séverine, raised an eyebrow and tilted my head in Cranwell's direction.

She finished chewing her bread. Sighed. "It is difficult, the legends of King Arthur and what is known about his relationship with the queen. The knowledge expands through the centuries of the Middle Ages, and this is the reverse of what we expect during this time period. So what is true, and what is a tale? It must depend on the writer and on the nationality Guinevere is given."

"What nationalities has she had?"

"Roman, Welsh, Celtic, British. She is like Mariamne, the symbol of the French Revolution; her attributes change according to the decade."

"So she's a symbol, not a person?"

"In some ways. She is a symbol of the changing thoughts of women. In any case, we know Guinevere to have been the focus of the attentions of many different men. Whether this is because she is abducted against her decision or because she chooses to run away, it is difficult to say. But always, she is married to Arthur, a man she respects but does not love. And always she is in love with someone she can never have. And this passionate but chaste affair of the heart destroys the finest kingdom on Earth. That is the tale of King Arthur and his Queen." Séverine picked up her new tray and headed toward the stairs.

"Thanks. You seem to know as much about Arthur as you do about Alix."

Sévérine paused, and then turned, her face hidden in the shadows. "I learned these stories on the knee of my father as a child."

Pulling up the neck of my angel blue angora turtleneck, I rolled my eyes as I went to portion out dessert. Cranwell and Sévérine may have been having a fling, but it was not the same thing. I was right, and I knew it. A love as passionate as the Durocs' was rare.

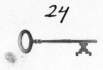

24

*T*he next morning after they had finished breakfast, the Durocs decided to go for a walk. They asked me where they might go, and I directed them down the drive and toward the path I'd made during my jogs through the forest.

They went upstairs to retrieve their coats and then came back arm in arm. Sophie paused as they walked down the front steps to tie an Hermès scarf around her head and pull on delicate leather gloves.

Though I meant to push the door closed behind them, I stopped halfway and leaned against the doorjamb. I hadn't meant to, but I sighed as I watched them walk arm in arm down the drive. A shiver overcame me, and I wished I'd thrown my cardigan on over my tank top.

Cranwell and Lucy had come up behind me, ready to start their own morning walk, but Cranwell stopped to watch the Durocs with me. It looked as if he were prepared for some serious tramping, wearing wide-wale brown corduroys and an olive barn jacket.

"You know they're not married, don't you?"

"Cranwell!"

"They're not."

"Of course they are."

"They are not."

I watched as Sophie picked her way across the gravel, careful not to scuff her high-heeled shoes.

"Cranwell, that's blasphemous. You just automatically assume the worst about everyone."

"Bet?"

He stuck out his hand, and I gripped it with mine. "What's your bet?"

"I win, you go with me to the Pointe du Raz."

Pointe du Raz? The rock-strewn westernmost tip of France at the opposite end of Brittany. It was a bit too far away to be labeled a day trip, but then I wasn't planning on losing.

"I win, you prep my garden for spring. Deal?"

"Deal."

We shook on it and then turned back to the couple, watching as they swayed down the drive, blurred into the forest, and disappeared.

That evening when they appeared in the dining room for dinner, Cranwell was building a fire for me. As before, Sophie was wearing a stunning gown.

M. Duroc pulled her chair out. As she moved to sit in it, her hand fluttered to her throat. "*Le collier. J'ai 'oublié.*" She'd forgotten to put on her necklace.

"*Ça ne fait rien, ma biche.*"

She moved away from the chair and toward the entrance to the dining hall. "*Un petit moment.*"

"*Laisse-le.*"

"*Un instant.*"

We all watched her glide across the room.

"Your wife is an extraordinary woman." Cranwell said what the three of us were thinking.

M. Duroc inclined his head. After a moment he spoke. "She is not my wife."

Cranwell could have turned in that instant and smirked at me, but to his credit he didn't.

The old man's lips lifted in an ironic twist. "It is not that I have not asked. We encountered each other when we were eighteen. I knew within a week that I must marry her. We both did. But she was Jewish, and I was not, and so we needed time. To convince our families. That was 1939."

M. Duroc sighed and played with his watch. "We should not have cared so much for what other people thought. We waited, but we waited too long. The next year, our government began collaborating with Germany. I begged Sophie to marry me so that I could protect her. My family was prominent in Paris; she would have been safe. But she refused. She was afraid she would ruin me. And then after the war, still she refused. She claimed there were too many who were anti-Semitic. She would not marry me, yet she picked my wife for me. I agree with you. Sophie is an extraordinary woman. And she is not my *maîtresse*; she is the owner of my heart."

We heard the sound of Sophie's heels clicking down the hall.

M. Duroc clamped his hand around mine fiercely. "You have made happy the heart of an old man."

And he had disabused mine of some rose-colored sentiments that had begun an insidious creep around my heartstrings. Cranwell had been right. I don't know why I'd bothered to wager against him. After all, he was the expert in affairs of the heart. To see a couple like the Durocs had given me . . . what? Encouragement? Hope? Inspiration? To see a couple like Monsieur Duroc and Sophie had left me disillusioned. Sharing a passion is not the same as sharing a life. Anyone could have an affair. Not everyone could use that passion to build a life in common; it was an emotion that existed within a glass dome. Marriage removed the dome, letting that emotion become tempered by life. Anything can exist in a controlled environment. But in the wilderness of life? Only those with the most fortitude. While the sentiment my guests shared was beautiful, I feared it was, in fact, rather ordinary after all.

M. Duroc and Sophie left late the next day. It was as if they wanted to squeeze all the time they could out of their tryst together.

That evening, Cranwell and Lucy sauntered downstairs for dinner. Cranwell finished setting the table and propped himself on a stool at the island. He fiddled with the buttons on his black cashmere cardigan for a while and then with the collar of his black turtleneck.

"So, how about the Pointe du Raz?" Cranwell tried to look innocent, but failed.

"What about it?"

"When do you want to go?"

"It was your bet. Your choice."

"Tomorrow."

"Tomorrow?!"

"Do you have something going on?"

I sputtered around the kitchen for a few minutes before I gave in to him. What could I do? We'd made an honest bet. I'd just have to put off running errands until the weekend.

We had mushrooms with thick cream and *cassoulet* stew, and then tamped it into our stomachs with a citrusy *sorbet des agrumes*. It was during the espresso that the conversation got more serious.

"You know, Freddie, I have been wanted and needed, but I don't think

I've ever been loved." He plunked two cubes of sugar into his espresso and pursued them around the bottom of the cup with a spoon. "By anyone but God, of course. And my mother. And father."

"That can't be true." After spending hours on the Internet piecing together his love life, I knew he'd had more opportunity than most to find his soul mate.

"Believe me. It's true."

"Frankly, I can't. It's not like . . . "

He tilted his eyes toward me and crooked his mouth in a wry smile. " . . . it's not like I haven't had every opportunity." He played with the wrapper on the chocolate tablet I'd tucked on top of his saucer. Folded it up into a tiny square and then unfolded it. Smoothed it against the island's top.

Still not buying it, I shrugged. If there's one thing I'd learned how to do in France, it was shrug.

"There must be something I haven't figured out yet. Something I'm not doing right."

"How many dates do you usually go on before you sleep with someone?"

His brow wrinkled. "I don't know. It depends." He colored slightly. "Depended."

"On what?"

He took a sip of espresso, then stirred it around, again, with the spoon. "I don't know."

"You must know." He'd mentioned this before, and for someone so introspective, he was having a difficult time getting his thoughts together.

He took another sip.

"Personality? Common interests? Life goals?"

He refused to look at me.

"Cranwell?"

He snuck a look at me from under his eyebrows. "What about you?"

"What about me what?"

"Wanted, needed, loved?"

"Loved. I was definitely loved by Peter. Loved first, then needed and wanted." I popped a square of chocolate into my mouth and let it begin to melt. Absorbed its flavor. "I think we're opposites, Cranwell. You might never have been loved, but I've never been the object of anyone's desire . . . besides Peter's."

At that, he finally lifted his gaze from his espresso. But it settled on me with such intensity that my cheeks were instantly enflamed. "I find that extremely hard to believe."

The smoke in his eyes was doing strange things to my stomach. And when he shifted his attention from my eyes to my lips, I couldn't help it: I swallowed the rest of my chocolate in one long gulp. I could hardly find the voice to say, "It's true." And after I had said it, my mouth went dry.

So I moistened my lips.

At that, Cranwell's eyes imploded, and I felt myself drawn with them into his soul.

"I — " I was having difficulty forming a coherent thought.

"In fact, I know it to be false."

My scalp began to tingle, and I could feel my ears flush. Like a person in quicksand, I grasped at any branch to keep myself from drowning. I did not need, want, a relationship with Cranwell. And why on earth would he be interested in me? It was just more of his flirting. Anyway, he had Séverine.

He cleared his throat, but his words were still husky. "It depended on how long it took."

When I blinked, it broke whatever spell he had cast over me. And I noticed then that we were leaning so far toward each other that we were practically falling off our stools.

Straightening, I pushed my demitasse in between us at some attempt of defense. "How long what took?"

"At what point I slept with a woman depended on how long it took her to say yes."

My mouth must have dropped open because I found myself closing it. I'd heard about people like him, been warned about people like him, but I'd never actually met one. Known one. Been friends with one.

He settled back onto his stool. "And they usually did."

"What?"

"Say yes."

To his credit, he didn't look very proud of his past behavior. His slouching shoulders and hanging head actually indicated embarrassment.

But how do you respond to something so egotistical? So far was it from my way of thinking that he might have been speaking in Swahili.

"Well then let me give you a tip, Cranwell: The nice girls, the kind you didn't used to date but now want to marry? They generally look for love before they succumb to want or need. It seems to me you need to look for a woman who'll say no."

He shrugged. "I like women. Liked them. Like them still. I just don't know how to relate without trying . . . well . . . " He finally gave up.

My answer wasn't immediate because I couldn't tell how earnest he was. Thinking of his sheepish looks, his lack of usual confidence, I decided to offer my opinion. "That's the problem. You'll have to give up women if you ever want to find a woman." I looked in his eyes once more, impervious to the danger. "Maybe you're just scared."

The doors to his soul slammed shut. "Maybe." He drained the rest of his espresso and called to Lucy.

As she rose to her feet, he slid off the stool. "See you in the morning." He turned around as he reached the stairs. "Freddie?"

"Hmm?"

"Would you sleep with me?"

"No!" My indignation mounted as I heard him chuckle. Evidently the familiar Cranwell had resurfaced.

"Maybe there's something to that advice you gave."

25

*T*he next morning, I decided practical clothes were the order of the day. Especially if we'd be hiking over the jagged rocks of the Pointe du Raz. I wore jeans with a fuzzy fleece turtleneck. The hiking boots I laced on were a burnished brown.

Cranwell wore a thyme-colored wool polo-neck sweater over a pair of nice fitting jeans. He'd folded a heavy coat over his arm and had squatted to rub Lucy's stomach when I reached the bottom of the stairs. Séverine was leaning against the front door watching Cranwell. Considering the way Lucy always snarled at her, I didn't blame her for keeping her distance.

Cranwell looked up when he heard me.

His chest hairs were peeking out of the collar of his sweater.

Swallowing, I focused my attention on Lucy. I'd never said the man wasn't handsome. "Ready?"

"Ready."

We walked to the garage together. It was his idea, so Cranwell insisted on driving. I offered no argument; his black Jaguar beat my cream soda-colored Mini hands down. And his heater probably worked too. Though I still had money left from the settlement of my parents' estate, I didn't choose to invest it in a car. What I owned had four wheels, and it got me where I needed to go.

As I settled myself into the beige leather passenger seat, I sighed in pure bliss as Cranwell pushed his coat into the space behind our seats. He glanced over at me and started laughing.

At that moment, I didn't care: I liked the smell of leather, I liked the look of burled walnut trim. I liked nice cars; it just wasn't a priority for me to own one. "How do you come to be driving a Jaguar?"

"I like Jags. After I bought my first one, I promised myself I'd never drive anything else."

"So you had this one shipped to you?"

"No. I bought it in Paris and then drove it over here."

"And what will you do with it when you leave? Sell it?"

He shrugged. "Probably give it to a friend."

"Nice gift."

"I have nice friends."

He'd alluded before to the fact that he had friends in Paris, but he hadn't left my chateau for the city except when I'd forced him to in the middle of the month. Maybe, like most smart rich people, they spent their winters in places farther south.

Cranwell pointed out the heated seat feature and let me play with the adjustments while we sped away from the chateau. The ride was heavenly. The weather wasn't the best, but cocooned inside the Jag, it didn't matter.

The trip took three hours.

By noon, we had motored into Douarnenez, the site most closely connected with the ancient Legend of Ys. A quaint fishing town in the old Breton style, its fishing port is brightened by a string of buildings with colorful facades topped with black roofs facing off against the ocean. We checked into the hotel and had lunch at a restaurant at the

Port de Rosmeur along the water. Heat lamps made it warm enough to eat outside.

Then we drove to Pointe du Raz.

Cranwell parked his Jaguar at the far side of the parking lot. Can't say that I blamed him; with a car like that, I would have been worried about bumps and scratches too.

We walked together past the gift shops and snack bars and then began the hike over the hills and up toward the rocks until we could see the surf break now and then over the tops of jagged, jumbled stone.

When we reached an abandoned concrete slab at the start of the point, I crossed my arms and hugged myself, trying to trap some body heat inside my pea coat. "So how did you know they weren't married?"

"I know them."

"Know them?!"

"Not personally. But I know of them. Enough to know that Sophie has never been married."

Although I sent forth a fist to punch him, he captured it before it reached his arm and took it and tucked it into his coat pocket. Then he turned to me and smiled the most self-satisfied smile I'd ever seen him make.

And rascal that he was, I had to smile back.

Inside his pocket, he worked my fist apart and then entwined his fingers with mine.

I began to berate myself for not putting up a defense against him, but with the wind whipping my hair and the waves breaking far above the rocks, I decided that I didn't care anymore. Apparently he was like this with everyone. If flirting didn't mean anything to him, then why should it mean anything to me? Besides, it felt good to have my hand held; I had missed my companionship with Peter.

To cement my decision, I gave Cranwell's hand a squeeze.

He tightened his hand around mine for an instant, pulling it close.

Thinking he wanted to say something, I turned toward him and in doing so, my hair blew between us.

He backed away from the stinging strands, releasing my hand.

After using it to tuck my hair inside my coat, I turned back to him, but he was already several yards away, staring seaward.

Suddenly, he turned to me and yelled across the wind, "Come on!" grabbing my hand and yanking me forward. He wasn't content to just look at the edge of Continental Europe. He wanted to stand on it.

"Cranwell, I don't think — "

"Nothing says we can't climb out there."

Of course nothing said we couldn't climb out there. The French don't care if you're an idiot, risking your life scrambling over slippery, slime-covered rocks. And should you die, any French court of law would say it's your own fault for being stupid.

"Cranwell . . . " I dug my heels into those rocks just as far as they would go.

"Freddie!" He let go of my hand in exasperation. "What are you afraid of?"

"Heights. Drowning. Strong tidal currents. Undertows. Hypothermia. Breaking my head open and having to watch my brains leak out."

He broke into laughter, placed a hand behind my head, and pulled it close so he could kiss my forehead. "Is that all?" Then he pulled the tips of my coat collar up around my neck. "I'll take care of you."

And in that instant, he sounded so much like Peter that I couldn't help but offer my hand when he extended his.

He was able to push and pull me over a trash heap of huge tumbled boulders before I balked at the sight of what lay ahead.

"Don't look, Freddie." The words were whispered in my ear.

Grasping at Cranwell's hand, I gave it a violent squeeze. "If I don't look, I'll fall."

"I mean don't look at the waves, just look at the rocks below your feet. They're not going anywhere."

Ahead of us, the rocks abruptly gave way to the ocean, plunging downward at ninety degrees. In between the tip of the point and where I was standing was a half-cauldron filled with angry sea that crashed into the rocks sixty feet below us to send spray shooting up. Relentlessly, it fell back, gathered strength, to begin another assault. I could feel the vibrations of those onslaughts in my chest. The only way forward was to skirt the semicircle of the cliff. One misstep meant certain death or dismemberment . . . maybe both.

"Step where I step."

"Cranwell—" Before I could stop him, he'd jumped forward onto another rock.

I looked back from where we'd come. Forward toward Cranwell. He was looking still forward to that beckoning jut of rock at the very tip of the point. Then his shoulders dropped and he hopped his way back to me. "Never mind."

"Go. I'll wait here." I sat down, leaning back against the rock above me. "I'll be fine."

He helped me up by the elbow. "Let's go back."

As he raised me to my feet, I looked up into his eyes, and instantly, I knew I couldn't, wouldn't, turn back. So I let him help me up and then ducked around him and started picking my way forward along the edge of the cliff.

How I did it, I'll never know, but the image of the top of my boots is indelibly etched in my memory. As I crested that final rock, a spray of salt water came spurting up from the sea.

Caught off guard, I threw up my hands against the cold wetness and teetered on the spine of the rock.

I felt strong hands grip my shoulders.

Turning, I saw Cranwell beside me. He slipped an arm around my waist to steady me. "We did it."

"We did."

We stayed there, enjoying the reward of our labor. Before us, beyond a lonely lighthouse, the sea stretched, endless, and merged with the mist. Somewhere out there was the Ile de Seine, portal to druidic paradise, but according to my eyes, before and beside us was nothing. We were truly standing on the last piece of continental soil. The last stanchion against the ocean. Several times we were drenched by spray, but the sensation of being the last two people in the world was so strong that we were powerless to turn back. And when the spell had finally dissipated, I found myself bound much tighter in Cranwell's clasp than I would have chosen to be.

We turned around and headed back toward the mainland. The return seemed much easier than the hike out to the point had been.

When we'd passed the worst of the slippery boulders and when the danger of falling into the ocean had passed, Cranwell stepped up onto a boulder beside me and gave me a half hug. "Thanks."

Not needing him to know that I'd almost had a heart attack from fear of heights, I shrugged as if it were nothing. Still, it had felt exhilarating to stand on the edge of the continent. If I'd had to decide right then, I would have said I was glad I'd done it.

⚜

As we sped back to the hotel, I began working on my hair. I figured it would take at least an hour to pull all the knots from it. Much as I had enjoyed the sea spray, it had only served to lacquer the tangles together.

Cranwell glanced over at me. "Don't comb them out. Let's go back tonight."

Working on a particularly stubborn knot, I frowned. "I'm sure the park closes at sunset."

"It doesn't matter. We can hike in."

"That's dangerous."

"Nonsense."

Although I was proud of myself, as far as hiking out to the point went, once was definitely enough. "Why can't we just go out for dinner like normal people?"

"Because there's nothing to be gained by living an ordinary life."

The knot wouldn't budge. "I'm not hiking back out to the tip of the point."

"I'm not asking you to. I just want to see what it looks like in the moonlight."

Oh, please. I threw him a sharp glance. He wasn't usually so cheesy.

Finally, I jabbed my fingers into the knot and pulled downward in desperation. It didn't even budge. Cranwell had a point; if we went back out, it would be a waste of time to untangle everything.

"What do you say?"

"Fine. Let's do it."

Dressing warmly for our evening adventure, I wore nearly everything I'd brought: a cotton turtleneck under a jewel-toned wool crew neck. It was one Peter had bought for me in Peru. I pulled tights on before I slipped into wool flannel pants, then tugged on the same lug-soled leather boots I'd worn earlier that day. Gloves and a hat were tucked into the pockets of my pea coat.

Cranwell met up with me in the hallway. He had a wool scarf tossed around his neck and underneath his black coat, he wore a roll-neck sweater and those tight-fitting jeans.

"Don't you think you'll slip and slide in those?" I was looking pointedly at his black loafers.

He held up a pair of well-worn hiking boots he'd kept hidden behind his back. Smiling, he gestured me ahead of him and down the stairs.

We ate dinner at a crêperie. Defying logic, this crêperie, like all the others I'd visited in France, took forever to serve our dinner. I can make a crêpe in three minutes; two crêpes take me ten minutes at the most. And between the two of us, two crêpes are all that we'd ordered.

Did I mention that we were the only customers in the restaurant?

⁓҉⁓

It felt very naughty to step over the chain that roped off the park from the main road.

"Do you think there's a guard?" His question might have sounded cautious, but Cranwell was already out in front, leading the way at a quick pace.

"No. This is Europe. If you want to be stupid and kill yourself, they don't care."

Cranwell broke his stride to look over his shoulder at me. "Then come on."

At his prodding I started moving again, grabbing onto the hand he was holding out to me. It made me feel more safe. "Can't we walk in the shadows?"

"Why? You just said there's probably no one here."

"Just in case."

Cranwell relented, and we walked to the left toward the shade offered by the shelter of the restrooms. As we were engulfed by the shadows, I began to feel better. It was a beautiful night. We could hear the surf pounding the distant rocks, the full moon shone bright, and the stars were out in scores.

But then I heard something. Stopping suddenly, I pulled his hand to my side. Then I dragged him toward the building. "Someone's coming."

He stopped for a moment and listened, his eyes directed toward the left.

My loose hand found a fistful of his jacket.

He placed me behind his back, sheltering me against the wall.

Involuntarily, my hands wended themselves through his arms and around his waist. My eyes tightly shut, I tried to distinguish human sounds from the relentless assault of the surf. I could hear nothing but the beating of my heart.

His hand gripped one of my arms, stopping it, keeping me still. His body went tense with the effort it took to listen.

The sounds of the night became deafening: the surf, the wind, the sound of my heartbeat in my ears, Cranwell's breathing, the sound of a footfall on the concrete path.

My hands flew up toward Cranwell's chest, and I hid my head between his shoulders. I couldn't stand to look.

Cranwell covered my hands with his own and it was then, when I felt the warmth of his skin on mine, that I realized how cold my own hands were.

He noticed too, for he pulled my arms forward, bringing me closer to his back, and then he cupped my hands and began to blow into them.

The warmth of his breath spread from my fingers to the rest of my body as if a furnace had suddenly fired. It took the sound of another footfall to steer my focus from Cranwell to the precarious situation we were in.

"Freddie—"

Before he could say another word, I clamped a hand over his mouth.

Another footstep fell.

Cranwell gently pried my hand from his mouth.

I buried my head deeper between his shoulder blades.

He began to kiss my fingers. My knees sagged, and I leaned into his back.

Another footstep fell.

It sounded as if it were almost opposite us, but my eyes were screwed so tightly shut I couldn't see. Didn't want to see. I was flying, I was soaring. What could possibly interest me on earth?

The next footfall sounded like it had passed us. And by that time, it was all I could do to keep standing. Cranwell had worked his way to my ring finger.

And then he came to my ring. Peter's ring.

He slowly released my hand and walked away down the path through the hills.

The sudden lack of support made me pitch forward, but I caught myself before falling. Sliding down the wall, I shivered from the sudden absence of his warmth. I sat there for a full five minutes, trying to recover my breath and put my thoughts in order.

Robert Cranwell was a very dangerous man.

26

*E*ventually, I joined him on the old concrete slab, hunched into my coat with my hands shoved in my pockets.

"Are you cold?" He leaned my direction as he spoke, but he didn't look at me.

"No."

He crooked his arm for me, keeping his hand in his pocket. I hooked my arm through his and then returned my hand to my own pocket. Standing there, facing the wind, I reminded myself again that he flirted with everyone. Clearly he was involved in a relationship with Séverine. The wind blew any romantic fantasies out of my mind.

"I'm sorry, Freddie. I had no right to do that. You always seem to be the victim when my old nature rebels against the new one."

I could think of no reply.

Cranwell walked us to an area of rocks that jutted up from its neighbors but was sheltered from the prevailing winds. He climbed up onto the highest of them. I nestled into the rock below it, leaning back against his legs, and drawing my own up in front of me.

Then Cranwell began to talk. "I'm not used to having a relationship with a woman that isn't based on things physical. Freddie, I like you. You're like no one else I've ever known. In my former life, the highest honor for that designation would have been to sleep with you. Of course, now, that should be the furthest thing from my mind. But it's not. And I don't know how to tell you how I feel about you without using my body to show you."

Cranwell's speech was very pretty. How he could have such high aspirations when he was sleeping with Séverine was a little hypocritical in my opinion, but then, he never stopped and asked for my thoughts, so I kept them to myself.

"Every day I pray for the strength to respect you. And most of the time, I do. But once in a while, I don't think, I feel. And that's when the problems start. So, more than anything, I want you to know how much you mean to me. And I want you to know that I don't ever want to hurt you. Or be the cause of delay on your way toward God."

"Do we have to talk about Him all the time?"

"Freddie, how can we not talk about Him? Spoken or unspoken, He's the cause of your being here. Why did you move to the chateau? — to flee from Him. You can't flee from something unless it has presented itself. By your own flight, Freddie, you proclaim that God exists. If He didn't, you wouldn't have anything to run from. You believe, Freddie. If you didn't, you wouldn't hold such interest for me. And then there's me: why did I come to your chateau? — to learn how to establish a life with Him. Away from everything I used to know. I could have gone anywhere, but I chose you because of Alix. Think how far back, how long ago, God planned this and how he reached back through history to bring us together. He amazes me."

We stayed so long that I saw the stars shift in the sky. The thudding of the waves and the low whistle of wind through the rocks lulled my mind into numbness. I realized at some point that Cranwell had slid down his rock and that I was no longer leaning against his legs, but against his chest. I looked down, in wonder, to see his arms clasped around me, his knees drawn up next to mine.

Looking back on that night, I have no memory of how long we sat like that, but it was long enough that we were breathing in unison; his body had molded so close that it felt like my own.

"We need to go."

He brought his mouth close to my ear. "Wait."

"We need to go."

Although I didn't mind being Cranwell's friend, I was not going to get into a relationship with him. Not while he was with Séverine. I couldn't trust him.

Clambering to my feet, I realized for the second time that night just how warm Cranwell had kept me against the chill.

We hiked back down to the car and snuck as quietly as we could back up to our rooms.

The next morning, it took three rinses of conditioner to get the knots out of my hair. And I was trying to do it in a standard French hotel bathtub/shower which had no shower curtain. By the third rinse, I was extremely peeved at Cranwell and the game he was trying to play.

With great impatience, I pulled on a pair of slim black pants and an ice-blue turtleneck sweater. After tugging on a pair of black square-heeled boots and winding my hair into a knot, I tramped downstairs to the dining area.

When I rounded the corner, I saw that Cranwell was already there. He was wearing an outfit I was wild about: black wide-wale cords and a tweedy charcoal roll-neck sweater. He rose from his table when I entered the dining area. If he were a scoundrel, at least he was a gentleman about it.

He must have read my mood, because he didn't try to speak to me but kept his nose stuck in an *International Herald Tribune* newspaper. Every time he turned a page, whiffs of his cologne were propelled in my direction.

The coffee was sour, the bread was stale, and the croissants were greasy. But a hungry girl has to eat. When the bread was finished and I'd read the entire front and back pages of Cranwell's paper, I scraped my chair back from the table.

Cranwell got up too, folded his paper, and tucked it under his arm.

He walked me back to my room, but before he passed by and down the hall to his, he leaned against my doorjamb.

It blocked me from opening the door.

"The bread was stale and the croissants were greasy. You are a much better chef, Freddie. I thank God every day that I stay with you."

With that, he sauntered down the hall, leaving me to wipe a silly grin off my face.

I hated him.

❧

The next week, Cranwell decided he needed to visit Dinan and he asked me to come with him.

"Have you ever been?" He was composing a *tartine*, carefully buttering a length of baguette. I knew from experience that in another moment, he would just as carefully spread jam across it.

"Yes, Cranwell." A hundred times at least. And every week since he'd come to stay. I was not the hermit he had supposed me to be. The closest Carrefour and Monoprix were in Dinan. I did most of my shopping around the periphery of the town in the newly built areas.

"I need to see it because Alix accompanied Awen there at least once when he went on business."

And there went the jam.

In a major feat of self-control, I tugged the corners of my lips back down. For all the masculinity of his roughly knit rust-wool turtleneck sweater and espresso-colored moleskin jeans, he looked like a six-year-old boy.

I could have cared less about Alix, but there were a few things I needed, like garbage bags and toilet cleaner. "What time would you like to leave?"

"How about now? I'll drive."

After cleaning up from breakfast, I ran upstairs to change, pulling on a pair of black twill slacks. I chose my black boots, and then I buttoned a black leather jacket over my funnelneck sweater and wrapped a blue and plum scarf around my neck. I took my black leather gloves with me but decided against a hat. I didn't think we'd be outside in the weather much. We left Lucy with Séverine. I don't know why he didn't ask Séverine to go with him, but I wasn't going to inquire: I needed garbage bags. It was possible they were having a lover's spat. Lately Séverine's moods were oscillating faster than a floor fan.

Cranwell looked to me for directions, and I had him turn north on D71. We wound through the morning mist for the first thirty kilometers of our journey, and then a stiff breeze pushing inland from the ocean began to lift it before us in swirls and we drove out into the rare, bleak winter sun.

"Could you get my sunglasses for me? They're in the dash."

In a moment I found them and unfolded the arms, so he wouldn't have to fumble with them as he drove.

It's possible that he winked at me, but I couldn't be sure because his shades were so dark. I decided to give him the benefit of the doubt and be agreeable. Especially as he was driving with both hands around the leather-wrapped steering wheel. Men who drive with only one hand make me nervous. I always wonder what they intend to do with the other.

Since we had broken into the sunlight, Cranwell sped up. Way up. I've found that on tight, curvy country roads, the best thing to do when someone speeds is to close my eyes. Or grab the chicken bar. Jags don't come with chicken bars so I closed my eyes. Tightly.

"You're missing the scenery, Freddie."

"It's going by my window so quickly that it doesn't matter."

He downshifted, sending the car lurching.

My eyes sprung open.

"You don't like speed?"

"Not when it threatens my existence."

"On the autoroute?"

"On the autoroute, on a sunny day, with no wind, no other cars, and no police, then, yes, Cranwell, I like speed."

"You're no fun."

"I can be very fun. Under the right conditions."

He turned to look at me.

That was not what I had meant to say. Or rather, what he understood was not what I meant. Besides, I hate it when men wear sunglasses. I can't see their eyes.

It seemed like an eternity that he looked at me, and when he looked away, he gasped and yanked the steering wheel to the right.

It was such a violent movement that it practically threw me on top of him, but it did have the result of avoiding a collision with an oncoming truck. The road had made a tight turn to the right while Cranwell had been distracted.

"I'm sorry, Freddie," he said, once he'd yanked the steering wheel back to the left to avoid sending us sailing into the ditch. "You have to stop doing that."

"Doing what?"

"Propositioning me."

"Prop—?" My face immediately flamed, but then I remembered what men of his type are like. They flirt with everyone. "Cranwell, if I ever proposition you, you'll know it."

He turned to grin at me. "My mistake."

"Drive."

Cranwell accompanied me to the grocery store, and after that, he insisted I accompany him into the historic center of Dinan. I didn't protest too much. Dinan is a charming town with the oldest network of ramparts in Brittany. We drove, as closely as possible, around the walls so that Cranwell could get a good look at the dimensions of the medieval city.

We stopped at St. Sauveur, leaving the car to take a look inside the basilica. Then we drove up and down the more touristy streets, filled with old half-timbered and stone houses. I pointed out the missile-shaped Tour de l'Horloge, the clock tower that postdated Alix by half a century. It was Thursday, so we ate lunch at Place Duguesclin market, picking up *rillettes* sandwiches and Cokes. Then we decided to tour the rest of the city on foot. After passing several old convents, another church, city hall, and the municipal library, we walked through the old commerce streets where fishmongers, iron workers, tailors, and other merchants had hawked their wares in Alix's time.

Cranwell was forever asking me to translate the historic signs fixed to buildings or perched on poles in the middle of the sidewalks. He wanted to make sure he didn't write about things not present in Alix's era.

Finally, we paid an entrance fee to the Maison du Gouverneur to see exactly what the inside of a fifteenth-century half-timbered house had been like. They also had a good collection of regional furniture on display that Cranwell took some time to sketch.

By five that afternoon, he'd seen what he'd come for and had nearly scribbled through his notebook noting his impressions, so we decided to walk to a nearby restaurant and then head home.

"I'm low on gas," he commented as he started the car. "Should I get some before we leave?"

"It's only about 75 kilometers."

Cranwell gunned the engine and we peeled out of the parking garage. "We should be fine."

With night falling, I decided to direct Cranwell to take a slightly larger road. While less picturesque, it wound through fewer towns and should have been an easier drive. At least it was a beautiful drive. Twilight had always been my favorite time of day, and that evening, the trees seemed to lengthen, then loom. In the stretching shadows, their silhouettes formed a tunnel over the road.

At one point, it looked as if there were a board lying in our lane up ahead. Cranwell must have seen it also, because he slowed the approach of the car. But he didn't steer around it, he drove right over it. He must have been thinking about our near-miss that morning. And that was his mistake. The moment he hit it, the car seemed to deflate.

Cranwell pulled the car off onto the narrow shoulder and got out to inspect the damage, slowly walking around the vehicle. I saw his mouth moving, although I couldn't hear any words. Then he hiked back down the road. Turning in the seat, I could see him pick up the board and examine it. Then he flung it into the trees.

When he got back into the car, he slammed the door shut. And as he turned to me, I could tell from the flint in his eyes that the news was not good. "Do you have a cell phone?"

"No."

"All four tires are flat. That board must have had about fifteen nails sticking out of it."

I wasn't prepared for that. If winter days were mild in Brittany, the nights could kill. It's not that they were frigid, but they were damp, and if you didn't keep moving, if you didn't keep your blood circulating, you could get hypothermia.

"Where exactly are we?"

"We passed Montauban about fifteen minutes ago." At least I remembered that much. And I remembered more. "The next town, Iffendic, isn't for another six kilometers." We really were in the middle of nowhere. "I've seen police on this road before. They may patrol it. I think waiting here, inside, is safer than leaving. Besides, we'll stay warm for a while."

"Agreed." In turning on the ignition briefly, he glanced at the gas gauge. His eyes grew wide.

"Isn't it two kilometers to the mile?"

"Roughly. It's actually 1.6."

"I miscalculated. I'm sorry, Freddie."

"Are we low?"

"Past empty . . . I probably drove too fast."

No "probably" about it. He'd definitely driven too fast.

"I can't leave the engine on, but we can have some heat for a few minutes at least."

He turned the heat on full and moved his seat back and down, then he stretched out his legs, cracked his knuckles, and folded his arms under his head. "So what do you want to talk about?"

The warmth from the car's heater didn't last long. An hour later, I had drawn my legs up onto my seat and had my arms slung around them. I remembered from some water safety course I'd taken in junior high that this modified fetal position helped to trap body heat.

He turned the car back on for about fifteen minutes to restore the heat. It felt good, but with all the layers that encased my body, I began to sweat.

"Do you want my jacket?" Cranwell leaned toward me and reached an arm behind my seat for it.

In spite of seeing me shake my head, he kept looking, and when he fished it out, he made me wear it.

"Don't you want it?" I figured he should have dibs if he needed it.

It was as if he were dressing a child. He guided one of my arms into a sleeve and then the other. "I'm fine, Freddie. I dressed for the weather."

He was right, but I frowned at him anyway.

"Don't scowl at me." He reached through my leather jacket and began to unwind the scarf from my neck.

Closing my hands over his, I tried to stop him.

He gently disengaged them. "If you tie this over your head, it will keep you warmer."

He was right, so I let him wrap the scarf, Grace Kelly-style, over my head and around my neck.

"Just call me babushka."

"Or we could braid your hair and call you Gretel."

When he said that, I knew that I must have looked about twelve years old. It was the curse of my round face and my big round blue eyes. The freckles scattered lightly over my nose didn't help any.

"What were we talking about, Cranwell?"

He went back to his side of the car and stretched out like before, but folded his arms across his stomach. "What was it like? With Peter?"

"In the beginning, it was wonderful. It was what I'd dreamed. Toward the end, his job had begun to devour him. He wasn't there, physically or emotionally. His mind was always on his job, but we couldn't talk about it. It was the only way he could protect me."

"And by protecting you, he pushed you away."

"Basically." My temperature was beginning to moderate, and I was no longer sweating. "But I wasn't going to let him push me far. He was an honorable man, a decent man. I was in love with him. And I respected him. We just had one more month, and then we would have moved on, started over again. Whatever had burdened him would have been left behind. I was not unhappy being married to him." It was important to me that Cranwell understand.

"But were you happy?" Cranwell never failed to understand.

"Happiness is transient. You might as well try to trap the ocean. You've never been married."

"No."

"Happiness is not enough to marry for."

"So does that mean you weren't happy?"

"No. But I was not happy every single minute of every single day."

"But—"

"There were moments of incredible happiness strung together with real life."

"Do you believe in soul mates? That there's just one person on Earth? A person reserved just for you?"

"No. Do you?"

"Yes."

Now that was an interesting piece of information. "And you haven't found her yet?"

He rolled onto his side, facing me. "I might have."

The way he was looking at me made my eyes dive toward the floor of the car. But they couldn't stay away for long. His eyes were magnetic, so I closed mine and reminded myself of Séverine. Then I changed the topic. To what, I can't even remember, but I know we spent almost an hour on it.

And then, I felt myself shiver. Somehow, the perspiration trapped between my body and my cotton turtleneck had grown clammy. And my feet were freezing.

The next few minutes I spent concentrating on my toes. They were so cold I could hardly move them.

"What's wrong?"

"My toes."

"Move them."

"I'm trying."

"Can you still feel them?" A note of concern had crept into his voice.

"Yes, Cranwell, I can, and they really hurt."

His teeth glinted in the dark, and I saw the condensation curl from his chuckle.

I moved my shoulders farther up my neck.

It was exasperating that we hadn't seen a single car up to that point. I think I would have even flagged down an axe murderer. Was there no one in all of Brittany who was partying until the wee hours of the night?

Experimentally, I wriggled my fingers inside the sleeves of my coat. They were cold, too. I was beginning to think that staying put hadn't been such a smart idea. I was scared. Opening my mouth, I asked the first question that popped into my head. I always get chatty when I'm nervous. "What's it like to date movie stars?"

"What's it like to date anyone?"

Touchy, touchy.

Cranwell sighed. "Some are workaholics. Some are egotistical. Others are the nicest people I've ever met. They're people, Freddie. Just like you or me."

Maybe like him, but definitely not like me. "How about the rock star?"

"How about her?"

"What was the attraction?"

"We were young." He snorted. "It was the eighties. We were both on top of our games. Life was one golden, glamorous party. We looked good with each other. The photo ops were tremendous." He sighed then, a long heavy weary sigh. "If I had it to do again, I would do it so differently. I just didn't realize there could be so much more. With so much less. I am so grateful for God's grace."

"I read about you becoming a Christian."

"That made the news here in France?"

"No. I was surfing the Internet." How did I always get myself into such embarrassing situations? I dipped my chin toward my chest so that my face was shielded by the lapels of Cranwell's coat. "I did some research on you."

"Pardon me?"

There was no help for it. I batted away the protection of the coat and turned to face him. "I did some research on you."

His smile was apologetic. "My reputation precedes me."

My smile must have been rather thin. I tried to shrink down into myself, knowing that if I could make myself smaller, my body heat would go farther. I know I closed my eyes. I must have let my chin drop, because the next thing I remember is Cranwell shaking me and my head jerking up.

27

"Freddie, listen to me. You can't fall asleep."

The yawn could not have been stopped if I'd tried. "Of course I can." He could be so overbearing sometimes. "I'm really tired, Cranwell." I let my head drop back down. It was so heavy.

Cranwell grabbed me by both shoulders. "Freddie. You must not fall asleep."

"But I'm so tired."

He took off his gloves and cupped my face. "Freddie, you're freezing."

It was true, I *was* cold. I had been shivering for at least an hour, but his coat was so big, I had managed to hide it. "I know. And Cranwell, I'm so tired."

"Freddie, come over here to my side."

"Not enough room." My lips and my cheeks were so cold it was hard to form words.

"Freddie, move it!"

He must have been mad at me, because I'd never heard Cranwell yell before. But he was yelling then. At me.

The difficulty in unfolding my legs and pushing myself across that short distance between the seats is indescribable.

By the time I reached him, I was crying.

He must have seen a reflection from my tears because he quickly wiped them away. "Shhh. Don't cry."

" . . . mad at me."

"No, Freddie. I'm not."

" . . . yelled."

"I didn't mean to, I'm sorry. I was worried about you."

" . . . cold."

He unbuttoned the coat around me and then pulled me against himself, stretching the sides of the coat as far around him as they would reach and clamping them to his sides with his arms. We were chest to chest and my head was pressed against his shoulder.

"I know you're cold. You'll be warm again in a minute. Just don't cry anymore. It will make you colder."

" . . . not mad . . . "

He pressed my head against his shoulder with his chin. "No. Freddie, I love you." His arms tightened around me.

" . . . can't breathe . . . " It took me an enormous effort to get those words out.

He loosened his hold, but not by much. "Let's sing. What do you want to sing?"

" . . . bright, coppered kettles . . . "

He groaned. "*Sound of Music*? Freddie." He sounded disappointed in me, but he joined me anyway. By the time we were done, I felt marginally warmer.

"No more Julie Andrews. Something else." He didn't sound like he was joking.

A song popped into my head. It wasn't one that I wanted to sing, but the longer I refused to sing it, the louder it echoed in my thoughts.

He shook me. "Freddie!"

" . . . Jesus loves me . . . "

He finished the line, " . . . this I know . . . "

"For the Bible tells me so." By alternating the lines and joining in on the chorus we finished the song, albeit slowly and with not a lot of rhythm.

"'Jesus Loves Me?' I knew you believed. You just had to stop trying to convince yourself you didn't."

My lips had thawed enough to smile against his scratchy sweater. To this point, my head had rested against his shoulder, nose first. Now I had the energy to turn it and nestle it into the dip of his collarbone.

He laid his cheek against my head. "Someone will come soon."

My eyes closed again. His scent was intoxicating: wool mixed with soap and aftershave and a hint of mint in his breathe. I felt my head begin to spin.

He shook me slightly and my eyes flew open. "Freddie, who's your favorite author?"

I smiled to myself. " . . . trick question . . . "

He laughed. And with my head against him, I could hear it start deep inside his chest. "No, seriously."

" . . . Jane Austen . . . "

"Movie?"

But I wasn't finished. I shook my head. "And Byatt."

"A. S. Byatt?"

I nodded.

"Good, Freddie. Movie?"

"*Sense and Sensibility*."

He groaned. "You're a romantic too. I never would have guessed it. And I suppose you thought Willoughby was handsome."

No. I shook my head. "Colonel."

"Colonel? You liked the colonel?" He bent his head to whisper in my ear. "Maybe there's hope then for an older man." I could have sworn he kissed my ear.

"Color? No, wait. Let me guess: blue."

Yes.

"And a good choice with the color of your eyes. Food?"

"Chocolate."

"A woman after my own heart."

He babbled something else, but I don't remember what it was. I started getting cold again, and this time I couldn't keep myself from shuddering. It came from deep within me.

It seems to me that Cranwell shook me, yelled at me, and threatened me. I think at one point he even swore he loved me, but I had no strength left to respond. I watched in a stupor as lights flashed blue against the windshield.

And then I was being lifted into a different car. A police car. We streaked through the silent, frigid night, screeching to a halt in front of a hospital. I was bundled inside to a room, was told to undress while hot water was being prepared.

"What are you doing?"

It took a full minute for my lips to thaw enough to answer Cranwell's question. "They told me to undress."

"Why?"

"Hot water."

"Of all the medieval—!" He tugged my coat back on and then lifted me into his arms. "We're leaving. Nobody in their right mind asks a hypothermia patient in your condition to undress themselves and then hop into a bath." He stalked down the hallways muttering about the ineptitude of the staff, then talked the receptionist on duty into calling a cab for us by barking 'Taxi!' at her. I must have fallen asleep on the way to the hotel.

When I woke, I was on a bed in a room ablaze with light. Cranwell was working to pull my boots off. I moaned as he pulled them from my frost-swollen feet.

He unbuttoned his coat, which I was still wearing, and deftly worked it from my arms. And he unwound the scarf from my head and pushed my hair away from my eyes. His face loomed in front of mine, and he searched my eyes. "Freddie, stay with me."

My sweater was being pulled over my head before I could protest. Then he stood me up. Leaning my body against his and holding me around the waist, he worked my pants down to my ankles. I was reduced to my bra and panties, and all I could do was watch him.

He pulled a corner of the duvet and the sheets from the bed, and then he placed me there and covered me with them.

My shivering was uncontrollable.

After a moment, he climbed into bed behind me, and pulled me toward him. "Heaven help me." It sounded like a prayer the way he breathed it into my hair.

Cranwell folded my arms across my chest and then crossed them with his own, fitting his hands over mine. He molded his legs to mine and somehow managed to clamp my feet between his own. Against my icy body, he felt like a furnace.

My last thought before succumbing to sleep was, "Thank goodness I didn't wear my holey underwear."

When I first stirred, light was streaming through a window directly onto my face. I wrinkled my nose at it, and I did what I always do in the morning. I stretched. At least I tried to, but my arms were bound to my chest and my feet were being held in captivity. I tried to turn my head, but even my hair had been pulled taut.

While I was making exploratory movements, something moved behind me.

Fighting against panic, I smothered a scream.

"Freddie?"

"Cranwell?"

"Thank you, God." He rolled up on an elbow, releasing my hair, and leaned over me. His other hand he fit around my neck, leaving his thumb free to caress my cheek. "How are you doing?"

Blinking, I suddenly remembered the previous night. I felt tears well up. "You saved my life, didn't you?"

Those magnificent brown eyes clouded for a moment, and then a corner of his mouth turned up. "Just call me your knight in shining armor."

Turning toward him, I wrapped my arms around his waist and hugged him. "Thank you, Cranwell."

His hand around my neck pressed my head toward his, and he planted a kiss on my forehead.

I realized then what I wasn't wearing. But before I had a chance to feel awkward, he had reached around and unclasped my arms. And then he pulled up the duvet and tucked it under my chin. "Don't move. I'll have breakfast sent up." He gathered my hair with his hand and smoothed it over my pillow before turning away from me to pick up a telephone from the nightstand.

As he ordered, I closed my eyes and luxuriated in the warmth of the sun and the duvet. I fell back asleep.

The valet's knock woke me. As I stretched beneath the sheets, Cranwell answered it and then brought the tray to the bed. He was fully clothed in the rust-colored turtleneck and moleskin jeans he'd worn the day before, and he smelled as if he'd just taken a shower. He set the tray between us and then punched his pillow down between his back and the wall. "*Bon appétit.*"

As I began to sit up, I remembered that I was only wearing a bra. I caught up the duvet just in time.

Cranwell jumped up and went into the bathroom. He returned with a hotel bathrobe, handing it to me before turning his back so I could put it on.

After, he offered me a cup of tea, but I was in the process of trying to push up the sleeves of the robe. They kept falling. He set the tea down in order to help me turn up the sleeves.

"They didn't have coffee?"

"Last night, the doctor told me tea."

"What doctor?"

"The one I called in L.A."

"L.A.?"

"The one I interviewed when I had to research hypothermia for a book I was writing. That's when I found out that too much movement or too rapid reheating could kill a victim of hypothermia."

He hadn't been kidding when he'd called himself a knight in shining armor. "But I don't like tea."

"It doesn't matter if you like it. Think of it as medicine."

I took the cup from his hand and plunked four cubes of sugar into it. At least he let me have the *pains au chocolat*. I was ravenous. And since he refused to let me have coffee, I drained the pot of tea.

As I finished it off, he perched his glasses on his nose and took up the newspaper the hotel had sent up with the tray. He passed it toward me. "Section?"

Declining, I shook my head. "I think I'll take a shower." I threw back the duvet and walked toward the bathroom.

"Take a bath."

So now it was okay to bathe? "But I don't like baths. By the time the tub fills up and you can actually enjoy it, the water starts to get cold."

He looked at me sternly over the top of his glasses. "The doctor said bath."

"How about I promise to stand underneath the shower for at least twenty minutes?"

"Bath."

So, for the sake of Cranwell's conscience, I took a bath. For a good long hour. Every time the water started to cool, I turned the faucet on and warmed it up.

And then I did the one thing I'd never done before in a bath: I closed my eyes.

It's a good thing Cranwell knocked on the door, because I had started to doze.

Startling awake, I sunk into the water up to my chin.

He cracked open the door. "Freddie?"

"Yes?"

"I had some things brought for you. I'll put them right by the door."

He slit the door open, set a stack of boxes on the floor, and pulled it shut.

It wasn't until after he had gone that I realized I had been holding my breath.

Grabbing a towel, I pulled the plug on the tub and dried myself off. I approached the boxes with suspicion and delight. I didn't know what Cranwell was up to, but the French wrapped purchases so elegantly that the stack of boxes looked just like Christmas.

The smallest, at the top, was pink and tied with a black ribbon, and I knew immediately what was in it. I slid the ribbon off the box and opened it to find some of the most luxurious lingerie in France: Aubade. The next three boxes were marked with the name of a designer so prestigious I'd only heard rumors of him. The first contained a pair of medium-blue leather pants. The second a gloriously soft and thick cashmere sweater to match. The last, a pair of blue leather wool-lined boots with stiletto heels, along with cashmere tights.

When I lifted the top of the last box, I couldn't believe my eyes. I plunged my hands into the most extravagant fur I'd ever seen. I lifted it out by the shoulders and gaped. The floor-length fitted body was of silky black fur and the collar, cuffs, hood, hem, and opening were lined with an explosion of the fluffiest of sable in charcoal gray. It was beautiful. It was gorgeous.

For five long minutes, I argued with myself about whether or not to accept Cranwell's gifts. I felt again the buttery-leather pants, the soft cashmere, and the silky fur. If Cranwell hadn't tried anything romantic last night, I rationalized that he wasn't going to. From this perspective, his gifts had no strings; there was nothing he was trying to buy from me; he was simply being friendly. Friendly at my income level usually meant a nice houseplant. Friendly at his level . . . was very nice indeed.

He knocked on the door again. "Freddie? You ready to go? The auto shop was supposed to have delivered the car by now."

"I'm coming. Give me five minutes." I was afraid to put the clothes on. I'd walked down rue Faubourg-St. Honoré in Paris many times, and I knew at a minimum what they must have cost.

After trying to use the hotel's built-in hair dryer, I gave up: the air pressure was too low, and it was only distributing further the smell of cigarette smoke that permeated the room. I ran my fingers through my hair, gathered it in a hand, and tied it in the usual knot.

Makeup? I had none. I pinched my cheeks to make some color rise. It would have to do.

And I was left with having to put on my new clothes.

The pleasure was indescribable. I don't know how Cranwell managed it, but everything fit perfectly. I could have done without the stiletto heels on the boots, but aside from those, I felt like at least $200,000.

When I placed my hand on the doorknob, I suddenly felt shy.

There was a soft knock on the door. "Freddie?"

Putting a hand up, I stroked the door above my head, knowing exactly, from experience, where his face would be. I caught myself smiling. I opened the door.

"Cranwell—" Whatever it was that I was going to say died on my lips. The way he was looking at me sent a tingle down my spine.

"Wow." He bent at the waist, made some silly gesture as if he were doffing his hat, and then offered me his arm.

"I don't know how to thank you."

"Just give me your hand and tell me again that you didn't freeze to death last night."

He let me slip a fur-covered arm under his. "But —"

Cranwell covered my hand with his. "It was nothing. I've never known a woman to want to wear the same thing two days in a row. My car and my own stupidity put your life in danger. It's the least I could do."

He stopped on our way out the door to grab a piece of designer luggage. "I'll carry this out for you."

"It's not mine."

"It's got your things in it, so I guess it is now."

This I've learned in life: If you don't believe in Santa Claus, he can't bring you any presents.

I believe.

Cranwell's car was waiting for us in front of the hotel. It didn't look anything like the arctic coffin it had seemed the previous night.

A valet opened the door for me. Cranwell helped me in. It made me feel just like a model.

As we dashed through town, I noticed the clock on the Tour de l'Horloge. It looked as if it were already afternoon.

Cranwell must have read confusion on my face. "It's about two o'clock. After what we went through last night, we needed the sleep."

Involuntarily, I shivered. I never wanted to be that cold again.

We reached home about an hour later. Cranwell parked in front of the steps and then came around to help me out.

Not being used to the stilettos, I teetered on the first stair. Cranwell reached an arm around my waist to steady me and then decided the better of it and lifted me easily into his arms. He marched up the steps and set me carefully on my feet in the entrance hall.

"Sorry about those heels, but that's all the designer carried this season." He flashed me a grin and then jogged back down the stairs to park the car.

"Frédérique? Robert?" Séverine's call advertised her advance up the stairs from the kitchen. She burst into sight, followed, from a distance, by Lucy. "I was so scary." She put a hand on my arm "You are well?"

"I'm fine. Didn't Cranwell call you?"

"*Oui.* Robert called last night from the hotel. But he told me near to nothing. He was very occupied."

"Preoccupied." I could imagine.

For several minutes, I petted Lucy and listened to Séverine chatter. I heard Cranwell crunch through the gravel across the drive and shuffle up the steps. The great oak door opened behind me.

Giving Lucy a final pat, I started toward the stairs. I thought I'd give the lovers a chance to be alone.

"Robert!" I heard Séverine kiss Cranwell's cheeks and begin to accost him with questions.

I picked my way up the first spiral of the staircase.

"Freddie?" His voice broke free from the conversation. "Are you okay?"

"Fine."

After walking up another turn of the staircase, I sat down on a step in my fur coat to take off the boots. I just wasn't a stiletto type of girl.

"I'll bring up your bag when I come."

"Thanks." I was beginning to feel tired again, though I'd only been awake four hours. I trudged up the stairs to my room and hung my coat in the armoire before I collapsed on the bed. I was overcome by gratitude: I was alive. Every day I would live after that was a gift. I curled up on top of my duvet and marveled at this miracle. I allowed myself to drift off to sleep.

When I woke, the sun had set. I was surprised I hadn't become cold, and then I realized I was snuggled underneath my duvet. I thought for a moment that I had done this in my sleep, but when I got up to walk to the bathroom, I saw my new suitcase on the floor beside the armoire.

Cranwell.

Again.

my sixteenth year
the first year of Louis XI, King of France

day of Saint Michel

My lord was angry this night.

We were having a fête special for Saint Michel. I was wearing an houppelande of velvet the color of the summer sky with sleeves very close and the lining beneath and below of the furs of squirrel. I wore also a chemise of silk the color of straw, the neck being straight and low and the chemise showing itself beneath the houppelande. My ceinture was of gold and fixed to itself with a jeweled clasp. My headdress, shaped as a butterfly, was more comfortable than my henin and less tall. It is of gold and studded with pearls and beryls the color of water.

This feast day, the comte de Dol had honored us with his presence. The comte is very old. He has at least fifty years and only half of his teeth, and difficulties with hearing.

The comte bowed low to me and made homage.

I replied to him, My lord, and he raised himself. And he looked at me and I did not like it.

The comte demanded of me how many years I had and I told him. Sixteen.

And he demanded of me from where I came. And I told him. The country of Touraine.

Anne and my lord came and joined us. And the comte bowed low and made homage, but I made note that he did not look at her, but kept his eyes on me.

I placed myself near to my lord, and put my hand on his arm and he covered it with his own.

The comte told Anne that her cousin is very beautiful and certain he is that she searches a husband. He told her also that she should have no problems with such a body for bearing children and so fair a face.

And I had the realization that the comte believed that I was the cousin and Anne was the wife of my lord.

And my lord apologized for the comte mistaking himself, and he made an introduction of myself, his lady, and Anne, his cousin. This he had need to repeat three times before the comte was able to hear it.

And the comte turned to Anne and looked at her and then made a bow and excused himself.

She must not have pleased him, though I know not why.

I think of this and realize that this is the first time I am glad of being wed to my lord and not still a girl. I must write my father and thank him strongly for making this match. I have been saved from many worse things.

But I do not think it is that which made angry my lord.

He watched me all the long of the night.

I am ignorant of why.

Everyone else made much over Anne. She was clothed in crimson velvet and glowed like an ember. Around her neck were the pearls she had received from my lord. She was talking and laughing much with many of the men.

And then the dance.

My lord and I led the danse basse large as we must. But we have danced it as never before.

As my lord bowed to me, he lowered not his eyes. And dark as they are, they smoldered in his head, sending their heat to all they looked upon. And they looked upon my lips and my cheeks and my own eyes. Even to my shoulders and lower. And this I do not understand: it had not at all the same effect as when the comte had done the same thing.

And from this start, I could not escape those eyes.

It seemed to me that I was trapped with him in the dance. In the rhythm of sliding back and forth and raising up and coming down. If his eyes had arms they would have seized me. I am certain of it.

And after the danse basse large, the trihoris. And as we turned toward each other and then away and came close to each other and parted, it seemed to me with each step, whether in or out, he pulled me closer to him. And as my feet kept the music, my ears heard it not and I saw, still with all the people in the room, only him. As if my sight had been blocked from all but his face.

There was trouble with my breath. It would not come. And I could feel my color rise.

He did not move his hand from mine and it burned beneath my palm.

But though I wanted, I could not turn away from the dance.

After, when I took my rest, I was making conversation with Agnès and watching the musicians and jongleurs toss their toys. But my lord was brooding.

When the musicians made a pause, he got up from his chair, slapped his hand to the table, and pointed at me. "She," he spoke in a loud voice, meaning me, "is my lady."

All the world fell silent.

Then the men left the side of Anne and made homage to me.

When the men were done, my lord took my arm and made me leave
with him. He placed me in my room and left.

Later this night, my lord came to me. Not to speak of stories, but
to demand my pardon. He told me he had caused me dishonor by not
honoring me among his people.

I am ignorant of what this means.

three days before Saint Dynys

My father has replied to me. There is a chevalier of the viscomte
de Rideau of good reputation and newly widowed. He has thirty-five
years and is possessed of property. He will do for Anne when the hour is
arrived.

two days before Saint Dynys

Last night, my lord came to me.

He settled himself on the bed as he has the habit. Then he told me a
new story: about two men named Ioen and Herik and a woman named
Klaoda. Ioen is fiancéed to Klaoda and has twelve less years than she.
Herik is her cousin and lover. As Ioen becomes older, Klaoda comes to
love him. She does not know whether to send Herik away or to keep
them both.

My lord demanded of me what I would do.

I did not know what to answer. Is it right to send away someone that
you have loved? Is it right to keep two lovers? I decided finally that the
wife, Klaoda, has wronged the husband by taking the cousin as a lover.
It is to the husband that she owes loyalty, and not to the cousin. Had the

cousin been honorable, he would have refused her advances. Had she not taken a lover, she would not have a problem. That is what I told him.

He sat up then on the bed and demanded of me if it made a difference if the woman loved them both.

I demanded of him if it were even possible to love two persons at a time.

He answered yes.

Then I reminded him of duty. Duty is present in the one case and absent in the other.

He repeated that word, Duty, in a strange tone and he demanded of me then what I should think were I the husband?

I laughed and pushed him so he fell onto his back on the bed. I demanded of him if I looked like the husband.

He grabbed my wrist and pulled me onto the bed on top of him. He assured me that I did not look like the husband.

I think I must have shivered for he demanded of me if I had cold.

I must have told him so, for he threw back the covers and set me in them and then demanded of me if he might cover himself too.

This was strange, for it is the end of October and we have an été de Saint Michel. It is much more warm than the night he came the last time. I thought perhaps he might be ill and not know it, so I told him he should do as he pleased.

He stood away from the bed then and removed his houppelande, keeping still his blouse.

I could not look too long and be immodest, but the light of the fire shone through the weave of the blouse and placed his form in silhouette. I could not keep my eyes from him. Everywhere I am soft, he is hard. Everywhere I curve, he is sharp.

It is strange that a bed which seemed to me so big just the night before could then seem so small. The smell of the linens, of lavender and sandalwood to which I have become habituated, was overtaken by his scent. I was not sure what to do or how to turn for sleep.

I decided to watch the fire for some moments and drew my feet under me. When I turned from its light, I found my lord watching my face.

I could not look elsewhere for his eyes.

They caught mine and would not let them go.

A tingling went over me from my scalp to my toes. And of a sudden, my mouth was dry. I told him that I thought I was falling ill.

He replied me that he thought he was falling in love. Then he placed his hands on my neck, drew me toward him, and kissed me.

I demanded of him to speak to me of other things.

He demanded of me how many years I have.

I told him. Sixteen. And strange it was that so many wished to know it.

He put a finger to my lips and kept me from speaking and demanded of me to call him Awen.

I replied to him of course, my lord, and then we both laughed.

He kissed me again.

And then he spoke to me. He told me that he suffers. He cannot sleep, though he tries. He cannot eat though he tries. He has melancholy and even baths and the letting of blood do not help.

I have fear for him, for as I looked, he did seem more pale, more sad, more listless.

I demanded of him if there is anything that might help.

He replied to me that being near me brings the only cure. And then he kissed me again. And he told me I might do the same, and so I tried, but I have fear I did not do it right, for he smiled. And then he laid me on the bed and brought his head near. He bid me do it again, for he told me it heals him.

And so I did, and this time, his lips moved over mine. And together they did a sort of dance. A long, slow dance, like the danse basse, with much sliding about and approaching and then pulling away. And the more it was done, the easier it became. And somehow his hands became tangled in my hair. And I realized that my hands gripped his hands.

He slept all night with his arm around me and his face to my hair.

I slept not at all.

one day before Saint Dynys

He came to me again this night. This makes only one night since he has been here last. I did not expect him for one month. He did not want to tell me a story. He wanted only to lie in bed and kiss me.

It made me want. What, I do not know.

one day after Saint Dynys

He did not come this night.

two days after Saint Dynys

He did not come this night.

three days after Saint Dynys

He did not come this night.

I am a crazed creature. I do not take food. I cannot. I have no hunger. I cannot sleep. I can think only of him. Of Awen. I have gone to the chapel and have repeated Ave Marias without cease, but my eyes remember neither altar nor candles. My ears remember no words.

I find myself at meals watching him. I am fascinated by him. By everything about him. I have not read a book since one week. I try. I read a whole page at a time, and at the end, I cannot remember what was read at the beginning.

I do not understand the ways I feel.

eight days after Saint Dynys

He came this night.

At the sight of him, I wept.

He sat beside me on the bed and drew me onto his lap. He pressed my head to his shoulder and then circled his arms around me. I clasped my hands around his back. He called me his little one, and demanded of me why I have sadness.

I replied to him that I have not sadness, but confusion in my head.

He kissed my head and stroked my hair and demanded of what I was confused.

I replied to him of everything. Of nothing. Of how I feel and why.

He demanded of me if he makes me unhappy.

I replied to him on the contrary. He makes me happy. More happy than I know why or how. That I have hunger not for food, but only for him. And even his presence does not satisfy me. I do not understand.

He put me away from him and says me that there are things he must explain to me. Then he bid me take off his houppelande.

This I did. I placed it on the chair in front of the fire. I prefer it of those he wears. The color is oxblood and it makes somehow glints in his eyes. It is lined with fur of ermine and made fancy with broderie of gold thread.

Then he sat down in the chair and bid me take off his shoes.

I sat beside him on the floor in front of the fire and I did it.

He took my hands in his then and he told me there is a conjugal debt in marriage.

I demanded of him then what I owe.

And then he bid me take off his blouse.

I tried, but fumbled with the button. It is a sphere and seemed too small for my fingers, and more, it slipped against the green silk. He placed his hands over mine to help me. They are large, much more large than mine, and his fingers are thick and squared where mine are long and slender. They are covered on the backs with dark hair. Mine are bare.

Even with his fingers so large, he unfastened the button. He bent his head to me so I could lift the fabric over his head.

I demanded of him again what I must owe.

And he had nothing on save a large chain of gold and his leggings of the finest silk.

As I watched he reached around his neck to take off the chain. This he placed into my hand and closed around it with his own.

He told me that the conjugal debt is a debt of flesh. That in a marriage, a husband and wife have rights to the body of the other. And that when one desires it, the other must yield.

This being said, he had me place the chain on the mantel. Then he reached for my hand and placed it on his chest saying that it belonged to me.

I watched the reflection of fire off his chest as I felt its warmth. His muscles tensed at the touch of my fingers.

I took his hand in my own and placed it on my chest saying that it belonged to him.

He took my hand from his chest and placed it on his cheek saying that it belonged to me.

I spread my fingers over that jutting plane and felt the growth of his whiskers.

I took his hand from my chest and placed it on my cheek and leaned into it, bowing my head saying that it also belonged to him. Heat burned in my cheeks as he brought his other hand to my face and cupped it between the two.

He brought himself to stand more close to me and I could look nowhere but into his eyes. And I only saw reflected in them myself and the fire. And I felt as if it was burning inside me. I would have taken off my night robe if there had been anything beneath it.

And as if he read my thoughts, he began to untie my laces. And I felt as if I could not breathe. And a feeling of birds flying from the pit of my stomach overtook me and my hands closed on his and blocked him from the laces.

He bent his head to my lips and began to kiss me. And it stole my breath so that I closed my eyes and my knees became weak.

And as if he read my thoughts still, he lifted me into his arms and carried me to the bed. And he whispered in my ear. "We will wait little one, until you are ready, but it is only because you submit to the conjugal debt that you have hunger for my touch. And I have hunger for yours. And this is good, my Alix, because we have the right. We are wed."

nine days after Saint Dynys

This night my lord, Awen, did not come. I was awake long after the fire had extinguished itself and the moon had passed from one window to the next. I heard a noise in the hall.

I opened the door a small little to look. It was Anne. She hit softly at the door of my lord. It opened and she disappeared inside.

I watched for a long time, at least the time of two masses, but she did not come out. As I could not sleep, I took the duvet from the bed and wrapped it around me and waited beside the door for Anne to come out.

When the sky began to lighten, she opened the door of my lord and returned to her chamber. I waited to see when my lord would appear.

It was soon after.

I opened my door full and let him see me, standing in my nightrobe, wrapped in the duvet.

He stopped in his stride and stared at me.

I cared not that he saw the tears on my cheeks.

He began to start toward my chamber, but I closed and bolted the door against him. He hit the door softly and whispered my name. I made much noise in my chamber so he knew that I did not listen.

After a time, he went away.

I demand of God why it is arrived that my husband be stolen from me when he has only just come.

février

Le court et fievreux février,
le plus court des mois,
est de tous le pire à la fois.

February

Feverish February,
the shortest of months is,
of all of them, the worst.

29

"*W*e need to have a wedding feast."

"What?!"

"A wedding feast. So I can write about it in my book."

"A feast generally means more than two people, Cranwell."

"There's Séverine."

"Feast implies at least twenty people."

"I'll pay for it."

The problem was that I had researched medieval cuisine when I had first moved into the chateau. I had vague recollections of what it involved. "Cranwell, that would mean a whole roasted pig, a whole side of beef, and at least ten to twelve other dishes. A feast is five or six courses with five dishes in each course."

He shrugged. "Invite your friends."

"Invite *your* friends. You said you knew people in Paris. They could stay here for the weekend."

"I guess I could." He took a sip of espresso and let the subject drop.

Later that evening, I surfed the Internet on the subject of medieval food and feasts. They were even more elaborate and time-intensive than I had remembered. Out of curiosity, I flipped through the cookbook Cranwell had given me for Christmas. The recipes and text were fascinating, but would require a fair bit of research to translate and time to find equivalencies for ingredients.

Two days later, he dropped his bombshell. It was over dinner. Up until that point, it had been a relaxing dinner. I'd made a *navarin d'agneau*, and we had enjoyed the tender chunks of lamb with its accompanying root vegetables. It was when I started on my custard-filled pastry *mille feuille* dessert, the one that I'd been looking forward to the entire day, that Cranwell made his announcement.

"They're coming next weekend."

"Who's coming next weekend?"

"My friends. For the wedding feast."

"What?!"

"Remember, Freddie? The wedding feast? The one we were going to have so that I could write about it."

"*Next* weekend?"

"Next weekend. On Friday."

That was only ten short days away.

"How many friends?"

"Twelve."

"Twelve!"

"Twelve. You said a feast was at least twenty people, but I knew you only had seven rooms." He hesitated. "Well, six rooms plus mine. So that makes fifteen of us. You and myself and Séverine included."

"So, these people will be taking up how many of my rooms?"

"The other six."

I exploded. "Cranwell, this is not your house. I can't just order a whole pig and a leg of venison and a . . . " I couldn't stop thinking of that long list of dishes I'd found on the Internet. I was overwhelmed.

"Just add the rooms to the month's bill."

My eyes ducked away from his. I was overcharging him as it was. I compromised with myself. I'd add it to his bill, I just wouldn't charge as much as I should. He was giving me free publicity.

"And don't give me any deals. These are my friends, not yours."

How was he always able to read my mind?

❧

The next morning, I started working on the feast, cursing Cranwell's name all the while. He had absolutely no idea.

It wasn't that I had no period recipes. Among them were those in the book he'd given me for Christmas. But to turn a period recipe into one that worked with modern tools and ingredients required a lot of experimentation and quite a bit of time. And it wasn't as if these people could be faked out with a platter of oversized turkey drumsticks.

The first thing I did was pray that his friends would cancel.

The second thing I did was to try and settle on some sort of menu. I discarded recipes with ingredients I knew I couldn't get on short notice. That meant no berries, no grapes, no red fruits, no leafy green vegetables.

Why couldn't he have had his brainstorm back in October when game would have been plentiful, wild mushrooms would have been in season, and fruits still available?

Medieval meals involved different courses, much as modern formal meals would, but the medieval courses were self-contained. At each course, there would have been some sort of meat, an accompaniment, a starch, and a dessert. So a four-course meal would have been the equivalent of four meals, if a person were a large eater. In effect, I would have to prepare not one meal, but four.

It was easiest to start with meats. I decided on lamb, venison, fish, and fowl. Chicken would have been eaten by only the poorer classes. Beef was rarely eaten as a cow was more valuable alive than dead. I might have chosen goat over lamb, but I knew that lamb was more readily available. Not to mention the fact that I'd never cooked a goat before. It would have been an interesting experience, but I simply didn't have the time.

We'd have a soup. That much was certain.

At least several of the meats would be in pie or turnover forms. With limited utensil technology, foods were served in ways that made them easy to eat with the hands. Of course I wouldn't deny my guests forks and spoons, but I did want the meal to be as authentic as possible.

Fruit tarts were a good idea, but I would have to research the availability of citrus fruits in fifteenth-century France. Would apples have been available in a medieval February? Dried apples, perhaps.

For drinking? A nice red wine and hippocras — a wine spiced with ginger, cinnamon, nutmeg, and sugar — with dessert. Cider was also a possibility, but I would not serve ale. Ale was confined to England during that time period. No water either; it wasn't commonly drunk. Absolutely no milk for drinking, unless it was for a child. And no coffee or tea; they were unknown in medieval France.

As I tore through my cookbooks and scoured the Internet for information, the thought occurred to me that it might be Cranwell's secret wish to drive me insane.

My dinner menus that week were uninspired: quiche; *boeuf bourginon*, and from it, a *tourte bourginon*, meat pie; *endives gratinée*; and *poulet*

rôti with a few potatoes and garlic cloves tossed beside the chicken in the pan.

Cranwell never complained. At least, I don't think he did. If he did, it made no impact on me. My energies were entirely devoted to the feast. I read, tested, and tasted recipes during the day, and then I would dream about them at night.

The longer I worked on my menus, the greater my fear became. Unless they were superhuman Frenchmen, I was almost certain they wouldn't like the meal. The medieval style of eating was the polar opposite of the basic tenet of modern French cuisine: sweet and seasoned foods must never be mixed. For example, just the suggestion of the classic American peanut butter and jelly sandwich would make a French stomach churn. Baked beans would be equally as revolting. Serving bread and jam was expected at breakfast, but at dinner? — never. Most French even go so far as to ban salted butter from their tables, because the seasoning clashes with the sweet cream base. The French like sweet food, it's just that they like it confined to dessert. My medieval feast would propose that my guests intermingle sweet and seasoned foods at every course.

At that point, I made an executive decision about the third thing I would do: hang Cranwell from one of my towers by his toes.

It took effort, but I tried to remind myself that I was making this meal for Cranwell and not for his friends. I was sacrificing my better judgment for the sake of his novel. Maybe I'd get some sort of mention in the dedication.

Maybe not.

When I warned Cranwell to tell his friends not to expect great things, he just laughed at me and his friends came anyway. And by the way, Cranwell neglected to tell me that his closest friends in France were among those Frenchmen best known overseas.

"You didn't tell me *he* would be here," I hissed at him as I followed him down the stairs that Friday. The person I referred to was a well-known French actor who had starred in several of the films adapted from Cranwell's books. In fact, most of the guests were related, in some way or another, to his books.

"Had you asked, I would have told you."

An actor married to an actress. A producer and his model girlfriend. A composer, several writers, and a haute couture wardrobe designer. I had a Who's Who of the French entertainment industry gathered together in my chateau that weekend.

Cranwell had asked me to set the table for fourteen. I counted only thirteen people in total.

"Who are we missing? The Prime Minister?"

"Everyone's here."

"I only count thirteen, Cranwell. Twelve guests and yourself."

"And you."

"Me?"

"You. You're the hostess."

"No, you're the *host*. I'm your *chef*."

"Hostess. Come on, Freddie, you've worked so hard on this; enjoy it."

"Who's going to serve?"

"Séverine." He had it all figured out. He always had everything figured out.

"Cranwell, I'm the chef; that means I cook. I can't be a hostess and cook at the same time."

"I thought you'd been cooking all day."

"I have."

"So what's left to do?"

I surveyed the kitchen. "A little bit of everything. The finishing touches that have to be done at the last minute. No one wants to eat their food cold."

"I can't imagine anyone in the Middle Ages ever eating their food hot. It will be more authentic this way. Just leave a note for Séverine and tell her what needs to be done."

And if Cordon Bleu could have devised a degree by correspondence, I'm sure they would have done it by now! Frankly, I just didn't want to do it. I needed an excuse. A better excuse. I thought of Séverine and her magic charm; she should have been the one sitting at the foot of the table.

"Nonsense," Cranwell scoffed when I presented my argument. "And we can't have thirteen people at the table. It's bad luck."

Since when?

Séverine saved me by appearing in the kitchen at that moment. I explained to her the situation and suggested that she could help me best by playing hostess.

Defying all my insight into her personality, Séverine adamantly refused. At the time, it was mystifying. "But no, Frédérique. You are the *chatelaine*. Robert is correct. You must not serve. It is to me to do this."

"But — " The rest of my words refused to follow when I saw daggers she was throwing with her eyes. Threatening and dangerous were the words I would have used to describe her at that moment. And suddenly, I no longer had any interest in refusing her.

Séverine turned her back on me, took an apron from a drawer, and tied it around her waist.

At Cranwell's prompting, I wrote the notes for Séverine.

Then he spun me around, took my hand in his, and marched me up the stairs. He led me directly to my bedroom door as if, without his supervision, I might have tried to run away.

And I might have. I'll never know.

As Cranwell pushed the door shut behind me and left for his own room, panic engulfed me. Looking at my wardrobe, I realized that I had nothing to wear.

People say things like that all the time, but for me at that moment, it was the truth. I wished the clothes Cranwell had bought me would have worked, but I had the feeling they would have been too casual. I hadn't bought any new clothing for the previous three years; not since Peter had died and I had moved from Paris. To be in the presence of a collection of fashionistas, and to know that the average French woman buys thirty pounds of new clothes each year, meant catastrophe.

Not that I cared.

I must have stood in front of my armoire for at least ten minutes rationalizing why I could not be seen in any piece of clothing that I owned.

After glancing at my alarm clock, I abandoned that task and decided to direct my energies toward a shower. Fifteen minutes later I was standing in front of my mirror, towel wrapped around my body, agonizing over how to wear my hair.

There was a knock at my door.

Startled, I scampered across the floor and opened it a slit, hiding my body behind the stolid oak of the door.

Cranwell pushed past me anyway.

"Cranwell, you can't just — "

"Why aren't you dressed yet?"

"Because I have absolutely nothing to wear."

"That's ridiculous." He strode across the carpet and threw open the doors of my armoire. He shoved a few hangers back and forth before seizing on a robe of steely-blue velvet. Just seeing it brought back skin-numbing memories of the night back in October when he had nearly kissed me.

"I am not wearing my bathrobe to dinner." I tore it out of his hands and tried to replace it on its hanger. When my towel started to sag, I let the robe drop to the floor. But I did manage to glare at Cranwell while I refastened the towel around my chest.

"Why not? I need a muse."

"A muse?"

"An inspiration. It isn't enough to partake in a feast. I need to be able to imagine what the people would have looked like."

"I will not wear a bathrobe." Granted, it looked as if it had been purchased at a Renaissance costume shop. The Basque waisted skirt began well below my natural waist, in the style of late medieval fashion. The upper body was cut on the bias and it molded around my torso as if it had been tailor-made for me. In fact, I rarely used it because it hugged my body too tightly.

"Please, Freddie." Cranwell had picked the robe up and given it a shake, holding it up by the almost nonexistent shoulders. The bodice had a two-inch roll of material that framed the neckline and covered the seam of the close-fitting sleeves. "Please."

At least he had an idea. I could offer no alternative.

Shoving damp strands of hair behind my ears, I tried to hold up my towel with the other hand. "Fine."

"Wonderful!" He leapt forward as if he were going to kiss me but then held himself back and thrust the gown into my hands instead. "Give me five minutes and I'll be back to do something about your hair." He slammed my door shut behind him.

Something about my hair. Of all the nerve! I decided to take care of that possibility myself. I spent the next four minutes bent from the waist, aiming all the ferocity of a high-speed, high-heat blow dryer at it. And I finished fastening myself into the robe only seconds before Cranwell burst into my room.

30

"Don't you knock?"

"Do you have a comb?"

He took the one I offered, and then he slid a chair away from the wall and motioned for me to sit. He drew my hair up and over the back of the chair and began to comb it with gentle strokes. I closed my eyes and told myself to relax.

"You have beautiful hair, Freddie."

"Thanks." My scalp was beginning to tingle with pleasure. He followed each stroke of the comb with his hand.

After another minute, I felt him part my hair down the middle and he handed me the comb. I was disappointed he had finished so quickly. But he wasn't done with me yet.

He ran his fingers through my hair, separating the locks, and began to twist them, strand by strand, along the side of my head.

"How do you know how to do this?"

"My sister. She liked to play Maid Marian when she was little. The only way I could get her to leave me alone was to 'do her hair like a princess.'"

He twisted the other side too and then must have tied a lock of hair around the ponytail that hung down my back. He opened a sack I hadn't realized he had; it was filled with ivy.

"From the chateau walls?"

"From the chateau walls."

He tried at first to fashion a length of it into a crown, but the leaves were too large and the gaps between them too huge. He settled on pulling off leaves and pushing them into the twists of my hair.

When he was done, he took my hand, pulled me to my feet, and then stood back from me and stared. He stared for the longest time. And then he smiled.

It was a smile that made my legs turn to *gelée*.

"Go look."

As I stood in front of the bathroom mirror, I was astounded. Cranwell had transformed me from a twenty-first-century chef into a fifteenth-century lady. He was right: The bathrobe was perfect. And what he'd done with my hair reminded me of paintings I'd seen by Botticelli. I was ethereal. I was celestial, graceful. I was . . . beautiful.

Cranwell appeared beside me in the mirror.

"You are perfect, Freddie."

Looking at myself in the mirror, with him standing beside me, I believed it.

Cranwell escorted me to the top of the stairs and then offered his arm to me. It seemed natural to slip my hand around it.

I felt a muscle tighten. He hadn't struck me as muscular before, but I could tell at that moment that I'd been deceived. He was wearing a black cashmere turtleneck with a black wool sports coat. His black pants were the kind I'd always associated with the wealthy: formed of the finest, lightest wool, they were impeccably draped and held in place by a slender belt with a discreet silver buckle. His hair was slicked back, and his glasses were sliding down his nose. The glasses ruined the picture, but I knew him well enough to know that he must have been sneaking in a few extra moments of work on his manuscript before he'd come to my aid. With my other hand, I reached around and pulled them gently from his nose.

He caught my hand and brought it to his lips and kissed it. "My lady."

My cheeks grew hot. It was probably caused by the exertion of breathing after being stuffed into such a tight-fitting gown. Bathrobe.

When I lifted my eyes from my hand and glanced down the stairs, I saw all the guests gathered in the hall.

And they were staring at me.

Cranwell must have heard my indrawn breath, for his hand closed over mine and gave it a squeeze.

At the bottom of the staircase, he unwound my hand from his arm, and then drew me forward so he could place an arm about my waist. "May I present Madame Frédérique Farmer."

"*Bienvenue au Chateau de Kertanuan.*" I greeted my guests, stuck my nose into the air, and led them to the dining hall.

Cranwell's words echoed through my head all night.

You are perfect, Freddie.

ᴖᴖ

Séverine, bless her, had lit the fire, the candelabras on the table, and the sconces on the walls. Firelight illuminated our faces, softening our features and sparking our eyes. I could easily imagine myself six hundred years in the past. From the hidden CD player, Renaissance music was piping. The recorders, pipes, and drums created a festival atmosphere.

The actor and actress were very pleasant company. The model had the huge eyes and the over-awed demeanor of a kid sister. The producer said little. The wardrobe designer sent glances in my direction throughout the night. And all of them hung on Cranwell's every word. He must have told a hundred stories. He was an artist: spinning, weaving, painting with words.

Seated at the opposite end of the table from him, it seemed as if he were speaking just to me. By the end of the evening, with a full stomach and a head numbed with hippocras, I had planted my elbows on the table and propped my chin up in my hands. Cranwell had just finished telling a joke, and the other guests roared at the punch line. It had to have been past midnight, but I couldn't know for sure; I'd left my watch upstairs so it wouldn't clash with my attire.

Cranwell's eye caught mine, and he smiled the most gentle smile.

It warmed the places in me that the wine had not been able to touch. I was too tired to remember that Cranwell flirted with everyone, so my lips stretched wide before I could stop them.

Cranwell pushed his chair from the table and stood; the others followed suit. I watched, from my seat, as he walked around the table toward me.

Someone said, "*La petite a du sommeil.*" The little one is sleepy.

Had I not been so tired, I would have objected to the patronizing tone. In a daze, I removed my elbows from the table, took the hand Cranwell offered me, and followed him up the central staircase.

It was difficult to lift my feet off the floor; I was that tired. Midway up the first coil of stairs, my slowing footsteps had led to a growing gap between us.

Cranwell felt me tug at his hand. He stopped and turned around.

"I'm just so tired, Cranwell."

He descended several steps to mine and then scooped me up in his arms as easily as if I'd been a child.

"I know, Freddie."

It's possible I told Cranwell I liked him, or some other nonsense, because I know that he smiled. I felt the tightening of his cheek and then his lips against my forehead.

Then I remembered how he was. "I don't think I should trust you."

His arms tightened around me. "You would do well not to Freddie. You're much too beautiful."

He must have been mistaking me for Séverine.

Somehow he opened my door and nudged through it into my room. He set me on the bed. Before slipping out, he kissed me on top of my head.

Several long minutes passed as I sat in the darkness, rubbing that spot, wondering what he thought he was doing.

Finally I rose and got ready for bed, slipping into silk pajamas. I pulled the ivy out of my hair as I crossed the room, moving in and out of the moonlight that streamed through my slitted windows.

Then I stopped so quickly, I nearly fell.

Something was not right.

Standing in the middle of the room, in the darkness, I knew that something had changed.

After retracing my steps toward the bed, I started once more for the rug, but before I reached it, I stubbed my toe on a stone that was sticking up slightly above its neighbors.

It was the rug that was wrong. I had positioned the rug so that stone had been covered.

Someone had moved the rug.

And suddenly, being alone didn't seem like such a good idea. I turned on my lamp and took a good look at my room. Had I not noticed the rug, I might not have noticed the furniture, but as I looked around me, I realized that everything was slightly out of place. And looking inside the bathroom, I noticed several places where something sharp had left marks in gaps between the stones.

That scared me.

I did what anyone in my situation would have done. I ran out of the room.

"Come in."

At least Cranwell hadn't been sleeping. From the looks of his desk, he'd been at work on his manuscript.

"Someone has been in my room."

"What?" Cranwell looked at me over the top of his glasses.

"Someone was in my room tonight."

"Are you sure, Freddie?"

"Positive."

He went back to my room with me, keeping me always behind him.

On entering the room, Cranwell stopped by the bed. "What makes you so sure someone was here?"

"The rug. I arranged it so that the uneven spot in the floor was covered. I must have stubbed my toe on it a dozen times before I put the rug on top of it."

"Very practical."

"Cranwell—"

He held up a hand, as if to stop me. "Is that it?"

"No. All my furniture is slightly skewed. Like the bed. I had it lined up between two stones." I walked toward the bed to show him, gesturing for him to follow.

"Did you look underneath the bed?" he whispered as he approached.

"No." I whispered back.

"Why not?"

"What if someone had been there?"

"Then you would have known."

"Cranwell!"

He was laughing at me. He crouched down and looked under the bed. Then got to his feet. "Nothing."

Grabbing his arm, I drew his attention to the headboard. "See, I had it lined up between this square stone and that one." The bed was clearly off center.

"What about the other furniture?"

Touring the room, I showed him exactly where everything had been and how I'd known they had been moved. I was feeling proud of myself when Cranwell ruined it.

"That's very anal of you, Freddie."

"Anal?"

"Must everything be exactly lined up at right angles to everything else?"

"Well—"

He paced past me to examine my bathroom.

"Anything disturbed here?"

"Look at the grooves between the stones."

He put his glasses on and looked around at the walls. At the time the chateau had been built, a small spiral staircase allowed access from a corner of my bathroom to the attic. During renovation, I had it blocked. Cranwell had started halfway up the stairs. "Any reason anyone would want to go up there?"

He motioned me up and extended a hand for support. Above him, the stones blocking the access had been chipped at repeatedly.

It was menacing; I shivered.

"Would you like me to stay in your room tonight?"

"No."

"Do you want to stay in my room?"

That was exactly what I wanted. I nodded.

"I'm working. I hope the typing won't disturb you."

"I'll be fine."

We made sure the door to my room was locked, and Cranwell made a thorough search of his own room when we got back. I stood on the area rug beside his bed hugging myself and trying my best to keep my feet warm. I hate cold feet. They bring back bad memories.

His search done, Cranwell pulled the covers back from the bed. I didn't need another invitation. I scampered in. Cranwell was offering me what I wanted the most: safety. I doubt if I could have slept as soundly if he hadn't stayed up all night typing. The sound of his fingers tap-dancing across the keyboard assured me of a human in proximity. Of a friend.

Once, in the darkness of my dreams, I found myself fighting with an unknown assailant. An assailant with a heavy crowbar. I must have cried out, because I thought, for a moment, that Cranwell sat beside me, smoothing my hair across the pillow, whispering soothing words. But then sleep claimed me, and I remembered nothing, but a phrase. It echoed through my head all night.

You are perfect, Freddie.

31

I began to come awake in small degrees of consciousness from a pleasant dream. Luxuriously I stretched. It was warm in bed. Sighing, I nestled more deeply into the warmth. Sliding my hips toward it, and burrowing my back into it. And I breathed deeply, drifting back into sleep.

In my next dream, an arm reached out from my memory and held me close. Somewhere in the darkness, I found Peter's lips and began to kiss them. My fingers remembered the path up his neck and behind his ears to his beautiful blond hair, and they wove their way through it. I traced the line of his familiar jaw, ran a finger over his eyebrow. Then I recalled that there was something I needed to tell him. I needed to tell him that I was sorry. And then I was overcome with guilt. And the guilt is what wrenched me away from my dream and abandoned me in reality.

Of course, it wasn't Peter at all. It was Cranwell. He was lying on the bed, on top of the duvet, like a true gentleman. And I was lying on top of him, kissing him. Just like one of his actresses or models.

At that moment, Cranwell woke up. I saw his eyes flare in surprise and then melt into glowing pools of amber. He whispered my name.

I began to sob.

At that instant all I really wanted was to be taken into those strong arms. And I wanted him to make the awful guilt go away.

But he searched my eyes, and as I looked into them, I could see them cloud with confusion.

Leaving him there in his bed, I ran up the stairs to my room. It was only when I put my hand to the door to open it that I realized the key was down in Cranwell's room.

Banging on the door with my fist didn't yield any results, so I leaned my head against it and cried. I cried for Peter. For the fact that he was probably living in eternal hell. For the fact that I could have told him at any time about having a relationship with Christ, about believing in God. But I didn't. I let his claims of being an atheist go unchallenged. I gave up my relationship with God for a relationship with a man. Cranwell was right: Of course I believed in God. I just hadn't been able to get past my guilt. I was too ashamed to face Him.

I cried from frustration. As I wept, I was filled with a loneliness that for months I had held at bay, hoping secretly that Cranwell would provide the cure.

I cried from shame. I couldn't believe I'd been making out with Cranwell. Throwing myself at him in his own bed. Those tears, the tears shed in humiliation, were the worst.

Cranwell must have come up the stairs silently, for suddenly he was beside me. At least he had sense enough not to touch me. He simply turned the key in the lock and pushed open the door, leaving me to find my own way inside.

I took my time showering. I had to think. When I went downstairs I would run into Cranwell, and I had to decide right then what I would do. I couldn't just pretend things were normal. My actions had changed everything. I couldn't imagine sitting down to breakfast and dinner with him as we'd been doing for the past six months. How could I bring myself to look him in the eye?

But then, he'd probably had women throw themselves at him all the time. How could my actions have been any worse? He was probably used to dealing with women like me. *Like me!* How could I have turned into a woman like that! Maybe the only thing *to* do was pretend like things were normal.

My guests solved my problem for me. There was always something that had to be done or someone, other than Cranwell, to talk to. Of course, whenever I came within proximity, I spoke to him just so he would know that as far as I was concerned, nothing had happened. But where before I could read his eyes, now they were blank.

At least they were when he looked at me.

I knew if I could just survive until Cranwell finished his novel, then he would be gone, and my life would be my own again.

I would survive if it killed me.

Everyone left on Sunday evening. I don't know why. From experience, I knew that traffic surrounding Paris on Sundays was horrible from 3:00 in the afternoon until 10:00 at night. But maybe sitting in a Lamborghini or a Ferrari was pleasurable whether the wheels were turning or not.

Cranwell was late in coming downstairs for dinner. From the sound of their footsteps, both he and Lucy seemed subdued, as if each step on the stairway was leading them one step nearer to doom. I already had a piece of *flamiche aux poireaux* cut for both of us and waiting on the island. In spite of my knotted stomach, I was looking forward to the creamy leek pie. The only thing I hadn't done was pour the wine. I hadn't done it because that was Cranwell's job.

He paused at the bottom stair, his forest green crewneck and dark gray slacks blending into the shadows. When he looked at the island, his face registered surprise. He queried me with his eyes.

"If you'd like to open the wine, then we can eat before it gets cold."

Lucy let out a great sigh, which managed to lighten the air around us. We both smiled as we watched her settle herself on the floor. I was still smiling when I looked up to find him watching me.

Grabbing the corkscrew, I handed it to him, and then we settled on our stools to eat.

For the first time, there seemed to be nothing to talk about. Fear washed over me. It wasn't going to work. Beginning to feel more and more self-conscious, it seemed like the sound of my chewing and swallowing had been magnified over a loudspeaker.

"Cranwell—"

"Freddie—"

We had spoken at the same moment, so we laughed, embarrassed.

"You first." He was insistent.

I'd completely forgotten what inane thing it was that I was going to say. So I took a deep breath. And staring hard at my plate, I said the first thing that popped into my mouth. "About yesterday morning."

In my peripheral vision, I saw Cranwell freeze.

"I'm sorry. I had a dream." That sounded lame, even to my own ears.

"Peter?"

I nodded.

"I guess it's never easy competing with a ghost."

"I'm . . . well . . . attracted to you." It was the truth. My cheeks flamed as I said this, but I tried to ignore them and kept on speaking. "You told me once that I needed to move on. That I had to get over Peter. And I am. I'm trying. It's just that I've known about God since I was three years old. I always went to church, before I went to college. I knew everything there was to know about God, Cranwell, but I never told any of it to Peter. If he's in hell right now, it's all my fault."

He bowed his head at that point and was still for several moments before he spoke.

"Freddie, it's not your fault."

"It is."

He raised his brown eyes to mine. "Wait. Just listen for a second. It seems to me that everyone is responsible to God for the state of their own soul. He's left it up to each individual to make a choice — for themselves. Maybe Peter would have become a believer if you had talked to him, or maybe he wouldn't have. Sometimes people won't listen to those closest to them. Sometimes they need a stranger to tell them. Sometimes they don't need words at all. God doesn't need anybody to tell others about Him; He's arranged the world itself to be His testimony. Let Peter go, Freddie. If there's anything I've learned in the past year, it's that no matter how much you wish, you can never change the past. The only thing you can do is change the present."

He reached for my hand and took it in his. "Please don't be embarrassed about yesterday. I wish I *had* been the object of your affection. I've never met anyone like you, Freddie. And I don't think I ever will again."

The corner of my mouth turned up in the start of a smile. "Thank God."

Cranwell began to smile too. "Thank God."

He lifted his glass. "To us."

I clinked it with mine. "To friendship."

Something close to gratitude passed between us after that as we sat and ate. What we had said to each other would never be said again, but it had made that morning romp a squall passing through our relationship rather than a hurricane stalling over it. And after that, there were a million things to talk about.

In hindsight, I was glad I'd had the courage to say what I did. I would have missed the companionship had I sent him upstairs.

Several hours later, he left with Lucy to return to his room. He stopped on the first stair and turned around to face me. "Freddie —"

I held my breath.

"Thank you."

Bringing the dishes to the sink, I washed them with shaking hands. Then I went up to my lounge and spent most of the night going over grant applications for the foundation.

⚜

"Let me help you."

I peered between my legs.

Cranwell was standing on the garden path, so I stood up for a stretch. Planting gardens made for backbreaking work. I put my hand to my lower back and arched my spine, trying to pull the kinks from it.

"What can I do?"

He was standing there in his suede leather jacket, Italian leather loafers, and brown moleskin trousers. I tossed my braid behind my shoulder and pulled my hat farther over my ears. "Unless you want to ruin your shoes and permanently stain your pants, I'd just stay right where you are."

He looked down toward his feet. "These? They only cost two hundred dollars." He stepped carefully into the plot and made his way toward me.

Lucy, disdaining the dirt, found a comfortable flagstone and curled herself upon it.

Unbuttoning my brick-colored corduroy jacket, I tossed it to him, and then I pushed up the long sleeves of my thermal shirt. Looking down, I saw that my faded jeans were already stained with dirt, along the hems and the knees. They'd wash. I tried to think of something that Cranwell could do that would keep him from becoming too soiled. I finally decided he could follow behind me, sprinkling seeds into the holes I'd dug.

We worked for a good hour and a half before I declared that it was time to stop. I put my jacket back on, becoming cold after the sudden halt to our labor.

We returned the tools to the garage and walked together back to the kitchen where we perched ourselves on stools.

"Would you mind just giving my back a little push, right there?" I pointed to a place near my spine on my lower back where my muscles had spasmed.

"Where?"

Pulling up the back of my jacket, I pointed.

He put a hand on my shoulder and the other to my spine, grinding a knuckle into my muscle. "Too hard?"

"Not hard enough."

Cranwell took his hand from my shoulder and reached it around my rib cage to support the pounding he was giving my back. "Better?"

"Yes."

He moved up my spine slowly, pushing first with his fist, then with his knuckles and fingers. His hand at my rib cage splayed to keep me from being pushed over by his efforts.

He happened onto a knot.

I cringed.

"Does that hurt?"

"Like torture."

Using a thumb, he tried to relax the spot. It refused to loosen. "Just a second." He lifted the hem of my shirt and slid his hand up against my skin.

The effect was electric.

A tingle went from my scalp to my toes, leaving my senses heightened in its wake. His massage slowed.

The room was growing warm. My clothes were stifling. There was a buzzing in my ears. Without asking my permission, I felt my body lean into his.

His breathing fanned my hair. And then stopped.

Then, at an instant, as if a bomb had exploded between us, we hurled ourselves away from each other.

"Thanks, Cranwell. Perfect." I bent at my waist to the right and left to demonstrate my newfound mobility. "Wonderful. Thanks a lot. That was nice of you." I sprinted toward the stairs. "I'll see you at dinner."

As I zipped up the stairs and past the entry hall it occurred to me that this was the first time I had ever run away from my own kitchen. The kitchen was *my* refuge.

Slowing to a walk, I then stopped altogether. It wasn't right that I should be run out of my own kitchen.

Reversing directions, I descended the stairs, determined to face the situation between us.

As I reached the bottom of the stairwell, I saw Cranwell was still there. He was seated at the island. He had stretched his upper body across the marble countertop, arms bent and his hands clasped over his head. It was a position of utter defeat or extreme pain.

Not wanting to startle him, I cleared my throat.

He scraped himself off the marble and turned on his stool to face me.

I'd never seen him look so haggard.

He pushed off the stool and walked with wooden legs toward the stairs, Lucy following behind.

"See you at dinner."

"No." He didn't even turn to look at me. "Not tonight, Freddie. I just can't do it."

I sat on his abandoned stool and stayed there for a long while. When I got up, I revised the evening's menu. The pork cutlets I had intended for dinner, I put in the fridge; they would keep for the next evening. Two of the *île flottantes*, I poured down the sink, using hot water to melt them; I set one aside for Séverine. There was no point in saving the others; the meringue dessert wouldn't last through the night. And at that moment, I wasn't hungry for dessert. In fact, I was hardly hungry at all.

A humble dinner of a salad, a ham and gruyère *crêpe*, and a small bottle of *cidre* sufficed. I tried, while I was eating, to remember what I had done at dinner before Cranwell had shown up at my chateau.

I couldn't remember.

nine days before Saint Simon

I am stupid. In the wonder of what has happened, I understand everything now. I know why Agnès has not liked Anne. I realize why Anne is by times so kind and then so cruel.

Awen and Anne are lovers.

I do not know what to do. Do I want a husband more than I need my friend? What should I do in this strange country without her? And how should I manage the chateau?

I must speak to Agnès. She is the only one I can trust.

My friend the most close is the lover of my husband and has been these three years.

❧

I have spoken with Agnès.

Agnès demanded of me if I had become a wife.

I did not understand. Of course, yes. Three years since. And she had been at the noces.

She took me toward the window and then sat me down. She demanded of me to tell her exactly what happens at night when Awen comes. She warned me to speak to her the exact truth.

So I did.

She kept demanding of me if there was nothing else, but there is not.

What more could I reply to her than this: he speaks to me of stories until I fall asleep and then stays until the fire goes out. At least he did until more recently.

She told me then what a man does to a woman to make her his wife. That I had choices and I must make a decision. If I tell father what has happened, Agnès says me that I do not have to be married to Awen any longer and that I can go back to my country, Touraine. She says me that the church will annul the marriage.

She says me that I could continue here and leave things the way they always have been. She says me that it is not uncommon for a man to have a maîtresse and that this is not the worst of things.

Or she told me that I had the right to demand Awen as a husband. And as his wife, I had the right to send Anne away.

I must think.

I must pray for to be wise.

eight days before Saint Simon

He came to me this night, but I did not open the door to him.

six days before Saint Simon

If I were a crazed creature before, I now feel as shriveled inside as a prune. If I go home, father will find for me another husband, I am certain. But would this new husband please me?

four days before Saint Simon

He came to me this night, but I did not open the door to him.

three days before Saint Simon

I cannot go on as if I understand nothing.

two days before Saint Simon

He came to me this night, but I did not open the door to him.

one day before Saint Simon

Do I want a husband? Must I have one? If only I could live alone. But I cannot. I am much too valuable. If I return to home, if the marriage is annulled, I would be fiancéed within one month.

How much more easy it would be to just leave things as they are. And pretend as if I understand nothing.

day of Saint Simon

He came to me this night, but I did not open the door to him.

one day after Saint Simon

By times, I truly hate him.

I cannot have him as my husband and leave him also Anne. I would never have any confidence. I would never have my own life. It would always be shared. With her. In addition, it is me the wife. It is mine the marriage. If there remains something which can be blessed by God, it is my life and my marriage, and none belonging to Anne. It is she the penitent and me the righteous.

Anne must go.

two days after Saint Simon

He came to me this night. I unbolted the door to him, and then walked toward the fire. My soul sought all the warmth it could find.

He pushed the door open and stood in the doorway, searching my eyes.

I turned away from him, back toward the fire.

He closed the door and came to me.

I backed away from him, toward the windows, as he advanced until I discovered my back was against the wall.

I warned him not to come near.

He would not stop.

I touched the cool stones and felt their strength.

He stopped just in front of me.

I took my hand from the wall and slapped him across the face.

He spoke no words, but drew me into his arms.

Women are weak, for I could not save myself. I wept. But I would not be held. I broke from his arms and he let me. I went to stand in front of the fire and he let me. But he stood behind me and placed his hands on my shoulders.

I closed my eyes and tears fell from them. I wept for all the sweetness and trust which had gone from us. I could now never maintain my honor. I felt stupid. Bête. For Anne had done the thing with him that I do not. Since three years.

I told him he had made me so happy I thought my heart would burst of it. And he had made me so sad I thought my heart would die of it. I told him all this and had no strength left. No strength to cry, no strength to stand.

I shook off his hands from my shoulders and placed myself by ground on the fur in front of the fire. I wanted only to be alone.

But he would not leave. I heard him sit behind me, but he did not touch me, not for the time it takes to repeat ten Ave Marias.

Then he put a hand to my hair and ran it all the length.

I had tired of tears. He must have known it, for when I moved, he let me curl in toward him, like a dog, and rest my head on his thigh. He stroked still my hair and I closed my eyes to listen to the fire snap.

He explained to me that he had loved Anne when he had seen her the first time. And she him. And because their bloodlines were so close, they knew they could never be married. And when first he had seen me, I seemed to him the same as his sister. And thinking of her, he could not be a husband to me. And these three years, I had become grown and he found that he had grown to love me. And the night I had seen Anne go to him was the last they had spent together.

I told him, with my eyes closed still and my head against his thigh, that she must go. That my father had found for her a chevalier possessed of a good property and age. I told him if he wanted me, I would have him in whole, but not in part.

He made no reply, but stroked still my hair. And with the heat of the fire and the feel of his hand, I found sleep there on his thigh, although when I woke, we were in bed, together. He heard me stir and placed his arm around me. I came close to his warm body and slept still more.

mars

Malgré le mauvais temps,
mars prépare en secret le printemps.

March

In spite of bad weather,
March prepares in secret for spring.

33

All havoc broke loose in March.

It began, innocuously enough, with a visit from my contractor.

When I'd first purchased the chateau, his name was given to me by the real estate agent as an expert in historical renovation. The chateau had been vacant for years before I purchased it, and the last "renovation" had been done in the 1920s. It had taken weeks to get an appointment with him, but as soon as he stepped in the front door, I knew he'd been worth the wait. He spent the entire day crawling over the chateau and the grounds, tapping at windows, knocking on wood, chipping at masonry, and scribbling comments in his notebook. At the end of the day, dust and cobwebs obscured his thinning blond hair, and dirt was caked into the wrinkles of his fifty-year-old face, but his blue eyes were twinkling, and his head nodding in an ever-more-confident cadence. He told me he'd be back the next weekend with some plans and an estimate.

I drove back to Paris right after he left and waited that next week with trepidation, having no idea the cost of such an undertaking.

The next week, we met again at the chateau. Thankfully, M. Mailly was convinced the chateau was structurally sound. His main concerns were updating the wiring and the plumbing. Fortunately, the former owners hadn't done much besides install "modern" bathrooms and a kitchen, phone lines, and electricity. At least I would not have to undo anything they had done. We talked, at the time, about the stable. He commented that at a minimum, it needed reroofing, and to convert it into any sort of living quarters would require doing everything. I had decided to use it as a garage while I pondered what should be done with it. M. Mailly had many ideas: a restaurant, groundskeeper's quarters, a conference hall, an interpretive center, luxury suite accommodations. I was hesitant to pour more money into the estate than was absolutely needed . . . especially when I wasn't sure how business would be.

There was no doubt in my mind, however, about letting him manage the renovation of the chateau. I was even able to convince him to let me be the on-site supervisor. After that meeting, I returned to Paris, put in my notice with my landlord, and packed up and moved into a small room in the chateau.

It had been fascinating to watch M. Mailly's subcontractors dismantel centuries-old walls and ceilings, perform their work, and then erase the evidence of their tampering. As the work came to an end, I agreed to call M. Mailly when I was ready to work on the stable and talk about creating a formal garden out in front.

Considering the number of guests I turned away, I decided that moment had arrived. My flow of revenue could only increase. And Cranwell was right, I needed to join the land of the living.

M. Mailly appeared exactly at 9:00 a.m. that morning. I'd just had time to change out of my working clothes and into slim black pants and a cadet blue spread-collar long-sleeved shirt. I tied a colorful scarf around my neck and drew on a short-waisted tailored black blazer. If we spent any time outside, as I expected, I wanted to be warm.

I met the contractor at the door and offered him an espresso.

He looked as if he was going to turn me down, but then he surprised me by accepting. After installing him on the settee in the reception hall, I went downstairs to fix a tray.

Cranwell and Lucy were there, just back from a stroll. He had already peeled off his barn jacket.

"Anything I can do to help you?"

"No. Thanks. I have a meeting with my contractor."

"For what?"

It was on the tip of my tongue to say, "Contracting," but then I thought better of it. "I'd like him to begin work on the stable."

By that time, I'd started the espresso-maker, so I began putting together a tray of sugar and spoons. When I turned my attention back to the espresso, Cranwell and Lucy had gone.

Upon entering the reception hall, I found M. Mailly investigating one of the fireplaces, mumbling.

"*Quelque chose qui ne va pas?*"

"*Non. Du tout. C'est superbe ce travail.*"

Thank goodness! I was afraid that he'd discovered some flaw in the mantel. A mantel I'd paid 7,000 euros to have restored.

We stood at the *dressoir*, sipping espresso and looking at M. Mailly's previous recommendations for the stable. I was especially interested in how it might be turned into a private suite. Cranwell's stay had made me realize the value in having quarters that would accommodate a long-term visitor more privately. The contractor had also brought plans for a garden. Though I wasn't interested in landscaping yet, it cost nothing for me to listen to his enthusiastic sales pitch. At the end of his spiel, I shrugged and suggested we take a look at the stable.

When we approached, I was surprised to find Cranwell and Lucy waiting for us.

"I thought you just took a walk."

"We did." Cranwell refused to elaborate on the subject and didn't appear as if he were leaving anytime soon, so I introduced him to M. Mailly. Never having had the need to speak with the contractor in English, I was surprised at his fluency when Cranwell engaged him in conversation. Apparently, Cranwell's profession wouldn't allow him to pass up the opportunity to consult an expert on historical buildings. I didn't mind sharing my contacts, of course, but I did get impatient when, after half an hour, we were no nearer the topic of my plans for the stable.

"*Excusez-moi de vous deranger . . .* " I interrupted the men as politely as I could, and then I took M. Mailly by the arm and steered him inside. My relationship with the contractor had been established in French, and despite Cranwell's presence, it seemed somehow artificial to me to conduct our business in English.

M. Mailly wanted to reinspect the building. To think of a French stable as a barn would be incorrect. The two buildings have always served very different purposes. This stable was not original to the estate, but dated from the late 1600s. As such, it displayed the characteristics of the period; of stone construction, the one-story building had a rather large entry area, for storing conveyances, and one long, wide central hall, lined on both sides with stables. Each stable had a door on the wall that opened to the outside. The floor was pieced of stone cobbles which could be easily cleaned with a wash of water. It still smelled musty from generations of straw and excrement that had been ground between the stones.

Cranwell and Lucy accompanied M. Mailly and me on our investigation. Several times, I saw the contractor frown as he tapped on a wooden door or glanced up to see light filter through the roof. At last he finished his prowling and we stepped outside to talk.

"*Le problème est que c'est une écurie.*" He glanced at Cranwell as he said this and stopped to repeat it in English. "The problem is that this is a stable. One has gaps in the stones. One has holes in the roofs. One has doors which do not fit correctly."

"*Mais c'est peut-être . . .* it is perhaps less difficult to convert because one must tear down for that we can build up. And this is easy to tear down."

M. Mailly and I spent a good hour talking about the feasibility of my plans. And all that time, Cranwell refused to leave. I finally ignored him and tried to help M. Mailly do the same by keeping the conversation in French. It would have taken twice as long to translate every phrase into English. And besides, Cranwell had no stake in the matter.

It was decided that M. Mailly would contract an architect to draw plans for splitting the stable into a garage and a residence. He thought that the beamed ceilings could stay and that the stone pavers could be removed, the ground cleaned and leveled and the pavers replaced in a concrete foundation. He warned that the walls would need insulation and more windows would need to be added — at least in the residence area. I agreed with all of those suggestions. I did, however, want to keep as many of the doors as possible.

The contractor asked if he could check the attic in the chateau. I remembered that during renovations, he was concerned that there might be leakage in the roof if work was not properly done in the varied angles around the towers. Although we'd blocked access to the attic in my bathroom, we'd decided to install a door in Séverine's bathroom that would allow direct inlet to the area which had most concerned M. Mailly.

As we walked back to the chateau, I recalled that Séverine was in Rennes, working at the University. I grabbed the master key and led

M. Mailly up the central stairs to her bedroom. I had misgivings about going into her apartment without her knowledge, but I decided I could let her know later that evening. It wasn't as if we were being deliberately nosy.

Walking into the apartment felt like walking into another world. I had decorated my chateau in period furnishings from different eras in French history. Séverine had decorated her space much as I imagine it would have looked in Alix's time. There were several oriental rugs hung on the walls, there was a fur on the floor in front of the fireplace. She'd hung blueberry-colored drapes around her bed to match the duvet. The only thing marring the illusion was her study area. It was barricaded by piles of books, most of which looked to be about the legend of King Arthur. Fixed to the walls were charts, maps, and drawings in a handful of different languages. Some were on gemstones, others seemed as if they detailed foreign alphabets. Another was a map of the Forêt de Paimpont, punctured with a scattering of map pins. I'd thought she was researching Alix. King Arthur, if he'd ever lived at all, had died centuries before. While I was extremely impressed with the depth of her research, I decided not to mention our foray into her room.

M. Mailly crawled around in the attic for a quarter of an hour before reporting that he was satisfied with the condition of the roof.

He left around 1:00 p.m. Just in time for Cranwell and I to have lunch. I made it easy on myself and served *croque-monsieur* sandwiches and a tossed salad with mustard vinaigrette.

After discussing the latest draft of Cranwell's manuscript, he asked me about M. Mailly. "He seemed very competent."

"He's the best. At least in this part of France."

"So what did he say?"

"He's going to have an architect draw plans for making part of the stable a residence and leaving part of it as a garage."

"Practical."

"I think so. The next time someone like you comes, they can have the whole place to themselves."

"Do I bother you that much?"

"No! It's just that I was thinking you — or someone like you — could get more work done if you had your own space."

Cranwell shrugged and picked up his *croque-monsieur*. "I've never seen you speak French before. You're fluent."

"I've had lots of lessons. And my grandmother was French."

"You become a different person when you speak it. You hold yourself differently, your tone is different. Even your lips move differently."

"Different how?"

"More confident. More secure."

"It was business. And the French use muscles differently when they talk. If you look at older French women, they have a lot of wrinkles between their nose and their lips. American women wrinkle more toward the corners of the mouth." I had noticed myself doing this a lot lately: contributing my observations to Cranwell's pool of general knowledge.

We ate in silence for a minute before Cranwell spoke again. "Maybe you should make that stable into a manager's apartment."

"Why? I like my room just fine."

"Not for you. For a professional hotel manager. You could hire someone to run this for you. It would give you freedom. I'm sure it would get you more business."

"But then what would *I* do?"

"Whatever you wanted."

At that point, the chateau was my life. I couldn't imagine what I would do without cooking, without keeping it for guests, even when I didn't especially want them. Some people dream of a life of leisure. I was not one of them. The prospect of a calendar filled with long blank days filled me with dread.

They were what I had left Paris to escape.

⁂

The beginning of the end came the following Wednesday. The weather was nasty. We had news of an unusually strong wind that would blow a storm in from the sea that night. It was one of Séverine's days at the University and as I thought, that afternoon, of her long drive back to the chateau, I began to worry about her. The road from Rennes wound through the countryside, and while not normally dangerous, it could easily become treacherous in a strong wind and driving rain.

The only thing I could do was to call her and tell her to stay in Rennes, but first, I had to find her number.

After having spoken to at least four unhelpful phone operators, I was finally transferred to the University switchboard, at which point I was passed to the Department of Celtic Studies.

When I asked for Séverine, there was a long silence from the woman on the end of the line.

She transferred me to the head of the department.

"*M. Dubois à l'appareil. Je peux vous aider?*"

"*Bonjour, Monsieur Dubois. Ici Mme Farmer. Je cherche Séverine Dupont.*" M. Dubois and I had met when I had given Alix's books and journals to the University. He was a scholarly gentleman of about seventy years and had held his place on the faculty for at least half of his life.

"*Ça fait longtemps qu'on n'a pas parlé. Et vous cherchez Mlle Dupont. Pour quel raison?*"

I explained about the coming storm and how I just wanted to tell her to stay put.

"*Mais, elle ne travail plus ici depuis six mois.*"

It sounded as if he had said she hadn't worked there for at least six months. That would have been shortly after she started living with me.

"*Exactement, madame.*"

After hanging up the phone, I felt rather unsettled. Séverine had been working on her PhD, but her behavior had become erratic and she had been asked to leave. About six months previously. If she was not working on research, then why was she still living with me? From the looks of her bedroom, she was obviously still hard at work on something. And according to M. Dubois, it wasn't on Alix.

There were a thousand questions I would have asked M. Dubois if only I hadn't hung up the phone.

I sat for a long while, marshalling the facts I knew about Séverine. They were actually very few in number. I culled my mind for memories of my interactions with her. Generally she was a sincere, honest person. Except for the time when she lied about the butter. Usually she was very dependable. Except when she disappeared in a hurry the week that I hosted the conference. And she seemed lucid except when she'd told me about her father and when she'd been so strange the night of the wedding feast. Those daggers in her eyes still gave me the shivers, though I hadn't seen any more of them.

And that got me to thinking about sharp pointy objects. Like dinner knives, and whatever had dug into the mortar in my bathroom. And the long object that Sévérine had concealed behind her back the night of the first frost. What *had* she been doing outside that night? Lucy had barked as if there had been an intruder in the woods.

For that matter, Lucy had never liked Sévérine.

There was a stirring on the staircase and I jumped. My eyes searched the darkness of the stairwell and came to rest on a familiar figure. Lucy. And behind her, Cranwell.

Cranwell, who had been sleeping with Sévérine. Cranwell, who always seemed to be watching me. Cranwell, who had the ability to appear noiselessly at my side. What exactly was Cranwell doing with Sévérine? Were they working together on some . . . scheme?

"What do you know about Sévérine?"

He shrugged. "Not much more than you do."

"Why did you come here?"

"To write my book. Freddie, what is this about?"

"What is your relationship with Sévérine? If you don't tell me, I'm calling the *gêndarmes*." I put a hand on the phone.

"Freddie, the first time I met Sévérine was the day I came here. You know that. What's wrong?"

Outside, thunder cracked and bushes strained to rake the windows. I felt like I was trapped in a B-grade horror movie.

"Cranwell, I'm only going to ask you this one more time. What is your relationship with Sévérine?"

"I don't have one other than our interest in the journals."

I knew for a fact that wasn't true. "You've been watching me."

"Of course I've been watching you. I find you incredibly attractive."

"Then why have I seen Sévérine come out of your room in the morning?"

Suddenly, he didn't seem so composed. "Sévérine? How did—? I swear to you, Freddie, it was not the way it looked. I swear it. Can you tell me what's going on?"

At that moment, the lights flickered once and then were gone. The power was out.

"Cranwell, if you move, so help me . . . "

"I'm not coming anywhere near you. Trust me, Freddie."

Lucy sighed in the darkness. I felt a sudden pang of guilt, knowing that it was her dinner time.

Lightning flashed, illuminating Cranwell's face. True to his word, he hadn't moved any closer. He had found the last step and sat on it. There was nothing of a monster in his face, just an easily read confusion.

So I made a decision.

34

I decided to tell him everything I knew. "Sévérine was kicked out of the university. About six months ago." I watched Cranwell's face as I talked, and I could tell that this information surprised him.

"For what?"

"Her department head called it 'bizarre behavior.'"

"And you just found out?"

"About three minutes before you came downstairs."

"Did you ever talk to her about her work at the university? Did she openly lie to you about being a student there?"

That made me think. "On her 'university days' like today, I've always said, 'Have a safe trip into town,' or something like that, but she's never corrected me. I don't think she's ever lied to me either."

"What was your employment agreement with her?"

"It didn't hinge on her studies. It was free room and board in exchange for help with the guests. We didn't even have a contract. Do you think she's dangerous?"

"I don't think so. It might be nothing, Freddie. It's possible she was just embarrassed to tell you."

"But why would she still be here?"

"Maybe she hasn't found another job yet; she might not be in a position to finance a move."

"Then where does she go on her 'university days'?"

"I don't know."

We stared at each other through the flashes of lightning.

"Can I get up off this step? It's killing my back."

"Of course. I'm sorry. I just . . . I didn't know what to think. And I'd seen you and Séverine together . . . I saw her come out of your room."

"Freddie, do you know what the odds were in seeing us that one night in my entire stay here? I swear to you that — " He'd started to place his hands on my arms, but then he read the warning in my eyes and dropped them. "Never mind." He reached his arms up behind him, lacing his fingers together at the back of his head, and sighed. Then he released them, running a hand through his hair, and finally folded his arms in front of him.

Those arms. Those arms I had been surprised were so strong. Strong, but dangerous. I shivered. Then everything began to come together.

"Cranwell. The night of the feast. Séverine was the only one who wasn't at the table. She had to have been the one in my room."

"You can't know that. She was in the kitchen all night. Anyone could have prowled around without her knowledge. And the rest of us were in the dining hall."

"And during the *Journées de Patrimoine*, she was the only one on the second and third floors. And she was probably the one who jumbled up my fruit boxes."

"What proof do you have?"

"I don't need any, Cranwell. I just know." I had no doubt that it was Séverine. She was searching for something. The question was, for what?

"What are you going to do?"

"Do you think she's dangerous?" I was still trying to make sense of M. Dubois' information, still trying to redraw my image of Séverine.

Cranwell shrugged. "I think she's been dishonest, but I don't think she'd harm you."

"But what's she looking for?"

"It's got to be something to do with Alix."

"But what if it isn't?" I might have thought so too, but I had seen her room. And aside from decoration, nothing in it had indicated to me that she had any interest in Alix.

"What are you thinking?"

I didn't know. I just knew Alix no longer made sense.

Cranwell began to pace. "Let's think about where she's been looking."

"Outside. Inside. In the kitchen, my room . . . maybe even your room?"

"So it can't be anything very big if she thinks she could find it in our rooms. Everything's been constructed of stone."

"And most of the walls were torn down and put back together. During renovations."

Cranwell's eyes fixed on mine. "Does she know that?"

I shrugged.

"Is there anything — any room, any area — that wasn't renovated?"

I started to say no, but then stopped myself. "The attics. They were reroofed and wires were run up through the floors, but that was it."

"Any other rooms?"

"They didn't touch the cellar, except for stringing wires along the ceiling."

Cranwell sat for a long while, gazing into space. "How about the floors?"

"Every floor was renovated. All the rooms were redone."

"But the actual flooring?"

"I never touched it. It's all stone."

He leapt to his feet, grabbed my hand, and ran me up the back stairs to my room. He opened the door, walked to the rug, and began rolling it up.

I bent to help him.

"Where's that stone?"

"Which stone?" The whole room was made of stone.

"The one you said you trip on."

I scanned the floor looking for it, but couldn't pick it out from its neighbors. The light was dim — the storm had taken care of that. And the stone had never stuck up very far. Just enough for me to notice that it wasn't flush with its surroundings.

"Which one?"

"I don't know. Just a second." I walked over to my bed and then turned around. Started walking as if I were headed toward the bathroom. But I didn't feel anything. I went back to the bed, took my shoes off, and did it again. Still nothing.

Cranwell was kneeling now, his head against the floor, arm stretched out in front of him, sweeping back and forth across the stones. "Try it again."

"I can't. You're in my way. And you're making me nervous."

He rose to his feet, crossed his arms.

I tried one last time. And just at the point when I thought for sure I'd missed again, I felt it. I didn't dare pick my foot up for fear of losing the spot. "It's right here."

"There?"

"Right under my foot."

He knelt beside my foot, put a hand around it.

I bent to place a hand on his neck for balance.

"Don't move."

"I'm trying not to."

He slid my foot back and placed his hand where it had been.

I straightened, my eyes focused on the stone.

Cranwell was probing the edges with his fingers. "I need something with a sharp edge. And a flashlight."

I wished Séverine were there. We could have asked to borrow whatever she'd been using to gouge around my chateau. "I'll be right back." I ran straight down to the kitchen and grabbed an arsenal of sharp pointed implements: knives, scissors, an ice pick, and a cleaver. Pulled a flashlight from my desk drawer. Ran back to my room. I laid them all on the floor in front of Cranwell.

While I held the flashlight, the scissors and knives cleared centuries of dirt from the stone's edges. The ice pick, used as a lever, loosed it from its place. I held my breath as Cranwell wrestled it from the hole. At the bottom, covered in dust, was a slim rod.

Cranwell fished it out, blew the dust from it. Then laid it on the floor beside the stone.

He turned the stone over, bent closer to look at the underside. It had been carved. Not much. But enough that the rod had not been crushed.

I picked it up. It was lightweight. It was plain, except that there was a design along one end. Some markings and a ring of jewels along the top. I had just held it closer toward the flashlight when I realized that Cranwell and I were not alone. "Séverine."

Cranwell turned around. Scrambled to his feet.

Séverine left the doorway and walked toward us, shrouded in

shadows. She stopped in front of the hole in the floor. Her gaze never left the rod in my hand.

I tightened my hold on it. Lowered my arm and brought it close to my body.

"That is mine. I have been searching for this. Thank you, Frédérique, for finding it." She held out her hand toward me.

So compelling was her demeanor that I found myself stretching toward her, holding out the rod.

Cranwell's hand grasped my forearm, pulled me up from the floor. When I was standing, he stepped in front of me. "It belongs to Freddie."

"It belonged to Alix. It was from her mother. If you give this to me, I will put it in the body of research with all the other artifacts."

I stepped out from behind Cranwell. "At the University of Rennes?"

She didn't even blink. "Of course."

"I talked with M. Dubois this afternoon. He asked you to leave. Six months ago."

"But you see, it means nothing. Still I searched and look what I have found." She smiled. "Now they will beg me to return."

"Why didn't you tell me they had asked you to leave?"

"Access to the journals is sometimes only granted to thésardes and professeurs. It was me the expert on Alix. And they wanted to give the journals to someone else to work on. I was angry. And why did I not tell you? Why did you need to know? I had to stay here. I knew what I would find in this chateau. I had only to search it."

"But I looked on you as a friend."

"You looked on me as your door against the world. I used you. You used me."

Cranwell stepped beside me, as if to offer support.

"*Et vous, Robert?* All I ever hear from you is Freddie. Freddie think this and Freddie do that. I am sick in the stomach of Freddie. I will only ask this one time more: Give it to me."

"It's not yours to have." I placed it behind my back.

"I must have this."

Cranwell stepped in front of me again. If we kept this up, sooner or later, we'd both be standing in the hole. "It's not yours to keep."

"I must have it. You know what this is? It is a scroll. It is written by Joseph of Aramithea and it may reveal the location of the grail. And if I can find the grail, then I will be named. And if I am named, then I will exist."

I grabbed Cranwell's hand and tugged him closer to my side. "But you can't make your father love you."

"Love! I do not want his love. I want his pride. I want his honor. I want him to look at me. I just want him to see me. Give me the scroll."

"I can't."

She lunged toward the floor, picked up one of the knives. "Give it to me."

Cranwell shoved me behind him. I ran for the door.

Séverine was brandishing the knife at Cranwell.

"You don't want to do this."

She sprung at him.

Cranwell dodged.

Séverine lost her balance, fell to the floor. She hurled the knife at him.

It missed. Fell into the hole in the floor.

She looked at it for a long moment and then began to scream. Clapped her hands to her ears.

Cranwell knelt beside her.

"Leave me!"

He put a hand to her arm.

She twisted, picked up another knife, plunged it into her thigh. "Leave me alone!"

As Cranwell pried it from her grip, I ran to the lounge and grabbed the phone. Called emergency services.

By the time I got back to the bedroom, Cranwell had gathered all the sharp objects and deposited them on my bed. He'd also tied one of my scarves around Séverine's leg.

She was still on the floor, but she'd drawn her legs up to her chest and was rocking back and forth, staring off into space.

I knelt beside her, placed a hand on her back. "Séverine? Do you want me to call your father?"

Her eyes never moved; she didn't quit rocking, but she nodded her head.

"Who is he? Where does he live?"

I had to ask several times, but finally she told us. I dialed the operator, had her place the call. When her father came to the phone, I introduced myself, told him Séverine needed him. Desperately.

"Séverine? Séverine who?"

"Your daughter."

"I have no daughter." He hung up before I could respond.

I could only stare at the phone, wondering what sort of parent would pretend a child didn't exist.

When I walked back into the bedroom, Séverine paused in her rocking. "He will not come, Frédérique?"

I shook my head.

"He will never come."

By the time the ambulance came, she was curled on the floor in a fetal position, humming scraps of a tune I recognized as a French nursery-school song. They took her to the regional hospital for evaluation.

Cranwell brought the leather rod down into the kitchen after Séverine was taken away. He placed it in the middle of the island. We each took a stool, sat down, and stared at it. It was innocuous. Only a foot long, and two inches in diameter, it didn't look like anything important. The leather had worn to a smooth patina, but the amethysts still glittered. And etched into the leather on one side was a curious-looking 'N' with a wavy line set on top of it.

After a while, I got up, opened a drawer, and took from it a butter knife. Then I reached for the case and gently probed for an opening. Finding a slit near the top, I pried it open.

Inside was a scroll. It was not very big. Perhaps the size of three normal sheets of paper set side-by-side.

Cranwell left his stool and came to stand beside me.

The lines of script were very small and very tight. As little as I knew about Near Eastern script, the letters looked to be formed by a disciplined hand. I looked at it from every angle and felt cheated when it revealed nothing to me.

Cranwell reached out to finger a corner. It looked like vellum. He rolled it up and then fit it back into the case.

The next day, I drove it to Rennes and entrusted it into the care of the University of Rennes II.

The next week I received an enthusiastic letter from M. Dubois. In collaboration with the University of Nantes, the scroll was to be analyzed and translated. He promised to keep me informed of the progress and invited me to visit at the first opportunity. At the very least, he wanted me to know the scroll was 1,900 years old and that its author was a Joseph or Yosef of Arimathea.

It turned out that Alix was probably a Jew. At least on her mother's side. In the 1300s, one of the French kings ordered all Jews expelled from the realm. Many who lived near Brittany went to Spain or Italy; others went to what was then called the Kingdom of Provence. Some kept their faith, others converted and tried their best to disappear or blend in with the culture around them. After several generations, some even journeyed back to the northern parts of France.

It's possible that Alix's father never knew his first wife's origins, but I suspect he did. Why would he otherwise have given the scroll to his daughter? Jewish identity is passed from mother to child. Alix's father might not have been a Jew, but she would have inherited that identity from her mother.

If the scroll were determined to have been written in ancient Hebrew, how did Alix's mother come to have it? It's likely that the ancestors of Alix's mother originally came from the northwestern region of France, the part that bordered the old Kingdom of Bretagne. It's also possible that the legend is true: that Joseph of Arimathea did flee from Israel to Gaul after the death of Christ.

Julius Caesar conquered the region in the first century BC and Gaul was integrated into the Roman Empire. If Joseph did flee to Gaul, he may have brought the grail with him. If he brought the grail with him, he may have written about it. He was a member of the Sanhedrin, the Jewish Supreme Court. In order to have been a member of the Sanhedrin, he also had to have been a master student of the Torah and highly educated. There's no disputing that he knew how to write.

Family heirlooms have been passed from generation to generation for hundreds of years. Why could the scroll not have been passed down through generations? Why could family legend not have imbued the scroll with enough importance that it was regarded as a treasure to be kept safe and protected?

Sévérine must have recognized the Hebrew letters Y and A from Alix's description of the baton, the container of the scroll. In Hebrew, each letter is also assigned a numerical value. The initials of Joseph of Arimathea, or Yosef of Arimathea, would have been Yod, Aleph. The letters Yod and Aleph taken together add up to eleven.

Eleven symbolizes incompletion.

From her study of the journals, Sévérine knew that the twelve stones that decorated the lid were amethysts; Alix had said so herself. And from her studies of ancient texts, Sévérine knew that the amethyst represented the number twelve.

Twelve symbolizes completion.

If the scroll belonged to Yosef of Arimathea, as the initials indicate, why did he use twelve amethysts when his initials totaled eleven? Perhaps because the instructions inside would lead to completion. To the grail. To a symbolic communion with Jesus, where he again would join his disciples.

At least, that had probably been Sévérine's reasoning.

Why my room?

The scroll, the books, and the journal were entrusted to Agnès. And Agnès was the maid of Alix's mother. Why can we not assume that she also knew the value of the scroll? Otherwise, she would have put it in the trunk with Alix's journals and books.

If she did not hide it with the books, what other place was left to her to hide it? Her room. The maid's room and other servants' rooms would have been on the top floor of the castle. Exactly in the present location of my bedroom.

Cranwell insists he never slept with Séverine. He claims that they were discussing the journals when he got a horrible headache and asked Séverine to leave so that he could sleep.

When asked, Séverine verified that she had drugged him lightly, just enough for him to fall — and stay — asleep. The lacy black underwear had been a ruse, just in case I saw her leaving Cranwell's room. She had determined that his room would have been the one Alix had used, and she had searched it. She searched it thoroughly enough to know that the scroll was not hidden in his room, so she decided to search mine.

And to think, to me that stone had just been a nuisance.

I had to admit that I was wrong about Cranwell and Séverine. And I was completely wrong about Cranwell himself: He really did seem to have changed.

Does the scroll contain the secret of the grail? I leave it to the Universities of Nantes and Rennes to decide.

In the calm of the aftermath, Cranwell wrote, and I cooked.

one day before Toussaint

I insisted this morning that Anne be brought to my room, and Awen, still in my bed, and he must tell her of the marriage arrangement which has been made for her.

He says me that he could not.

I told him I would be present, but he must do it. If he could do anything for Anne, it must be to give her leave and the liberty to go. Had I not loved him so much, I would not have insisted. But I do.

I called Agnès to have Anne brought, and it was done.

Awen spoke through clenched teeth and did not dare to look at her as I did.

He had to do it. He cannot live divided. And he is my right.

Agnès smiled to hear it.

Anne spoke not one word.

one day after Toussaint

I have sent a messenger to my father to tell him of the coming of Anne. She will leave in two weeks time.

two days after Toussaint

I paid a visit to my lord this night.

I hit softly on the door, but he would not open it.

I remembered of Anne and how she came to him, so I spoke my name.

He opened it quickly to me.

I demanded of him to show me the way to pay the debt I owe.

He bid me come to his bed.

And this time, when he began to untie my laces, I let him.

day of Saint Malo

Awen has made me his wife. He comes to me by day as well as by night. I feel on fire with the heat of it. I am wanton. I have found happiness enough to last eternity.

We made no note of the going of Anne until this day, the day after she has gone. I remember myself of that morning of yesterday and recall that Awen had been in my bed. And I smiled at the memory of it and lifted my head from this journal and found that he had been watching me all this time. And I am putting down this work and going to him.

four days before Sainte Cécile

I find I have been selfish. All these years I have spent reading and studying when it would have done better to attend to my affairs.

I am a woman. I am a wife.

I had given up my duties for my pleasures, and all had turned upon itself. What if I had been a wife to Awen for several years past?

Anne would not have been in my place.

And what am I to do without Anne? I know not how to arrange a chateau. I know not how to command a servant. She has done all this, but I had allowed her to do it. I have been punished for not performing my duties.

I have kept the Book of Days of my mother; I fail to see how keeping it would do me harm, but I have given up what rests of my books; even the scroll possessed by my mother. For I confess I slit the top of the baton for it seemed to me hollow. And from there I took a scroll inscribed in a language I have never seen. I have demanded of myself what people could write in such a language of heavy lines, but as I have no teacher, I have no hope of being able to read it.

I have placed my journals in my chest and when I am done writing this day, I will demand of Agnès to take them all: the books and the journals. I care not where.

I must attend to life.

avril

Avril et mai, de l'année,
font seuls la destinée.

April

April and May alone craft destiny.

36

As the days passed, the tragedy of Séverine's breakdown and the shock of her betrayal shifted from the foreground of my thoughts to the background. I thought about looking for someone else to replace her and then thought about taking a break. I considered for the first time what I would do if I didn't have my chateau. I didn't arrive at an answer, but at least the question itself no longer scared me.

Without Séverine's arms to push Cranwell into, my thoughts about him had no lightning rod. They crashed and blazed and thundered in my mind without anything to ground them. If he didn't belong to Séverine, then he was no longer off limits. But that didn't mean that he was mine or anyone else's.

I was like a person who plans to drink flat water and swallows a mouthful of sparkling water instead. It takes a while for the mind to process the difference, even while the taste buds are transmitting the new information.

So Cranwell was unattached. He was the person he'd proclaimed himself to be and not the lout I had assumed he was. But what difference did that make in our relationship? And what sort of difference did I want there to be? If I had met Cranwell under different circumstances, if there had been no actresses or models, no Alix or Séverine . . . then he wouldn't be the man he was. And he wouldn't be staying in my chateau.

In spite of how hard I'd tried to keep my distance from him, I enjoyed everything about him. What's not to like about a man who volunteers to do his own vacuuming? And mine too?

Lucy came down one afternoon to find me. I assumed it was because Cranwell was talking to her about the same amount he was talking to me: very little. He was absorbed in editing his manuscript. I considered asking her if Cranwell ever spoke to her of me; if he were looking forward to going home; if he played with the collar of his shirt when he thought of what to write next, or if he'd already decided. But those questions seemed too intimate. Too indiscreet. Like asking the Queen's butler if she used a teaspoon or soup spoon to eat her cereal for breakfast. They were the sort of questions I wanted the answers to only if I could ask them of Cranwell myself. So I spared Lucy the indignity of having to answer them.

Cranwell offered no clues. No changes in the way he had always related to me.

As much as I longed to erase Séverine from the equation, she had become a ghostly place marker between the knowns and the formulation of the unknown. And I had been unknown for too long. With Cranwell's departure, there would be no one left who knew me.

But isn't that how many people lived their lives? Why should I be any different? What right did I have to demand anything more than what I already had? I wasn't true to Peter in life. Not really. But was there anything to be gained in trying to be true to him in death? Did the dead require such sacrifices of the living? Could they? Did it do anything at all to guard my heart for the ghost of unresolved guilt? Maybe that's why I couldn't ask for what I wanted. Maybe I didn't think I deserved to be loved.

Did anyone?

What was I supposed to do? Was there anything to do? What would happen if I did nothing at all?

Then when Cranwell was finished, he'd go. He'd find another place and write another book. And another and another.

What would happen if I did something?

Then when Cranwell was finished, he'd . . . go write another book.

So if I did nothing, Cranwell would leave and if I did something, Cranwell would go, so what was the best use of my pride?

Do nothing.

Do something.

I passed those days in suspension between doing something and nothing. I had forgotten how to reach for the things I wanted, if I ever had known how in the first place.

If anything were to happen, it had to start with Cranwell.

But then what did I want Cranwell to do? What did I want him to do that wasn't already tainted by memories of his past? What could I offer him that would be any different from what he'd already had? I had shared one man with a job. I didn't want to share another with the past.

I wasn't searching for love; I was searching to be known. But then love required knowing. And loving Cranwell required knowing him, and aren't we all made up of pieces of the people we've had relationships with? How could I successfully grapple with the weight of all those casual affairs? Knowing there was a past hanging over him just wanting to be repeated? How could love bloom under such a rain cloud? And what would it matter if I never loved anyone again?

I tried to talk myself into looking forward to Cranwell's departure. Tried to goad my thoughts to create reasons to look forward to his leaving. I couldn't think of very many. And then one afternoon, Cranwell's footsteps fell on the stairs. I heard him coming before I saw him. Being in the middle of a *sauce béarnaise*, I couldn't — didn't — look up.

"Pop open the bottle of champagne. I'm finished."

When I could glance up, I saw that he looked satisfied, relaxed. It seemed the burden of writing had lifted.

"You're finished," I echoed. So that was it. He'd pack his bags. He'd leave. I'd clean his room and rent it to someone else the next weekend. "Congratulations."

"Thank you."

"So who did your Alix turn out to be? A spy or an innocent girl?"

"She was an innocent. And regarding her husband, she decided to claim what she had a right to."

Recalling what I knew of Alix, Cranwell's plot made sense. She was the one married to Awen. Anne was too close a blood relative for the church to have approved a marriage. Alix had a right to Awen and the power to send Anne away. In a time when marriage was sacred, that was very smart. "So it came down to rights." It always did.

Taking the saucepan from the stove, I set it on the marble island. Then I opened the fridge and pulled out the bottle of champagne we had been saving.

Cranwell pulled a stool out, slouched onto it, and crossed his arms on the marble of the island. "Rights? Not at all. It came down to what she wanted. Her rights were what she used to get it."

After setting the champagne on the countertop, I reached in the cupboard for two flutes. "What she wanted . . . A woman in fifteenth-century France had the guts and the ability to do what she had to in order to get what she wanted. And here I am in twenty-first-century France and . . . "

"And what?" He was there, right behind me. As I closed my eyes and let the tears fall, he turned me around and gathered me to his chest. "What do you want?"

"I don't want to be alone anymore."

"Neither do I."

"But you've had actresses and models and . . . anyone you've ever wanted."

"No, I haven't. I've wanted you." He spoke to me softly, gently, as he covered my hands with his. "I can't change my past, Freddie. I have been with a lot of women. I admit it. But mostly, they were just flings. That's it."

That was *it*! My mind rebelled as my heart shattered into a thousand tiny splinters. But it wasn't *just* it; *it* was everything. I was not one of that group. I have never been one of the beautiful people; I have never been one who has only to want in order to make something happen, to make something mine. Only at the best of times have I ever seen a head turn to watch me walk down the street. I had no experience in casual sex. I didn't even have experience in casual wine or coffee drinking. Cranwell might as well have been living in the deepest jungle in South America: that's how far apart our worlds were.

"But I want all of you." I just couldn't stop myself from saying it. *Not in part.*

He still held me by the wrist. The only thing I wanted to do was get away, but he held onto me like a vise. Those brown eyes bored straight into mine.

Then I couldn't take it anymore: the admission of what probably amounted, in his mind, to a crush. The humiliation, the pain. I cursed Alix and the chaos she'd wreaked on my solitude.

He wouldn't let me go, so I slumped, like a child, to the floor. An unstoppable flow of tears made rivulets down my neck.

His grip tightened for a moment and then released. He was done with me.

Praying, I begged for the floor to swallow me whole.

But instead of leaving, he squatted in front of me, cupped gentle palms around my elbows, and pulled me toward himself.

Abandoning my body to his pull, I clung to him like a person in danger of drowning.

Cranwell enfolded me in his arms as if he too were afraid I would disappear. I breathed his soapy scent as he wound his fingers through my hair. He grabbed a handful and with one insistent tug, he drew my head back, baring my neck. With soft, reverent kisses, he traced the path of my tears. His lips grazed my ear. "You're the only one I want."

Trembling as he returned to my neck, I dared to ask the question, "But what about the others?"

He raised his head. "I didn't know there was a person like you waiting for me. And I didn't have God then to help me be strong. I wish I could change the past, but I can't. If you can forgive me, then I'd like to change the future . . . starting with the present."

"But—"

Taking my face between his hands, he looked into my eyes. There was no hint of a smile in his lips. I had never seen him look more serious. "I love you."

He'd said it. He loved me. I wanted so much at that moment not to think. I wanted to throw myself at him. But the voice of reason would not be stilled. People rarely change. Even with God's help it's hard. If Cranwell had slept with people at whim in the past, whom else might he sleep with? How many other urges would he give in to? Could I trust him?

"Trust me, Freddie."

Oh, how I wanted to.

"Freddie." He was demanding an answer.

What could I do? What could I say? My eyes searched his. There was nothing hidden. Looking into them was like diving into the depths of his soul.

How could I trust him?

How did Alix trust Awen? *Did* she trust Awen?

Cranwell got up and drew me with him. He picked me up and set me on the counter.

"Freddie?"

We were at exactly the same level. Eye to eye. The only option left me was to meet his gaze.

I did it.

And then I closed my eyes, wrapped my arms around his neck, and found shelter in his embrace. It came to me then, as I allowed myself to accept the warmth of his love, that Alix might never have brought herself to trust Awen. But it didn't matter; she gave from her wounded heart what she could. She gave him what God had given her. What God had given me.

She gave him a second chance.

The End

A Letter from the Author

Dear Reader,

Chateau of Echoes is one of my favorite books. It's the sort of book I would choose to read myself. I hope the following is conveyed through the words you have just read: my love of France, my love of French food and wine, my love of legends. My love of people who aren't perfect but who are trying; my love for a God who understands each of us, who doesn't assume any of us is beyond reach, and who moves through time and history to reveal himself to us.

The writing of this book began with Alix. As much as we'd like to think we'd be the same enlightened people in a different century, our modern assumptions about the world make us unfit for the eras that have passed before us. When Alix started speaking to me, I began to wonder what it would have been like to be married at such a young age. And then I began to picture what being a child bride would have involved, and I decided I just couldn't do that to her. She was too innocent. So I had to give her a husband who would let her grow up. A husband with a reason to let her grow up.

Freddie came second. The first scene I imagined her in was one in which she was talking to someone named Cranwell. There was something courageous and sad and grumpy about her. She was the sort of person you'd like to hug, if only you were certain she wouldn't brush you off. She made sacrifices for marriage her first time around in terms of her faith and her dreams. She's determined not to make those same mistakes again. How many of us are like that? How many of us have regrets about our past? And feel guilty about having regrets.

And King Arthur? The idea of writing a story about a story is irresistible to a writer. Especially a story that has survived centuries.

When I think of this book, I think of a world where mists swirl around a timeworn castle; where the scent of coffee mingles with the scent of musty, dusty old books; and where the sound of clanging pots mixes with the shuffle of footsteps on stone stairs.

After I finished this book, I often wished I could retreat to the little world I had created. A fantasy that existed only in my dreams. I'm so glad that my own little world can now be part of your world too. And I hope this story lingers in your memory as it has lingered in mine.

Sincerely,

Siri Mitchell

P.S. Please visit my website at http://sirimitchell.com to find out more about the legends of King Arthur and life in medieval times.

Brittany

Only the smallest child would not feel the weight of history in Brittany.

At twilight, it is easy to imagine that you can hear the echo of sounds that are not a part of the modern world. Or see shadows flitting through the trees that are not birds, or smell the memory of fires from ages passed, as if some long-ago quest was being perpetually launched.

The land is ancient.

It is Brocéliande, home of the Breton people. And home before them of the Franks, and before them, the Gauls, and before them, the Celts — and with them the druids — and before them, some nameless race who vanished into the mists of time, leaving only massive standing stones to mark their passing. The legends say that some of them still walk the forests as if shipwrecked . . . out of sync with the tides of time.

The legends also say that King Arthur and his knights scavenged through these forests, looking for the Holy Grail. And it is here that some seek it still.

If you look far enough back through the legends, the search for the grail is not a search for a chalice. And those who concentrate on the chalice tend to lose their way, just as those who pursue happiness seem never to quite find it. The search for the grail is a search for a mystical union with God, a search for wholeness. It is the relentless pursuit for a second chance to commune with Christ. And after all, isn't that what Christianity is all about?

Things You May Not Know About Brittany

*B*retons were the inventors of crêpes. The poor soil of the inland regions was fit only for growing buckwheat. When ground into flour, the fruit of this plant lacks gluten and so it doesn't rise like wheat flour. By binding buckwheat flour with eggs and milk, a batter for making thin pancakes was created. Through the centuries, instead of relying on the staple breads of the rest of France, Brittany's population survived on buckwheat crêpes, also known as *crêpes sarrasin* or *galettes*. Traditionally they are served only with savory fillings. The crêpes made of wheat flour, which most people are familiar with, are traditionally served only with sweet fillings in France.

The term Châteaubriand was applied to a writer before it became applied to a steak. François-René, vicomte de Châteaubriand, was born in St. Malo, France. He first achieved popularity with his book, *The Genius of Christianity*. It provoked a post-Revolutionary revival in France. He was also known for the exotic novels he wrote about America. At its conception, the culinary dish Châteaubriand was a recipe, not a cut of meat. It was created for the vicomte by his chef. History is silent on the exact details of the recipe, but the version passed on to me is that a top-quality filet was sandwiched between two lesser-quality steaks and then cooked. This method gave the filet more flavor.

Mont St. Michel is hotly disputed territory: both Normandy and Brittany have traditionally laid claim to it. Mont St. Michel has been a monastery, a church, a fortress, and a prison. It still houses a small monastic community, and it holds the distinction of never having been captured. The island of Mont St. Michel is separated from the mainland at high tide by almost a kilometer of sea. There is a forty-foot difference between the tides. Before a causeway between the island and the mainland was built in 1880, the tides rushed in at a speed of up to 10 miles an hour, and when they went out, they left an ever-changing field of quicksand. In earlier centuries, the only time pilgrims could reach the island was at low tide, through the uncharted fields of quicksand. The pilgrims would entrust that treacherous journey to God, knowing that if their prayers had found grace and favor, then they would pass unharmed. And if not, then they had been judged for their sins.

Brittany is home to dozens of megalith sites totaling thousands of stones. Most of these sites are three thousands years older than Stonehenge. Carnac, in southern Brittany, houses one of the largest megalithic sites in the world. It includes not only the remains of a stone circle, but 3,000 standing stones (*menhirs*) strung out for over one kilometer. Although closed to the public, the visitors' center interprets the site. The words *menhir* and *dolmen*, used to describe features of megaliths, are taken from the Breton language.

Breton is the only Celtic language still spoken in continental Europe. It is part of the family of languages that includes Welsh and Cornish, and possibly the extinct languages of Cumbric and Pictish. During the Roman occupation of Britain and Gaul, Latin loan-words invaded these languages; eight hundred of them still survive in the modern versions of Breton, Welsh, and Cornish. Breton is still spoken by 500,000 people in Brittany; before World War II, this figure was closer to 1.3 million. The first dictionary in France, published in 1464, was a trilingual dictionary including Breton, French, and Latin.

Pierre Abélard, half of Abélard and Héloïse, one of the most famous couples in history, was born in Le Pallet, near Nantes. An itinerant student, he traveled from school to school and from teacher to teacher before arriving at the school of Notre Dame de Paris. He remained there until he defeated his instructor in a debate, causing him to found his own school. Soon he was offered the chair at his old alma mater: Notre Dame de Paris. It was there that he fell in love with Héloïse, the niece of the canon. She was known for both her intelligence and beauty. Abélard talked himself into being appointed her tutor, and they commenced what would become a legendary love affair. Héloïse's uncle separated the couple when he found out about their affair, but Abélard continued to see her in private. When she became pregnant, he took her to Brittany to have the child. The couple was married in secret so that Abélard could continue advancing in the church. But like most secrets, this one was not kept, and when the news was made public, Héloïse had no choice but to deny it. And then retire to a convent. Convinced that Abélard was trying to dump his bride, the uncle had him castrated. The couple now shares a tomb in Père Lachaise cemetery in Paris.

Medieval French Calendar

January

6 Les Rois Mages (Epiphanie)
14 Saint Hilaire
21 Saint Agnès
25 Conversion de Saint Paul

February

5 Sainte Agathe
6 Shrove Tuesday (1459)
7 Ash Wednesday (1459)
10 Sainte Scholastique
17 Shrove Tuesday (1461)
18 Ash Wednesday (1461)
22 La Chaire de Saint Pierre
24 Saint Matthias
26 Shrove Tuesday (1460)
27 Ash Wednesday (1460)
29 Leap year (1460)

March

2 Shrove Tuesday (1462)
3 Ash Wednesday (1462)
12 Saint Grégoire le Grand
16 Saint Grégoire d'Arménie
17 Saint Patrice
21 Saint Benoît
23 Good Friday (1459)
25 Easter (1459)
    (Annonciation)

April

3 Good Friday (1461)
5 Easter (1461)
11 Good Friday (1460)
13 Easter (1460)
16 Good Friday (1462)
18 Easter (1462)
21 Saint Anselme
23 Saint Georges
25 Saint Marc

May

1 Saints Jacques et Philippe
3 Ascension (1459)
6 Saint Jean Martyr
13 Pentecôte (1459)
14 Ascencion (1461)
22 Ascencion (1460)

24 Pentecôte (1461)

27 Ascension (1462)

June

1 Pentecôte (1460)

6 Pentecôte (1462)

11 Saint Barnabé

14 Saint Basile le Grand

24 Saint Jean-Baptiste

29 Saint Pierre

30 Saint Paul

July

22 Sainte Marie-Madeleine

25 Saint Jacques le Majeur

26 Sainte Anne

August

4 Saint Dominique

10 Saint Laurent

12 Sainte Claire

13 Sainte Radegonde

15 Assomption

21 Sainte Bernard

24 Saint Barthélemy

28 Saint Augustin

September

14 Saint Etienne

21 Saint Matthieu

29 Saint Michel

October

9 Saint Dynys

28 Saint Simon

November

1 Toussaint

11 Saint Martin de Tours

15 Saint Malo

22 Sainte Cécile

24 Sainte Flora

30 Saint André

December

6 Saint Nicolas

11 Saint Damase, pape

13 Sainte Lucie

21 Saint Thomas, apôtre

25 Noël

26 Saint Etienne

27 Saint Jean, apôtre

28 Les Saints Innocents

29 Saint Thomas Becket

Lexicon of French Cooking Terms

Apéritifs — Drinks served before dinner to stimulate the appetite. Traditionally they have been sweet fortified wines (Banyuls, Muscat, Frontignanc), liqueurs (Porto, Madeira, Samos, Pineau), Vermouth, drinks with a wine base (Martini, Byrrh, Campari), anise-flavored drinks (Pastis, Ricard), whisky, and grain alcohols (gin, vodka, aquavit, sake).

Armagnac — Grape brandy produced in the Gascony region of France that has notes of prune and plum. The best Armagnacs come from the Bas Armagnac (lower Armagnac) district. Unlike the double distillation process for Cognacs, most Aramagnacs are distilled only once and then aged in oak barrels. They are distinguished by designations such as VS, VSOP, and XO, which designate the youngest liquid used in the blend, by the age of the brandy, and by their vintage if the blend of grape juices used in the mix is from the same year.

Baguettes — The classic French bread, it is a crusty, elongated yeast bread made with wheat flour, water, salt, and yeast.

Béchamel sauce — The classic white sauce. Made with butter, flour, milk, and seasoned with nutmeg, salt, and pepper.

Blanquette de veau — A ragoût made with veal, leeks, carrots, and onions. The thickening of the sauce is done with egg yolks, cream, and lemon juice. Traditionally it is served with white rice or steamed potatoes and a Saint-Joseph wine.

Boeuf bourguignon — A ragoût made using tougher pieces of beef, onions, carrots, bacon, mushrooms, tomato paste, a bottle of red burgundy wine, and seasoned with a bouquet garni and garlic.

Bouquet garni — Sprigs of parsley, thyme, and a bay leaf tied together and used to flavor a recipe. It may also include sage, celery, or rosemary. This "bouquet" of herbs is always withdrawn from the dish before serving.

Braisé de boeuf — Braised beef, cooked with onions, white wine, lemon, garlic, diced bacon, and flavored with parsley, thyme, and bay leaf. Braising is a cooking technique in which tougher, less expensive cuts of meat are steamed in a covered pot with very little liquid.

Brioche — Sweet yeast bread made with butter and eggs, it can be baked in different shapes of molds. The dough must go through three periods of rising before being baked.

Bruschetta — An Italian appetizer made of thickly sliced bread, traditionally grilled and rubbed with garlic. It is served with olive oil and salt. Many times it is garnished with tomatoes, herbs, cheese, or other accompaniments.

Bûche de Noël — A French Christmas tradition, this pastry is most often made of a thin rolled cake frosted with chocolate, vanilla, or coffee-flavored butter cream, to look like a log, and decorated with meringue mushrooms and almond paste holly leaves.

Carte Noir — A popular brand of French coffee that can be purchased at a grocery store.

Cassoulet — A hearty stew from southwestern France, this ragoût mixes white beans and meat in one of three styles: Castelnaudary is made with pork (ham and sausage); Carcassonne is made with mutton and partridge; Toulouse is made with pork, mutton, and local sausage.

Cidre — Hard apple cider. It is fermented without the addition of sugar or yeast. Often identified with the Breton and Norman cuisines and regions of France.

Civet de sanglier — A ragoût made from wild boar simmered with red wine; a civet is always finished with the addition of blood from the animal being cooked (or pig's blood in a pinch) to thicken the sauce.

Confiture — Jam or preserves made with cooked fruit and using sugar as the preserving agent. In France, commercial jams labeled "extra" contain at least 45 percent fruit. Regular confiture must contain at least 35 percent fruit.

Confiture de figues et marrons — Fig and chestnut jam.

Coquilles St. Jacques — Sea scallops. Their season runs from September to May, and there are two varieties: Atlantic or Mediterranean. The classic preparation is served in shells with shallots and mushrooms in a béchamel sauce, garnished with mashed potatoes piped along the edge of the shell.

Cordon Bleu — Founded in 1895, Le Cordon Bleu offers instruction in cuisine and pastry as well as degrees in different areas of hospitality and a Master of Arts in Gastronomy. According to their promotional literature, "The origin of the expression 'Cordon Bleu' comes from the 1578 foundation of the Order of Knights of the Holy Spirit. The members of the order wore a medal suspended on a blue ribbon and their spectacular feasts became legendary. The expression 'Cordon Bleu' was then later applied to mean an outstanding chef." Le Grand Diplôme Le Cordon Bleu may be earned in nine intensive months of study.

Cornichons — These miniature cucumbers conserved in seasoned vinegar are a classic accompaniment for cold and boiled meats, pâtés, terrines, and are also featured as an ingredient in many sauces.

Crème anglaise — Cream made with milk, vanilla beans, egg yolks, and sugar. Always served cold, it is used as an ingredient in various desserts, as a base for ice cream, and for drizzling over cakes and other sweets.

Crème caramels — A custard or flan cooked in a caramel-lined mold or ramekin.

Crème fraîche — The product of skimming whole milk, this cream is the consistency of sour cream but with a sweeter taste. It is used in many sauces, as a thickening agent in various dishes and as an accompaniment for desserts.

Crêpes — Of Breton origin, these flat "pancakes" are made with flour, milk, and either salt or sugar depending on whether they will be used for a sweet or savory dish. Traditionally crêpes made with buckwheat flour, *galettes sarrasin,* or *crêpes noires*, were used for savory dishes and crêpes made with white flour were used for desserts. In general, crêpes are served simply in France. For lunch or dinner with fillings of ham, cheese, egg, and/or mushrooms. For dessert with sugar, chocolate, fruit, jam, or nutella.

Crêpes suzettes — A dessert crêpe in which mandarin juice and curaçao are added to the crêpe batter. It is served spread with butter mixed with mandarin juice and zest, sugar, and curaço, and may be garnished with sections of mandarin and syrup made with mandarin zest. It should *never* be served flaming.

Croissants — Although associated with France, this crescent-shaped flaky butter pastry is actually of Viennese origin. The best are usually purchased from a pastry maker at a *pâtisserie*, as opposed to a baker at a *boulangerie*. It is generally preferable to eat them plain, although they may be served with jam, baked with ham or cheese, or glazed as a dessert.

Croquembouche — A cone-shaped, tiered dessert, a croquembouche is formed by stacking small caramel-coated cream puffs intermixed with dipped fruits, coated almonds, or sugared flowers and then is surrounded by a cage of caramel.

Croque-monsieur — Grilled ham and gruyère cheese sandwich. The addition of an egg turns the sandwich into a croque-madame.

Digestifs — Alcohol or liqueur served at the end of a meal — traditionally Cognac, Armagnac, or Calvados.

Endives gratinée — Endives wrapped with ham and cooked au gratin in a béchamel sauce.

Espresso — Suffering from much the same weather as the Pacific Northwest, those in northern France and Brittany drink a large amount of espresso. In fact, ordering *un café* — a coffee — in France will get you a shot of espresso served in a demitasse cup.

Filet mignon de porc — Pork tenderloin. May be cooked as one piece, slit and stuffed, sliced and served as medallions, or cubed and used for shish kebabs.

Filets de pintade aux cèpes et aux girolles — Guinea fowl filets cooked with porcini and chanterelle mushrooms.

Fines herbes — A mixture of freshly chopped parsley, chervil, tarragon, and chives.

Flamiche aux poireaux — A savory leek and egg tart from the northern French region of Picardy.

Foie gras — The liver of a force-fed goose or duck. Traditionally, these fowl were handfed on corn every day for two or three weeks, mimicking the natural tendency for water fowl to gorge themselves for several weeks before beginning migratory flights, to store excess fat in their livers. Associated with the cuisine of southwestern France, foie gras is also produced in Alsace and in Brittany.

Fruits verger — Orchard fruits: pears, apples, plums, quince, etc.

Galette des rois — This "kings cake" is traditionally served on Epiphany to celebrate the three kings' visit to the baby Jesus. Made of flaky pastry and filled with frangipane, a fava bean or small ceramic favor is hidden and cooked inside. The person who receives the piece with the prize is king or queen and must choose his or her queen or king. The galettes are usually sold with paper crowns.

Gâteau au chocolat — Chocolate cake with the intense flavor of a truffle and the texture of a mousse.

Gâteau aux trois chocolates — Chocolate cake made with white, milk, and dark chocolate.

Gelée — Gelatin used as an aspic in savory dishes or as a dessert with a base of fruit, wine, or liqueur.

Gnocchi — A hot baked dish served au gratin. In France, *gnocchi à la parisienne* is traditionally prepared with cream puff dough. Gnocchi may also be prepared with corn flour and boiled with parmesan or made with potato dough and cream.

Gougère bourguignonne — A bread made from cream puff dough with grated gruyère cheese, it is shaped into balls or into a wreath. It is served as an hors d'oeuvre or appetizer.

Gratin — A method of cooking in which grated cheese, white sauce, or bread crumbs added to the top of an oven-cooked dish turn golden and crusty from the heat.

Gratin dauphinois — Sliced potatoes cooked au gratin with a white sauce and grated cheese.

Gruyère — A cheese that is made of heated milk and is shaped into a large wheel. In taste and appearance, it is similar to "Swiss" cheese. Gruyère itself does not have an AOC (*appellation d'origine contrôlée*) and therefore is not regulated by the French government in terms of place, method, or quality of production. Only 36 cheeses in France are AOC, among them several gruyère-style cheeses: comté and beaufort.

Haricots verts — Green beans both narrower and sweeter than the common North American varieties. Their season runs from May to October, although imports from Kenya or Senegal may be purchased during the winter months.

Île flottante — Floating island; a dessert consisting of meringues "floating" in a lake of crème anglaise.

Jambon au cidre — Ham cooked in hard cider.

Joue de lotte — Jowls of the monkfish.

Laurier — Bay leaf.

Limoncello — Italian liqueur made from fermented lemons. The best limoncello comes from the Amalfi Coast and the island of Capri.

Macaroni — French elbow macaroni is smaller than its American equivalent. As a side dish, it is usually served buttered with chives.

Magret de canard — A tender filet of meat taken from the breast of a duck. It is cooked much like a steak and served rare.

Maury wine — A sweet wine fortified with clear brandy, and made from Grenache noir grapes in the Maury commune in the Côtes du Roussillon-Villages area of southern France. The wines have notes of red fruits, cocoa, and coffee. It may also be drunk as an aperitif.

Mille feuille — A dish traditionally made of flaky pastry layered with fillings. The dessert version contains sweet fillings such as pastry cream or whipped cream and is topped with fondant or powdered sugar. Contemporary versions of Mille feuille may also be made with savory fillings, or may use an alternative to the layers of flaky pastry, as in the recipe that follows this section.

Mont d'Or — or Vacherin du Haut Doubs, this dessert cheese has an AOC by which the government controls the place, method of fabrication, and quality of the cheese. Mont d'Or lies near the Swiss border, and this winter cheese has been made in that region for two centuries. Sold in a box and encircled by a length of pine wood, it continues to ripen until it is eaten. It is produced over a period of three weeks and then finished on spruce planks, where it is regularly flipped and rubbed with a canvas soaked in brine.

Moules marinaire — Mussels cooked in a marinade of white wine, butter, thyme, bay leaf, onion, and parsley.

Mousse de potiron au gingembre — Pumpkin and ginger mousse.

Navarin d'agneau — A ragoût of mutton or lamb cooked with potatoes and vegetables. Traditionally made in the spring with baby vegetables, it is seasoned with white wine, garlic, nutmeg, and a bouquet garni.

Oeufs en gelée — Hard-cooked eggs halved and then individually molded with Madeira-flavored gelatin, ham, and an assortment of chopped vegetables.

Pains au chocolat — Flaky croissant-like butter pastry baked around tablets of dark chocolate.

Pâté — Most often based on meat (pork, veal, fowl, game, and/or their variety meats), traditionally, a pâté is a meat stuffing wrapped in dough and baked. It may or may not be molded; it may be served hot or cold. A looser definition includes a pâté meant to be served in slices, cooked in a terrine dish and served cold, known as a *pâté de campagne*; or a pâté meant to be spread, i.e., foie gras.

Pâté de lapin aux noisettes — Pâté of rabbit with hazelnuts, seasoned with Porto, sausage, chicken livers, onions, chervil, thyme, and bay leaf.

Pintade aux figues sèches — Guinea fowl cooked with dried figs. A guinea fowl may be used as a substitute in recipes using pheasant or partridge.

Poulet rôti — Roasted chicken most commonly prepared on a rôtisserie.

Profiteroles — These miniature cream puffs may be stuffed with savory filling and served as an appetizer or with pastry cream, whipped cream, or jam and served as a dessert. Most common is a filling of vanilla ice cream with a garnish of hot chocolate sauce.

Ragoût — A dish combing two cooking methods: browning and simmering. The food is first browned, and then slowly simmered in an aromatic liquid. Flour is used as a thickening agent.

Ratatouille — A ragoût of vegetables originating from Nice in southern France, it includes onions, zucchini, tomatoes, peppers, and eggplants seasoned with garlic, olive oil, bay leaf, and thyme. Ratatouille is often used as an accompaniment for meats. It may be served hot or cold.

Rillettes — A spread traditionally made from pork or goose cooked in its own grease. It may be spread on grilled bread as an hors d'oeuvre, used as an ingredient in canapés, or used to make sandwiches. Rillettes from the area of Tours are darker and of finer texture than those from Mans or Sarthe in southern France. A stamp of *qualité supérieure* on the jar notes a product with less fat than a rillettes *traditionnelles*.

Roquefort — A blue cheese and the first cheese in France to be given an AOC, which controls the place, method of fabrication, and quality of the product. Roquefort is ripened in natural caves in

Mont Combalou in the commune of Roquefort-sur-Soulzon for at least three months, but generally from four to nine months.

Salade composées — A salad served as an appetizer that has been artfully arranged on individual plates and that generally uses a wide variety of ingredients such as meat, liver, shellfish, foie gras, lettuce, potatoes, apples, mushrooms, etc.

Sauce béarnaise — A sauce made of egg yolks, butter, and lemon and seasoned with shallots, tarragon, chervil, thyme, bay leaf, white wine vinegar, and white wine. This sauce should be made just before serving and should obtain the consistency of mayonnaise.

Saumur-champigny — From the Anjou-Saumur region of the Loire Valley, this wine is a light, lively red with notes of red currant and is made from a blend of cabernet franc and cabernet sauvignon grapes. It may be produced in any of nine communes within the Saumur-Champigny district. Wines carrying this designation must be aged at least a year. This wine is a good accompaniment for duck.

Sauternes — A white dry, sweet wine from the Sauternes, Barsac, Bommes, Fargues, or Preignac subregions of Bordeaux. The best come from Sauternes and Barsac. Made from a blend of sémillon and sauvignon blanc grapes, a later harvest in fall allows the development of mold on the fruit, which dehydrates them, thereby concentrating the sugar in the juice. Due to the concentration of sugar, the fermentation process may require up to a year, after which it is aged for at least two years in a cask.

Sorbets — An iced dessert made from sugar syrup and a fruit purée or fruit juice, wine, or alcohol. A sorbet recipe may also incorporate a meringue to give volume to the mixture.

Sorbet des agrumes — A sorbet of citrus fruits, including oranges, grapefruit, mandarins, clémentines, lemons, kumquat, Satsuma, and tangelos.

Tagliatelle — Fettucine. Made from egg dough, this pasta is formed into large ribbons; the pasta may be colored green with the addition of spinach to the dough.

Terrine — Traditionally, a pâté to be served sliced made with pork, fowl, or game. Currently, the term is also applied to molded dishes made with fish, shellfish, or vegetables, which often use gelatin to bind the ingredients.

Three-star restaurant — France's Michelin company rates restaurants each year on two scales: luxury and quality of food. The luxury scale rates from one to five crossed knives and forks; the food scale rates from one to three stars. There were only ten three-star restaurants in Paris in 2003. Restaurants are rated by Michelin's anonymous critics who note such things as food quality, setting, decor, restrooms, linens, service, kitchen, and wines. A three-star restaurant must have exceptional cuisine, superb food, fine wines, and faultless service that make it worth a special journey to visit.

Tourte bourguignon — A meat pie made with beef, onions, carrots, bacon, mushrooms, and tomato paste and flavored with a bouquet garni, garlic, and red burgundy wine.

Veal marsala — Veal cooked in marsala dessert wine from Sicily and seasoned with sage.

Recipes

My friend Kerrie Hecker created these recipes especially for the readers of this book. I met Kerrie when I was living in Paris. While I was working a desk job, she was having five times the fun taking courses at *Le Cordon Bleu, Paris*. In March 2000, she graduated with the grand diplome, cuisine and pastry, with honors. For the past seven years, she's been teaching cooking classes from her home.

Roasted Peppers with Goat's Cheese

STARTER COURSE

8 servings:

4 large red peppers (green are not suitable)

9 T. extra virgin olive oil

2 cloves garlic

400 g (1 lb.) soft, round goat's cheese (cylindrical for you to cut or
precut rounds). Most common is *Crottin de Chavignol.*

Freshly milled black pepper, salt

1 small bunch fresh basil leaves, washed and dried

2 T. balsamic vinegar (optional)

Pine nuts (optional)

PREPARATION:

1. Preheat the oven to 180°C/ 350°F.

2. Wash the peppers, cut them in half, even the stem, trying to keep a
   part of the stem on each side. Keeping part of the stem is optional,
   but it helps to keep the shape of the pepper as it cooks. Remove the
   seeds and membranes. Drizzle 1 T. olive oil in a shallow baking dish
   large enough to hold them without overlapping or layering. Place
   the peppers open side up in the baking dish.

3. Peel the garlic and slice them thinly and divide the slices equally
   among the peppers.

4. Drizzle 1 T. of olive oil over each pepper, and salt and pepper each as well.

5. Place the baking dish in the center of the oven on the highest shelf. Bake for roughly 50 min. to 1 hr. You don't want the peppers to burn, but you want a nice roasted, nutty color and flavor. Remove from the oven and place roughly 50 g (2 oz.) of soft goat's cheese in the middle of each pepper. Return to the oven until cheese is warm and slightly bubbly.

6. Depending on the size of each pepper half and how hungry your guest is, each guest should get one to two pepper halves on an individual plate. Be sure to give each serving plenty of the pan juices, ensuring all guests get some of the warm oil and roasted garlic slices. For each serving, drizzle ½ T. balsamic vinegar over the peppers and sprinkle with basil leaves and pine nuts. Serve warm or at room temp. Focaccia bread would go well with this dish to soak up all the lovely juices.

Grilled Salmon with Asparagus, Balsamic, & Parmesan

MAIN COURSE

4 people:

4 pieces skinless/boneless salmon, each weighing 50 g (2 oz.)

20 spears green asparagus, medium thickness

3 T. unsalted butter

1 T. olive oil

3 T. balsamic vinegar

1 T. lemon juice

Wedge of parmesan

PREPARATION:

1. Clean salmon by rinsing with cold water. Pat dry with paper towel. Lay salmon flat in the hand so it bends on either side of the hand. Check for bones by running your finger against the grain of the salmon. If you find any bones, pull them out in the same direction they're sticking out. Pat dry with paper towel. Grill either on an outdoor grill until no longer raw or broil in an oven, roughly 15 minutes at 400 F. Keep warm.

2. Take 20 spears of green asparagus; wash thoroughly and dry. Hold each asparagus toward the end/base of the stalk and bend it until it breaks. This causes the asparagus to break off at the point of freshness. To make a neater presentation, cut off ends close to where

they broke, and furthermore, cut all to be the same length. In a sauté pan, heat 2 T. unsalted butter plus 1 T. olive oil. Sauté asparagus over medium heat until slightly browned, roughly 10 minutes. Lower the heat and sprinkle 1 T. balsamic vinegar over the asparagus and heat for 1 minute. Remove from heat and place asparagus in a heat-proof bowl covered with aluminum foil to keep warm.

3. In the same pan that you used to sauté the asparagus, heat the remaining 2 T. balsamic vinegar for roughly 30 seconds. Off the heat, add the tablespoon of lemon juice and tablespoon of unsalted butter, swirling in the pan to make a cohesive mixture. Keep off heat.

4. Place 4 stalks of asparagus on each serving plate in a row and then place the fifth stalk diagonal on top of the other 4 stalks. Finish off with grated parmesan cheese. This can be accomplished by using a peeler over the wedge of parmesan. Finish each plate with a piece of salmon and drizzle one fourth of the balsamic vinegar mixture over salmon.

Millefeuille aux Mascarpone avec fruits et Coulis

Layered Mascarpone with fruit and fruit sauce

DESSERT

4 people:

1 C. Mascarpone cheese

1-2 T. powdered sugar

150 g (1/2 C. + 1 T.) blueberries, strawberries, raspberries,
blackberries (any diced fruit) NOT FROZEN

12 thin cookies store-bought or homemade, such as almond or sugar.
Make sure all are uniform in size.

Raspberry Coulis:

125 g (1/2 C.) frozen raspberry pieces (*or other fruit*);
can use fresh as well

Powdered sugar

PREPARATION:

1. Mix the mascarpone cheese with the powdered sugar. You can add more powdered sugar if the mixture isn't sweet enough. Wash and dry fresh, diced fruit then add to mascarpone cheese. If doing this step in advance, be sure to place in refrigerator or cheese will soften and be runny. DO NOT use frozen fruit or it will discolor the mascarpone with all the juices after thawing.

2. On the individual serving plate, place a dab of the mascarpone (some without fruit) on the plate then a cookie on top. This stabilizes the cookie to the plate. Place 1/8 C. of the mascarpone cheese (may use less depending on the size of the cookie) on top of the cookie; spread evenly with the back of a spoon then place another cookie on top of that. Do this one more time, creating 2 layers of cheese with 3 cookies.

3. Make the raspberry coulis by straining thawed raspberry pieces. Pass through a sieve to remove seeds. Whisk in powdered sugar to taste. Strain if it has lumps. If using fresh fruit, simply purée in a food processor then strain; add powdered sugar as directed.

4. Ladle the raspberry coulis around the cookie. Sprinkle some powdered sugar on top of the cookie and serve. Fresh mint always adds a nice touch to the top as well.

Reader's Guide

1. Which fairy tale or legend do you most wish were true?

2. Do you prefer reading fact or fiction?

3. Is it easy or difficult for you to give people second chances? Can you think of times when you've been given a second chance?

4. What is your responsibility for others' salvation?

5. If something violates your sensibilities, should it violate everyone's sensibilities?

6. Is it possible to love a person you can't trust?

7. After Awen claims Alix's mystery as his own, they have this dialogue: "On the return, my lord demanded my pardon for claiming the mystery for his own. I replied to him that I understood the why of what he had done and I thanked him. For had he not claimed it, the mystery would never have been heard. By any. And he recalled to me that in all cases, it is for God the glory of such a work and not man. And this I know, and this I had intended, but it does not make the offense seem any less." What were your own reactions to their meeting with the priest? Would you have been as understanding as Alix?

8. When Freddie contemplates her marriage with Peter, she realizes that, "I'd never before stopped to consider how very great a distance there was between believing in something and believing nothing. There may have been less of a culture clash had I been married to a Hindu or Muslim. At least we both would have been approaching life with the idea that there was some sort of higher purpose for it all." What do you think about these statements?

9. At one point, Cranwell apologizes to Freddie for his behavior: "I'm sorry, Freddie. I had no right to do that. You always seem to be the victim when my old nature rebels against the new one." Can you think of times when your old nature has rebelled against your new one? Who always seems to be the victim?

10. Have you ever been betrayed by someone? How?

11. How do you view marriage? As a union of bodies, hearts, minds, or souls?

12. When Freddie learns she has lost her bet with Cranwell, she states that, "Anyone could have an affair. Not everyone could use that passion to build a life in common." Do you agree with her?

13. When addressing Freddie's guilt, Cranwell makes this argument: "It seems to me that everyone is responsible to God for the state of their own soul. He's left it up to each individual to make a choice — for themselves. Maybe Peter would have become a believer if you had talked to him, or maybe he wouldn't have. Sometimes people won't

listen to those closest to them. Sometimes they need a stranger to tell them. Sometimes they don't need words at all. God doesn't need anybody to tell others about Him; He's arranged the world itself to be His testimony." Do you agree with him?

14. Do you spend more of your time living in the past, the present, or the future?

15. Freddie acknowledges one of her fears in this passage: "As the days passed, the tragedy of Séverine's breakdown and the shock of her betrayal shifted from the foreground of my thoughts to the background. I thought about looking for someone else to replace her, and then thought about taking a break. Considered for the first time what I would do if I didn't have my chateau. I didn't arrive at an answer, but at least the question itself no longer scared me." Do you have any questions that you're afraid to answer?

Bibliography

Arbez, Emmanual. Pommiers.com. Emmanuel Arbez. 2005. http://www.pommiers.com/.

Barbieri, Fabio P. "Chapter 7.2: 442–468: a historical Reconstruction." *History of Britain*. Fabio P. Barbieri. 2002. http://www.geocities.com/vortigernstudies/fabio/book7.2.htm.

Bennett, Elizabeth. "About King René and the Tournament Book." *King René's Tournament Book*. Elizabeth Bennett. 1998. www.princeton.edu/~ezb/rene/renenote.html.

Binkley, Peter. "Medieval Calendar Calculator." wallandbinkley.com. Peter Binkley. 2000. http://www.wallandbinkley.com/mcc/mcc_main.html.

Brekilien, Yann. *Contes et Légends du Pays Breton*. France. Nature et Bretagne, 1996.

"Burgundian Dance in the Late Middle Ages." An American Ballroom Companion; Dance Instruction Manuals c. 1490–1920. The Library of Congress. 1998. http://lcweb2.loc.gov/ammem/dihtml/diessay1.html.

Casteland.com. 2000–2004. http://www.casteland.com/.

Chateaux Celtes et Chimères. 2004. http://pages.infinit.net/celte/
bienvenue.html.

Comité Départemental du Tourisme de Hatue-Bretange, Ille et Vilaine.
Haute-Bretagne, Ille-et-Vilaine. 2005. www.bretagne35.com.

Creasy, Rosalind. *The Edible French Garden*. Singapore: Periplus
Editions (HK) Ltd.

Culhwch and Olwen. Translated by Lady Charlotte Guest.

Eckford, Teresa. "Life in the Keep & the Chatelaine." All About
Romance. Laurie Gold. 2004. http://www.likesbooks.com/
lifekeep.html.

"Epiphanie." Lafete.net. 2005. http://www.lafete.net/epiphanie/default.htm.

Falling Rocks, Daniel and de l'Estrangere, Roselyne. "The Brussels
Manuscript: Transcription and Translation." The Letter of
Dance. Mark Waks. 1993. http://www.pbm.com/~lindahl/lod/
vol2/trans_brussels.html.

Fenmere, Janelyn of. "Stepping on Our Toes: Some Background on
Branles." The Letter of Dance. Dani Zweig and Monica Cellio.
1993–1996. http://www.pbm.com/~lindahl/lod/vol3/branle_
background.html.

Ford, David Nash. "Mark, King of Cerniw & Prince of Poher (born c. 480)." Brittania.com. David Nash Ford. 2000. http://www. britannia.com/bios/ebk/markcw.html.

Friedman, David and Elizabeth Cook. "The Little Things." Cariodoc's Miscellany. David Friedman and Elizabeth Cook. 1992. http:// www.pbm.com/~lindahl/cariadoc/little_things.html.

Gilberts, Rachel. "Travel and Trade." E-museum @ Minnesota State University, Mankato. 2001. http://www.mnsu.edu/emuseum/ history/middleages/trade.html.

Gode Cookery. Matterer, James L. 1997–2005. http://godecookery.com/.

Greenberg, Hope. "15th Century Female Flemish Dress: A Portfolio of Images." Society for Creative Anachronisms, Alice Nele's Collection. Hope Greenberg. May 1998. http://www.uvm. edu/%7Ehag/sca/15th/index.html.

Guice, C. Preston. "Rene D'Anjou." Le Bon Roi Rene. C. Preston Buice. 2005. http://kingrene.guice.rg/renentro.html.

Harbaugh, Molly and Carla Emmons. "Medieval Garb by Molly (Harbaught) Overholt." A World in Progress. July 2004. http:// green.seagull.net/garb/women.html.

Harmand, Adrien. Jeanne d'Arc, ses costumes, son armure: essai de reconstitution. Paris: éditions Leroux. 1929; source: Le Rozier des Guerres. http://lerozier.free.fr/index.htm.

Heinonen, Meri. "The Medieval Love Sickness." Wind Mills the Middle Ages. 1999. http://www.tkukoulu.fi/tiimalasi/en/en-lemmensairaus.html.

Heise, Jennifer. Zajaczkowa, Jadwiga. "Scents of the Middle Ages." Jadwiga Zajaczkowa's Page. 2000. http://www.lehigh.edu/~jahb/herbs/scents.html.

Hermé, Pierre. Larousse des desserts. France: Larousse. 2002.

Joyeuse-fete.com. 2005. http://www.joyeuse-fete.com/.

Julien, Stéphane. "Le Temps de Noel." www.jour-de-l-an.com. Stéphane Julien. 2005. www.jour-de-l-an.com/temps.htm.

Kennel-Renaud, Élisabeth Kennel-Renaud. 2005–2006. http://yz2dkenn.club.fr/index.html.

King Arthur and the Knights of the Round Table. Nathan Currin. 2001. KingArthursKnights.com.

Kuehl, Barbara J. "Medieval & Renaissance Theme Wedding FAQ: Questions about the Feast." Medieval and Renaissance

Wedding Page. Barbara J. Kuehl. 2000. http://www.drizzle. com/~celyn/mrwp/faq6.html.

"La condition des femmes au moyen age." Ivn.com. 1998. http://www. chez.com/ivn/.

"La loire de Saumur À Angers." francebalade.com. 2005. http://www. culture.gouv.fr/culture/medieval/francais/index.htm.

La Peinture Médiévale dans la Midi de la France. Aurélie Delbey. http://www.culture.gouv.fr/culture/medieval/francais/index. htm.

Ladnier, Penny E. "Color in Elizabethan Dress." The Elizabethan Costuming Page. Drea Leed. 1996. http://costume.dm.net/ lizcolor.html.

Légendes. http://www.bagadoo.tm.fr/kemper/legendes.html.

Levallois, Marie-Pierre. *Larousse de la Cuisine*. France: Larousse. 2004.

Mabinogion. Translated by Lady Charlotte Guest.

Mairie de Chateaugiron. Ville-Chateaugiron.fr. 2005. http://www.ville-chateaugiron.fr/.

Marr, Charles. "Vegetable Garden Calendar." SavvyGardener.com.
    November 1992. http://www.savvygardener.com/Features/veg_
    garden_calendar.html.

Medieval-Weddings.net. World Web Design, LLC. 2000. http://
    medieval-weddings.net/medieval_weddings_copyright_notice.
    htm.

Merrien, Nathalie. *Mystères de Bretagne*. Luçon: éditions Jean-Paul
    Gisserot. 1991.

Poisson, Henri and Jean-Pierre Le Mat. *Histoire de Bretagne*. Spézet:
    éditions COOP BREIZH, 2000.

Rivard, Claude. Calendrier Rural Traditionnel. Claude Rivard. 2005.
    http://chez.com/ceher/calndr/calendr.htm.

Ross, S. John. "Medieval Demographics Made Easy." The Blue Room.
    S. John Ross. 2005. Version 3.0. http://www.io.com/~sjohn/
    demog.htm.

Saints and Angels. Catholic Online. 2005. http://www.catholic.org/
    saints/.

Solé, Jacques. *Etre Femme en 1500*. Mesnil-sur-l'Estrée: editions Perrin,
    2000.

The Catholic Encyclopedia. 1913. http://www.newadvent.org/cathen/.

"The Legacy of the Horse, chapter 2A." The International Museum of the Horse. 1998. http://www.imh.org/imh/kyhpl2a.html.

"Treasures of Fresno: 'Galerie Francaise de Femmes Celebres.'" The Costumer's Manifesto — Costumes.org. 1996–2005. Sanoian Special Collections Library. http://www.costumes.org/HISTORY/100pages/famouswomen.htm.

Velde, François R. "Nobility and Titles in France." Heraldica. 1995–2003. http://www.heraldica.org/topics/france/noblesse.htm.

Watson, Sonny. "Basse Dance plus Hautes Dances." StreetSwing.com. Dance History Archive. Sonny Watson. 2005. http://www.streetswing.com/histmain/z3basse.htm.

Watson, Sonny. "Galliarde." StreetSwing.com. Dance History Archive. Sonny Watson. 2005. http://www.streetswing.com/histmain/z3galrd1.htm.

Watson, Sonny. "Passpied." StreetSwing.com. Dance History Archive. Sonny Watson. 2005. http://www.streetswing.com/histmain/z3paspd.htm.

Watson, Sonny. "The Branle." StreetSwing.com. Dance History Archive. Sonny Watson. 2005. http://www.streetswing.com/histmain/z3branl1.htm.

Watson, Sonny. "The Minuet." StreetSwing.com. Dance History
Archive. Sonny Watson. 2005. http://www.streetswing.com/
histmain/z3minuet.htm.

Watson, Sonny. "Torch Dance." StreetSwing.com. Dance History
Archive. Sonny Watson. 2005. http://www.streetswing.com/
histmain/z3torch1.htm.

Acknowledgments

To my agent, Beth Jusino, who believed in this manuscript, and to my editors, Rachelle Gardner, who sharpened my vision, and Darla Hightower, who polished my words. To Emily Locke, my first reader, who read this manuscript by installments when she should have been studying. To Mick Silva for his enthusiasm when all doors seemed shut and locked. And to my WriteHands comrades-in-pen — Lisa Crayton, Ginger Garrett, and Sue Lang.

Author

With a degree in business from the University of Washington and experience in working at all levels of government, *Siri Mitchell* has lived all over the world as a military spouse. Together, with her husband and daughter, she enjoys experiencing a variety of cultures — whether that means becoming fluent in French or mastering the art of sushi making. This is her first novel with NavPress.

She came to conquer a king
but discovered a man and,
in the end, saved a nation.

Chosen

GINGER GARRETT

1-57683-651-7

What really happened in Xerxes' palace? Queen Esther's secret diaries tell all. Few knew she kept a private scroll of her deepest thoughts. From her days as a poor market wench through her rise to queen, she recorded it all—the sights and scandals—hoping that one day, others would learn the truth.

Visit your local Christian bookstore, call NavPress at 1-800-366-7788, or log on to www.navpress.com to purchase.

To locate a Christian bookstore near you, call 1-800-991-7747.

NAVPRESS®
BRINGING TRUTH TO LIFE
www.navpress.com